NUMBER 1129 RIDGE AVENUE

The man who built it committed suicide on the eve of the mansion's completion.

Its first tenants enacted a grisly tragedy that would forever haunt its walls.

For 20 years it had stood vacant, until Thomas Alva Edison dared to conduct a revolutionary experiment that would change his life forever . . . and unleash evil upon the modern world.

Other Leisure Books by J. N. Williamson:

**THE TULPA
PLAYMATES
THE LONGEST NIGHT
NOONSPELL
BABEL'S CHILDREN**

J.N. WILLIAMSON

HORROR HOUSE

LEISURE BOOKS   NEW YORK CITY

For my cherished wife,
Mary,
with undiminished loving gratitude,
and
for such youthful "entities"
as my own children—
as well as my new grandchildren!

A LEISURE BOOK®

April 1991

Published by

Dorchester Publishing Co., Inc.
276 Fifth Avenue
New York, NY 10001

Copyright© MCMLXXXI by J. N. Williamson

All rights reserved. No part of this book may be reproduced or transmitted in any form or by any electronic or mechanical means, including photocopying, recording, or by any information storage and retrieval system, without the written permission of the Publisher, except where permitted by law.

The name "Leisure Books" and the stylized "L" with design are trademarks of Dorchester Publishing Co., Inc.

Printed in the United States of America.

Our minds and our bodies represent the vote or the voice . . . of our entities. . . . Once conditions become unsatisfactory in the body . . . the entities simply depart from the body and . . . either enter into the body of another man or even start work on some other form of life. . . . Entities live forever, you cannot destroy them, just the same as you cannot destroy matter.

. . . I do hope our personality survives. . . . This is why I am at work on the most sensitive apparatus I have ever undertaken to build, and await the results with the keenest interest.

Thomas A. Edison, as quoted by B. C. Forbes (founder of *Forbes*), in "Edison Working on How to Communicate with the Dead," *American Magazine*, October 1920.

Preface

Amazingly, this is in part a book of fact. The house on Ridge Avenue existed during the period stated, and it was destroyed in the mysterious way I describe. The valuable lot has remained vacant—uninhabitable—for some *fifty* years. It was, my research suggests, a demonically haunted house and, in most details, much the way you find it described. The Congeliers and Brunrichter apparently did what I report, ghastly as it was; Essie, Charles, the young ladies and the Italian laborers seem to have gone to their graves—perhaps not to their rest—in the way this book suggests.

The concept of "entities" certainly existed in the mind of Edison—a mind which gave us electric lights, phonographs and movies—and they may exist in fact. Moreover, all evidence clearly indicates that this century's foremost inventor *was* working on a machine with which to contact the dead. Somewhere, it, too, may exist in fact.

Events described in contemporary times are almost entirely fictitious and any similarity between these characters and living human beings is, as they say, purely coincidental.

Gratitude is expressed to Nancy Osbourne and Richard Winer for introducing me to Ridge Avenue's awful mansion in their exciting *Haunted Houses* (New York: Bantam, 1979). Other sources of reference include *Edison* by Matthew Josephson (New York: McGraw-Hill, 1959); *Light for the World* by Robert Silverberg (New York: Van Nostrand, 1967); *Thomas A. Edison: A Modern Olympian* by Mary Childs Nerney (New York: Harrison Smith & Robert Haas, 1934); and *Thomas Edison, Chemist* by Byron M. Vanderbilt (Washington, D.C.: American Chemical Society, 1971).

Sincere appreciation is also expressed to those persons or groups who have nobly assisted in the completion of *Horror House*, among them the following: Richard "Ric" Hase; John Cowell; WTAE-TV, Channel 4, Pittsburgh; Carnegie Library, Pittsburgh; Eliza Smith, Pittsburgh History and Landmarks Foundation; David Mendenhall; Karen Hassos; North Eastwood Library, Indianapolis; James Zunic; and Mike Mullen, Pittsburgh Mapping Department. Additional thanks are tendered to Nancy R. Parsegian, then of *Playboy*, and to my former literary agent, Ray Puechner.

Prologue

Winter, 1871.

Wilhelm I was proclaimed kaiser, and Bismarck became the German chancellor. It was the year of Chicago's "great" fire. Lewis Carroll, a mathematician, published his incomparable *Through the Looking Glass.* And the mysterious Rasputin entered this world—appropriately. But the location that concerns us here is Pittsburgh, Pennsylvania, and the events are even more mysterious and bizarre.

By the time Charles Wright Congelier, his Mexican wife and the lovely Indian lass had moved their unholy triumvirate into the handsome new house on prosperous Ridge Avenue, the middle-aged carpetbagger didn't know which living repository of supernatural conviction tended to annoy him more, wife or servant. Each of them had a way of talking about frightening, other-worldly things that seemed stuff and nonsense to Congelier, even when it scared him a little. He was a practical man, after all, a dodger of bullets, a one-time escapee from strong hemp. He was also a man with more than his share of enemies.

"Old Charlie," as they called him, had survived the Civil War by being inordinately adaptive, amiably meandering through the battle-torn young nation with no passionate involvements with anyone but himself. After the war, a born opportunist, he made more money than he ever thought existed and didn't, as a rule, question where it came from. One acquaintance was quoted as saying, not without a soupcon of admiration, "Old Charlie might wind up owning all of Texas, except for one little fact: so many people consider him a miserable turncoat that he'll be hanged the minute his damned luck runs out."

Congelier listened well to comments of that sort. Always prudent where his lanky six feet of well-tanned, ageless hide was concerned. Old Charlie didn't wait for his luck to turn. He bundled up his money, his wife and his prized servant girl and headed north a good five miles ahead of the latest frustrated possee.

It won't startle you to learn that Charles Congelier had little interest in matters of the spirit. Deep in his head, buried beneath a thousand questionable escapades and a handful of secrets nobody knew, he remembered attending church when he was a tad, in an old frame building that had served as the school five days a week. And, when pressed, he might recall a superstition or two about how to get along with Indians and how to survive in the wilderness. But, by and large, matters of faith—orthodox or unorthodox—had always left Old Charlie cold as the Colorado in January. And *now*—now that he'd come across the country to retire, now that he was finally safe in his own house—to hear these constant declarations of how his soul was surely lost . . . well, he felt it was more than a man should have to bear!

Carping on the one hand was Lyda, his wife, an overripe thirty-year-old who had aged in a manner Charlie felt unforgivable during the saddled-up three years of their marriage. She usually wasn't much of a talker—he'd give her that—but whenever her early Catholic indoctrination was triggered by his taking the Lord's name in vain or some other egregious blasphemy considered routine in a man's world, she was good for an hour's lecture.

Lyda was particularly loquacious and shrewish, he felt, whenever she had a mind to harp on her favorite theme: Old Charlie hadn't told her, before she married him, that he'd been married before. Since he had conveniently neglected to apprise her of that, Lyda said plainly, they were both living in mortal sin, and their souls were surely jeopardized.

For his part, while feeling fenced in and ornery on the river steamer that brought them north from Texas to Pittsburgh, Congelier thought that he'd have greater sympathy for Lyda if she would accept his angry suggestion and simply leave him. The longer he looked at gorgeous Essie, his servant, the more he felt it wouldn't be too hard to get along without Lyda. Her refusal to leave indicated to Old Charlie that Lyda preferred squandering his ill-gotten fortune to protecting her precious soul. God A'mighty, he hated a hypocrite! He'd take a good, honest cutthroat or gunman any day, and twice on Sunday.

On the other hand, there was the succulent Indian maid, Essie. Essie's age was not a matter of record, and that was OK with Charles W. Congelier. Age could be of no conceivable importance when a man cast his eyes on her waist-long raven's-wing hair, her great shining eyes and her buxom frontage. Trouble was, Essie seemed to have spent her entire girlhood rounding up every supernatural tribal myth she could absorb. She knew amazing stories about bearded old men who built boats to save their people from great floods, like Noah and his ark, even though that was patently impossible. Sometimes, staring into the midnight sky and bathed in such moonlit glory that her skin turned to alabaster, she told him things that came true in a few days. How'd she do that? Essie would simply smile shyly and shake her gorgeous head.

Thank heaven, Congelier thought, there was no concept of sin in her native tongue. But *there*, he suspected when he longed for her mouth, resided a sweet honey on which a man might become forever intoxicated. He'd flat-out insisted that Essie come with them to coal country for the simple but unstated reason that he hoped fervently, one day, to sip that honey. If he could ever forget for a night that he still adored Lyda.

So it was that the ill-matched trio bought and moved into the two-story mansion at 1129 Ridge Avenue—from which none of them would leave unscathed.

The house was still vacant nearly a year after construction, because the man who built the place had committed suicide the same night he assumed tenancy. Local burghers said they had heard rumors that the builder had been driven to killing himself by ghosts who'd moved in the morning the doors were opened. They felt uncomfortable because of such rumors; even those who didn't believe in ghosts planned to wait a prudent period of time before making an offer for the property.

But things like suicide, evil spirits and civil manners didn't concern Charles Wright Congelier. He figured 1129 Ridge was as fine a place as any to settle and avoid the countless enemies he'd acquired after the war. After all, he was anxious to get on with living the full, rich life of his dreams. Fulfillment had always been just beyond his avaricious grasp, but no more, b'God. He planned to buy half of Pittsburgh and, in time, to install himself as mayor. A mansion erected by a galoot crazy enough to hang himself wasn't going to stand in Old Charlie's way. The place was clearly a good buy, especially when the realtor came down in price.

Congelier was dead-sure that this was where he would begin his uphill climb to respectability, and more. Who knew how far a man like him could go if he really put his mind to it? The governorship?

Consequently, the carpetbagger was feeling both expansive and charitable on the day his little brood moved in. When Essie began making her strange remarks and bizarre proposals, insisting they absolutely had to protect the place against evil spirits, Congelier sighed and turned to her with his full attention.

According to beautiful Essie, her people always believed that spirits inhabited the land itself, the very ground and grass, the trees and flowers. Human animosities were made and wars initiated when the land was not properly propitiated. "Mighty warriors of past will not rest till they have been shown proper respect," Essie claimed, her eyes wide and eager. When a house was constructed, she persisted, these spirits—happy or unhappy, good or evil—moved in along with the living occupants. To get them on one's side, therefore it was necessary to do certain things. Even Lyda raised her brows.

"*What* things, girl?" Congelier demanded, anxious to be done with this nonsense.

It was just beginning to snow outside, and none of them had seen much of it before. The effect of the unfamiliar weather on the Mexican wife, Lyda, was disturbing. Weary from the difficult cross-country journey and as fearful of the keening howl of winter as she was of growing ill again, she stirred uneasily and did not seem to hear what her servant said. "Charles, we must have a padre—a priest—come here soon to bless thees house. Please!"

Congelier gave her a vague nod. His black agate eyes were drawn to Essie's lively face; they darted boldly to the full bosom pressing against home-sewn clothes, and he licked his upper lip hungrily. "What crazy things do we have t'do *this* time, girl?"

"Not crazy, Charles!" she asserted. Then she saw that he would probably grant her wish and allow her to sanctify the premises, and a flicker of a smile appeared on her lips. "Is important that the spirits be greeted OK."

"Damn it!" He draped a long, playful arm around her shoulders without seeing Lyda move, wraithlike, to the stairs. "Little girl, if y'don't tell me exactly what you want to *do*, I'll wring your purty heathen neck!"

Essie glanced at Lyda, shrinking against the wall on the stairs, and then to Congelier. She was eager now. "First I must get bread. Then I walk into all rooms of the house. And salt, too," she added earnestly, "with bread."

"Salt, eh?" He rubbed his lantern jaw and spread one wing of his moustache taut against his cheek. "White people got a superstition about salt, too. When we spill it, we gotta toss some over our shoulder. Right, Lyda?" He turned his head to Lyda.

The Mexican, her hair in a fistlike bun at the back of her head, was unnaturally pale as she stood watchfully on the second step of the stairway. A shawl was pulled tight around her somewhat meaty shoulders, and a necklace of perspiration beads shone on her forehead. She nodded absently, without answering.

"You not pick up salt when Essie throw it!" the Indian girl commanded, frightened now. "Bread help make spirits know us friends. Salt let 'em know we're boss in house!"

"How's that?" the carpetbagger asked, curious despite himself.

"Spirits must count every grain of salt," she replied with a flash of snow-white teeth. "If we throw lotsa of salt, that means spirits got to spend a long time counting! Keep 'em busy!"

Congelier threw back his head, laughed hoarsely and hugged the young woman against his angular chest. "OK, then, girl. I'll go along with that one, but don't waste too much salt. Now, what else you gotta do t'keep the ha'nts away?"

"One thing more, that's all," Essie replied, pleased with her progress.

Throughout the discussion she had kept her hands together, beneath her breasts. Old Charlie had thought she was merely cold. Now she extended her hands to him, revealing a small bundle covered by bright Indian cloth.

"What the hell y'got there?" he asked, squinting at it.

She took the gaily colored cloth by a corner and pulled it back with a proud, delighted flourish.

"Jesus H. Christ!" Congelier exclaimed, taking a backward step as the smell reached his nose.

Spread before him, on Essie's brownish palms, was the decaying corpse of a small maggot-eaten animal. It was impossible to tell what kind of beast it had once been.

She looked happily up at him. "I put this in walls of house, or maybe what you call cellar. Then spirits *real* happy. Dead animal take the evil away with his spirit."

Lyda, forgotten on the stairs, had leaned forward to see. Now she sobbed and, turning on one heel, ran quickly upstairs, covering her mouth with her hand.

Torn between the two women and his own disgust at the object, Charles paused, then glared down at his Indian servant. "Get rid of that damnable thing!" he ordered.

"I can put it in cellar?" she pressed fervently. "Essie hide it good! So you not smell it anymore!" In her religious zeal she had put her pretty face only inches away from Congelier's long face. "Then we all be happy always in Pi'sburgh!"

Her sensual lips were parted. When Congelier stared at her intent face, fresh desire for her swelled in him. "OK, honey, you can do that." He frowned in comic revulsion. "But I don't want ever t'see that goddamn mess again! Y'got me?"

Essie turned with delight, clutching her loathsome offering, and ran toward the door that led to the cellar. The carpetbagger could not see the smile of covert triumph cross her face. Instead, Charles Wright Congelier stared at the woods-taught gracefulness of her youthful body until his mouth began, quite literally, to water.

Somehow, he thought, swearing it to himself, I got to git *into* that squaw! Soon!

The pressure of a troubled conscience, the memory of a child aborted before starting her hazardous journey, and the cold shock of alien winter were too much for Lyda Congelier. After dining with her husband on their first night in the Ridge Avenue manse, Lyda retired to their bedroom and remained there throughout the night and all the next day. That evening, though, she summoned her waning strength to go downstairs for dinner. After only a few tentative sips of soup, she found herself so weak that she excused herself and hurried upstairs to her lonely bed.

If only Charles would bring a padre to bless this

house . . .

For many people, thirty is an age of small importance, only a late stepping-stone of ongoing youth and vitality. But for the inhabitants of Lyda's tiny Mexican village, thirty had always signaled the turning point toward old age and the clammy reach of death. Such stepping-stones led to the grave.

She recalled these things clearly, and it is impossible now to know to what degree her own expectations contributed to her debilitating illness. The workings of the human mind were still challenging, enigmatic in the big cities of vast America and rarely discussed at all in Mexican villages. All Lyda understood, alone in the unfamiliar bedroom of this strange house in a strange city in a strange country, was that everything about her was alarming. Always spoiled by her adoring Catholic mother, who had wanted the girl to join a convent, Lyda had no way to recognize the difference between physical sickness and a psychological breakdown born of dislocation and uneasy conscience. There are those, too, who believe that she was pregnant with a child whose birth could not be allowed in a region where entities of sheer evil were stealthily, invisibly gathering to produce a century of periodic terror and unspeakable tragedy.

The curtains were drawn, as usual. Lyda had tried for two hours to sleep but found that she was oddly restless and that sharp-edged images of terrible things kept filtering through her mind. For a time she strove to read the Spanish language Bible that was her treasured possession and which she had kept near her at all times during the travail of her river voyage.

But it was hard to concentrate when, from the corner of her eyes, she kept sensing movement—motions that, when she raised her dark eyes to see, seemed to scuttle into corners of the room like unseen rats. Sighing, trying mightly to ignore her apprehension and focus on the sacred words, she turned on her side and propped the Bible against the other pillow.

She heard it then, for the first time.

Noise, unaccountable noise, was seeping fluidly from the walls of the room.

For a moment Lyda tried to tell herself that it was only the voice of her husband beneath her, moving from room to room on the first floor, talking to himself. She clutched the Bible tightly in her hands and stared into first one corner of the room and then another. It *had* to be Charles!

But it wasn't. Lyda pressed herself against the pillow and, dropping the Bible, tugged the blanket to her neck. The sounds were everywhere—nowhere—taunting, whispering sounds. *Voices.*

Voices trying to communicate with her. To tell her . . . *something.*

Essie had half forgotten the name her people once called her, but that didn't concern her. Life was good now, full of fine food anytime she wanted it and full of time to think the thoughts that even her own people hadn't wished to hear. The awful cold outside was kept at bay by this fine, sturdy house. And, best of all, she had her own room for a retreat.

She'd had little enough to do the past few days, with bossy Missus taken ill; it was a luxurious feeling to do whatever she pleased. In her memory existed vivid, hateful pictures of the way she had catered to every whim of her aged parents and her muscular, handsome brother. Her entire girlhood had been spent working, serving the constant demands of her family. Without being aware of it, Essie had grown to nurture a hatred for them that permeated her soul and aroused in it a tribe of evil longings that continued to march, even in her fine new home.

With such unhappiness in her father's house, it had not taken Essie long to say yes when Charles explained that he wanted to buy her. But even the parting was bleak, because her parents sold quickly and got little in return. Still, the chance to travel far beyond constant heat to places her people could never go had been the most glorious opportunity in her young life.

Essie had never had sexual relations with anyone, but it was commonly accepted by her tribe that the woman servant in a house was obliged to do anything asked of her. When Charles Wright Congelier tapped softly at her door that evening, then slipped into the room without waiting to be asked, it took Essie only one look at his face to know what he had in mind. Which was all right with her. When Old Charlie began to remove his clothing, she merely sat up in bed to throw back the blanket.

Congelier's dangling moustache jerked as his lips quivered. He looked longingly at her bare brown body and soared with lust. She gestured to him, and still he continued to stare, unmoving—because it had occurred to the white man, still just enough in control of his faculties to notice it, that there was something distantly peculiar in all this.

He had craved Essie's warmth since hiring her, but he had always held back, knowing how terribly upset it would make the faithful Lyda if she found out. The truth of the matter was that, before coming to Pittsburgh, as late as the time when he bought the house on Ridge Avenue, Congelier had gone on loving his Mexican wife, and it had mattered greatly to him that their marriage remain intact. Sure, Lyda drove him crazy with her religious crap, but he'd always complained about the way of womenfolk and gone on admiring them. After all, Lyda had been basically a good wife these past three years, and in Congelier's opinion a child could make all the difference in the world to their marriage. If they hadn't lost the one she was carrying, he felt, this relationship might have been the single decent achievement of his life.

Now here he was, just a few days living in the only respectable house he'd ever owned, taking an immoral step he knew was fraught with hazard. Lust was nothing new to him, but he'd always kept things in perspective, before—like all the times he'd moved in on a woman when her husband was safely out of town.

And here he was, too, he realized, more charged with rutting desire than he'd ever been his whole life! Lord, he'd never seen himself this way before, Congelier thought, looking down at his swollen member. It was already enormous, even before touching the girl! Why, he was positively shaking with want of her, trembling like some stupid young fart who'd never been with a woman before!

Suddenly he felt dizzy and reached out for the

bedpost with his hand. It was all wrong, somehow—
out of kilter. For an instant his inflamed eyes swept
the room, and Old Charlie had the sensation of the
walls being somehow sloped inward, nightmarelike,
at insane angles, as if they'd no longer support the
ceiling and it would gradually slide downward to
crush him. Heart pounding in his ears, he gazed
toward the window and saw the way it, too,
appeared distorted, out of proportion: it seemed to
move! He thought it damned near *breathed*!

And he saw the yowling winter night beyond
the window, black in a way he'd never seen
darkness before—an unholy ebon until it was
sheared by a jagged bolt of fierce lightning. Lightning during a snowstorm? Congelier shuddered.
The world—everything in his world—was becoming
peculiar.

Then he saw Essie on the bed, a few feet from
him, sprawled out with her long black hair sweeping
sensually over the burgeoning bare breasts. Her
legs were parted—not brazenly, but in a straightforward utilitarianism that Congelier's pragmatic
mind realized. She was his, something cried in his
head, his to do with as he pleased: ready, docile,
eager to learn! The possibilities raced through his
fevered mind.

"Show me, Charles-sir," Essie called. Somehow
her voice echoed off the distorted walls of the small
room. Her mouth, parted, appeared hungry. "Show
me how."

Congelier forgot everything then but the universe of desire opening before him, and he threw
himself upon the bed to grapple with the virginal,
superstitious Indian girl.

HORROR HOUSE

Neither of them heard Lyda's bell jangling from above them.

Some remember that night in Pittsburgh, or say that they do. They claim there has never been a snowstorm so vicious in intensity nor a wind so angry in its soulless, shrieking search for winter victims. They say there was, indeed, unnatural lightning which pierced the violent skies.

Some remember it because their parents or grandparents told them what happened next—told them in the way that certain elders enjoy frightening the young half-silly.

And some say that they remember it because to pass through that section of Ridge Avenue in the old coal town is to feel the relics of bygone savagery stir in the dusty air and cling to the cringing skin itself.

In her bedroom, Lyda listened to the whispered voices below her, then nodded and staggered out into the corridor. She was panic-stricken by confusion; she could not quite understand the maddeningly distant message of the voices, and she had grown angry because neither her Indian servant nor her husband would come to her aid.

She started down the steps. No one can say what the shadows looked like on the unfamiliar walls as she descended the staircase in the storm-lashed house. Surely, as lightning flashed surreally through the windows she passed, the forms on the walls must have seemed like gnarled trees whose branches reached coldly, graspingly, for the innocent stranger.

Stumbling, half falling and sobbing, Lyda Congelier made her way through rooms on the first floor. She could not recall where the furniture had been placed; it did not seem to be where she thought she'd left it. Bruising her thighs, Lyda tottered on. "Charles! *Charles!*" But her voice was swallowed up by the booming thunder, and Charles seemed to have disappeared.

Lyda found Essie's room, and grateful for human companionship when she saw candlelight beneath the closed door, she paused to catch her breath and quiet her tortured nerves.

"Again, Charles-sir!" gasped the servant's voice. "Ah, yessss . . ."

With awful clarity, Lyda knew that the other, muffled sounds were those of her husband.

And now, at last, she understood the words latent in the whispering sounds that had hissed tormentingly at her in the lonely bedroom upstairs. *Instructions!* Yes, *that's* what they were!

She whirled away from the servant's door and rushed—falling, clambering to her feet, falling again and rising—to her kitchen. There, she found what the voices had recommended. Branches beat the house in a fury of anticipation as she returned to Essie's room, eager to share her discovery.

Her hand knotted in a fist and gripping her find, she beat upon the door. At once, within, all sounds ceased. A shocked and embarrassed silence filtered out to Lyda's attentive ears. With one sane part of her mind she heard mumbled syllables tumbling from Charles's lips and shocked questioning from her maid's.

Footsteps inside. Approaching.

HORROR HOUSE

Then the door opened. The candle inside the room threw a huge, sharply defined shadow: a sensual silhouette of a lovely and sated naked girl resting on her knees in bed, arms raised, her breasts jutting proudly.

"Lyda, what're you doin' down here?"

There was an intant's pause as she stared at Charles's angry, shocked expression. His fingers were scurrying like white mice as they fastened here, fastened there. His moustache appeared damp and glistening. His shamed eyes followed Lyda's rising arm.

Lyda hadn't known who would be first. It hadn't really mattered. The meat cleaver in her hand came down on the forehead of her husband, then was jerked free and raised again. As if suspended, he seemed to hover in front of her. And Lyda, her brain clotted with whispered psychic urgency, lifted the cleaver again and again.

On the fifteenth lowering of the arm, Charles's skull split like an orange; and he fell, supported by the framework of the doorway. He was quite dead now; still, Lyda continued her work. Crying in mad frustration, she hacked away until shards of skull strewed the hallway and a crimson-shadowed pool of blood with grayish lumps of brain flowed turgidly back into Essie's room.

When the murmuring, persistent messages hesitated, at last, Lyda heard the terrified screams of the Indian girl. Placing the bloody meat cleaver beside the battered body of her husband, Lyda quietly picked up the *other* tool she'd been told to bring.

George Caldwell had sold the house at 1129 Ridge Avenue to Charles W. Congelier and, being a courteous chap in his late thirties, anxious to get along in the world, decided it was proper to look in on the new owner. After all, Mr. Congelier paid in cash, and there was no way of knowing how well he might do in Pittsburgh.

Personally, Caldwell had considered it absurd for anyone to care about rumors of dead Indians haunting the property. He had heard and dismissed them so many times that he'd sold the place to Congelier with an absolutely clear conscience. What earthly difference could it make that the house, only a few blocks from where the Allegheny and Monongahela rivers met to create the Ohio River, had been erected on Indian burial grounds? And who cared about a stranger's suicide?

There were festive Christmas wreaths hanging on the front doors of neighboring houses, and as George Caldwell climbed from his carriage in front of 1129 Ridge, he thought it passing strange that there were no decorations on the new owner's house. Didn't the Congeliers have a single dash of Christmas spirit?

Asking the coachman to wait, Caldwell approached the front door, which he now saw was gaping open, several inches of snow molded to the frame and melting into brown puddles on the foyer floor. Concerned, he quickened his step and entered the house.

"Mr. Congelier?" he called. "Mrs. Congelier? Are you about?"

Caldwell was to say, later, that he'd never before heard such an absolute silence. He was stunned by it. For a while it seemed gravelike, but, upon further reflection, he thought it wasn't that at all. Because a gravesite should feel devoid of ... presences.

Across the foyer, Caldwell caught a glimpse of light fingering its way beneath the parlor door. And for the first time he heard something: the slow, steady creaking of a rocking chair. Caldwell never confessed to the feeling of apprehension he experienced; yet he would not have been human had he not paused, just for a prudent instant, the winter breeze a chill clutch at the nape of his neck, in this house where no one replied, yet someone, or something, waited.

As he drew near the parlor door, Caldwell heard another sound: the soft keening of a woman's voice. It sang a wistful lullaby in a language he did not know. He stepped into the room, then froze in his tracks.

Lyda Congelier rocked quietly in her chair before the curtained window, her unwashed hair, freed from its bun, sweeping down the back of the sweat-stained, frayed nightgown. Something in her lap held her unswerving attention. *God on high,* Caldwell prayed for a witness, her gown and bare arms were *drenched* with blood. It was as if she'd waded and splashed in a tub of gore.

Lyda did not lift her eyes to look at Caldwell until he was halfway across the parlor floor, hat in hand and filled with the stupefying realization that he had blundered upon a playlet produced in hell.

Even after Lyda peered in his direction, she did not see Caldwell. She merely smiled distantly, as if responding affectionately to some vagrant line of the wistful song wending its way through her tormented mind.

Caldwell stopped before her. His eyes fell to the bundle in her lap, something the poor woman's hands were caressing lightly. It was wrapped in a pink child's blanket. Caldwell was puzzled. The Congeliers had no children, of that he was certain. Then, what did this pathetic soul clutch so sweetly in her lap?

When he took it gently from her, without protest from the blood-spattered Lyda, the blanket unfolded and the object within dropped to the parlor floor and skittered away, finally halting by the fireplace hearth.

George Caldwell screamed his terror as he vaulted back, away from Lyda. He is on record as admitting that he'd never been so shocked—so unforgettably *horrified*—in his entire life.

The object that lay before the fireplace was covered by matted raven's-wing hair and grimaced up at him with snow-white teeth daubed with blood. *It was the severed head of the lovely Indian servant named Essie.*

Children came again onto Ridge Avenue, after a couple of years had slipped away and their mothers had begun to forget. But children are fascinated by the horrible, and they remember it, and so they ventured near number 1129 once more.

No longer did they come to admire the handsome brick and mortar mansion—the finest house in all the neighborhood—but to poke each other unsubtly in the ribs and mutter challenges to one another. "Bet y'can't go up to the front door," one child would call. And another replied warily, "Darers go first!"

Eventually, of course, one brave and bold darer would indeed sidle up the front lane of 1129, with his heart in his mouth, and shakily touch the door to validate his claim or, very rarely, actually peep through the bay window.

Sometimes he would fly back to the relative safety of the sidewalk populace and insist, with the boundless passion of childhood, that he had seen somebody in there—"an ugly ole woman carryin' a human skull."

And the others would shower obloquy upon the courageous one but go home shuddering, to have nightmares about the "haunted house" at 1129 Ridge Avenue.

There were rhymes created by uncelebrated poets, little odes devised by the careless cruelty of the very young, awful and gruesome paeans to a death that none of them feared because that was a millenium in the future for each child. And they spoke and sang of Lyda and her husband, Old Charlie, and of their beautiful maid, who together wandered into a fugitive wind of madness and were swept away one night to the kind of dark immortal renoun that no sane man has ever sought.

But none of the children, when reaching what passed for maturity, really believed—down to his toes—the genuine, real-world *facts* of the matter:

Dwelling in the house at 1129 Ridge Avenue, existing there in wait for the next tenants, were creatures who would become known to a truly great man as *entities*.

Because 1129 Ridge Avenue was, in point of absolute fact, quite hideously haunted.

One
THE WRETCHED WRAITHS OF RIDGE AVENUE

I think as you do that death ends all, yet I do not feel certain.

Thomas A. Edison

1

Spring, 1920.

Civil war erupted in Ireland over the question of Home Rule, and people began to die. They died, too, in Poland: Russia, the Big Bear, had flexed its muscles and declared another war. The world wept anew and counted its widow's beads. Prohibition brought tears to the United States, too—but a new use, other than bathing, sex or drowning, was discovered for the common bathtub. Joan of Arc was canonized, at last, this year; but in Pittsburgh, Pennsylvania, a different kind of remembrance of the dead took evil shape.

When a tree falls in the forest and no one is around to hear, asked the philosophers of the fifties, *is* there really any sound?

When a house stands empty for nearly twenty years, nothing inside it alive, are there really malefic spirits haunting it?

Many of the good burghers of the eastern coal town said yes, remembering the terrible things that happened *after* the Congeliers—things that would not be recalled in detail for more than sixty years. Those who said no, in 1920, were nevertheless careful to avoid lingering near 1129 Ridge Avenue.

Now and then there were tentative offers to buy the place, generally tendered by innocents from other places; but a scant few minutes spent in the nearly half-century-old mansion convinced the prospective buyers that their money was better spent elsewhere. Whether 1129 was haunted by Indian savages, the ghosts of the Congelier trio and those who followed their bloody footprints or merely—as some boasted—a house grown old without love and care, out-of-towners spread the houses's scary story all over the populous eastern seaboard.

In Pittsburgh itself there were speeches made, on occasion, urging that 1129 be razed; several times it almost felt the breath of the torch. Such hands were held back by the city fathers, who remembered the house had commercial value: it had become a point of interest for tourists.

When a city has little to boast of except a baseball team—and bowlegged all-star shortstop Honus Wagner was getting along in the tooth— almost anything is welcome that is an attraction, a lure for the tourist dollars. And so the reputation of 1129 Ridge spread, fueled by the intentionally husky whispers of the town fathers. People began to come from far and near to stand outside the deserted mansion, shuffling nervous feet, mumbling in hushed tones, snapping pictures. Some claimed that the photographs, when they were developed, had caught spirit glimpses of tear-stained, gaunt female faces floating bodiless behind broken window panes—relics of the monstrous Dr. Brunrichter, who followed the Congeliers into tenancy. Some said, too, that they had lost sleep for days after an exposure only to the proximity of this house of multiple deaths; one woman said, indeed, that she lost her baby because she had visited and come too close.

Not that anyone went inside. The city of Pittsburgh, grudging inheritors of 1129 Ridge Avenue, did not care to be responsible for what might happen within, real or fancied. "The floors are rotting out," was their public explanation.

Such matters concerened the *outside* of the house. What was going on *inside*?

Time is not only relative but a useful invention of man, a tool of measurement as one's hand or foot once was. Time measures the passing of earth day to night, and the concept of weeks, months and years was basically the way early man chose to keep his records—a sensible way to plant and harvest his crops. Man notes, too, when he is born and when he dies, calling that period of sunrises a lifetime.

But what if there *is* no life to measure? What if death itself has been accepted, finally, and has no more meaning to the one who experiences it than time to the lad who thinks he will experience life's pleasures forever? The boy does not care about his elders' arbitrary commitment to time and lives (when he can) as he pleases—casually, freely. For him, manhood, middle-age and old age are events of a future too distant to fear.

Death has no more reality than fairies, St. Nicholas, the city of Paris, the red planet Mars or one million dollars for teenage boys. For that which is in the midst of death itself, life holds even less reality.

Such stark similarities may be advanced a final step.

When our careless boy is, at sad last, whimperingly confronted with the obligation of seeing and recognizing death, experiencing it secondhand at the passing of a friend or kinsman, he may be filled with revulsion as well as a kind of terrified hatred. He would cheerfully do away with the Reaper, wipe the earth clean of its baleful power, its inescapable hint of inevitability.

And so the phantom, is haunted. Haunted, when he—or it—is confronted with the direr fact of life. When encountering it, thinking of or remembering life, he is suffused with revulsion, and envy. The spirit would, it seems safe to say, do away with life, would cleanse the shadowed and tormenting chambers of his imprisoning house of each haunting reminder of an inevitability he has forever lost, an inevitability that has come and gone.

So the entities at 1129 Ridge Avenue drifted powerlessly in their eternal, time-stripped warp. At times they forgot the lives they once lived, as one alive loses sight of childhood past. The secret, never-spoken worry that they might be obliged one day to experience life again, reincarnated, was similar to the anxiety about death experienced by the living.

At 1129, because they were dead, the spirit presences feared nothing about death itself. There was, in fact, a diminution of feeling, of all caring, hunger and basic need. But there was also an absence of pain. Pain of a fleshly sort, no, but ceaseless. Pain of the bereft spirit.

The psychic pain experienced on Ridge was immense, and raging. Because the entities here were basically evil and hopelessly mad, they suffered from an anguish of loss—loss of the ability to bring agony and insanity to others. Locked in a gray and ectoplasmic union composed of murdered carpetbaggers, soul-shriveled Mexicans, superstitious lunatic Indians and unnamed dreadfuls from one thousand years of bloody killing on this plot of earth—thrown together, despised souls from an amalgam of centuries and no common bond but a hatred for life—they had become a soupy morass of crushed individual egos unable to unite with a single voice, incapable of frightening even fellow members of their nightmare broth.

At one and the same instant, they dreaded the visitation of the ego-spurred living and longed for it with all the horribly husbanded powers they possessed—powers that could only be adequately "appreciated" by those of flesh and warm, oozing blood. Powers that could bring amusing madness, delicious dismemberment and the welcome icy embrace of death. Powers that they practiced and assiduously developed as they wafted restlessly to and fro between the cracking walls of the dark mansion, shrewd and cunning in a fashion that only Untime teaches.

And as they studied and improved their moribund skills, they, too, heard whispered messages over the years.

The messages implanted themselves on their senses from some subterranean source so malefic that even the spirit presences blanched and sought concealment behind half-closed closet doors and beneath beds that departing humankind had left behind.

The substance of the message that motivated them was unfailingly, relentlessly the same. *"Bring them to me,"* it hissed. *"They shall be mine."*

In November of that year, an old man descended from a train and paused for a moment on the platform to get his bearings, choking a little on the dust enveloping him. He was at once an imposing figure—with a mop of white hair that insisted upon falling lankly over his wide forehead, a prominent nose, and tufted gray eyebrows that extended a full half inch—a man who could physically have been almost anybody. He'd never quite been able to remember to be tidy about his person; there were multicolored stains on his vest and, he noticed absently, on his familiar drooping string tie as well.

When a blast of Pittsburgh's early-winter air struck at the old man's face, his jaw moved and his false teeth clacked with a chicken's sound. Embarrassed, he swiftly raised a massive, chemical-stained hand to his lips. Recently, unfortunately, some of his original teeth had become infected. Rather than identifying the culprits, he had simply and incredibly ordered *all* the offending teeth extracted.

"I know what X-rays can do to a man," he had growled at Mina, defying dispute, "and they ain't using their damned machine on *me*! I'll just get 'em out all at once!" And he had added "store-bought" dentures just as rashly.

This was his first visit to Pittsburgh for years without a welcoming committee. It would have been child's play to get half the town out to welcome him, but aging Thomas Edison was here on strictly private business, and he didn't care to advertise his arrival. Clutching a medium-sized box tightly against his side, hidden beneath his dark topcoat, he summoned a jitney and sank down on its back seat with a sigh. He averted his gaze, trying to ignore the flicker of pleased recognition clearly crossing the cabbie's face.

Foolishness, he thought to himself after announcing his destination. He'd lived over seventy years just to succumb finally to Everyman's complaint. Pure tomfool *foolishness!* Yet he settled the box cautiously on the seat beside him, to keep it from jostling, then rested a wide, protective palm over it. The pressure applied was light, almost gingerly.

If it don't work this time, the hell with it. Mina convinced me that it didn't function before because the other houses weren't really haunted, and I guess she's right. But this is the last time I try to summon the dead! Three failures is too many at my advanced age!

It wasn't a lengthy ride to the restaurant up the street from the Ridge Avenue region, but it allowed him a moment to think. Tom Edison was grateful for those chunky flakes of snow which steadily covered the Pittsburgh streets, forcing pedestrians into their homes, assisting him in his desire to remain an unknown visitor. He'd always had a strong feeling for the masses, sometimes even preferred an anonymous crowd of fascinated strangers to the handful of cherished friends who made up his circle. You could say no to strangers on occasion.

But these days, with his hearing getting so damned bad and all, it was difficult as Harvey Hell to put up with large numbers of people—especially nosy reporters.

He slapped his free hand against his knee, thinking wryly as he often had, over the years, about how incredibly ignorant people could manage to be, individually or taken as a whole. For years they'd criticized him because he wasn't a religious man; some well-meaning Nosy Parkers had even plotted to kidnap him, by God, and haul him off to some orthodox church! Damnation, he could have told them a hundred times that he honestly felt there might be immortality for man—that there could conceivably be a caring Omnipotent One. It just hadn't seemed to be any of their goddamn business! Besides, none of that was scientifically proved. *Not yet, anyway,* the old man thought with a secret smile.

Here he was in a spanking new decade when other Americans were fairly breathing *joie de vivre* and it was people who weren't alive anymore that had piqued his curiosity. A British scientist and spiritualist called Sir Oliver Lodge had begun studying the supernatural in ways Tom Edison approved—scientific ways. Old Lodge was even documenting spirit contact through his son, Raymond, who died five years back. Real contact hadn't even surprised Sir Oliver, who had somehow known it could happen. Privately impressed by the Englishman, Edison had eventually erred in saying publicly that he calculated a man was, in reality, a "vast collection of myrids of individuals."

Then he'd said a lot more rash things, too, to that boy business reporter, Forbes, who'd upped and published it in his magazine just last month. Tom didn't mind helping young Forbes advance his ambition to make the magazine successful but pressure had made him obliged to recant, or try to do so. Hell's bells, any self-respecting inventor ought to've known to keep it under wraps—

Till the experiment itself worked or flopped.

Still and all, the *Forbes* article hadn't been in vain. Tom grinned at the recollection of his pal, ever-admiring Henry Ford, who'd been downright relieved by the prospect that his dear old friend Edison might be saved from hellfire! Henry'd told the world: "The greatest thing that has occurred in the last fifty years is Mr. Edison's conclusion that there is a future life for all of us."

Good ol' Henry and his mechanical coach! Let him think what he pleased; Ford meant well. Besides, life wasn't just to please him or Thomas A. Edison. He and Henry were only a couple of tinkerers who were getting on—not pure scientists like Sir Oliver or that hunchbacked fellow Charlie Steinmetz. Maybe Ford was just trying to help Tom get the religious bos off his back, the ones who didn't care for his entities—his own version of man's soul—and the loonies who had stuffed his mailbox full of hate mail for the past month or more.

Getting down from the jitney in front of Hale's Bar & Grill, the old man bent toward the wet window to pay his bill. Before the wide-eyed driver could seize his last opportunity to ask, the old inventor winked at him. "Yep, I *am* Tom Edison," he confessed, "but here's something extra t'keep it between the two of us. All right?"

Edison tromped, grinning, through the caked snow and pushed his way into the almost deserted restaurant. He squinted—beneath great tufted brows—into the gloom. There! He gave a quick smile and headed for the booth.

"Good of you to meet me here, Fred," he said, putting out his hand as he slid into the booth. "And to keep it all quiet."

"Anything for you, Mr. Edison," Frederick Parlock said, shaking the gnarled hand warmly and inadvertantly making Tom's arthritis twinge. In his twenties, Parlock was a minor executive in the Pittsburgh Edison General Electric offices—the inventor tended to think of 'em that way, even though they had dropped his name over a dispute—and a frustrated inventor himself. Edison remembered the humble, entreating letters he'd received from Parlock in recent years and felt the man could be depended upon. "I brought the key to the Ridge house, just the way you asked me," the boy added.

Edison lit his twelfth cigar of the day and turned his large head to blow out a gust of nearly lethal fumes. "You won't regret this, Freddie," he said warmly.

"You must be tired, sir. May I order something hot for you, or perhaps you'd like to take something a little more in keeping with the weather?"

Edison scowled. The heavy brows curved in a W above the thrusting nose. "Can't eat much of anything anymore, Freddie. Stomach's shot to hell. But I can drink all the milk I want."

Parlock grinned, glad to be of service, and hastily beckoned a bored waitress. The old man averted his famous face as she approached. "Bring this gentleman two large milks and me some more coffee, if you don't mind." Once she had yawned her way back to the counter, Parlock leaned his lightly pockmarked face across the table. "I hope you know what you're up to, Mr. Edison, if you'll pardon me for mentioning it." He paused. "Do you realize everyone says 1129 is *really* haunted?"

The aging inventor grunted. "It best be. I've come a ways longer than I care to travel at my age because of the reputation your place has."

"Oh, it's not mine!" Parlock laughed nervously. "Are you allowed to tell me just what you are trying to accomplish? If you don't mind my asking?"

"I'm allowed everything that I want, so long as Mina isn't around," Edison rejoined with a smile. He puffed on his stogie and coughed a little. It sounded like a bark. "Every man's permitted the same damned thing, but he don't take advantage of his freedom the way I do."

"Well then?" Parlock pressed anxiously.

The wind outside Hale's Bar & Grill gusted past the windows, and a surge of snow lathered there drew the old man's attention for an instant. It reminded him of a clown, making faces. Suddenly he longed to be home with Mina in the great room they shared at Glenmont. It was possible he was getting a spot old for this kind of adventure. Shouldn't he really be spending more time with his grandchildren, considering the way he'd halfway ignored his own kids much of their lives?

Time—once there'd been so much of it that he had reveled in it, working almost incessantly and sleeping in shifts, tumbling minutes and hours over and around him like a joyous juggler. Thomas Alva Edison sighed, and the familiar brilliant light twinkled again in his crinkling blue eyes. "Well, Fred, it all goes back half a century or so."

"Really, sir? So does the haunted house, if you don't mind my saying so?"

"Please stop making that irritating apology. Freddie," Edison answered. "I don't mind much at all what you're likely to say or do. All right? Well, around '75 or so I was makin' stock printers and doing right well. An electric pen was in the works, but what really fascinated me was a strange new force. An *etheric* force, I called it."

Parlock's bland gray eyes widened. "But wasn't that radio? I mean—"

Tom lifted a palm. "That's how the idea worked out, how it was used—for the development of that damfool radio of mine. I guess I could have used the same knowledge and become inventor of the wireless. That's what they say, anyhow. But, Fred, I was fascinated by other possibilities, other applications of the etheric force. Charlie Steinmetz, he said I was a fool, because he didn't believe in other. 'Course, that was before radio." The old man chuckled softly and put his cigar out in a single crunching motion. "Lots of things are superstitious nonsense till y'figure out how to use 'em. Anyway, I was inclined to see this new force as a means for contacting the entities of people who had passed on."

"Beg pardon, sir. Entities? Do you mean *souls*?"

"I mean what I say, Freddie; always." Edison folded his large hands together comfortably, assuming the scholar's role. "They have both mass and weight, although they are microscopically small. After all, there's no limit to smallness any more than there is a limit to largeness. Right?"

Parlock nodded, wide-eyed as a boy.

"These entities dwell in communities of the body we term 'cells,' but don't go confusin' them with cells themselves. The cells are just their, um, residence. Entities are in charge of what our minds think, what our bodies represent. They live so long as the individual man does; then they move on"—he paused—"because they live . . . *eternally.*"

"Then, aren't they sort of like the soul?" the young man interjected.

"It's all how you look at it, Freddie," Tom said.

They paused while the waitress deposited two huge glasses of milk and then departed.

"Where was I?" the old man asked, taking a sip. "Oh! Well, Freddie, these entities are not only immortal, but they can assume any form—if a new human being isn't around to attach themselves to." He looked with amusement at Parlock's expression of shock. "As I see it, they're adaptable buggars. Now, sometimes, I guess, they tend to become 'stuck' on one place, like this so-called haunted house of yours. For some reason, as I say, they cannot move on. And that gives me a golden opportunity to test my *new* apparatus."

Parlock glanced for the first time at the box beside Tom Edison. "That's what you're going to use to contact the *dead*?"

"I'm going to try. Talk to 'em and hear what they have to say. It's failed twice before, this experiment of mine—flat-out didn't work. Mina thinks that the places I visited weren't haunted." He squinted at Parlock. "I'm depending on you, Fred."

Parlock lifted both palms as if he'd touched something hot. "As I told you, sir, the things that have happened at 1129 Ridge Avenue are beyond human ken. Not just the murders, you understand, but the way that ordinary people seem to have been influenced by what dwells in the old place. Folks in this city say that the house will get you, one way or the other, if you spend much time in it."

"Then, how come you agreed to show me the way?" the old man asked softly.

Parlock flushed. "Let's just say, if you don't mind, that I'm no genius but I'm smart enough to know I've been asked to help this century's most important man. When you're no great shakes yourself, it's pleasant to touch greatness." Embarrassed, he pointed to the box. "How does it work, Mr. Edison?"

"It's pitched between long and short waves. Marconi is doin' something similar, trying to record voices from the *past*. He don't advertise that much. Of course, my gadget doesn't record."

"Why not? I mean, you really should have a phonograph to record it." Then the General Electric executive colored richly. "Oh, sir, I didn't mean to be so presumptuous, but—"

"I will come back and record it, *if* there's anything significant that develops scientifically, Freddie." The old man licked at the cream moustaching his lips. "As you know, I've always done things one at a time, and I always will. People say I waste a lot of time by not figurin' things out in logical theorem first, by doing several things at once. But I have my methods." He reached down to pat the box. "Years ago, young man, I felt that I could invent something to be used by personalities that have passed on to another existence. But I let the apparatus sit awhile because I didn't know where in hell to *point* the damn thing—not until I thought about haunted houses." His smile was nearly shy. "I think it'll at least give the folks who come after me a better chance than tilting tables and spirit photographs like that Doyle fella in England swears by. I'm inclined to think he should have stuck with Mr. Holmes of Baker Street." He polished off his second glass of milk and placed his palms on the table. "Any reasons why we can't go out to Ridge Avenue now?"

Deep in the snow on the front porch, it took young Frederick Parlock some time to get the old lock to work, but, when it turned at last, the front door of 1129 Ridge Avenue seemed to swing back almost as if pulled from the inside.

Edison stepped into the foyer first, Parlock hanging back for a moment. The inventor appeared taller than his five-ten and larger than his consistent weight of one hundred and eighty pounds. Despite the bowed shoulders and the sweep of white hair, he had an ambience of greatness that gave him, for Parlock, a suggestion of considerable bulk. "Hope you brought the flashlights," Edison called affably over one shoulder. "Dark as hell in here."

Parlock stepped beside the old man and shone a beam into the entrance. Cobwebs glittered like silver. "You picked the right simile, Mr. Edison."

Edison took the flashlight pressed into his hand and led the way. It occurred to the business executive Parlock that the flashlight never even existed before this incredible old character came along. "I can surely see why they say it's haunted." Edison chuckled appreciatively. "Looks like everything was furnished about the time Adam and Eve moved out of the garden, dispossessed by their Landlord."

"Are you truly aware of the people who have lived here, sir?" asked Parlock as the two men moved carefully down the corridor and past two closed doors. He tried not to tremble at the cold that exuded from the rooms. "The terrible history of the place?"

"You mean Congelier and his charming family? Dr. Brunrichter and his amateur foray into science?" There was the open rumble of the old man's laugh, audible sunshine, as he led the way into the living room. "Truly engaging history, Freddie. One of the major reasons for my presence here tonight."

"Why is that, Mr. Edison?" He nearly added, "If you don't mind my asking," but caught himself.

"Because a discarnate entity surely derives from tragedy, sudden death such as from murder foul and the like. Otherwise, it would be able to move on and assume a fresh role in a newborn child. Well," he said, stopping so suddenly that Parlock collided lightly with him, "this looks like as good a place as any."

Edison casually dropped his flashlight on a table with dust coating it like fur and placed his box beside it, more carefully. Illumined by Parlock's torch, the inventor seemed almost ghostly himself with his white hair and heavy brows. His practical dark suit merged with the darkness. He dug into the box with surprisingly nimble fingers and drew something out with a satisfied sigh.

It was possibly a foot square and gleamed metallically in Parlock's beam. There was a dial, the young executive saw, a single lever and a series of enameled black numbers. That was all he could make out in the gloom. He was going to ask Edison to explain the device further, when *it happened.*

The thing that once had been a man seemed to enter from the doorway they had vacated. It was tall and lanky, with a black moustache waxen against its sallow cheeks. It required no illumination, because it somehow provided its own—a sullen, yellowish cast that led upward from where no feet could be seen, highlighting the ghastly head. Parlock gasped. From crown to nose, the skull was split apart so that the fragmentary sides dangled from threads of flimsy grey flesh, giving the creature a slightly walleyed expression. And one of sinister, dark terror.

" 'And whatsoe'er may be his prayer/Let ours be for his soul,' " murmured the old man.

"What?" Parlock piped, his own voice high with fright. "What?"

"Byron, Freddie." Edison was rooted to the spot as he calmly, curiously regarded the drifting apparition. "Perhaps," he whispered, "perhaps we shall not even require my apparatus."

But before he could turn to address the thing, it had vanished.

Parlock's delicate nose wrinkled in disgust. The creature had left behind a lingering odor of rotten eggs. Not quite that, but it was close enough.

As if nothing special had happened, Thomas Edison was quietly fiddling with his new machine.

"Doesn't that c-convince you, sir?" Parlock demanded. "Isn't that—that *thing* enough for you?"

Edison flicked a glance from the corner of his perceptive eye. "It did not see fit to address us, Fred. I want to communicate with the entities—remember?—not merely register my surprise at their concepts of how they looked at the point of death."

"*Concepts*, Mr. Edison?"

The inventor nodded. "I told you I was in two other places similar to this, and I've thought it out. My theory is, they are still in shock from what happened to them. And what they show is how they felt they looked at the moment of death. All is vanity, as the psalm says." He shrugged lightly, and the machine on the table began to make encouraging clicking sounds. A light glowed dimly from its heart. "These poor folks want sympathy, Freddie, as much as anything. Or so I think."

"If you say so, sir."

Edison smiled to himself. They weren't going to earn a lot of compassion from this young man, he thought. The poor fellow was scared stiff. The inventor picked up his apparatus as well as his flashlight, hesitated, then headed toward an aged rocking chair across the living room.

"We may as well be comfortable," he observed, indicating a stool beside the ancient fireplace and comfortably taking his seat in the darkness.

Then, to Parlock's amazement, Tom Edison produced an ordinary cigar from his breast pocket, struck a match and leaned back contentedly to rock and smoke.

Parlock shook his head. He slumped to the stool and nervously jabbed his flashlight beam from corner to corner. The unnatural silence crowded in on the young man, suffocatingly. He had to admit it to himself—this place was unnerving. For the first time it occurred to him that his admiration of Thomas Edison may have got him into a tight squeeze. Considering how he could best propose that they depart, he turned his head to the old man, the flashlight beam with it.

The apparatus nestled in the inventor's lap began to thrum sonorously, to rise warningly in pitch, and then *she* was there, coming toward the two men from across the wide room, apparently a materialization from the web-strewn wall. Parlock's nerves chittered upon seeing her. Her dark hair flowed down her back; her eyes, seemingly unaware of the intruders, darted wildly from side to side. To Parlock's horror, she carried, in a filmy right hand, a gigantic butcher knife. It looked frightingly real to him.

Daring a hurried glance at the old man, he saw that Edison was fiddling confidently with his device. He looked like a calm man at home, tuning in a radio, and the incongruity of the image scared Parlock almost as much as the Mexican woman—who now seemed to be floating directly toward him.

She stopped perhaps nine or ten feet away. As the two men watched, a door materialized in front of the apparition. It was ajar. The woman reached inside and silently tugged with all her strength. Then her mouth was open wide, as if she were shouting, but no sound came as she pulled from the unseen room the naked form of a young woman with reddish-brown skin.

The apparatus worked! Without warning it suddenly achieved the right level of intensity, and both men heard the shriek of the terrified Indian maid. The Mexican woman's arm flashed from side to side, then shot forward swiftly. For a moment the Indian lass was shielded by the other woman's filmy form; then both of them were sprawled on the floor.

Now *quite* on the floor, Parlock noted with horror—because they seemed to hover quite inexplicably some six inches above the moldering carpet. The businessman turned away, sick from the ghastly reenactment, at the point he saw the Indian girl's head part from her lovely body. The Mexican woman straightened, satisfied again, holding the head dangling by its loose, long hair, the full lips parted in a cry that would echo through eternity.

It was then that the madwoman's eyes *acknowledged* the presence of the living. It was almost as if she had dutifully completed her repeated task of murder and could now hone in on the present. She stared fixedly at Thomas Edison; Parlock could hear her panting from the exertions as the apparatus continued to hum softly.

"We have not come to harm you," Edison said gently into the machine. His own gaze did not leave the pale face of the dead Mexican woman for a second.

But there was no reply. Instead of answering, the crazed apparition of Lyda Congelier knelt beside that of the Indian maid and picked up the hand fallen to the floor. Without looking at the human beings again, Lyda slipped the dead member between her lips and began to chew. Parlock felt faint, but still he could not tear his eyes away.

The old inventor was puzzled. He had never heard of cannibalism in connection with this case. Was it possible, he wondered, that the entities were free to do anything they wished in this awful house? Could they go beyond what they had actually *done* in life? He twisted the dial on his machine just slightly and spoke into it once more.

"Do speak with us, Señora Congelier, *por favor*," Edison pleaded. "Tell us, please, what it is like to be in your state? Tell us how we can perhaps free you to go on to other human lives."

"Lives?"

The voice was immediate. Both men jumped. The reply had come in the form of a loud roar. The apparatus quivered in Edison's lap, jerked.

"*Human lives?*" There was a note of such scorn in the bass voice that Parlock flinched away from it. Lyda continued to look at them, and her lips moved, forming the words that they heard; but no female voice, living or dead, had ever sounded so incredibly low or had ever roared with such ferocious anger and virility. *"Do not speak to me of human lives! They are nothing but food for me—food that generates my power, my everlasting strength!"*

Tom Edison blinked as Lyda's face faded and was instantly replaced by another, then another, in a lengthly parade of unfamilar feminine faces. It occurred to him that he should have been counting. Were these the faces in the Adolph Brunrichter case? The case so ghastly that few reports had been written of it to this day?

Each face in turn, Tom saw, continued to mouth the words pouring in unbearable rage and hatred from Edison's connective device. "Who *are* you?" he demanded at last, his voice strong and unafraid. "Are you the infamous Dr. Brunrichter?"

"Not yet!" the voice exclaimed. "He still lives; so I have not yet absorbed him." The deep voice chuckled. A taint of insanity flickered among the basso notes. "The good doctor has more to do for me—years from now, in the decade of the eighties."

Fred Parlock looked fearfully from the shifting faces before him to the puzzled expression on the inventor's face. Edison seemed to be mustering his courage to ask a certain, inevitable question. And yet, Parlock thought with admiration and frustration, he might merely be absorbed with the performance of his latest incomparable invention.

"Why can't these pathetic souls who have occupied this house, and this land, go on to other lives? Why can't they enjoy other existences in life?"

"Oh, they *shall!*" The booming voice laughed its private pleasure. "One day in the future, I shall free them to reach *many* other lives. But that time is more than sixty of your years from now. Tell me, Mr. Edison, would it intrigue you to know that your little toy will become the source of our liberation—and the downfall of many human lives?" The hilarity in the deep tones was clearly building, broadening, as another tormented face replaced that of Lyda Congelier. "Would you care to know that *you* have paved the way for *my personal release* upon *your civilization?"*

The old man quietly looked down. The entire machine was shuddering each time the voice became louder, vibrating in a perilous vibrato that threatened to bring the walls of 1129 Ridge Avenue crashing down upon their heads. He twisted the dial, sought to diminish the voice level; he knew instantly it had done no good.

Then Edison raised his curious blue eyes to the shifting apparition before him and whispered the question, "Who *are* you?", again.

A last face assumed form upon the shoulders of the ghostly Lyda Congelier.

Fred Parlock took one look only; then, screaming at the top of his lungs, he dropped his flashlight and ran to the doorway. His body caromed off the old walls as he fled. Falling, he leaped erect and propelled himself toward the foyer and finally through the front door. He was still screaming hysterically when he stumbled out into the Pittsburgh winter.

The front door of 1129 slammed behind him, leaving an old man alone—with the Destroyer.

Thomas Edison had not believed in the concept of evil before, not as a conscious force, nor as one stemming from a single unspeakably hideous source. Now he found himself gaping bravely at the face before him as—from the apparatus keening in his lap—the ineffably ugly thing hurled lunatic litany and spewed the hatred of Hades into the nightmare room of the dead. The taunts, the insults, the blasphemies seemed nearly tangible; Edison felt that they were filling up the floor, reaching above his shoetops like so much grasping, adhesive fertilizer.

Before his trembling fingers could quite shut off the apparatus, it leaped in his lap and the bass voice managed to speak a final time.

"Do not take *all* the credit for our release upon your silly shoulders," it urged him. "We shall escape quite soon, but it will only be our initial step. The significant step toward liberation of my entities and me will occur long after you are dust, some twenty-five years from now—when the atomic power of which you, yourself, have spoken becomes a reality. Ah, that"—the demoniac bass voice rose in piercing glee, rattling the very windows of the ancient room—"*that* shall be *my* doing alone!"

With a shudder Edison snapped the switch of his apparatus. The Lyda body, evil face before him, faded slowly. The head itself appeared to drift backward across the room until it vanished and was diffused throughout the intricate patterns of the wallpaper. Then, quite simply, the headless form shrank to a dot of light, and was gone.

The old man sat for a while longer with the machine still in his lap, the batteries of his flashlight growing weaker and weaker. For a time his thoughts were a nightmare jumble of considerations; for a time, too, he could think of nothing—only experience fear and doubt. At last, with the utmost effort, Edison pulled himself to his feet and very slowly, haltingly, left the house of horror.

By the time he had boarded the train, he knew that he would never be the same again. The house at 1129 Ridge Avenue had claimed its greatest victim.

2

February, 1922.

Archaeologists discovered the tomb of King Tut, revealing its priceless treasures—and a large part of the world yawned. Pope Benedict XV went to his presumably not inconsiderable reward—but Mohandas Gandhi was thrown into prison like a sack of potatoes. In the U.S.S.R., Joseph Stalin showed enough vindictive promise to be named Communist secretary-general. Again the world yawned, T.S. Eliot published *The Wasteland*. In Pittsburgh, Ridge Avenue had become a fiendish wasteland itself, but one at which no man yawned.

For a while it was as if 1129 Ridge Avenue wore a disguise. It seemed to be just another house in an old city. Adrift in Untime and soothed by beloved memories, recollections that would surely torture normal beings, the entities were pleased with themselves. After all, through the leadership of their feared Destroyer, they had disposed of a most celebrated challenger.

That shaken old man, Thomas Alva Edison, was soon quoted in the press again. The tone of his remarks seemed different, somehow, to his public. He declared, "I believe in a Supreme Intelligence pervading the universe and have stated it hundreds of times." Followers of the great inventor could be forgiven if they could not readily lay hands on such statements.

He had, of course, every sound reason now for believing in an afterlife—even if his exposure to one facet of it had proved to be the most terrifying and troubling event of his long, productive life. Privately Edison was deeply concerned about what he had encountered and the prophetic remarks he had heard. The possibility that he might, however inadvertently, provide aid or comfort to a chief entity whose identity he did not dare confront—not even in his own private thoughts—disturbed him enormously. He began laying plans for ways to conceal his work.

Meanwhile, the house and its inhabitants remained quiescent until, in 1922, the noted psychic Julia Murray became the latest in an extensive string of psychic mediums to insist upon an audience with 1129's vicious and discarnate spirits.

Julia was a woman whose appearance did not suggest any particular age. Whatever her chronological age of the moment, it was concealed by two huge dreamer's eyes and a pleasant vagueness of manner that bolstered her prestige with followers and lowered it in the view of those who put no stock

HORROR HOUSE

in her passions. Neither polarized group tended to recognize the considerable courage of the small woman—a trait often evident in people who dare to dally with demons. It took persistence and cleverness to talk her way into the mansion at 1129 Ridge, more than people were inclined to give the demure lady credit for. And this year, at last, she persuaded the city fathers. They granted her permission to spend a single night on Ridge Avenue alone.

Regrettably, there is no happy ending to this story. The night became one Julia Murray could never forget. Afterward, it is said, memories of those awful hours came peeping like fugitive gargoyles into her other psychic visions. Often Miss Murray was left weeping and shattered.

To start with, Julia did not stay the entire night. She could not. A few hours before dawn she broke through the front door and, with the abundant dignity allowed her by vast experience, walked quickly on fear-stiffened legs to the heart of town. There she found a jitney and rode shakily home to the comfort of her favorite Bible

When a measure of composure was regained, later that day, Julia told reporters what had happened in the haunted house.

"There was a presence to be felt at once, the instant I entered," she began, those dreamy eyes assuming the expression of a doe that has peered into the uncaring eyes of a hound. "It was more than that of spirits on the other side, mere discarnate souls who needed to find a way home. Much more, I fear." She paused. "It was—a dark presence of sheer, unadulterated evil."

"Was that your first experience with such a force of evil?"

She tried to keep her fingers from dancing in her lap. They weren't part of her today, somehow; they leaped of their own volition. "No, it was not, but it was the first time I felt it in such malefic openness, as if it felt no need to disguise itself." She sighed. "Well, I went upstairs to the room in which Lyda Congelier had slept and sat there in the sole chair remaining, my intention being to communicate with the spirits and explain that I had friendly, Christian intentions, that I wished to help the spirits, to release them, even to sing the praises of Paradise if that proved necessary."

The reporter saw the shy smile on Miss Murray's lips. "But that underlying presence you mentioned—it did not want the other entities released?" He saw the psychic nod. Despite himself, despite the fact that he hadn't wanted this story and had very little belief in anything except his twenty-dollar paycheck and the Pittsburgh Pirates, the reporter was impressed by Julia Murray's obvious sincerity. "What happened then?"

Julia simply stared at him. "I do not think I can tell you."

"Sure you can," he coaxed her.

"Not in detail. It is not for a lady to discuss." She lowered her eyes; her lips trembled. Beside her, a matronly friend reached out to squeeze Julia's hand. Making a clear effort to gather her nerve, Julia went on haltingly, "When I was—forced—to descend to the first floor, I walked slowly through all the rooms of that dreadful manse, using a lantern with which I had provided myself. I passed

HORROR HOUSE

through the—laboratory and examining rooms which Dr. Brunrichter had employed for his loathsome purposes. You may have heard of his terrible deeds." She hesitated again and gratefully sought the warmth of her friend's kind gaze. "Things— were hurled at me there. Some I could not identify, which may in truth be best." She swallowed. "Other things seemed to be levers, leather straps, buckles, bizarre instruments that I dare not describe. There were, as well, things I could not see with my eyes but which were—*cold* against my arms and legs."

The reporter leaned forward assiduously. "Go on," he prodded, gently for him.

Miss Murray shook her head. "I cannot. I dare not. It is—unseemly—repugnant and repulsive to me."

There was silence. Soon, seeing that Julia Murray would not proceed—or could not proceed— the reporter, sure there was more to the story, reluctantly arose, thanked her and made ready to depart.

"There is one thing I can tell you." The psychic spoke in tones barely above a whisper, but her inflections seemed to radiate in the air about her small person. "One important thing."

"Yes?" The reporter eagerly flipped his notepad open.

"That presence," she began softly, "will kill. It wants to kill—anyone—horribly. And—and . . ."

"And what, Miss Murray?"

The medium steadied her gaze. "It will not remain confined to Ridge Avenue. It will reach out —eventually, in the future—to take other human lives unto itself." She had spoken steadily, but now her eyes clouded, as though seeing more deeply into a dimension others might not perceive, and she gasped. "It—sponges up human souls. The presence is thriving, and it cannot be stopped!"

When the reporter, dazzled by the story, had departed, Julia's matronly companion closed the door on him and bustled across the room. She sat beside the psychic and took her friend's hand. "Tell me, Julia," she begged, her upper lip damp, "what *did* happen in that mad Lyda Congelier's room?"

Miss Julia Murray stared at a distant corner of the room, above the table where so many peaceful, satisfying seances had taken place, where gentle and genteel spirits spoke through her, offering words of solace to the loved ones left behind. "It made—propositions to me. It whispered ugly sexual things." Suddenly she realized that she wanted —no, needed—to wash her hands.

The older woman appeared disappointed. She squeezed Julia's arm lightly. "And downstairs, dear? What did the presence do when you were in that terrible laboratory?"

Julia shuddered. For a time it appeared that she would not answer. Finally she turned to look at her old friend with immense, frightened, disgusted eyes. "It—pressed itself against me. A clammy, masculine form. It"—Julia swallowed—"was exposed and unbelievably enormous." She swallowed again. "It—tried to—to *put* itself into my hand." Suddenly Miss Murray burst into helpless tears, then leaped to her feet, unable to sit another instant without bathing her hands. "My God, Anna," she exclaimed in a fever of clear recollection, "that revolting, despicable thing—*had a sexual orgasm right against my body and my hand!"*

Julia ran for the bathroom, leaving her friend pale, with fingers pressed to her lips. Alone, Julia thought she saw pustules beginning to form on the balls of her fingers. Her palms appeared red. She took the dress she had worn the night before, picking it up quite carefully with the end of an office ruler, and dragged the affronting garment through the halls of her house and outdoors, to a trash incinerator.

She could never forget the sticky substance in her hands, how bitterly, eternally cold it had felt. For a long time Julia Murray stood in the chill February evening to make sure that the dress burned. She stared at the cleansing fire, black smoke rising into the palid Pittsburgh sky like an Indian message above the line of peaceful homes.

It's begun, she thought; it's reaching out. Things in this city will never be quite the same again. Things in the world beyond the coal town were also in danger, she felt, and in her uncanny mind's eye she saw a road sign appear before her, indicating a location: INDIANAPOLIS CITY LIMITS, the sign read. Julia tried to sense if it was now or later that her vision suggested. The best she could do was realize that the significance of what she saw lay in the distant future.

Poor people of Indianapolis, she thought with anguish. And the tears in her eyes were not from the smoke alone.

Another nine years crept by, unheeded by the spirits at 1129 Ridge Avenue. The Roaring Twenties faded and died. In October 1931, the Sino-Japanese war was under way and Spain was in the throes of a famous revolution. At Invergordon, Scotland, there was an actual mutiny; and at Loch Ness, also in Scotland, a mythical monster achieved fame.

Someone who was already famous knew that he was dying. Eleven years before, his life had changed forever when he took his unscheduled, unannounced trip to Pennsylvania; and four years before, the aging inventor knew that a ghastly explosion had demolished the old and mysterious Pittsburgh mansion.

At first Tom Edison had greeted the news with exhausted relief. The world was better off, the old man had felt with utter certainty, with that terrifying window on another world smashed to smithereens.

Then Edison began to hear what people were saying, here and there: that 1129's murderous specters had only been released into the world, to what hideous purpose no one knew. And he was deeply troubled, unable for long to lift his thoughts from the things he alone knew. In dreams and awake, Edison was nagged by the indescribable face he had glimpsed at 1129 Ridge Avenue and by the diabolical words it had uttered: "The significant step toward liberation of my entities and me will occur long after you are dust, some twenty-five years from now."

But twenty-five years had not yet passed. And Edison knew that, though he might be a bit frail, rid hard and put away wet, he was still flesh and blood. Yet that ugly presence had seemed so *sure* of what it was saying! Clearly, it had been considering a greater escape than that which might have occurred with the demolition of the house.

And that implied a time in the future—some fourteen years hence—when something else would happen; and a time beyond that, he judged, when another curious person might once more use his apparatus. Why anyone would choose to do that, to bring the entities together again, he could not imagine. But he could believe that atomic power would be developed, just as he himself had envisoned, and that it would surely aid the presence and the spirits it commanded to harm or to influence innocent human beings well beyond the boundaries of the Keystone State.

It was during this phase of his life that Edison made such public remarks as, "We do not know one millionth of one percent about anything"—and his chill warning that would be quoted for many years: "There will one day spring from the brain of science a machine or force so fearful in its potentialities, so absolutely terrifying that even man, the fighter, who will dare torture and death in order to inflict torture and death, will be appalled, and so abandon war forever. What man's mind can create," Tom Edison had thoughtfully added, possibly not with his own aparatus in mind, "man's character can control."

It had been a bold statement with a nugget of optimism. Increasingly now, the aging inventor thought that he might have spoken too much from wishful thinking. He'd found he was human.

What was impossible, he knew, was "uninventing" anything. Mau was a user, a consumer;

what he envisioned he tended to create, and what he created he tended to use—come what might. In the future, he sensed, man would one day want desperately to undo his discovery of atomic power, and he knew that it would be a futile try. Even, he thought sadly, as he could never return to Pittsburgh, Pennsylvania, to undo his own nervejangling confrontation.

Success was a funny thing, Edison often mused during the final, increasingly ill five years of his long life. He himself had been successful in proving that entities existed, that his apparatus would, indeed, contact the dead, even as other men of science would one day soon succeed in releasing the power of the atom. But how long might it be before mankind in general was the better for either scientific success? At least he could refuse to look deeper into the mysteries of the atom, delay its cosmic liberty by the exclusion of his own brilliant investigation. But what could be done about the apparatus?

Theoretically, he mused, it was possible to dismantle the damned thing, burn the blueprints for it, determine never to add it to his all-time record number of patents—a record that he felt would always endure. Already he'd decided not to patent the death apparatus, in order to slow things down just a trifle, and he'd talked to paltry few people about it. Poor young Freddie Parlock wasn't about to mention it; the G.E. executive worked late every night simply trying to forget about the visit he'd made to 1129 Ridge.

But what a fella conceived of and put substance to, old Tom understood, could no more be expunged from this earth than the memory of the fella himself. Somewhere, he had privately concluded, expressed and enacted ideas were "stuck" by nature on an otherworldly shelf, and later other fellas would reach up blindly to get 'em down all over again. Ideas were, after all, what made a man immortal. Every truck driver or waitress who cursed President Hoover, for example, brought the chief executive closer to defeat or even to death, whichever happened first. The spoken ideas of the least important human being were more powerful, he thought with a chuckle, than the heaviest truck or the darkest black coffee ever poured!

Well, thank God—He absolutely *had* to exist, right along with that accursed presence—for Glenmont and its beautiful, sweeping sixteen acres of land in West Orange, New Jersey. That sweet mansion in Llewellyn Park had been Tom's private pride and joy since he and Mina, his second wife, moved into it during April of '86.

He loved lifting his gaze to the high windows in the library and admiring that ornate Bordega statue with the incandescent lamp in its hand, the thing he'd brought from Paris three years ago. He loved the display of cartoons on walls everywhere in Glenmont. They depicted great historic moments, as did the photographs of the famous that were autographed to him. Once, in a pique, Tom had nearly tossed darts at 'em, further to puncture man's unwieldy ego.

The great chandeliers that he'd hung, three or four to a room, were symbols of old Tom's most brilliant triumph. But there were also collections of ore and rare minerals, bottles of shiny crystals from the days of X-ray experimentation; and here and there, throughout vast and beautiful Glenmont, stood towering stacks of books, correspondence and packing cases full of manuscripts. He had never been able to throw away a damned thing in his life, because he remembered every iota of detail and treasured the memories things brought back to him. Well, sometimes he couldn't quite remember where in hell he'd left his false teeth!

And he loved, as well, Mina's lovely room above the porte cochére, sporting separate desks and crammed bookshelves for each of the Edisons. She'd wanted the room to be Tom's, too, so he'd always feel welcome in it and so they could spend more time together. He cherished the many gables and vivid stained-glass windows throughout the sprawling chateau, the gaping staircases and the broad vestibule, the red damask-covered furniture and his own ridiculously variegated collection of oil paintings.

And Mina, of a certainty, topped the list of things he loved, especially this past two years of misery, when he often found himself too weary to go to his laboratory. She was forever appearing before him, tucking a snow-while napkin beneath his chin to protect him from the glass of milk she inevitably pressed on him. Mina was always after him to take little daily motor trips, "just to get outside awhile and see what your world's become." Mina thought of it that way, as Tom Edison's world, since he *had* invented so very much that was in it.

The old fellow sighed as he sat up in bed and wished he could summon the strength to venture over to the upstairs den and do a spot of work. Then he smiled feebly, privately. They'd all thought he was a goner two months ago, but he'd rallied again, amazingly, with the help of that newfangled air conditioner. Edison shook his head at the memory. It was easy to understand how something practical like that might go over, but he was still astounded by the success of his contributions to the phonograph, the radio, even the telephone. Most of it—but for the beloved light bulb—was tomfoolery in his opinion. Mere grown-up's toys.

He remembered with satisfaction how he'd pestered Dr. Hubert S. Howe for information about his procedures, telling Howe that he wanted to know everything, all the details of his illness, because such information was fascinating and helped a fella get well. After Howe had taken another of his interminable blood tests, Edison had snatched away both the slides and his own chart, peering at them before Howe could get 'em back.

Observing the notation "Downhill," Edison had rebuked the physician in typical fashion: "Not a particularly scientific word, Howe."

But by now, this day, almost all the strong fight had oozed from the old man. He could scarcely read half of even one of the eight daily newspapers he subscribed to and had previously devoured, determined to keep modern, to stay on top of every development. "You have to know what the people need, "Edison said once, "but also what they *want*, if you hope to make a dollar at it."

Now he could no longer manage even to work abed. The dim highlight of his long day was when one of the technical assistants came to visit and report on how things were progressing at the lab.

Edison had probably hung around as long as he had only because of his work. He was always genial and witty when the work was going well, moody and snappish when his employees voiced an objection to the same seventy- or eighty-hour week their renowned boss put in.

"I can improve machines," he'd confessed wryly to the press, "but I can't improve men."

Well, *thank the good Lord—and ain't I thankin' Him a helluva lot lately?* Edison mused, turning with some pain onto his side—that the apparatus for contacting the dead was safely put away in the attic. Men would need to be improved a good deal before using a thing like that!

Whatever Tom didn't regularly use, for a period of nearly forty-five years, he had unceremoniously tossed into a cavernlike room in the attic to gather dust and grime. Memorabilia and valueless souvenirs lay in cramped quarters and oddfellow relationship with abandoned projects of an incredible range —the sort that would puzzle many Edisonians for half a century or more. The treasure-trove of furniture, gadgets, toys, well-thumbed books and magazines, and half-finished inventions so filled the great room that it was hard to pass through from the door to the cobwebbed far wall.

And a year or so back, when some groaning sense of internal abandonment informed him his lengthy life was drawing to a close, Edison had climbed the stairs at the end of one nightlong period of labor to stick that internal death apparatus out of sight. He'd hidden it in a trunk, without blueprints or instructions, with some machines that had never worked properly. Most likely, Tom had figured at the time, his tufted eyebrows and mane of white hair coated with dust, they'll never figure out what in tarnation it was *intended* to do!

Thomas A. Edison, the man who had invented America as much as Christopher Columbus was said to have discovered it, tried to turn on his other side and closed his eyes, unaware that, when they opened next, he would no longer be the same.

As he turned, his hip inadvertently knocked an issue of *Scientific American* to the floor beside other magazines and books accumulating there. Concerned, Mina approached the bed. The fact that he did not answer when she called his name did not worry her. Tom had been deaf for years. But she soon found he was incapable of answering her and, her heart beating heavily, she summoned Dr. Howe.

"I fear it is a coma, my dear," the physician murmured softly. "I doubt that Mr. Edison will awaken from it. Really—hard as it is to say—this is something of a blessing for him. The *pain* . . ."

That Saturday evening, Edison regained consciousness. As others marveled at his will, his intelligence, his constitution, the old man insisted upon being placed in a chair beside a tall window in his bedroom. There, in the gathering gloom of twilight, he stared intently down upon the great green lawn and stately beeches. He seemed to be memorizing every blade of grass, every bending bough.

Mina looked at his stooped shoulders with fond tears in her eyes. "Are you suffering?" she called in a loud voice.

For a moment it seemed Tom had not heard her. Then, without turning his head, he replied simply,

"No, just waiting."

Hours dawdled, clumping and lugubrious things that appeared to have nothing whatever to do with such an industrious, active and vital human being. In the absence of his enormous nonstop labors, time was confused, inclined to suspend itself guiltily and wait for Edison to regain his eighty-year pace.

Downstairs, below the inventor and his adoring wife, reporters from almost everywhere joined in the waiting with a patience uncommon to their brisk trade. Son Charles Edison looked in as the nurse was tucking a blanket around Tom's fleshy, unprotesting form. The old man suddenly shuddered, flickered his long eyelashes and straightened in his chair. A frail white hand lifted, almost as if indicating—or discovering—something.

Conversationally, yet with a note of wonder they would not forget, Thomas Edison said clearly, "It is very beautiful over there." He then lapsed into an unconsciousness that was his personal forever.

Stooping to retrieve the fallen issue of *Scientific American,* Charles spied an old interview *granted by his father.* In it, Tom Edison had stated: "If our personality survives, then it is perfectly logical and scientific to concede that it retains intellect, memory and other capabilities and information learned on this earth." Charles nodded. His eye then fell upon a fascinating thought, heavily underscored by the old man's pencil: "I am prompted to believe that our intelligence and personality in the hereafter can affect matter."

HORROR HOUSE

The dead affect the living—not only psychically, perhaps, but in point of genuine, real fact? The son shook his head, wondering what discovery of his father's had prompted such an observation.

When he looked up, Charles saw that Thomas Alva Edison had died at 3:24 A.M., Sunday, October 18, 1931. With a heavy heart he went downstairs to acknowledge the fact to the waiting reporters. With proud tears gleaming in his eyes, he told them, "The light still burns."

Soon after, the son passed wearily through his father's library, a man suddenly become lonely, and saw something remarkable there: the inventor's cherished, enormous grandfather clock had stopped. At 3:27 A.M. And Charles recalled that old Tom had always complained about the clock running fast...

The next day, as life for the living continued and when it seemed proper to mention it, three of the old man's favorite workers tentatively reported their astonishment at having known Tom was gone *before* they had been informed. How could they have made such a strange statement? Because *their* clocks had also stopped, as they were sitting vigil for their famed employer, at precisely 3:24 A.M.

"*... our intelligence and personality in the hereafter can affect matter.*"

* * *

After that, there were reports published in magazines and newspapers from time to time to the effect that the spirit of the world's foremost inventor had been communicating to the living through mediums. Those who did not care for such topics scoffed at it. Others believed. Reportedly, the Edison of the beyond offered information about a strange device he had left behind him.

There were other odd reports in the same vein. Tom and Charles Steinmetz, the late electrical engineering genius, whom Edison had met personally in 1922—just two years after visiting Pittsburgh—were said to speak through mediums about technical modifications that would enable a certain machine to work properly again.

J. Gilbert Wright was interested, because he happened to *find* the machine in question. (And Wright was not a fool. A research scientist for Edison's old firm, General Electric, Wright happened to be the discoverer of putty.) Soon Mr. Wright claimed that he had, indeed, made the modifications described to him from the hereafter. And what were the results? Wright said that, although he could not contact Tom Edison, he had in fact established a successful and enlightening dialogue with the late Mr. Steinmetz. Tom, presumably, was out.

When J. Gilbert Wright himself passed away, in 1959, all the notes he had taken on both experiments—his efforts to make Tom Edison's apparatus work properly and his own tests meant to establish communication with the dead—were left untouched for years.

The location of the strange machine itself—the remarkable apparatus Edison had used to contact a presence at 1129 Ridge Avenue, in Pittsburgh, Pennsylvania—remained a mystery through the Kennedy, Johnson, Nixon, Ford, Carter and Regan years.

In short, as a matter of fact, until quite recently.

Two

MALEDICTION—THE ANGRY ANGELS OF THE APOCALYPSE

Mr. Edison had discovered "a radiant force... something radically different from what has been before observed by Science."

Dr. George M. Beard

And how does it work, Mr. Edison? What are its ramifications?
"I dare not say. A strange, new force."

Thomas A. Edison

3

Mid-February, 1988. Indianapolis, Indiana.

For three emotional hours in the soul-dark segment of night, a middle-class home in little Doyle, Indiana, was under siege. Objects a grown man would find hard to lift floated featherlike in midair, only to be smashed, with no warning, against the wall. Contrariwise, a feather duster had become imbedded by its handle in the ceiling and still hung there, vibrating.

The man and woman of the house cursed and wept, ducking ashtrays and books that flashed by their unprotected heads. Both were near the end of their tether.

Two figures remained calm, even quiescent, throughout the entire period: a pubescent girl, in cotton pajamas, with great, sad eyes, budding breasts and long red hair; and a slender, tall man who had seen this sort of thing before and survived.

When he decided it was time, when the madness was at its peak, he peered somberly yet affectionately down at the child and murmured, *"Now."*

Her eyes closed and her head dropped forward, slumped in sleep.

The feather duster fell from the ceiling to the floor; all activity in the living room ceased, and the only sound was that of a little girl breathing heavily in her troubled trance. Mother and father knelt on either side of her, their faces tear-stained; each of them took a small, limp hand in a mute gesture of forgiveness and love.

Martin Ruben, the parapsychologist, glanced briefly at them. "There is no ghost involved here," he said. "The poltergeist, as I suspected, is your child."

"Oh, my poor girl!" the mother sobbed. "She would never do such awful things if she could control it."

"She could not. It was her unconscious mind at work," Ruben continued, "as it generally is in such cases. There is frustration there, resentment and anger, typical of children entering puberty. Some such children handle it in this bizarre fashion."

"What in the name of God can we do about it?" the father asked, kissing his sleeping child on the temple.

"It is being done." The tall man turned his attention again to the girl but continued to address her parents. "I'll give her a suggestion that all is well and that she can deal with her problems, can verbalize them." He allowed a smile to touch his lips. "You'll have no more problems of this kind after tonight."

But before he could address the red-haired child, her pale face lifted to him, eyes still shut. The trio of adults could see those orbs move beneath the lowered, translucent lids and see, too, the worried frown that formed even before she spoke.

"Phone call," she said distinctly. "You had a phone call before coming here. And you made an appointment. For two or three weeks from now." She was addressing the parapsychologist in a conversational tone.

"Yes, I did," he confessed with no visible surprise. "What do you have to tell me about it?"

"Your friend," she continued, "is a publisher. Name, Ben." Suddenly she began shaking her head violently from right to left, long hair spinning like a sea of scarlet grass whipped by the wind. "Don't go, *don't go!* There is *danger* for you!"

"What in the world is she saying?" demanded the mother, anxiety in her eyes.

"Often," Ruben whispered, "a child relinquishing her psychokinetic energies is overcharged by them. She subconsciously resists giving up all her latent gifts and makes precognitive or other psychic comments. It is not uncommon, madam."

"I don't want my kid to be a freak!" the worried father blurted, reddening.

"She won't be, I promise you," Ruben murmured. "After tonight, your daughter will be perfectly normal." He paused. "As a rule, the remarks made in this odd state are both beneficial and surprisingly . . . accurate."

He looked back to the trance-bound child in time to see the tears on her fair cheeks. "Danger," she said again. "Oh, *awful* danger from—from Edison. No, Edison *machine*. Yes, that's it," excitedly now, but anxiously, "Edison *machine* will bring you—bring you—"

"Yes, darling?" Ruben pressed. "What will the Edison machine bring me?"

Suddenly her eyes shot open, blazing with fear and knowledge. *"It will bring you to the brink of hell!"* she exclaimed.

Why did secretaries always have to be so damned proprietary about their bosses? Laura glanced up again at the strikingly handsome black girl seated regally in her throne just beyond her employer's closed office. *His* throne room, she thought, feeling both a trifle suffocated and invisible. The secretary clearly had forgotten her presence.

Not that Carola Glenn—that was the name on the desk plate—had been rude. After all, no bosses allowed that for long. It was more like a frosty detachment, following on the heels of a grudging statement that, "Mr. Kellogg will be with you soon." Now Laura Hawks simply did not exist any longer for Carola Glenn.

As a rule, official secretarial frost didn't trouble Laura. One of the few certainties in her life was that she very much existed—and that everyone, everywhere, would one day be aware of it. The trouble now was that Laura found herself nearing thirty years of age, and too few people knew, or cared in the slightest, that she meant to become a best-selling novelist. Worse, her current unemployment was getting her down, and the feeling of not belonging, of fitting in nowhere, threatened to become ingrained before long.

Part of the long-range problem, Laura knew, was her own fault. She had remained in Indianapolis all her life with the avowed plan of putting the midwestern city on the nation's lips. There were lots of other reasons, she would tell friends with pride, to love this town besides that boring 500-mile race.

But when she found herself, like today, back on the pavement trying to be paid for her literary skills, she had to admit that while Indianapolis might be a great place to raise a family, it seemed to have about as much interest in the written word as said family's youngest child. Here she was, Laura Hawks—a budding Judith Krantz—on the verge of piling popularity and praise on her hometown, while every potential writing job was brushed off by the boss on to a secretary who couldn't spell *eleemosynary* or explain the difference between an adjective and a verb.

Laura shook her ash-blonde head wearily and crossed her silken legs, oddly drawn by the secretary's indifference to stare right at the woman. Here, declaring that you were a writer had the same general impact as announcing that you were a mountain climber or lion tamer. The question leaping to every mouth, though generally left unasked, went, "Why ever would y'want to do *that?*"

True enough, a lot of the problem was her own timidity. She worked her gloves nervously between long fingers as she made this confession to her own soul. Maybe *timidity* wasn't the word, but she'd always avoided asking the rude question, the sensible one that would keep her from misunderstanding or even prevent trouble. "Oh?" was just about the extent of her capacity for challenge. Yes, on paper she was a powerhouse, forceful, meaningful, purposeful—all the good, glorious things she had admired in literature since she was a girl. But in person, the lovely writer tended to be reticent, almost shy.

Laura sighed and cast a careful-not-to-offend peek at her watch. How could would-be employers be so miserably cruel? They always kept you waiting when you were really interested in the job! It was a damned sixth sense they had. Only five months ago she had sworn somehow to finish her first novel and sell it for a record amount without ever seeking employment again. But things like the furnace going out kept altering her plans. And someone had to take care of her mother.

If she could get *this* job, it wouldn't be quite such a cop-out. Actually, she told herself, she would be advancing her writing career. This publisher, Ben Kellogg, had asked her on the phone to mail in some samples of her work and, in a calm, mature baritone that gave away nothing, had added, "I'll call you for an interview if it passes muster." And sure enough, it had, and he'd called! Just last night, suddenly in a rush for her to come to his office.

An independent element of Laura's soul had told her to put the appointment off for two days, but something practical, even downright cold, had insisted that she get her buns over there just as Kellogg had requested. And now he kept her waiting!

She sighed and looked around, rather liking the set-up. Ben Kellogg's publishing firm occupied a twenty-year-old one-story building, a deep structure with huge, sunny windows. The deep-pile carpeting made Laura want to take off her shoes and wriggle her toes. There weren't many employees around, and that, too, was absolutely fine with Laura.

But what she didn't know, was the type of books Mr. Kellogg published. While she felt capable of handling technical writing in most subjects, most men would take one look at her soft ash-blond hair and subtle female curves and begin wistfully and obviously waiting for the next male applicant. Perhaps Mr. Kellogg—

The door to the publisher's private office opened, and he was peering out, directly at her, all sober brown eyes and dark beard—except for a welcoming smile! "Come in, please, Miss Hawks."

The door was left ajar for her, and she followed him in. Seeing him gesture to the chair in front of his long desk, Laura hurriedly seated herself. An attack of timidity made her wish to be smaller, and she was surprised to see Kellogg shyly ducking around to the other side of the desk. He seemed almost to be hiding. "Can I get you anything?" he asked abruptly, blurting it out. His eyes were pillow-soft, kind. "I can ask Carola to put on some coffee or something."

"No, thanks, I'm fine." From where Laura sat, she could easily detect the thick folder of writing she had mailed to him. The way the folder was sprung apart, she could tell that it had been thoroughly reviewed. "I do appreciate your asking me here today."

"Think nothing of it. I'm a publisher looking for a writer, and you're a writer." Ben Kellogg nervously clapped his palms together with a let's-get-on-with-it air. But his smile was friendly, and Laura found herself relaxing. The publisher went on, "I'm delighted to say that I was quite impressed with what I read."

"Grand!" Laura exclaimed, leaning eagerly forward. "Did you scan the two poems?"

"Poems?" He looked stumped. "No, not those. Sorry."

"My story about the Indian brave and the lonely medicine man?" she asked again, more slowly. "Did you read that, sir?"

"Uh, I don't believe so." Kellogg twisted uncomfortably in his chair, and, with a stunning flash of surprise and mean delight, Laura realized that she was interviewing him! "I haven't had a lot of free time these days, Miss Hawks, so basically I, um, sort of *briefed* everything." He gestured vaguely to the folder.

A writer wants her material read. Laura recrossed her legs. "I see," she answered with dismay.

"But what I did read was very, very good. Quite competent, I think." He picked up a yellow pencil and began turning it over, end for end. Silence threatened to invade, and he jumped in ahead of it. "We are *self-publishers* here, Miss Hawks."

"Call me Laura, please," she offered in a low, modulated voice. Once, that pitch of voice had cost her hours of effort. She had a theory that high-pitched women's voices got them marked down as idiots.

Still, Ben was put off, somehow made jittery once more by her little intrusion. It was hard for him to pick up the thread. "We're self-publishers, which means that, well, fundamentally, I'm the company." He laughed awkwardly. "I don't go outside for manuscripts of any kind very often, and those books that I publish are generally sold through the mail. D'you follow what I'm saying? Kellogg Publishing is, well, *me*. And our books don't go into nice, respectable bookstores like B. Dalton or Walden—I peddle 'em through direct mail."

Laura sensed his discomfort in explaining all this and also her own quickened heartbeat. Was it just for the possibility of a job? Certainly, this man compelled her attention in a new way, she thought. Not from her need for a position or because he was even remotely authoritative—he'd probably faint if she said something rude!—but because it seemed important to him that she understand his meaning. Ben Kellogg was just as shy as she was, she realized all at once, and it was a genuine effort for him to conduct this interview. She couldn't resist a smile. Clearly, he was trying to overcome his nervousness by stressing all the important things and leaving his personal feelings completely out of it to the best of his ability.

Except—except he wasn't doing that. Laura knew, in an insight fresh in her experience, that Ben Kellogg really liked her and that he was drawn to her. Just as, she knew, too, he was a gentle and decent man.

"If everything you publish is written by you, Mr. Kellogg, why do you need another writer now?"

"Call me Ben." He paused and his eyes narrowed in another spasm of unease. "Well, I'm prepared to share the by-line with you. That is, with another writer I choose. Fact is, Laura, I have too many irons in the fire to handle everything." He grinned boyishly, and his beard popped forward with his chin. "I keep having these great ideas, you see, these scintillating, gorgeous ideas for projects of all kinds. And, well, I get halfway into them—or maybe not even that far—and nothing quite gets done, as a rule."

It was so strange, Laura thought. This man's decision would affect her future considerably, at least for months; yet she felt so much in control of the conversation. "I see," she murmured. "You want me—if I am hired—to complete a few of your books?"

"No, not that." He shook his dark head with surprising decisiveness. "No, Laura, I want someone to write a book from scratch upon subject matter I've already chosen. It is, I feel, an important and unusual subject." Kellogg ran out of the nerve to confide, again, as he sought to force himself to ask the question, "Laura, do you believe in ghosts?"

She would have expected any other question. "Why," she said, blinking her sky-blue eyes, "I haven't the foggiest notion!"

"Good, good." He nodded happily, the beard bobbing. "Your reply was important to me. I hoped that I'd seen an open mind in those writings of yours, and I was right!"

Laura tapped her gloves nervously on her knee, confused. "But I thought you did 'how-to' books, telling people how to get into various types of work."

"Oh, sure. I do. But my approach to that has always been different from that of other self-publishers. They'll tell the reader how he can invest money or save it, how to buy a franchise of some kind, or how to become an insurance agent or computer programmer." Absently, he scratched his sweater-encased shoulder. "But I write books, brochures and courses telling folks how to get into the professions that ordinarily aren't covered by anybody else."

"Like what?" she asked, pleased by how easy it was to chat with Ben Kellogg.

"Oh, how to begin your own magazine, for example, how to open a pet store, or how to get a break in show business. How to become a consultant to the TV industry, maybe, or how to start your own recording company." He indicated a shelf filled with softbound books just behind his head. "I research the topic thoroughly, talk to a few experts in the field and write it up. Candidly, I do ridiculously well at it."

Laura licked her lips. "How in the world, then, do ghosts enter the picture?"

Kellogg gave her an easy grin. "I want a book with a title like *How to Become a Psychic Researcher and Ghost-Buster*—something of that sort. You know, with a history of important spooks and spook hunters." He tugged the point of his dark beard a trifle defensively. "Look, I *do* know what I'm doing. Think of some of the books and films about ghosts over the past few years."

"It just seems—odd—" She paused. "I'm

sorry."

He leaned forward across his desk, earnest and more youthful than she suspected him to be. "People say we're all in the Aquarian Age now. From what I read, that means men and women are getting interested in all kinds of offbeat, occult things. But the trouble is, nobody explains *how* to get into the field as a vocation, a way to make good money interestingly. Now, lots of people want to know the inside of such a weird industry—whether or not they're even *aware* of it. And that's how I succeed in my publishing firm!" He was so serious she almost laughed. "As a writer, Laura, can't you imagine how easily a title like that can be advertised and promoted? It has worlds of possibilities—otherworldly worlds!"

Laura wanted to be honest with this man. She thought about it another moment and slowly nodded. Strangely enough, she *could* see the merit of his concept. And just as strangely, since she had just met Ben Kellogg, she sensed that he was the kind of man who made his ideas work. She decided, too, that she liked him a great deal.

"OK, I can become interested in your idea. But tell me something, Ben."

"Happily, if I can."

"Do you believe in ghosts?"

"Me?" When he laughed, it was soft and airy, gently teasing. "Well, probably not. Like you, I'm open-minded, or try to be. Although there are facets of this that trouble me." Obviously, he was verging on a personal revelation; but he changed his train of thought almost in midsentence. "Anyway, there's a large market for spirits, believe me. Will you write that book for me, Laura? Will you do the research and write a mini best seller for us?"

She looked happily into his earnest face—and made a decision that would bring her close to the point of insanity, and death. "I'd love to, Ben!" she exclaimed.

He leaned back, his chair creaking its protest. He was relieved to be done with the difficult part of the interview and to have made a selection. "I'm very pleased."

For ten minutes they spoke about the income Laura was to receive, and again she was surprised. The amount not only suggested Ben Kellogg's intrinsic generosity of spirit but provided her with an enhanced sense of her own dignity. It did not seem quite such a sell-out to abandon her own book, for a while, to work with this man.

Then Ben returned to the theme of the book she was to do for him. "You'll be basing your tome on a genuine, real-life haunted house in Pittsburgh," he told her as she dutifully took notes. "Or one, at least, that *did* exist. A damned scary place, I can tell you that!"

"Ben, you sound as if you believe it was literally haunted."

He frowned and tapped his index finger. "No. All I know for sure is that certain positively horrible things occurred there for a period of nearly fifty-six years."

Laura released an unladylike whistle. "Over half a century? The house in Amityville will have to be around a great deal longer before it's scared people over *that* long a period."

"That's quite true," the publisher agreed,

nodding. He reached an arm across the desk. "Here's a nice, thick folder of my research on the place. It even seems to involve Thomas Edison, the great inventor. We can't be definite at this late date, but the evidence suggests that Edison once visited the house and sought to use a peculiar device of his own construction. Afterward the old fellow's most productive years drew to a close." Ben's brown eyes danced with enthusiasm. "Possibly the house itself did something to him. Together, we'll learn about things like that."

"It's a fascinating story," Laura remarked, leafing through the folder, her blue eyes eager and attentive.

"I see it as the centerpiece, the major ghost story, for our book." He arose and went around the desk to her, leaning over her shoulder to look for material in the folder. "Take for example," he said, "this frightening episode in 1922. It's a classic by itself, really, and demonstrates how the spirits in the house didn't care whom they attacked, or why. . . ."

The weather was turning warmer when the Equitable Gas Company, located several blocks from the eleven-hundred block of Ridge, became an invigorating part of the Roaring Twenties. In 1922 the company was almost through construction of a great natural-gas storage complex, with one of the structures nearly three hundred feet in diameter and reaching to over two hundred feet above ground level. The world's largest gas tank—five million cubic feet—was supported by this structure.

HORROR HOUSE

Costs, of course, were enormous. To hold them down, immigrants who would work for less were speedily hired and put to work. Most of these men were Italians, delighted to have the chance to make some money. Several of them were placed in the house at 1129 Ridge Avenue, one of many vacant buildings being converted for the purpose of housing. Apparently the people who had assumed responsibility for the deserted mansion felt that the sincere and sweet Catholic prayers of the Italian immigrants would be sufficient to hold the spirits at bay. Or, just possibly, the feeling might have been —given the prejudices of the day—that it didn't quite matter what happened to the semiliterate laborers. After all, there were plenty of them around, and 1129 Ridge hadn't made a penny in years. Besides, with Nicola Sacco and Bartolomeo Vanzetti's well-publicized radicalism regarded as motive enough for the robbery and murder with which they were charged, the press daily droning its news of the trial ever since the preceding year, anti-Italian sentiment ran deep.

From a dozen to two dozen men moved into the Ridge Avenue two-story house for several months. Right from the start, odd things happened with regularity. The reaction on the part of the laborers, who needed the income, was guarded. Knowing that they were generally despised in the community, Federico Palermo (called "Feddie" by his friends and "Freddie" by Americans who mispronounced it) and his brother, Carlo, believed that the bizarre incidents were the work of pranksters and tricksters. As a consequence, instead of fearing the entities in the house, Feddie and Carlo merely prayed that the strange "little jokes" would not escalate into more open and harsh animosity on the part of the locals.

On an evening when the baking summer had just started to relinquish its hold to the onslaught of autumnal winds, the brothers Palermo were seated with twelve other muscular men at a crude dining table. The day's work had been endless and arduous; homemade wine was lavishly consumed with little thought for the Volstead Act or, for that matter, the next day's labors. The ancient house was growing chilly, and there was no way to heat it; so the workers tried to provide a measure of internal warmth.

"What is theesa comm'nism, anyway?" Feddie Palermo looked around the table with good-humored scorn. His swarthy face was lighted by two vivacious eyes that were almost feminine and a radiant smile. "Alla the money goes to the gov-'ment, right? And the gov'ment, she gives it right back to the people anyway! What'sa the harm, eh?"

Most of the others laughed merrily. An exception was Carlo. He'd always been the serious one of the pair, even though he was actually younger and hadn't received Papa's blessing before coming to this alien country. "Our family's always worked hard for its bread, Feddie," he observed with boldness, ignoring the amusement of his brother and friends. "We don't wanna handouts. Besides, it'sa not something to laugh at, I tell you! The bad ones have almost killed several of our people, remember—right in thisa house!" And the little brother piously crossed himself.

"I'm just makin' the jokes, Carlo, that's all."

Feddie gave a grand and sweeping gesture of his work-callused hand. "Justa the American jokes." He pointed to the dirty dishes spread before them on the makeshift table. "If you wanta do work so much, brother, why don't you get rid of these filthy plates?"

Carlo frowned darkly and passed a hand through his mop of dark hair. *"Ubi bene, ibi patria,"* he quoted as he rose, snatching up dirty dishes and piling them miraculously high on his muscular arm. "One day," he added firmly, "you all see what a grand place thees country really is—or will become!"

As Carlo left the room, Feddie chuckled lightly. Then he shrugged and poured still more *vino* for his friend Antonio, the foreman. Little Carlo, oh, he was so somber—*il penseroso*. Why, he should have been a priest! What Carlo could not see was that he, Federico Palermo, also adored this fine, new nation and understood fully that it would change one day, *poco a poco*, from loathing the Italians to loving them. Certainly! It *had* to change—for Italians were lovers and not haters, was it not so?

Feddie and the others drank and talked. Time passed, and Carlo did not return. Feddie sighed. Had that rascal brother become truly angry and gone to bed already? He planted wide palms on the tabletop and pushed himself to his feet.

Vino, he mused with a crooked smile, staggering slightly. It was like having one's mama with him. Carlo and *vino* and Mama all took hold of his senses and told poor Federico what to do!

He clapped Antonio's broad back and lurched amiably out to the kitchen, where a solitary light bulb dangled near the door leading to the cellar. He paused. Down there, rumor had it, an American Indian girl had once buried a mutilated animal to chase away evil spirits and somehow had released them instead, to flow into the very walls of this old place. Nonsense, it's just nonsense, thought Feddie Palermo, walking to the open cellar door. Such stories as these were not *ben trovato.*

He braced himself on the door frame and put his dark, handsome head into the gloom of the cellar entrance. This he did with care, all the same, but he could make nothing out beneath him. So dark! Slowly, he took a single tentative step forward into the murky cavity below—and screamed in horror as his eyes adjusted to the sight.

Paralyzed by the terrible scene beneath him, Feddie stared openmouthed down the long flight of rickety steps, his heart thudding with grief and fear.

Carlo Palermo, the little one, half sat and half lay on the cellar floor, looking like a man starting to arise from his bed. But Carlo would not be standing again. He was supported in the half-sitting posture by a yard-long sliver of ancient flooring that had pierced his chest and heart. Blood still pumped around that sliver, like a crimson fountain. Eyes open and blind, Carlo stared up at his brother, one hand yet on the steps in a beseeching manner.

I go to him! Federico thought wildly, taking three or four hasty, heartbroken steps downward before his life was irreversibly altered, wrecked.

The two were virtually simultaneous—the terrible shove at his back and the raspy, whispered exultancy of the remark: *"We have waited so long,"* said the satisfied voice in his ear, worsened by a nightmare stench just as the rude impact of the unseen hand struck him. *"We welcome you to join us!"*

In the mansion's dining room the remaining twelve workers were suddenly plunged into the darkness. One of the men later reported that he heard, just then, a rumbling, rough laugh.

Amid oaths and growls of fear and consternation, several of the men jumped to their feet and rushed toward the darkened kitchen, seeking a means of light. Antonio Cavetta, the silver-haired, middle-aged foreman who had sat affably beside Feddie Palermo at supper, fumbled in the kitchen's gloom for their makeshift icebox. Atop it, his groping fingers discovered the lantern they had left there upon arriving home.

Antonio struck a match. Yellow-orange illumination crept protestingly into the stale-smelling, haunted kitchen. "There!" Tony cried, pointing his finger to the open cellar door. He sensed that something was very wrong. "But be very careful."

With the lantern held high, the men in the kitchen crept through the cellar entrance, one by one, and started down the steps, hands trembling on the railing. They peered with a fear that was both superstitious and religious into the subterranean depths. Unearthly odors—a reak of hell itself —curled up to their noses.

And then, at last, they saw.

Two men swore at the horror they felt. Most of them muttered swift prayers, fingers flying to cross themselves.

Below the workers was, of course, the stabbed

and bloodied body of young Carlo Palermo. But *other* things were at the foot of the stairs, as well.

Carlo's older brother, Feddie, the happy soul, was dangling from a tangled electrical wire that had become lovingly wrapped around his throat. A myriad of lovely little lights leaped from the short-circuited wire and produced a halo from the handsome head above it. The fall, combined with the instantly tightening wire, had broken Feddie's sturdy neck, and the head appeared cocked, as if the young, dead Italian were *listening*.

Listening to what? Apparently untouched, the cellar door slammed shut behind the men on the stairs. One man shrieked in terror. Then all was still. Seconds crawled by as they froze, awaiting what? Then, closed up in their annex of hell, the workmen heard above them—in the shadow-steeped kitchen—the sound of a footfall.

To some of them, they said later at the double high mass, it sounded like someone—perhaps some *thing*—was doing a merry dance, a jig of sheer and quite devilish delight.

All the workmen left the house at 1129 Ridge Avenue within half an hour, most within ten minutes, never to return. No job, no new nation, was worth risking one's life—or one's sacred soul.

Laura finished reading and lifted her startled, puzzled blue eyes to Ben Kellogg's earnest face. "My God," she whispered, "it—it's fiendish!"

"Apparently."

"Is this report exaggerated?" she asked. "It is, isn't it? I mean, not all this truly happened, did it?"

Ben shrugged. "The two Italian workers died

there, just as the report reads, and their fellow workers cleared out." He smiled faintly. "I can't say that I blame them."

"And there's more about the Ridge Avenue house in this folder," Laura said, confirming it and watching him nod. "You may be onto something, Ben."

"I'm sure I am. You see, most haunted-house reports involve wayward spirits that are forlorn, sad, woeful things. A reader sometimes wonders, if he or she stops to think, why anybody was frightened at all. But there were numerous particularly ghastly deaths in Pittsburgh, suggesting to me that there might be some kind of—of evil force greater than that of discarnate former people!" He grinned. "Not that I'm even faintly convinced that the place was actually haunted, you understand."

Laura pursed her lips, then smiled. "Oh, yes. You don't *really* think it was haunted." While she talked, she had continued to glance through the contents of the folder. Now she raised a slip of paper with a name scribbled on it. "What's this, Ben? the name 'Dr. Adolph Brunrichter' is all you have here."

He perched on the front of his desk and gazed steadily at her. "He was an owner of the house between the period of the Congeliers and the brothers Palermo. Reports have been sketchy about the good doctor, and I have the impression that it's not because facts are unknown, but because they may be even more hideous—and therefore virtually unprintable—than what we have here. I hope we can dig out some information concerning Brunrichter."

"You mentioned that the house lasted fifty-six years," Laura said soberly. "Did someone finally tear it down?"

Ben shook his head. "Not exactly. There are those who say that God destroyed the place, at last, when He had finally had enough." He gestured with the yellow pencil. "If you'll glance through the folder, you'll find some papers headed 'End of the Beginning—1927.' I've already written a preliminary section of the book describing how it was destroyed."

She rummaged until she found the report. "Yes, I have it."

"It took one of the worst public calamities in history to tear that house down," Ben murmured. "But go ahead, if you wish, and read what happened. . . ."

"There were many people in Pittsburgh who either did not care about haunted houses or preferred not to notice them," read Benjamin Kellogg's report, "but every one of them noticed what happened on November 14, 1927—and all cared greatly, to the core of their beings.

"Whether there was something otherworldly about what happened, as some people believed, cannot yet be said with certainty. The circumstances involved the workers of the Equitable Gas Company, the firm for which Carlo and Federico Palermo had labored. On the date in question, sixteen men were searching for a gas leak, doing it the hard way: some 208 feet above the hard-packed autumn ground.

"Forty-three minutes later, they discovered the

leak—also the hard way. As if by magic, the silhouettes of two men suddenly were etched in clots of blood and ripped flesh as the workers were smashed against a brick building more than one hundred feet away.

"Tongues of unleashed flame lapped the morning sky for upwards of a thousand feet, spraying the sky with enormous black clouds. Human bodies, in maimed hunks and ugly segments—along with steep shrapnel and flying girders—became projectiles shooting in every direction as hell broke loose in the same general area as the house at 1129 Ridge Avenue.

"Was it God's sweeping revenge upon the haunted mansion or perhaps the work of the mansion's crazed denizens, seeking their liberty? No one can ever be certain.

"Before onlookers had recovered from their initial shock, four million cubic feet of gas contained in a secondary tank some two hundred feet away exploded—and another preliminary to the atomic bomb plumed heavenward.

"But what really capped it off was the third tank, partly full, which burst and added its uncontrollable violence to the nightmarish scene. For miles around, it was said, the murky fall morning—just days before Thanksgiving—was lit by all-engulfing flame. Almost instantly, smoke overwhelmed the fire and turned the morning to ebon, choking night. The screams of the injured and dying were locked in the old town's memory forever.

"Skyscrapers in downtown Pittsburgh shuddered from the explosions; some seemed about ready to topple, but miraculously stood. Windows in many businesses and homes imploded, showering their occupants with cascading torrents of broken glass. Water and sewer lines began bursting, spewing geysers of water into the streets and turning the city's north side into Dantesque oceans of flood and fire.

"There were good, religious folks who screamed of Armageddon, of the Apocalypse. Here and there, severed electric wires hopped about like so many possessed souls, shorting and shocking all who approached them.

"When people seeking to rescue those remaining on the scene began to arrive, shaken structures collapsed and pinned them. Several districts of the town were turned into flood areas by the water from the burst mains. The Union Paint Company, an across-the-street neighbor of Equitable Gas, was flattened quickly, and hundreds of human beings were temporarily buried alive, a few literally broken in two.

"Never before had there been such a disaster. More than six hundred citizens of Pittsburgh were seriously injured, or worse, before the manic blaze yielded to control; more than a dozen residents ended up missing forever. Commercial businesses, homes, warehouses and factories lay in warlike ruins; terrified friends and families roved the streets in a literal daze, and several were horribly killed when sections of the street buckled and were hurled into the air.

"Of course, on the surface, there was rather little mystery about the terrible tragedy. It was all too clear, really, too pathetically easy to figure out the mechanics of what had happened. But on Ridge Avenue other things would not be perceived so simply or quickly.

"Buildings on either side of the ancient haunted house at 1129 were damaged but intact. The house directly across the street was, as well, left in good repair. People who prefer an ordered world, one which makes sense, tended to say that these houses were simply too far from the gas company explosion to be leveled.

"Explain, then, the strange case of 1129 Ridge Avenue. Because the famous, or infamous, house that had brought so much grief to human beings for so many years was devastated—utterly. *In fact*, there was no trace, no sign, that a house had ever stood on the spot before! Not a stick of wood nor a patch of plaster remained where 1129 had stood for more than half a century. Instead, there was a vast and awesome pit: seventy-five feet in diameter, reports claimed, and eighty-five feet deep. At a glance, it appeared to lead all the way down to the doors of Hades.

"That's almost the end of the story, but it's really just the end of the beginning," Ben Kellogg's report continued, gripped tightly in Laura Hawks's trembling hands. "Two rescue workers, dashing up and down the streets of the neighborhood in search of the wounded, distinctly heard a rasping, rough voice rise triumphantly from the monumental cavity left behind: *'Free, free!'* cried the awful voice, wind-borne now, *'Free at last!'* "   Laura looked up at the publisher perched on the desk before her.

"I do not believe I've ever read anything so astonishing," she admitted.

"And it's apparently true, all of it." Ben reached behind him and found a scrap of glossy paper. He handed it to her. "By the way, I'm running a little ad in a number of newspapers around the country—with a special concentration in Pennsylvania—attempting to locate that machine of Tom Edison's, the one he was supposed to have been working on, to contact the dead." His brown eyes sparkled with excitement. "What a *coup* it would be to have photographs of that apparatus in our book!"

"Did you say it was a machine to—to *contact* the *dead?*" she demanded. "Are you serious about that?"

"I'm quite serious. Some of Edison's newer biographers ignore it, but the old ones told the story. I guess I have a particularly lurid imagination, Laura, but I simply can't help wondering."

"Wondering what?"

"Wondering what would happen if we should find that fascinating contraption. And *use* it." He hesitated, his brows curved in serious demeanor. "For the sake of both science and enhancing the credibility of our book, of course!"

"Of course." Laura laughed lightly.

But as she closed her notebook minutes later and rose to leave, she glanced again at Ben Kellogg and saw the glint of curiosity in his eyes. Curiosity and, she felt, something more. Was it possible he had a hidden reason for wanting those slender, creative hands of his on the vanished Edison apparatus? What was his *real* purpose for writing this book?

4

Early March, 1988.

There was, Laura Hawks had thought for some time, something almost breathtaking about beginning a new job. Part of the magic lay in the fact that an employer had selected *you* over all the other candidates and invested his confidence in your unique ability to perform an important task well. Part of it, too, was becoming an acquaintance or friend of the other employees, the challenging excitement of learning a fresh series of working procedures, and establishing a new routine involving transportation to and from work, finding new places to eat and shop on the lunch hour, and poking into various departments of the corporate body. It wouldn't be until much later, she knew—after you'd heard the awful gossip about the boss and his wife, absorbed a dozen passes from the male employees or clients and learned to what degree the boss had lied to you when you were hired—that it became just another job.

This one, though, was an entirely new experience for Laura. In the first place, Ben hadn't even talked to another applicant for the position. It had taken all his courage, he admitted when they had their first circumspect date, to ask Laura to come in for an interview. "I think," he told her with an embarrassed laugh, "that I might just have abandoned the book project if you'd turned out to be unacceptable."

Where making friends with other employees and poking into different departments to satisfy her curiosity about their roles were concerned, Laura was both slightly dismayed and, because of her innate shyness, rather pleased. Ben Kellogg had so few people working for him that it was hard to think of the little one-story building as housing a "company." There was a red-bearded, nonunion printer who toiled at Ben's modest printing equipment in the basement and, molelike, seldom ventured aboveground; two elderly people who came in three times a week to stuff envelopes of persuasive drop-mail literature; a part-time girl who proofed copy, did paste-up, occasionally answered the phone or ran errands for Ben; and Carola Glenn, Kellogg's indispensable secretary. Working procedures were left entirely up to her, since Ben gave her few orders and seemed preoccupied with his own work, performing in an atmosphere so quiet it was almost spooky.

Which was appropriate, given both the work Laura accepted and the dreams that began disturbing her at night. Unaccountably, since Laura rarely remembered her dreams, she began having a recurring nightmare in which she was pregnant and going to a handsome doctor for treatment. Unfaillingly, before the dream ended each night, the doctor changed into a disgusting monster, doing things to her that, in the blaze of sunlight, she could not remember in detail—always to her considerable relief. A few times Laura wondered if her unconscious mind might be trying to tell her something, even warning her to drop the project and return to the security of her own novel writing.

But that seemed to be total nonsense, since she enjoyed her new life enormously. That new life was inextricably bound up with Ben Kellogg, with whom she had had three dates. They were entirely innocuous occasions that felt natural to her when, working late in the evening, he would suggest that they "grab a sandwich and see that terrific new flick." Ben, she found, adored movies, and she was amused to sit beside him and see how intent and accepting he was and how easily the self-publisher was moved to emotion by actors on a screen.

To a woman with fairly limited experience, Ben was a different kind of man. Laura had never made a conscious decision to remain single, but the majority of men she'd dated before were so clearly determined above all to get her into bed that she grew bored with their shallowness and, beyond that, their apparent inability to see her as a person. Always independent, Laura avoided regular participation in women's-lib activism yet felt obliged to agree with much of what other women were doing. Except that, rather than finding men either disgusting or a threat, she tended to see them as overgrown, spoiled boys. A year ago she almost had an affair with a Carmel businessman, but his panting, hectic groping and obvious winning and dining of her had reduced her to helpless tears of laughter—and sent him motoring off, as she had told a girlfriend, "in a 1987 Huff."

Truth was, sex held few mysteries and no terrors for Laura—nor any magnetic attraction, most of the time. Her two affairs were remembered more with amusement than any other emotion—amusement and self-deprecation. Each time, she had talked herself into believing that she was falling in love merely to justify the fact that she was horny.

These days, sex seemed to Laura something that one did at appropriate times, along with dining, bathing and sleeping, paying taxes and observing Christmas. Except that you required a more acceptable accomplice than Santa Claus or the IRS for sex. The compulsiveness most men felt about sex early in a relationship seemed an overemphasized quality and eventually filled her with boredom. Only in the private recesses of her deepest thoughts did she ever confess to herself that, with just the right man, her attitude might conceivably change.

Benjamin Kellogg, she felt, might prove to be a different kind of bird. He had yet to become the lecherous boss of familiar repute. Other than a fleeting, brotherly peck on the cheek, he'd been content to sit for two hours in conversation with her after their third movie. It was this getting-acquainted kind of easy, amiable exchange that Laura had missed most with other attractive men, and it wasn't hard, with her writer's imagination, to think of falling in love with him. Or, she corrected herself sternly, to think of the *possibility* of it.

She was troubled only by a strange reticence about Ben that lurked beneath his outer candor, that unfolded in informal talk, something untold that bothered her. He refused to discuss his family or background, except for a reference to having attended Badler University. She decided he was sensitive enough of manner to be homosexual—most men, Laura felt, believed that any display of sensitivity was emasculating—but that seemed unlikely in Ben's case. It did not occur to her, either, how unfair it was even to have such a thought: the all-hands macho man was a letch, according to this thinking, and the gentle man was gay. Besides, when she had taken his hand in the darkness of the theater, an R-rated nude scene writhing before them, she'd easily sensed an intense, early response like electricity in his arm. Soon, she felt, he would overcome his own timidity and want to explore the sexual possibilities of their budding relationship. Just what her response would be, Laura had no idea.

Most of the time during the first several weeks in Ben Kellogg's employ, Laura found herself haunting the library and old, musty used-book stores, feeling a trifle quaint beneath the curious stares of librarians and proprietors. She was, she suspected, too pretty and young, somehow, to be properly intrigued by occult literature. Perhaps they thought she was the head of a coven.

And maybe that was what Carola Glenn, Ben's inestimable secretary, thought until yesterday, when they finally became friends. Until then,

Carola had barely spoken to her, and Laura was sure the young black woman had elected her Honky of the Month. Then, arriving at the office with arcane volumes piled in her little Toyota, Laura had gone around to the passenger's side and filled her aching arms with bizarre titles. Ben had given her almost a blank check for buying reference works, and she'd appreciated it until now, when she stared at the late-season sea of snow and ice between the Toyota and the office door.

She was almost ready to tackle it, when Carola had happened to glance through the front window and discover her plight. "Wait up, hold on!" Carola called, rushing out the door and hurrying down the walkway. She was wearing only a skintight green pullover and tailored skirt ending just above the knee, and Laura was afraid she'd catch her death of cold.

Without being asked, puffing from her run, Carola began taking half the volumes in her own slim arms. "Girl, you should have had those books delivered!" she exclaimed.

"You're probably right, but I needed them today," Laura replied, following the young secretary toward the building. The footprints they left in the caked snow were so much deeper because of the books they carried that Laura was reminded of the terrifying Devil's Hoofprints case. She said as much aloud, laughing.

"Ooo-*eee*," Carola yowled, slipping briefly but recovering her balance. "I don't need no footprints from any old devil!" She paused to yank the door open, then turned with a curious look. "What happened?"

"It was in Devonshire, England, in 1855," Laura remembered, tumbling the books onto her desk. "Hoofprints appeared one frightening night, materializing at one edge of town, going right through everything, then disappearing on the other side of town."

"Stop, I can't take it!" Carola exclaimed, clutching her bosom. "My heart!" She dropped onto the chair at her own desk with an engaging grin, the first of its kind Laura had seen there. "What d'you mean, 'going right through everything'?"

"Well, Carola, the hoofprints—cloven hooves—ran right up to the buildings or walls and then continued, directly, on the other side—as if something had literally walked through the wall or building. They never did find out what they were or who made them."

"Is *that* what Ben's having you do, Laura?" Carola demanded, hands on her hips. "Study terrible *crap* like that?" The writer nodded. "Well, he knew better'n to ask *me* to work with that kind of stuff! Lord, I'm glad you're just a researcher and writer."

A light dawned for Laura. "What did you think I was here for, Carola?" she asked. "To take over your job?"

Carola lifted a haughty brow. "Never know for sure what white people are going to do. Although," she added grudgingly, "Ben is all right, for a white man."

"I hope you'll give me a chance to prove that *I'm* all right," Laura said.

The lovely young black stared coolly at her.

"What'd you have in mind?"

"Picking me up tomorrow at Anson's Service Station." Laura laughed. "I'm having trouble with my Toyota, and I want to leave it for repairs. Could you drive me to the office?"

"Well," Carola replied, "if we're going to do things for each other, we may as well *try* to be friends."

Poring over her special material, Laura was surprised to learn that spiritualism had an official birthdate: March 31, 1848. It was then that the Fox family of Hydesville, New York, reportedly began active communication, through an eerie series of taps, with the other side. Here, as was the case with the mansion on Ridge Avenue in Pittsburgh, the house itself had had an uncanny reputation from the outset. Here, too, strange deaths had occurred, and fifty-six years later, a perfect human skeleton was in fact found between the two walls of the crumbling Fox home.

How odd! thought Laura. Fifty-six years was also the length of time that the Pittsburgh haunted house had stood!

Following the expressive spirit of Hydesville came a torrent of oddments related to ghosts continuing, basically unabated, to the present. Laura learned of the famous scientists, Sir Oliver Lodge and Sir William Crookes, who were fascinated with spiritualism despite the outrage of their fellow scientists—among them one Thomas Alva Edison, who'd corresponded with Sir Oliver. She read, too, of the incredible Scot, Daniel Dunglas Home, who could not be exposed as a fraud despite his fantastic levitations and materializations. And Sir Arthur Conan Doyle, Laura found, was more dedicated to spiritualism than to Mr. Sherlock Holmes of 221B Baker Street; Conan Doyle's work with the skeptical Harry Houdini was a story in itself.

Ghosts, of course, had not started to haunt midway through the nineteenth century. The history of phantoms was as old as mankind—appropriately, since ghosts were supposed to be people who had died. Around fifty thousand years ago, Neanderthal man was burying the artifacts of his deceased brothers, apparently from a conviction that the dead would return to life and need their things. The Etruscans, who occupied early Italy before the Romans, believed in a hereafter, and the Egyptian fascination for an afterlife was impossible to ignore, considering the unfathomable pyramids.

Reincarnation, too, was a life after death, and Laura found that its history could be traced not only to the mystic East but to the brilliant mathematician Pythagoras. He suggested that the soul had "fallen" into bodily form and was obliged to work its way back to Paradise through a series of lives in other human and animal bodies. But most reincarnationists thought people always lived in human bodies.

Ghosts and hauntings continued to modern times, and Laura was both touched and absorbed by the story of the late Bishop James Pike, who experienced a sense of responsibility for the death of his only son and subsequently seemed to have been contacted by the dead lad, even perhaps in a way that led to Pike's own desert death.

Sitting back and stretching, Laura glanced at her watch. Today Carola had brought her from the service station to work, apparently the soul of friendliness; then, half an hour ago, Carola had gone to an early lunch without asking the grounded Laura to go along! This meant she'd have to walk through the snow to Laughner's Cafeteria five blocks away, and she wondered if Carola was always this ambivalent about white people. Well, she'd wait until the pretty black woman returned before going for her own lunch. Who knows, Laura mused, maybe Carola will insist that I borrow her VW.

Laura was deep in study again at her desk when she heard a man clearing his throat.

"I beg your pardon," he said apologetically, seeing Laura's slight jump. "I did not mean to startle you."

Her curiosity deepened when she stared up at him. In height he was rather over six feet, but so excessively lean that he seemed to be considerably taller. His eyes were sharp and piercing, and his thin, hawklike nose gave his whole expression an air of alertness and decision. Yet there was a pallor to the man's face that suggested illness. Except for the confusing trace of a mustache beneath the long nose, the fellow appeared familiar.

"It's quite all right," Laura replied. "I'm afraid I was lost in thought."

"And where better to be lost?" he murmured, producing a business card from a vest pocket and extending it toward her. As her fingers touched it, however, his voice drew her eyes to his once again. "How are you enjoying your first excursion into the mysterious occult?" he inquired politely.

"It's remarkable material, and I don't know how much to believe." Then her light-brown brows lifted in genuine surprise. "How could you know what I was reading? Or that it was my 'first excursion,' as you put it?"

The slender man's eyes fairly glittered, and he put his hand over his heart and bowed as if to some applauding crowd. "A little trick of mine," he remarked lightly, then turned at the sound of a door opening. "Pardon me."

Ben Kellogg was standing in the doorway. His face lit up with joy when he saw his tall caller. "Martin!" he exclaimed, stepping forward with his hand outstretched. "Come in, please!"

The visitor stepped forward with clear pleasure to take Ben's hand, and the new animation of his face gave evidence of the more virile and healthy man he had been. When he and Ben closed the office door behind them, Laura realized with a smile why the man seemed familiar: he bore a striking resemblance to Basil Rathbone, the film actor who had portrayed Sherlock Holmes. Even his little deduction about her occult study was in character, and Laura was both delighted and puzzled.

She turned the card he'd given her and read, "Martin Ruben," and beneath that, "Consulting Parapsychologist."

By now Laura knew that a parapsychologist was a graduate psychologist who specialized in the paranormal—supernatural, ESP, incidents of an inexplicable nature—in an effort to test phenomena and get to the truth.

Inexplicable incidents, she mused, looking at Ben's closed door. Perhaps like a ghastly haunted house in Pittsburgh?

Ruben. Martin Ruben. The name, too, was familiar. She remained bothered by it for the remaining half hour until Carola returned from lunch.

"D'you know a man named Martin Ruben?" she asked in a low voice.

Carola finished hanging up her coat. "A friend of Ben's. He's a spook doctor." Carola grinned, obviously enjoying talking in her own patois. She didn't know Laura had discovered from Ben that the black secretary was a college graduate who had never received a grade below a B. "Is the good doctor with Ben?" Laura nodded.

Carola produced her keys and threw them in a quarterback pass to the writer. "Might as well take my VW and go to lunch, then, girl. Those two are *forever!*"

Sitting in a restaurant on Arlington Avenue, Laura suddenly put her sandwich back on its plate, startled by the realization: Dr. Martin Ruben had been in the headlines several years ago in connection with a terrible series of deaths occurring at a church in Carmel, the upper-middle-class town due north of Indianapolis. For a while, Laura seemed to recall, Ruben had even been a suspect!

What in the world could a parapsychologist caught up in murder have in common with Benjamin Kellogg? The connection escaped her, unless Ben seriously planned some kind of ghost hunt of his own.

Returning to the office, Laura caught a glimpse of faint lightning in the dark sky to the west and heard a rumble of thunder. It was odd, she thought, for a thunderstorm to be in the offing so soon after a snowfall. She tugged the lapels of her coat tightly around her and stepped into the office building with a slight shudder.

"Is it raining yet?" Carola Glenn asked, taking the keys that Laura returned to her.

"No, I'm not sure just what it's doing out there."

Carola presented her with a sparkling smile. "Well, in Indianapolis, if you don't care for the weather, wait around half an hour and you gets something different!"

Laura chuckled and returned to her own desk. Around four-thirty, weary and looking forward to quitting for the day, Laura glanced up with red eyes to see Ben beckoning to her from his private office. There was absolutely no use protesting that this meant they'd be working overtime. With her faithful Toyota being faithless at the service station and Carola living on the other side of town, Ben was her transportation home. Sighing, she got her notebook and a pencil and walked into Ben's quiet quarters.

"Ah, Miss Hawks!" cried the tall men from his chair to the right of the door. " 'Journeys end in lovers' meetings,' as the old play says."

Laura was startled to find Martin Ruben still present but gave him a shy smile. She'd assumed he'd slipped out sometime during the afternoon or while she was at lunch. But here the strange fellow was, sipping coffee, his penetrating gaze flickering over her face from his eyes sunken above prominent cheekbones. There was, though, a spot of color on each cheek now. His afternoon-long conversation with Ben Kellogg seemed to have restored him.

She took a chair beside Ruben, smoothing her skirt over her knees, and faced Ben Kellogg. Laura adored this cozy office with its two walls converted to wooden bookshelves, which were crammed with Ben's favorites. She had found all of Salinger there, and Updike, one or two F. Scott Fitzgerald first editions, and some of her favorite old Frank Yerby novels. There were sports biographies of Red Auerbach, Bob Knight, Howard Cosell, Hoosiers, something called *Tumultuous Merriment* by Heywood Hale Broun, which, Ben said, put sports in proper perspective. His catholic interests even extended to bios of film stars—*Cagney by Cagney,* the Higham books on Katharine Hepburn and Charles Laughton, and Peter Ustinov's witty *Dear Me.* On another wall was an original seascape in oil —"It's probably no good, but I like its wetness," he'd said—and, on the fourth wall, an autographed photograph of Peter Drucker, the business expert.

Beside Ben, always, was a stack of books and magazines—*Pursuit, Forbes, Baker Street Journal, Newsweek, Night Cry, Ellery Queen's Mystery Magazine*—which he had yet to read; and, in a single corner of his wide desk, a tape recorder with several appendages for use on the telephone in shining disuse.

Ben himself appeared more serious than usual. Laura thought, again, how ageless he seemed. After knowing him for several weeks, she still had no idea whether he was in his early thirties or mid-forties. Part of the secret was his neatly trimmed spade beard, of course, but more lay with the clear, undissipated brown eyes glowing with youthful enthusiasm and a zest for the world of ideas.

"Martin Ruben, here, is a parapsychologist, Laura." Ben toyed with a paper clip, but his eyes were fixed on Laura's face. "I've asked him to share our work on the ghost book. I think his know-how and experience will be important to us."

Stung by the thought of sharing her project, Laura turned to the thin man seated beside her. "I've been working hard, but I still don't know whether there is anything real enough about the Pittsburgh house to make it worth your time," she said. "But I'll have to admit your little guess at my reading the occult for the first time was proof of your know-how."

"I never guess," Ruben offered mildly, smiling. "It's destructive to the logical faculties. I have a turn both for observation and deduction, and I find this question of the Pittsburgh haunted house exceptionally fascinating. Frankly, I depend upon such things for my bread and cheese."

"How does that work?" she wondered.

His arresting gray eyes seemed to probe her soul as he spoke. "Well, I suppose I am one of only a few consulting parapsychologists in the world. Here in Indianapolis we have a good many professional psychologists—I was one myself, at Badler University, until my dismissal a few years ago—and numerous private ones. When these fellows are at loose ends because of esoteric questions, they come to me, and I usually manage to put them on the right track." He paused to look at Ben. "I have reason to believe that Kellogg, here, *is* on the right track. But a most dangerous one, if I don't miss my guess."

"I thought you said you don't guess," Ben put in, grinning.

"*Touche,* my dear Kellogg! A distinct touch!" cried Ruben admiringly.

"Are you also a writer, Dr. Ruben?" Laura asked, still trying to grasp the slender man's role in their project.

"Call me Martin, please," he urged. Then he lifted a languid hand and gave her a faint smile. "Alas, I am still awaiting my Boswell, my Watson."

"Then, what can you—"

"What can I suitably offer a literary enterprise? *Ms.* Hawks, I've had certain personal experiences with the supernatural. I proposed to Ben sometime ago that he was venturing into avenues beyond his expertise and suggested that he telephone to engage me when it was clear that he needed my stripe of know-how." He paused to shake his head at Ben. "These are deep waters, Benjamin."

"And no one should know better than you, Martin," Ben agreed soberly. "Perhaps you'd be good enough to sketch, for Laura's sake, some of the frightening things that have happened to you in recent years."

Laura saw, with surprise, that Martin Ruben's pale face indicated a clear resistance to the plea. But the parapsychologist saw the questions forming in her eyes and, putting his fingertips together and his elbows upon his knees, began to explain.

"You have probably heard of something called the Antichrist," he murmured.

"Well, I'd read *some* things even before I started working here," she replied slowly. "That he might come to the world in human form before the end of this century and that he'd be the son of Satan. But I guess it hasn't happened yet, thank heaven."

"Ah, there's the genius and the wonder of the thing," Ruben exclaimed, staring dramatically at the ceiling. "The creature assumed form in 1976, in Carmel, Indiana, yet no one knows of it to this day. Not even after a series of atrocious murders."

"It was in the papers, though, wasn't it?" asked Laura. "Your name—"

"—was dragged through the mud, as they say. And only parts of the story were printed, basically as rumor. They said officially that I went momentarily mad as a consequence of witnessing the hideous death of three good friends and a youngster called Robert. Oh, I was cleared, Laura, in the official sense of the word. My reputation, regrettably . . ." Ruben shrugged his narrow shoulders, and shivered.

Only in the past few days—when a revelation of her own surprising part in this had dawned, a revelation she still had mentioned to no one—had Laura been able to give credence to such occult matters. Now, sitting close to the parapsychologist and accepting his brilliance, she found that she believed what he was saying. "You're telling us, then, that the—the Antichrist was behind those deaths?"

"I had been continually conscious of some power behind the evil spreading in the world for some years. Again and again, as I read dreadful notices concerning young children slaying their parents, as I read of assassinations in civilized nations, I felt the presence of this force or power. Then, when little Robert Meggitt was on the verge of entering puberty, I learned—and was able to prove—that his unconscious mind contained all the accumulated evil in history. That, in point of fact, when he turned fourteen he would *become* the living Antichrist." Ruben's gaze seemed to turn momentarily inward, and he grew paler. "The malefactor, the organizer of all evil, detected and undetected. He would sit at the center of his great web, like a terrible spider, designing ways for man to kill his brother and deliver them both to hell."

Laura nibbled her lower lip agitatedly. "Where is this Antichrist today? What happened?"

Ruben peered at her with tortured gray eyes. "I only know that that boy, the container for the Antichrist, died at the hands of the Almighty. And that he has been born again, elsewhere." He inhaled deeply. "That, thank God, is the challenge of someone other than myself." He paused. "Meeting that force, just once, has all but destroyed my life. I do not care to meet it again."

"And he believes that our work might somehow bring the son of Satan back to Indiana," Ben Kellogg put in. His tone was polite but underlined by a faintly dubious strain.

Martin Ruben's head came up, and his eyes flashed at his friend. "I believe nothing of the sort!" he snapped. "Mortal man—especially mortal American man—has two outstandingly irritating qualities: he simplifies that which cannot logically be simplified, not because he lacks the insight to handle it well, but because he's irremediably lazy—and he believes in a wholly delusory personal immortality." He stopped in some exasperation, trying to gather his customary quasi-British charm. "Ben, old friend, there is more evil in this complex universe than that monster of an Antichrist I encountered." Ruben paused. "There is, for example . . . his *father*."

Laura paled. "Do you honestly think the devil himself is involved with the Pittsburgh hauntings?" she asked.

"It's difficult to say with certainty, lacking more data. But I trust it will not overwhelm you to learn that there are evil sources, roots of consummate evil, in addition to Satan." Ruben saw her surprise and sighed, breaking off to stare out the window at the darkening skies. "It is man's good fortune, I suppose, that he does not realize how many dark spirits seek his simple soul."

Ben's face softened, and his tone was gentle. "Look, Martin, if you'd prefer to go into this for Laura at a later date, we'll both understand. I realize these past few years have put you through a helluva lot."

"I cannot deny it, my friend—specifically, a 'hell' of a lot. Yet if my record were closed tonight, I could still survey it with equanimity. In more than a thousand bizarre cases of the paranormal, I'm not aware that I've ever used my knowledge for the wrong side. You and Miss Hawks need me now, whether you fully realize it or not. That is why I'm here. And I recommend to you, Laura, that you consider bowing out of the case *now*." He gave her an exceptionally keen, appraising glance. "Especially considering the secret information you've become privy to."

Laura blinked. How could *he* know that she had made a discovery of her own? For the first time she saw that it might be less than coincidental. Yet how could there be any danger involved in merely writing a book about haunted houses? The spirits within the Pittsburgh mansion dated back fifty years or more.

"Ben," she began as calmly as possible, "in the research I've done on 1129 Ridge Avenue, I have encountered something peculiar myself—a quite personal connection. Do you remember the psychic lady who went to the house to spend a night and later told reporters about the ugly, terrible things that happened to her there?"

He nodded. "I remember." And Ruben put in promptly, "Julia Murray, I think, was her name."

Laura swallowed. "My mother's maiden name was Murray. I checked it out and found, to my amazement, that Julia Murray was my own great-great aunt." She made a slight, helpless gesture with her hands, then hid them nervously in her lap. "Really, I couldn't back out now—even if I wanted to. What happened to Aunt Julia wasn't pleasant, and it begins to look as if I'm *meant* to be involved."

"A summons isn't precisely an invitation," Ruben murmured thoughtfully, "but I respect your position. And distrust coincidence."

"Very well, then," Ben said briskly, "I guess we're the Three Musketeers of Metaphysics from here on. One for all, and all that jazz." He saw them both nod. "All right, then, it's time."

He stooped to plunge his hand deep into a desk drawer. From it he withdrew, almost reverent in his care, a square object. As they stared at it in silence, a roll of thunder sounded eerily in the distance. Ben placed the corrugated box atop his desk and stepped back. Unaccountably, a shiver trickled along Laura's spine. She saw the intent, almost zealous glint in Martin Ruben's eyes as Ben began lifting something from the box. She saw Ruben's lips form the syllable, *"No."*

Fundamentally metallic, it appeared incredibly old; a heavy coat of dust lay upon its dials and lever. Ben rested his hand on it, more protectively than possessively. He looked closely from Martin to Laura Hawks.

"This," he said in his unassuming, soft voice, "this is something rather special, my friends. *It is the apparatus that Thomas Edison created over half a century ago."* Lightning flamed at the window, and Ben's eyes grew large with awe and delight. *"The apparatus he made for the specific purpose of summoning the dead."*

5

"H-How in the world did you get it?" Laura gasped, staring at the old contraption in complete fascination and yet, because of all they had learned about Ridge Avenue, with a measure of apprehension.

"It came in as a reply to one of the ads I ran," Ben answered happily. He pulled a long white envelope from the corrugated box that had contained the apparatus and slipped the letter from it. He held it up before unfolding it. "The writer of this letter is an elderly woman who lives in a small town in Pennsylvania, not far from Pittsburgh. She told me that much in lieu of giving her name. She didn't sign the letter because, she says, she never wants to hear about this invention again."

"Ben," began Ruben, raising a cautioning hand, his face drawn and concerned, "I must tell you frankly that you are beginning to meddle with things for which you have no training, no experience. I don't want to be rude, but I don't think this ancient device concerns you."

"Oh, it concerns me, all right, Martin." Ben smiled and waved the letter. "The woman who wrote this intended for me to *have* the machine." Laura saw that Ben could scarcely conceal his enthusiasm for this stroke of apparent good luck. "She wants *me* to keep it!"

"That is your misfortune, and I urge you to get rid of it," Ruben said tightly, leaning forward.

"I can't do that."

"You asked me into this case to offer my professional advice, and I'm giving it to you *now*: Get *rid* of that apparatus at your earliest opportunity—give it to a museum or foundation." He paused to look rather frostily at Ben. "I didn't bargain for *deus ex machina*. Or, for that matter, *diablos ex machina*."

"Your Latin is execrable, Martin," Ben replied with a laugh.

"Not as execrable as tampering in areas where the very roots of evil lie buried!" Ruben snapped.

"Ben, Martin," Laura interjected, leaning forward to them. "Look, we *have* gone this far, haven't we? I think we should at least hear the contents of the old woman's letter."

"What d'you say, Martin?" Ben called softly, looking like a little boy teasing his father. "It can't hurt anything merely for you and Laura to hear the letter, can it?"

Ruben pinched his narrow chin between long fingers and looked offended. "Curiosity, the cat and I," he responded with a sigh. Then he gestured with comic defiance. "Go ahead, then, Kellogg. Read your damned letter."

HORROR HOUSE

Ben grinned. "To avoid reading the whole thing to you, the lady claims that she came upon the Edison device after the death of a relative. She says he was a gifted scientist himself and passed away some twenty years or so ago. Well, it seems that the machine had been literally hidden away in her relative's effects. When she happened upon it, she also unearthed a page of very old handwritten instructions. Unfortunately, it crumbled away when she tried to read it; so we don't know exactly how the machine is meant to be used." Ben smoothed the letter out on his desk and indicated it with his forefinger. "All this lady knew for certain was that the apparatus once was the property—in fact, the *invention*—of Thomas Alva Edison." He paused. "But she learned one other thing."

"What was that?" Laura asked quietly, absorbed.

"That it changed her life," he replied soberly, meeting her gaze. "Very much for the worse, I'm afraid."

"Kellogg, it isn't too late to back out," Ruben said quickly.

"I just can't," Ben remarked simply. Then he held the letter beneath the yellowish light of his desk lamp and began reading it aloud. " 'I cannot tell you and offer proof, Mr. Kellogg, but I am certain that the apparatus or associations attaching to it brought awful tragedy upon me and mine. Nor can I tell you in precise detail all the terrible things that have happened to my poor family. Suffice it to say, there have been ghastly white faces peering through our windows in the dark of night, eerie hands materializing in our private bedroom, as well as crawling, lecherous things that have stroked and caressed my face and shoulders with the touch of the dead.' "

"My God," Laura whispered.

"I fear He has little to do with this matter, my dear," said Ruben, frowning with undiminished disapproval at his old friend.

" 'I shall briefly recount the fact that our small and helpless baby—who could not even sit erect without considerable assistance—was somehow drawn to his small feet with a look of stark terror written on his innocent face.' " Ben paused, shaking his head. " 'Ever after, our child has been disturbed by grotesque nightmares—haunted, I might say—which come to him almost nightly. When he reached adulthood, his solitary effort at marriage disintegrated in a shocking fashion, the nature of which I cannot reveal just now.

" 'I must report to you, Mr. Kellogg, so that you will be forewarned, of certain bizarre efforts to steal this fiendish contraption. I prefer to pretend that they were undertaken by people who simply sought to obtain something of value, but their efforts were strange. We knew of the machine's historic value from the start and attempted at all times to protect it for the time when posterity might be ready for it. Why, you ask, didn't we merely sell it or perhaps present it to a scientific organization of some kind? Because I remember my dear relative telling me, not long before he hid the apparatus and went to his Maker, that "the world is not able to withstand this machine or its effects." If anything should happen to him, he said, please protect mortal man from its hellish consequences, at all costs.

" 'Now, however,' " Ben continued reading after a pause, " 'I am ill because of my loss, apprehension, and continued exposure to this accursed device. One day I fervently hope to go to my Lord with a clean heart and conscience, and that day does not appear far in the future. Your advertisement was, to me in my growing helplessness of spirit, a Godsend. In the hope that you shall prove to be more courageous, resolute and resourceful a soul than I have been, Mr. Kellogg, you may now lay claim to Mr. Edison's old apparatus. And may God help you should you ever attempt to make *use* of it.' Well, that's it." Ben looked excitedly at Laura and Martin Ruben. "Isn't that something?"

"Oh, it's *something*, all right," Ruben replied testily. "And you don't even know who sent you that thing?"

"No, the letter is unsigned. My impression is that it's an elderly person who has a very vivid but dour imagination. Psychologists call it transference, don't they, Martin? Attributing to some outside agent the responsibility for life going wrong?"

The parapsychologist nodded. "I would say that she has very successfully transferred the outside agent that made her life go wrong—to *you*."

Suddenly a roll of explosive thunder burst above the one-story building, and the entire structure vibrated. Laura, tense from all that had happened, leaped uncontrollably and let out a tiny shriek of fear. Composing herself, she laughed and gestured to the old machine on her employer's desk. "Well, Ben, now that you've finally got your hands on the crazy thing, what do you plan to do with it?"

He gave her a positively beatific smile. "Do with it? Why, Laura, I have two plans for it. Let me tell you both my second intention first. Before long, I intend to fly to Pittsburgh and stand exactly where the so-called haunted house stood, at 1129 Ridge Avenue. Then I'm going to turn this machine on full blast—and see what happens!"

"Why, Ben?" Laura demanded. "I know you a little by now, and you aren't an impulsive man. You must have some reason for becoming this involved in the whole frightening mess. Why do you feel compelled to test the apparatus in Pittsburgh?"

He stopped smiling and gave her a rather wry, wary look. "You're right, Laura, I *do* have some personal reasons for wanting this book of ours written. But I think you may misunderstand me somewhat: I mentioned that I had two intentions, and the other one is very simple. I intend to use the apparatus immediately—*right now!*"

Shocked, Laura turned to Martin Ruben just as lightning again flashed at the window. She saw that he was perspiring freely even though the temperature in Ben's office was barely warm enough for comfort. The parapsychologist was not aware of her glance; his gaze, clearly, was turned inward—at what dark, grotesque things Laura could not even conceive.

But then he felt her stare and lifted his face to her. And never before, Laura thought, had she seen

HORROR HOUSE

an expression of such fear—of terror so absolute, so complete—on a human being's face.

6

"You cannot—you *must* not—use that device," Martin Ruben declared with intensity. The cords in his neck tightened, standing out like lengths of rope. "Not now, not *ever!*"

Ben Kellogg looked into his friend's pleading eyes, and, to Laura's surprise, an almost beseeching quality sprang into his face. "You don't understand, Martin," he said sadly. "For my own good reasons I feel that I must."

With that and before anyone else could speak, Ben leaned forward above the apparatus and raised the lever with firm determination. Rays of light formed around the machine, and Laura clearly perceived the faintest sound of humming.

Nothing, however, happened—at least, not in the publisher's office . . .

The 747 stratoliner was cruising comfortably, only easy miles from Indianapolis International, beginning its great drop from unreal heights. Its passengers could see the ground beneath the cloud cover for the first time since leaving Kennedy in New York.

"Begin instrument check," murmured Captain Dan Kinney, barely glancing at his copilot and friend. They'd flown together so many times that it was mainly regulations that made him issue most of his commands.

Steve Nolan absently replied, "Roger," and peered at his clipboard. That was when he felt Dan Kinney's muscular hand lock on his wrist, painfully. He glanced at the captain with annoyance, feeling his wrist begin to numb, but the words he was ready to utter stuck in his throat.

Dan Kinney's tanned face was contorted in an expression combining astonishment, disbelief and fear. Nolan had never before seen any of those emotions register on the captain's unflappable face.

He followed Kinney's pointing finger, then wished he hadn't.

Ahead of them, above the prototypically ordinary city of Indianapolis, an unbelievable scene was forming in the skies. Steve Nolan whispered, "My God," and it was a sincere prayer. The most solemn one of his life.

Spread across the entire visible arc of sky was a wave of bright, red flame. It was as if the sky had inexplicably turned to liquid fire—or as if the giant 747 were headed on a direct course into an ocean of hell. Spurting geysers of scarlet boiled madly upward. Explosions rippled, shot outward, seemingly groping for the approaching jet plane.

"Tell me I don't really see it," Kinney said in

low tones, his hands frozen on the controls. "Tell me, please, that I have simply gone mad."

Nolan risked a quick glance at the captain, saw his fisted hands and realized Kinney wasn't able to take action. *Whatever* happened up there, Nolan knew, there was something that could be done about it. Taking over for Dan Kinney, he banked the jet in as tight a right-angle turn as possible, slicing away from the roaring landscape of flame.

But ahead of them the enormous conflagration was beginning to assume another form. Before Steve Nolan's terrified eyes, it became a leering grin, a madman's smile that stretched across the horizon and, as Nolan watched, parted—to become a set of almost definable, devouring jaws.

Beside him, Dan Kinney screamed involuntarily and groped for the stick. Before Nolan could react, they were diving, plunging through the air, falling toward certain death.

"At least allow me to explain!" Ruben cried angrily. He was on his feet, obviously frantic, pale as any ghost.

Ben gaped at his friend, shocked. "Martin, what's wrong? What is it?"

"An impression, a feeling," Ruben gasped, and seemed to be on the verge of reeling—"that something has already happened!"

"You were never psychic before."

"No," Ruben muttered, his eyes rolling. "Not before—Robert." He stared beseechingly down at Kellogg. "Turn it down long enough to hear my reasons!"

Ben nodded. He throttled the aged lever. "All

right," he said. "I'll hear you out."

Sighing as if exhausted, Ruben settled back into his chair and mopped his damp forehead with a handkerchief. "I *am* the expert—and I admit to being terrified of this contraption." He looked intently at Ben, then Laura. "I have reason to believe that you may literally be unleashing the forces of hell itself."

The 747 was out of control. Dan Kinney was locked in the grip of his terrified determination, his face twisted into a mask of fear and persistence. Steve Nolan grappled with the captain's hand and wrist, trying to pull the jet out of its suicidal dive. Behind them, in the passenger section, more than a hundred people screamed their terror as they were thrown from their seats. Nolan was vaguely aware that two stewardesses had fought their way into the cabin and were staring at the pilots in voiceless horror.

As Nolan dug his nails into Kinney's hand, tugging, drawing blood, he turned once more to the nightmare scene that had created their plight—and saw with amazement clear, azure skies—even while they continued to plummet.

The jet could not be righted. It had been some sort of delusion, Nolan perceived—some killing game, or the challenge of an unseen force whose victory was achieved only when all their lives were lost.

In the midst of complete chaos, the last thing he heard before the 747 ripped into a nine-story building on the west side of Indianapolis was a piercing, nerve-shattering yowl of apparent delight or glee.

Then there was nothing at all.

"To begin with, I have a sixth sense about matters of this kind," Ruben told Ben and Laura. "Frankly, I'm rarely wrong when that sense is alerted. Now, it is one thing to confront a scene of poltergeist activity followed by the logical explanation that a child in the house has unconsciously caused the tumult and chaos through psychokinesis, but it is quite a different situation when I am trying to work with a man who's on the verge of entering diabolical experimentation with his eyes tightly shut."

"You seem to be saying that there's more to the haunted house in Pittsburgh than what they call 'discarnate spirits'—*more* than ghosts seeking their freedom." Laura was trying not to take sides, but, despite her warm feelings for Ben, she sensed that he was making a mistake. "You're implying that there is a distinctly evil source and that we may inadvertently summon that same evil—release it upon ourselves."

"That's accurate," Ruben conceded in firm tones.

"Well, I'm not even sure I believe in evil, Martin," Ben protested with a frown. "I'm a modern man. Mostly, it seems to me, people behave selfishly, greedily and just plain stupidly. I fail to see why we have to begin giving this matter some archaic religious interpretation."

"It needn't be a question of a specific religion which pinpoints the existence of evil, Ben. The dullest-witted teenager knows that certain acts are far more than wrong, that they are motivated by evil and—"

"May I finish my point?" Laura asked calmly. Each of the men stopped to turn to her. "While I'll grant you that I haven't yet had the chance to read everything about the occult, Martin, it would seem to me that ghosts are generally peaceful enough. They frighten more by merely appearing than any other means. They're entities who are 'stuck' here in some way, but striving to leave. Is that correct?"

"Yes, in all probability," Ruben replied. "Where the Ridge Avenue mansion is concerned I fear something far worse than discarnate spirits."

Something in his manner caused Ben to refrain from speaking. Ruben took a deep, trembling breath, arose and began pacing the length of Ben's office, suddenly charged with nervous energy, his hands tucked tight at the small of his back and his long chin thoughtfully settled on his narrow chest.

It occurred to Laura as she followed Ruben's silent pacing that he wasn't everything he seemed to be. For one thing, she detected a tender quality underscoring his aristocratic speech and manner, a true interest in his friends and a concern for society. Then, too, she sensed in him a fugitive yearning for the excitement he had known several years before. In a way, she thought, Ruben wants to become caught up with that apparatus yet is exercising his self-discipline by arguing against it. She found herself wondering if the man had some old score to settle.

Then Ruben flung himself onto Ben's couch with a sigh and stared up at them from lowered lids. "Please try to follow my thoughts. When a scientist has been exposed to incredible matters, those beyond his ken, and has no choice but to accept what his own limited senses transmit to him, he is a fool if he doesn't strive to get further answers. Hence, after certain friends of mine died so terribly because of the Antichrist, I vowed to learn everything possible about the essential, covert motivations of man himself. Motivations that begin in the cosmos, I find, in the nearly uninterpretable mind of the Almighty"—Ruben paused, then added, meaningfully—"and his counterpart.

"Thus, I worked feverishly, my friends," he continued, the piercing eyes roving like restless foxes from face to face, "exploring first one avenue of explanation, then another. No paranormal possibilities were too outre for my attention, at least momentarily. I devoured the works of masters in the occult field such as Colin Wilson, Lewis Spence and John Taylor, many volumes of my reading more abstruse and wildly speculative than what you have on your desk, Laura. Whenever possible, I tested things by the scientific method, hoping to anticipate where the other who sent the Antichrist to this planet would strike again, and in what fiendish way." He shook his head wearily.

Ben was in the world of ideas now, the favorite, precious world in which he came alive. "What did you learn, Martin?" he asked, almost breathlessly. The fever of excitement glinted in his soft brown eyes. "I can see from looking at you that you know *more*—more than you've told anyone until now."

Ruben inhaled in surprise and moved his long arms so that he could interweave his lengthy fingers in a restless clasp. He smiled. "Benjamin, you have a deductive capacity that's based on sheer intuition. Sometimes," he added with admiration, "I think that you can do more in a few moments with your inner impressions than I, with logical perseverance, can achieve in a month. It happens that you're right: I did learn something extraordinary."

"Can you tell us now?" Laura wondered, a trifle breathless herself.

Ruben sat up suddenly, sipped the remains of his coffee and made a bitter face. "I presume that you two are aware of Carl Gustav Jung's special contributions to the field of psychology?"

Laura nodded. Ben murmured yes.

"Then, you know about his 'collective unconscious.' "

"I have a—a layman's notion of what it is," Laura replied, thinking, "but could you explain it in some depth?"

"I shall try to be as concise as possible and focus on its applications to the situation we have in mind," Ruben declared. His gaze was fixed on a spot in the corner of the ceiling, and Laura could imagine the man back at Badler U., lecturing before forty rapt students. "Dr. Jung saw the collective unconscious as a sum total of the knowledge acquired by man, kept as a sort of repository—the telltale fingerprints, as it were, of man's ancestral experiences through the many generations of his existence. Now, Jung felt that the collective unconscious lay at the root of man's individual as well as collective experience. Man never entirely forgot it, he thought, but only unconsciously interpreted it in strikingly personal ways. These 'memories' of the ancestral past Dr. Jung called 'archetypes,' and they are, in a way, every man's bridge to all other men. Therefore, every individual man sums up prior human existence on earth, due to his memories."

"I don't see—" began Ben.

Ruben smiled, and it was warm, human. "Please bear with me, because you'll learn where I'm headed soon. Now, the collective unconscious can be seen as explaining *deja vu*—that odd feeling one has of having experienced something before, even though it's really a new experience. It also serves to explain how the same religious legends arise in disparate societies, Noah or the story of Eden appearing not only in biblical lands but among Indians or in the mountains of Tibet. In this way, friends, people are never quite 'modern,' never entirely freed of their pasts or even totally apart from all other human beings."

Ben sighed and glanced at Laura. Then he tapped his ever-present pencil on the desk and chose his words. "Martin, I think this is really interesting, but I don't see the connection with this contraption or with Satan—or even with your own awful experience with the Antichrist."

"I apologize, Ben," Ruben said gently. "Please bear with me just another few moments, and you will see." He pressed his fingertips together. "I've come to the realization that the force which is called Satan, the devil, Baal, or Beelzebub has a single truly distinguishing characteristic: it is the great distorter, the source of all confusion, the master . . . *of misdirection.*"

Ruben paused as Carola King entered unannounced to bring them a pot of fresh hot coffee. As

Ben and Laura murmured their appreciation, Ruben looked appraisingly at the lovely young black woman, content to wait for her departure.

He picked up his refilled coffee cup and the thread of his remarks simutaneously. "I do not want to appear to have all the answers, but I hope you appreciate how hard I have worked to acquire a few of them. Primarily, since little Robert was sacrificed on the altar of evil, I have learned that the immortal tale of the Antichrist—and his actual appearance in Carmel is *the mere tip of hell's iceberg*."

Laura's lips parted in new surprise. "From all I've read and heard over the last decade, I thought the Antichrist was the only one we had to fear at the end of the century, if all the terrible legends were to come true."

"Who else is there to fear?" Ben demanded, sipping his coffee.

Ruben ignored him and patted Laura's arm. "As terrible as the work of the grown child will be, wherever he is reborn, the Antichrist serves mainly as a maniac of confusion—as a diversion, averting man's attention from matters infinitely worse. And I fear that you, my dear Kellogg"—he stopped to shoot a piqued look at Ben—"may very well, by using this Edison device, bring that ultimate force of evil down upon us all. I am obliged by circumstance—to express that fear to you."

Peals of thunder underscored Ruben's last words and, when he raised his voice nearly to a shout to combat nature's volume, his intonation of warning blended to make an effective impact upon his listeners.

For a moment neither Ben nor Laura said a word.

"I don't see how this fits into the real world." Ben said at last. Quite clearly he wished simply to stop listening to the cautionary words that could turn him from the source of his curiosity. "How have you drawn your conclusions, Martin?"

"To start with," Ruben answered coolly, "in nature parapsychologists and occultists have found there to be an opposite for everything anyone can name. For cold, there exists hot; for man, woman. Together, opposites form a paradoxical whole, adding meaning to each part. Together, they are enlivened, regenerated and revitalized. They are never so powerful, indeed, as when they are viewed as total complements to one another: day/night; yin/yang; pleasure/pain; astral body and etheric body; love and hate; war and peace; mind/body; body/soul; anima/*persona;* objectivity and subjectivity—"

"Martin, enough," Ben wailed.

"Let me finish!" Ruben exclaimed. *Opposites,* man—thought/feeling; mind left and mind right; good and evil." He paused to gasp a breath of air, and to peer intently first to Ben and then to Laura. "*And* . . . divine, collective unconscious mind or— on the other hand—*evil collective unconscious*! Damnit, it's revolutionary. It's real!"

Ben blinked, twisted his pencil in his fingers. "I am not entirely following you."

Laura glanced soothingly at Ruben. "Are you proposing that Jung was . . . *literally* right? That all of us have some kind of access to a cosmic pool, a stockpile of racial memory and, in addition, that there is also a . . . a repository of sheer evil?"

Ruben lifted the curtain at the window to peer into the growing night. Rain washed the windows and, in reflection, turned his long face spectral. "Each exists as surely as God and the other. And no man slays either, my friends—I promise you that." He looked at Ben Kellogg. "There's a bit more, too. Are you familiar with Van Allen belts?"

Both his listeners nodded, Ben with slight rancor. "What do asteroids have to do with any of this?"

"Close, but no cigar." He strove to relax, to recover his poise. "James Van Allen is a physicist born here in 1914. He hypothesized high-intensity radiation of charged atomic particles circling the planet continuously which would penetrate, killing all life, except for the existence of protective 'belts' beyond the exosphere—some forty thousand miles above us, to be exact. Now, because there is such a belt guarding man's physical being from destruction, the law of opposites dictates that there must as well be another, complementing force." Ruben watched to make sure they were following him, looking penetratingly at them above the tips of his pressed fingers. "That complementary duality, therefore, *must* protect man's spiritual, or soul side, from annihilation."

"Annihilation?" Ben repeated curiously. "What earthly force could annihilate the 'soul side' of man, as you put it?"

"*No* 'earthly force,' " Ruben responded, imperious index finger lifted. "But the vast, evil, all-murdering radiation of the dark collective unconscious."

"That's only a logical proof—a proof done with mirrors, with words alone." Ben stood, stretched his cramped arms, then moved almost languorously around to the front of his desk. He leaned against it, and his smile remained amiable, even gentle, despite his words: "I want you to really *prove* it!"

"Ben!" Laura exclaimed. She thought he was being rude. Ruben had turned expressionless.

But Ben's gaze didn't swerve from the parapsychologist's hawk-nosed face despite Laura's indignation. "Martin, before I'll give up my chance to try this fantastic device, you're going to have to provide some evidence for your claims. In short, old pal—on this one, I'm from Missouri!"

Ruben did not take umbrage; indeed, he was relaxed and smiling, remarkably mild. "There's no real problem there, Ben, because I'm dealing with a fair, open-minded questioner. My dear friends, during the arduous study I've been undertaking, I became aware sometime ago of the existence of this awful . . . apparatus."

Ben looked at Ruben in astonishment. "You *knew* about it?"

Ruben nodded. "I also came to know where it was. Moreover, I learned something you do not yet know—that it has already been used. Precisely once." His alert gaze had been turned to Laura to discern her reaction; yet his eyes remained kind as they scanned her lovely features. "You see, that same, damnable apparatus has already brought severe problems for mankind."

"How?" Laura replied, dazzled by the man.

"When?" inquired Ben, openly amazed. "What happened?"

Martin Ruben, knowing he had his audience where he wanted it, leaned languidly back on the couch. Unable to control his dramatic nature fully, he closed his keen eyes for his best effect. "Evil has always existed in the minds of men, of course. It had to—as evidence that God lived as well, and for God's goodness to be expressed from time to time. However, before Thomas Edison came on the scene, evil was restrained—held in recognizable proportions, basically in check. There was a time of war, of occasional murder; there was the sort of mental detachment that permits other people to be starved or tortured. There was, of course, a general breaking of the Ten Commandments given Moses—yet in a fashion that, these days, a great number of ordinary people would find virtually amusing by comparison!"

"You're saying that evil was once simpler and more straightforward?" probed Ben. "That while men killed, it was with a rational if misguided purpose?"

"Perhaps even from necessity, such as to provide one something to eat or to feed one's family," Ruben agreed. "That's the way it once was—when goodness was in the *lead*."

"But what happened to alter things?" inquired Laura.

"My dear, after Mr. Thomas Edison used this machine of his—with the best of intentions, naturally; *he* was an honorable and gentle man who sought only to bring good to mankind—after it was created and he used it, well, the *quality* of evil was changed from that day forward. It worsened enormously upon this planet Earth."

A delicate smile moved Ben's lips. "I don't think you can prove that, even to this 'open-minded and fair man's', satisfaction."

"Perhaps I can't establish it in a court of law," Ruben replied. "But yes, in your own true, sweet reason I think I can." He narrowed his eyelids ruminatively. "Prior to the infernal use of this apparatus, Kellogg, man's terrible deeds were motivated by such elemental tools of the evil *other* as sheer, basic needs, as I mentioned. A need that overcame temporal rules or regulations, such as sexual lust, territorial imperatives which caused man to want and seek greater room, passing whims and, of course, actual madness. That, in short, was the way evil *used* to be expressed by mankind."

"And after the early twenties?" prompted Ben, listening attentively.

"After that year when Edison employed his device in that precious haunted house of yours, Benjamin, evil mounted—redoubled, became hideously twisted, often distorted to the point of being inexplicable. Nothing else can adequately explain some of the terrible things that have happened on this planet since then. The great distorter and confuser made hordes of people stand by disinterestedly while others plundered and raped. Think of the many men and women who turned their backs upon the Hitlerian Holocaust. Apathy, you see, is evil's most accessible weapon. Man began to rebel against God and the spirit of his laws—to foster revolutions out of sheer boredom, to behave in awful fashion because of passing dissatisfaction rather than from a sense of great cause or mission."

"Ben, I think he may be right," Laura murmured in hushed tones. "My own mother—many others have remarked on the way things are out of hand, out of control. The way we condone crimes so vicious that they once would have been considered acts of the devil!"

"And now, Ms. Hawks," Ruben said, "they're acts of true evil. Think of the assassins, normal till the second they strike, undetected by all. Think of the people with real grievances who strike but allow calamities to occur."

"I don't like this," Ben Kellogg growled.

"Rational people don't," Ruben snapped. "Think of the terrorists, of fanatics who provoke mass suicide. And what happened was that we began to see differences between one another that had not existed or been drawn before."

"Bigotry has always existed," said Ben.

"We drew increasingly into our tight, insular concerns as human beings. Consider the cities where, in an apartment, a tenant affixes four locks on his 'cave' and may not walk in his own neighborhood after dark. And, modified, the same evils exist in the hearts of those ordinary people who have hidden themselves from others with no willingness even to give them a chance—ever asserting their 'differences.' " Ruben snarled, "One turns his cheek today only to *spit*."

Laura's gaze upon the tall, high-keyed man was unblinking now. "Most of the Nazis themselves, I believe, did not actually hate Jews or foreigners. The plight was that the majority of people didn't *care* what happened to the oppressed—isn't that right? In a weird way, they were almost worse than Hitler and the others."

"Precisely," Ruben answered, inclining his head and glancing to the silent Ben Kellogg. "And not a few experts have suggested that there was *active, overt help* from hell backing the Hitlerian hordes—that he was a forerunner of the Antichrist, inspired by the lieutenants of the underworld. Just review what you read daily in the newspapers: spontaneous acts of cruelty, apparently with no motivation of understandable gain; gratuitous violence, such as the young monsters in this state who threw rocks at the gentle Amish people—and killed a babe in arms—because they were 'different;' people who burn their own neighborhoods, who fry their babies; teen-agers who mangle their parents simply out of boredom, because there's nothing else to *do* for the moment." Ruben slowly turned his whole body to face Ben, his eyes sad and earnestly fearful. "The evil that men do now lives with us, incessantly, and has *since 1921*. I shudder to think what is interred with their bones. A twenty-year-old radical with his grass in one hand and a homemade bomb in the other must make mighty, ambitious Caesar weep with shame."

"Perhaps," said Ben, barely above a whisper, "you are right." Slowly he raised his hand for the ancient apparatus. "Perhaps I can find some other way to learn what I must learn."

"I *am* right, friend," Ruben asserted, coming erect. His narrow upper lip twisted as he sought the right words. "Evil comes in many guises, you know. Another is that of the satanic divider, he who isolates man from his fellows and causes him to be able suddenly to make incredibly minuscule distinctions—distinctions on the basis of not only skin color or race but absurdities such as the way one's eyes are set, the way one walks, what he eats, reads, wears or believes in his daily routine. Man sees those who are different not only as being *apart* from him, but also—inferior."

"I'm convinced, Martin," Laura said simply.

He stood and offered her a grateful glance. "It has all been painfully different since '21. Of course, it's hard to see at first, since we were not around before that time; but the apparatus of Tom Edison, a man who brought much good to the world—this *device*, on your desk—dispersed sadistic entities of absolute evil. Somehow, they began influencing mortals—living human beings—influencing them directly, fiendishly." He hesitated, pursed his dry lips. "I believe I understand how this came about, but that's a story for a later time. The fact is, my friends, we were brought to the first confrontation with eventual apocalyptic doom in 1945 because 1129's spirits—plus, I suggest, a guiding force behind them—were released from their natural confinement within the old house. They were liberated to spread and to do their frightening things on a worldwide scope."

"In 1945?" Laura repeated, puzzled, and gazed up at the parapsychologist. She touched his sleeve. "You're saying that certain doom began to assume shape for man in 1945? What happened? Please explain."

"You are so young," Ruben said, as if he were an old man instead of someone in his mid-forties. He took her hands in his in a paternal way and looked down into her beautiful face. "Why, the release of nuclear energy—the discovery of the atomic bomb!" He smiled wanly. "And the plain, unassailably evil fact that *we used it* that year. Nothing will ever be the same again."

7

Laura lived with her mother in a thirty-year-old white frame house in Lawrence, a microscopic town northeast of Indianapolis. Ben, driving her home after the conclusion of the long meeting with Martin Ruben, found himself passing a miniature post office with the world's only cute police station across the street. He hadn't been to Lawrence for years, not until his periodic dating of Laura Hawks, and had forgotten that such a clean, friendly, well-organized town existed so close to metropolitan Indianapolis.

He had agreed to suspend further experimentation with the Edison apparatus for the time being, not because he was convinced that the machine might play into the hands of evil forces—he tried very hard to believe that no such things existed—but because he didn't wish to alienate Martin Ruben. While he'd told nothing of it to Laura or even his secretary, Carola, Ben had found Martin a source of comfort not long before—and, besides, he enjoyed the company of the eccentric Ruben. Anyway—he looked warmly at Laura, who was tired and glad to be riding home—she was convinced of the risk, and her feelings were growing important to him in a way that was new and surprising.

As they pulled up in front of Laura's house, there was an interruption of the music on the car radio, and they learned, with shock, of the crash in Indianapolis of a 747 jumbo jet. No immediate cause for the crash had been discovered. Laura shuddered and turned the radio off.

Her mother was spending the night with Aunt Flossie in Noblesville, and Laura paused only briefly before asking Ben in. "I'm not the world's finest chef," she began shyly, "but I doubt that I'll poison you. And I'd like to discuss this weird business a little more."

"You're undoubtedly an unforgettable cook," he replied gallantly, taking her keys and bending to unlock the front door. "Besides, I'm famished."

An enormous furry white animal with splotches of black bounded jovially toward them. Ben took an instinctive step backward, raising a protective hand. "Nigel!" Laura cried. She needed to stoop only a little to be greeted by the huge creature, whose hair was so long that he couldn't see well and careened into her legs. Then he lapped a happy tongue across her cheek and paused to regard Ben with an affably curious expression. The publisher saw that Nigel would unquestionably be wagging his tail, if he had one.

"What," he asked with a laugh, "is *that*?"

"Nigel is *not* a 'that,' I'll have you know. he's a *he* and canine of species. Nigel's our English sheepdog puppy." He licked her leg appreciatively.

"*That* is a puppy?" Ben reached down two inches to scratch the immense head, realizing that Nigel's friendliness matched his size. The great black nose nuzzled his hand. "This animal must be three years old!"

"Nope, he's only five months." Laura always enjoyed the reaction of strangers to her beloved pet. "Just push him aside and make yourself at home."

Ben, deciding to take Laura at her word, slumped into an easy chair that lived up to its name. She was too honest a person not to mean it. He kicked off his shoes and leaned back with a grateful sigh, watching the lovely writer bustle out to the kitchen with lovable Nigel bounding at her heels.

Ben felt cozy, instantly relaxed here and in Laura's company. What did all the talk of supernatural creatures and discarnate ghosts mean, when it was possible to come back to a real home like this? If it weren't for Mom, Ben mused, I'd abandon the entire project.

He scanned what he could see of the downstairs. It seemed decorated with the touch of an affectionate older woman, and Ben concluded that Mrs. Hawks ruled these quarters. Quaint Hummel figurines perched everywhere, on hutches and end tables. The furniture itself was a patchwork assortment, very old but covered with neat, homemade throws. Oddly, Ben did feel at home here, and still more of his customary shyness began to dissipate.

Laura fixed them each two positively obese curried pork chops with stuffing and a quickly whipped up salad. They dined on a sturdy oak table covered with a linen tablecloth that Ben was sure Mrs. Hawks saved for company. He sipped the first glass of milk he had tasted in years and enjoyed it. For Ben, used to the get-it-over-with life of the bachelor, eating out almost every night with his nose buried in a book in order to keep strangers at bay, the meal was a hugely pleasing and warming experience—marred only by Laura rebuking him when he tried surreptitiously to drop bites of pork chop to the gallumphing Nigel.

"He'll get fat," she wailed.

"I think your friend Nigel was born fat," Ben replied with a grin. "Besides, I'm pretty sure he likes me."

"Nigel likes everybody," Laura retorted, but she was pleased that Ben approved of the pup. "It's one of the charms of an English sheepdog." She paused when their eyes met and found herself groping for words. "Ben, how—how old are you?"

He peered up at her from half-lowered lids. His expression was one of concern. "Does it matter so much?"

Laura thought. "No, not really. I guess I had no business asking you that."

He frowned. "America has become so conscious of statistics that the stats are starting to form our key judgements for us." He spoke mildly, but she could tell that he was annoyed. "I've often thought that people who are overweight or especially thin tend to have it rougher than the rest of us. Being fat, at this juncture in U.S. history, appears to be a crime on the order of—of pandering." He sighed, then looked her full in the face. "I'll be forty-two later this year."

"*You?* In your forties? You must be kidding!"

"Nobody," Ben assured her earnestly, sipping his milk, "nobody admits to being forty unless he must. It isn't quite as criminal as turning thirty or sixty-five, but it's by-God bad enough!" Relaxing and grinning, he leaned forward suddenly across the dining room table. "So how old are *you*, Laura?"

She flushed. "I don't think—"

"One discourtesy demands another," he told her teasingly. "C'mon, lovely lady. How old?"

Laura made a face. "As you said, Ben, it's positively criminal. I'm almost thirty."

He jabbed a finger at her, and his beard jutted forward with his amusement. "Now, that is an obvious felony, if ever I heard one. Have you picked out your burial plot, old woman?"

"I wish you hadn't brought it up," she said with a comical sigh.

"But you did. At thirty, y'know, mature people think you still aren't old enough to go downtown alone, and teen-agers are certain you're over the hill." He placed his napkin on the table after patting away his milky moustache. "Honestly, I don't think age or background, color or race, or even size, tells us anything very useful about a person. But I am sorry if you believe I've been flying under false colors."

She reached across the table to take his hand. "Oh, you can't help it if you look like you're about thirty-four."

"God, I'm aging!" Ben moaned. "On our last date—you remember, you were pumping me for information?—you said I looked thirty!"

"Ben." Laura sobered swiftly when the thought occurred to her, and she tucked her folded hands beneath her chin to look seriously at him. "Please tell me, why is it so darned important to you to fool around with that dangerous toy of yours?"

He grimaced when she broached the topic. He stalled his reply by scratching behind Nigel's big, floppy ears. "Well, I wanted to do the book several years ago. In '81."

"Why then?"

"That was the fiftieth anniversary of the death of Tomas Alva Edison. I am a publisher, after all; that was a nice tie-in. But I didn't have his invention for contacting dead folks then."

Laura nodded but dropped her gaze, thinking. For awhile, she simply plucked at the napkin in her lap while Ben quietly poured fresh glasses of wine. At last Laura looked up, boldly, determined to overcome her natural reticence and ask what was on her mind. "There's much more to it than that, though. Isn't there? Ben, I don't mean to pry but I think I have the right to know everything since I'm writing so much of the book."

He didn't answer her for a moment. Lovable Nigel pawed lightly at his thigh; Ben didn't appear to notice. Outside, the formerly retreating storm was attempting to reassert itself and mumbling imprecations at itself and those who listened. "Laura, my mother's in an institution." Ben spoke levelly, carefully controlling his emotions. "We had to put her there—my brother and I." He swallowed hard. "She could no longer perceive the difference between reality and fantasies. Her fantasies."

Laura was sorry she'd asked. "I shouldn't have pushed. But what fantasies? What's the connection?"

Ben handed her her refilled glasses, sipped at his own. "As you've probably surmised, it's spook stuff—weird crap." A sigh. "For years, Mother considered herself a psychic of sorts, told my brother and me all manner of absurd but frightening things—like silverware leaping off the table during the night . . . with nobody there. Visits from the grave—with her dead Uncle Will. Eventually, when she aged, Mother started seeing ghosts"—he hesitated to find an image—"as if they were constantly close to us. Right in this room."

"How awful for growing boys." Laura shuddered. "Or for that matter, for caring, grown sons."

"The point is, it was awful for her, too," Ben continued almost angrily. "She'd talk to nobody anyone else saw and swear she was in deep conversation with deceased aunts or cousins, even celebrities. Historical figures. She bawled out FDR once, another time JFK. Because he wouldn't tell her how he died."

Despite herself, Laura's smile was visible.

"Be my guest," Ben shrugged. "She got to the point of believing she needed nothing to eat because she'd learned how to exist on the astral plane."

Laura was puzzled. "I forget what that is."

"Some call it 'OOBE' or 'out-of-body experience.'" When he paused, his embarrassment was obvious. "There are people who claim you can leave your body itself and travel almost everywhere on this astral plane. They call it astral travel, as well.

Their souls, I suppose, go off, attached securely to the physical body by a golden cord of ectoplasm or some such crap to get them back safely. And sometimes they go into the future and predict it. They can see what others are doing, across the world, and report on that. It's even said that the Soviets are so deep into this weird stuff that they have oobees leaving their bodies to snoop around for our secrets over here."

Laura interrupted as a light dawned. "Is that how you became a friend of Martin Ruben?"

"Exactly." Ben nodded. "I looked him up to see, for Mother's sake, if there was anything whatsoever to what she was seeing. There was a chance that it was legitimate, I guess; maybe I wanted to give her the benefit of the doubt. My brother and I thought that, just maybe, she might truly be psychically gifted. But Martin"—Ben scowled darkly—"Martin said that Mother might well be able to travel astrally but that, in terms of what she was reporting to us, she was merely seeing things, nothing more." He shrugged unhappily. "Simply—off her nut."

"Poor Ben," Laura said simply.

"Poor Mother. There's more, Laura. Martin did a battery of tests at her house just to be certain there wasn't an actual haunting occurring there. He says he has ways to tell. If there had been, he would have asked a lady psychic he respects to come and exorcise Mother's house. But the upshot of it is that there seemed to be no haunting at all." He turned his fork end for end, the way he was always doing with a pencil, and glared at the tines. "Except, of course, in the old gal's pathetic mind."

Laura rose to clear the table, pausing to stoop and kiss Ben's cheek in sympathy. Toting several dishes toward the kitchen, she called over her shoulder, "Just exactly what does all this have to do with Edison's device? I'm afraid I don't see the connection."

He rose, too, stretching and feeling better for having told her part of it. "Well, I set out to find that damned machine and literally prove that spirits do not exist. To be honest, I don't believe in them, never did once I was old enough to suspect that Mother was unwell. I decided to seek publicity, droves and reams of it, and I wanted a book on the subject that would demonstrate how we'd tried to contact the so-called spirit world with a machine made by the world's greatest inventor and found there was absolutely nothing there to contact, that there is no 'other side.'" He scratched his head and ambled toward the kitchen, at one point obliged to step over the sleeping Nigel.

"That way, Laura," he continued from the kitchen entrance, "those poor souls who heard of my fair experiment wouldn't wind up deluded the way Mother was. My notion is that if we can prove conclusively that there is no such thing as spirits, then that road to Crazyville and its destructive delusions might be sealed off forever—for a great many folks, at least."

Laura looked around at him from the sink in which she had been rinsing the dirty dishes, and a tender expression was on her lovely face. "I understand, Ben. That would give your poor mother's life more meaning, wouldn't it? It would make it all worthwhile?"

He nodded mutely and blinked back the tears that sprang to his eyes. Laura quickly dried her hands and went to fold her arms around him. For an instant, Ben stiffened with nervousness, and she was amazed once more by the man's shyness—and the boldness that it lent her. Feeling gorgeously brazen, she tugged his bearded face down to her and kissed his lips, gently rubbing her fingertips against the roughness of the beard.

Ben responded slowly at first. Then Laura's arms went around his waist and pulled him tightly against her—and then it was as if a switch had been thrown somewhere inside of the man. "Oh, God!" he moaned, kissing her lips, then pressing them against her neck.

Before either of them knew what was going to happen, Ben's fingers were undoing the buttons of her blouse, and Laura was letting him. Freed, the blouse slid down her soft arms, away from her high, pliant breasts, encased in a filmy white bra. Laura herself reached behind her back to unfasten the garment, to let this gentle man get closer to her. He buried his face between her breasts, sending an electric thrill down her body.

"The bedroom," she whispered hotly against his ear. "In there!"

Half locked in each other's arms, they stumbled into the room. Laura fell back on the mattress as Ben collapsed beside her. His starved lips moved swiftly from her forehead to the tip of her nose and her lips, from her throat to the warm place between her breasts. Hands working, he removed her skirt and then her panties—and then, for just a memorable instant, he drew back to appraise her with eyes of sheer wonderment. "You're the loveliest thing I've ever seen," he gasped.

Laura whispered one bold thing to him before her own hands worked at his clothing: "Darling—please make it work for me this time. Make it real, make it feel like love!"

Poised above her, his body taut and ready, Ben paused to stare fondly into her eyes. "Between us, how could it be anything *but* love?" he asked softly.

Soon the world became a sweet, delicious chaos, a timeless turmoil of their bodies and the windmilling of responsive arms and legs. When their release came, at last, it was a culmination of many things for each of them—and, Laura thought gladly as Ben pulled away and lay gratefully panting at her side, perhaps a beginning as well.

As Ben and Laura lolled in that vivacious mood of camaraderie of people who have made love for the first time and cast off their last defenses, Nigel came ambling in from the hallway and sprawled on the rug beside the bed, where Laura's dangling hand could reach out affectionately to rumple his furry head.

"I've always wanted a dog something like that," Ben said wistfully.

"Why haven't you bought one, then?" she inquired. "Money hasn't been one of your major problems, has it?"

He shrugged his shoulders. "You may as well ask why I put off a lot of things. It seems I'm always waiting for another person to motivate me and take the responsibility for the action. The last one I thought fit the bill"—he paused, wondering if he should express it to her—"married someone else.

A rather long time and many lonely nights ago."

"I'm so glad she did," Laura answered, snuggling against his chest. She liked the little patch of hair at its center and wrapped a few strands around her index finger.

"That's the kind of motivation I like," he said joyfully, pulling her even closer, beginning again to caress the soft smoothness of her body.

Then, unexpectedly, Laura said, "Ben, I never gave much thought to the possibility of an afterlife before I began working on this project. I suppose I never really believed in ghosts or even the concept of paradise."

He sighed, regretfully wishing she hadn't raised the subject just now. "You're probably typical of most people, who are generally unexposed to such considerations. I grew up constantly wondering about it—at times obsessed with fear of those on the other side, at times eager to meet them—because Mother virtually lived with deceased uncles and grandfathers after Dad died. But when I learned she was only imagining things—well, that was enough for me. It was clear that there's only this world of here and now. The only meaningful reality, in my opinion, is where I exist."

"In my research," Laura said slowly, "I read about a man named George Parsons Lathrop who quoted Tom Edison on the way human beings are actually *constructed*."

"Could we talk about it later?" Ben asked quietly, and resumed stroking her.

"No," she replied, playfully pinching him. "Lathrop said Edison believed it was possible to control all the atoms in one's body and tell a particular atom to go and be a part of a flower for a while. When it came back, he would know just what it was like to be something else."

"I don't think you can control all your bodily atoms," Ben said, squirming against her. "But wasn't Edison an atheist?"

She shook her ash-blond hair. "Not according to my research. He told Lathrop that the existence of God could 'almost be proved from chemistry.' I'm sure he invented his apparatus partly to prove God's existence."

"I wonder why *my* apparatus was invented," Ben whispered, thrusting a little and grinning.

"Don't be disgusting!" Laura exclaimed, grinning back and turning on her side so that he might make use of his other hand.

"If we're to believe that letter written by the woman who had the device," Ben said ruminatively, "he succeeded only in proving the existence of evil." Suddenly he threw the sheet down from them both and sank lower in the bed, much lower. "Take my word for it sweetheart. *This* is life and just about the best part of it. This is all there is."

For the next exciting thirty minutes—for Laura Hawks—that was all there had to be.

But when she finally lay cupped against Ben's comforting back, warm, relaxed, deliciously sleepy, her writer's imagination would not quite let go.

If what Martin Ruben insisted was true actually was, it would prove the inconsistent Ben wrong. Or maybe Martin was mad, a psychotic. But despite the parapsychologist's eccentric ways, Laura was impressed by him, very impressed.

Her eyes opened in the dark. *What if Ben is*

wrong, she asked herself, *and we prove to the world that ghosts do exist? That there is an afterlife—at least, one of sheer evil?* What if Martin Ruben was entirely correct and the spirits from Ridge Avenue in Pittsburgh were creatures of an earthshaking, diabolical nature? What if events proved them *real*? And what in the name of God would they do should Ben inadvertently liberate them?

Nigel moved restlessly beside the bed and she patted his head absently for a moment. At last she fell asleep, but she dreamed of monstrousities she had not seen since, as a small child, she'd believed in the creatures of dark nightmare.

8

Mid-May

Laura had half anticipated a great glassed-in, slime-slick pit where the sane might peer down in horror on the cavorting, foam-flecked, absentminded men and thank God for their own normality. She felt that she would be obliged to see sadistic guards and aides mistreating the poor souls, who would thrash about and vomit or wound themselves in their hysteria. Laura was, after all, a writer with a vivid imagination.

Instead, when she accompanied Ben on a visit to his mother, she found a respectable institution that reminded her of a nursing home for the elderly. It was not a place anyone would choose with joy for herself, but it was not, on the other hand, anything remotely resembling a snake pit. Inmates shared two-bed rooms without bars, and everything was scrubbed clean. The aides, rather than looking like youthful Hume Cronyns with dead-fish eyes, were jolly fat black ladies with every appearance of being dedicated to their enfeebled charges.

Ben's mother, Mrs. Kellogg, age seventy-eight, lay like the sheet on her bed. She was so thin that she barely ruffled the worn blankets and so pale she might already have been a spirit herself. Her face was notable only for the heavy eyebrows, which had remained thick and dark despite the whitening curtain of hair spread over the plumped pillow, and two lively eyes, fever-bright and, Laura thought, as mad as a hatter.

At first Mrs. Kellogg recognized the ill-at-ease Ben, and the two of them—mother and son—conversed in monosyllabic verbal shorthand, with many reassuring smiles and squeezed hands. But Ben's introduction of Laura Hawks to his mother was wasted. While she was yet herself, the old woman had eyes only for her son. As the minutes dragged and the antiseptic odor of the place began to get on Laura's nerves, the aged expression became anxious and fiercely determined, as if she were seeking a firm hold on the real world lest it slip through her corrugated and knotted fingers.

Laura, perched tensely in a chair while Ben sat near his mother on the edge of her bed, began to feel increasingly absorbed by the restless dark gaze of Mrs. Kellogg. The writer fidgeted and mused. While the brown eyes might not be able to identify her, they certainly appeared to be seeing something now—all at once—something not there. Laura blinked, troubled. She felt lightheaded, almost incapable of drawing away from those depthless eyes. *Whatever could she be thinking?* Laura wondered with a shiver. *What could she be seeing?*

For Edna Kellogg the hospital room was fading, beginning its terrible alteration. Neat, normal ninety-degree angles of sanity suddenly began to slope frighteningly; the floor seemed to rumple and ripple, suddenly turned to a lunatic soup. Ben—oh, Ben. He was gone now; the realization filled her with isolation; alienation. Even that woman he'd brought was gone, too. The room was losing shape, altering, beginning to be replaced, beginning to assume another shape.

The old woman moaned her psychic agony and waved her frail arms to and fro, groping for freedom from herself and having no idea that her son Ben quickly gripped them and strove to bring her back to the present.

Time was shifting, moving backward—her mind tried to register what was happening, sought to separate reality from fancy, fancy from memory—and she knew she had moved into another chamber of time. Odd, as the new room assumed the guise of reality, how a part of her mind knew that this was a different time. Odd, she mused, how she knew that the only time machine that had ever existed was this turbulent and liberated thing called a human mind—an inquisitive, rather birdlike creature that winged unknowing distances with a horrid inside-out liberty, quite without conscious volition or power of selectivity or . . .

Well, well, she thought, finally recognizing her location. She struggled to sit up and was surprised when she could without any difficulty at all. *Home.* Edna smiled tentatively. She was home. In a different time, one that did not exist anymore, but home all the same.

Her boys, bless them, were beside her bed. Could she remember the words after all these years? "What is it, fellas?" she asked.

They hesitated, pink little faces turning to each other, each wanting the other to speak. Willard, the larger one, finally elbowed the smaller one, hard. Little Ben came nearer the bed.

He cleared his throat, then spoke in his piping, lilting way. "We wanted to find out if you were feeling better, Mother, if you were OK."

The taller brother was emboldened by the little one's broaching of the subject. "*Are* you OK again, Mom?" he asked as he stepped forward.

She paused, not knowing her lines. Strange, it was her old bedroom at home, where she had spent most of her married life. The lace curtains fluttered against the window and, judging from the way the window was up several inches, it was spring.

"Was I ill?" she asked at last, careful not to frighten them. "Somehow I—I can't remember, boys."

Willard nodded, making do with that. Ben patted her arm. "Not sick exactly, but—you were upset all day yesterday. Because—because *they* came to see you."

Edna was puzzled. "Who was it who came to see me, Benjamin? Please tell me."

The expressions on their faces showed fear. Again they exchanged quick, worried glances. Again Ben answered. "Dead people," he said, spitting the words out to get rid of them. "Dead people in your family came to see you, you said. A-

And we w-were scared awful by it, 'specially when you went to b-bed in the middle of the d-day." He swallowed hard. "You s-said you had to m-make yourself available to them, so they could tell you about the f-future."

She remembered. God, after all these years, she remembered how it had been. Or at any rate, how it had seemed to her. How she had honestly, genuinely believed that an old uncle and aunt and cousin Phoebe had visited her from beyond the grave.

Now, after all this time, staring at the faces of boys she adored but who, she knew, were boys no longer, Edna Kellogg couldn't tell whether she had really seen them or just—made it up, because she had always wanted so badly to be important, to be *someone*, and nobody could prove she hadn't been visited by long-dead relatives.

Looking at her children, she saw their terror as well as their concern for her for the first time, and she began to cry. How could she possibly have been so blind? Why didn't she see what her prideful confrontations with spirits—real or imagined—were doing to her boys? How had it happened that she had put them second to those who had been gone from this earth for many years? Sobs racked her shoulders, and she put her face into her hands.

Then they were both on the edge of the bed, tentative but anxious to help, putting their little arms around her and urging her to be well, to be happy and normal again.

For the first time in her life she saw how she had terrified her children because of empty pride and realized, even as she appeared to be sitting in her old bedroom with years and years of beautiful time ahead of her, how she had marred their adult lives.

But at the pricise moment that she was drying her nose and getting ready to tell them the truth—that no one alive really knew what happened after a person died, and that it is natural to be curious but that she was wrong to let her curiosity dictate the way she led her life and worse than wrong, *terrible*, to put her doubts and fears on her children's shoulders—the room began to sway, the edges rounding, the floor buckling; and she knew that she was not going to be given a chance to change things after all—that this was just another cruel reminder, another fantasy, that showed her, too late, how she *should* have lived.

"Don't take me back to the hospital room!" she cried out, or thought she did. "Please—*please*, God—don't let it stay this way. *Don't* let it lead me back to that terrible, lonely room again. Don't let it—*don't let it!*"

But none of the words left her throat in any form that made sense. She had prayed to the wrong source for release, for He had not placed her there.

"Don't let it." These words were spoken in reality, not especially passionate, not with the impact Edna wanted them to have. Her despairing eyes fell upon the grown, privately haunted Ben Kellogg. Her manic and misunderstood eyes tried hard to communicate with him, to read the psalms of shamed sinfulness, to say simply, "I'm sorry."

But he could not hear her. "I think we'd better go," Ben whispered to Laura, stooping to kiss his mother's gaunt cheek. "Mother needs a sedative."

Please forgive me, my son, cried the glittering

brown eyes, the heavy brows arching as the son prepared to leave. *Please be happy. Drop this awful crusade of yours. Marry the girl; live a normal life. Just live! Don't let me carry this burden of guilt to my grave!*

But Ben was smiling serenely and unsympathetically to her from the doorway. He was waving. The young blond woman, so pretty, so nice and normal, was nodding at her in sympathy and in friendship. Edna wanted to nod back, to wave and to smile, but she knew that her appearance was frightening, her eyes bulging, her lips trying to work, to speak. She knew that she looked, in a word, mad. But she was helpless in the terror she had created.

A round black nurse was entering the room, bearing both an amiably reassuring grin and a shining syringe, loaded, looming large in a hamlike hand. God, *where* was she going *this* time! What antechamber of hell were they sending her to now!

Friday, one week later, Laura had been at work through the lunch hour when Ben arrived. Often he preferred to work at home, but usually he made it into the office by eleven. She had been expecting him for nearly two hours and had grown somewhat concerned about him. But she had not expected him to be in this state. His face was terrible to see. With the growing familiarity of a lover, Laura knew at once how upset Ben was.

Instead of coming to her desk to pat her hand discreetly, as he usually did, he stopped just inside the doorway. With pained eyes, he looked at her and at Carola and said, "My mother is dead."

Laura heard the undercurrent of bitterness in his voice. "Oh, Ben!" she cried emotionally, rushing toward him to kiss his cheek.

"I'm so very sorry, Ben," Carola murmured, her eyes filling with sympathetic tears.

"She seemed all right when we left her," Laura said softly. "Did—did something go wrong?"

He crammed his hands deep in his pockets and seemed, for a moment, to see beyond the women and his office to the sanitarium, where a vital part of his life had ended. "Mom got up during the night. There was an open door. Somebody made a mistake, just once. They saw her, at a distance, going out the front door—leaving. They yelled to her to stop and began moving toward her. And Mom called something to them—in a normal tone of voice."

"Do they know what she said?" asked Laura, her blue eyes round.

Ben's gaze moved down to meet hers, and she didn't like what she saw in his eyes. "She said, *'Turn on the machine.'* She said it two or three times, Laura, very clearly: *'Turn on the machine.'* "

"Ben," she began quickly, "your mother couldn't have known about your ——"

"And then," he went right on, ignoring her or not hearing her, "before they could reach her, my m-mother simply walked r-right out—in front of a speeding car." He closed his eyes briefly, squeezing them shut. "Killed her instantly, of course." Then he turned on his heel and headed toward his office.

Laura froze, unable to imagine what she should do. To her surprise, Carola grabbed her wrists. Tears stained the smooth dark cheeks. "Laura, help Ben—please!" The young woman's grip was like steel. "He's—he's the only decent white man I've ever known. Help him."

Laura gave her a kiss on the cheek and rushed to follow after Ben, panic welling in her bosom. Martin Ruben's warning rang in her ears like the voice of doom. Inside the office door, she saw Ben heading directly for his safe. *Don't!* she managed.

But his long fingers were already twirling the dial. Then the door was swinging open and he was reaching inside without hesitation, the image of oblivious determination.

"Please, honey," she said hoarsely, reaching out to touch his shoulder. "Please don't turn that thing on!"

His gaze flickered over hers, then settled on the machine. He clicked on a switch, the dial glowed, and, without further pause, he threw the lever up.

Laura inhaled in fright, but nothing seemed to happen. She stared at Ben, their eyes locked, their bodies frozen in immobility.

Faintly, then, came the whirring sound of before. Aimed at nothing, the thing creaked with the weight of age, as if gears moved or motors turned at some level submerged beyond man's vision. Then the sound leveled out and, without further warning, began to hum. It was a steady not unpleasant sound.

Laura backed away from it, her hip striking a chair; she looked wildly around Ben's office. She half expected it to be peopled with creatures from hell's backyard—grotesque trolls huddling with secret chuckles beneath his desk, ghastly ghouls yanked from their coffin tables to gnaw their nauseating way through the very walls and doors.

But, again, nothing seemed to happen.

Carola appeared in the doorway. Sweetly curved and looking like an ebon statue of Venus, she was the living opposite of anything spiritual. "You had a call, Ben," she said as lightly as she could, hoping by her tone of normality to make his burdens easier to handle. "It was the funeral director, about your mother. He'd like you to stop by this afternoon."

As Ben turned and nodded briskly, he struck the Edison apparatus with his wrist. It swiveled, centering quietly on the pretty secretary, and continued to hum, unnoticed by Ben. "I think we'll close up for the weekend, Carola," he said. "You can go on home."

"Is there anything else I can do?" she asked, bathed in the unwavering light of the device. "Just name it, boss."

"You're very sweet," he replied, "but there's not a thing just now." He patted her hand and waited until she left the room.

Then he whirled to face Laura and gave her a triumphant, embittered smile. It was terrible in its intensity, yet touching in its pained sense of triumph. "You see, darling?" he demanded, picking up the apparatus and aimlessly allowing its odd light to beam toward the office window, and the city of Indianapolis that lay beyond it. "No ghosts have showed up, not a damned one," he growled. "Absolutely nothing happened, nothing at all." Ben swallowed hard. "My mother lived her whole life believing in spooks and died for nothing but a lot of unadulterated bullshit!" He slammed the machine down on his desk, hard; it sputtered protestingly before it again settled to an enigmatic whir. Ben's gesture at Laura was almost fierce. "I want all this to be recorded for the book, Laura. Every damned word of it!"

She didn't know what made her say it, and later she would wonder if something had indeed caused her to speak. "Perhaps it just takes time. Perhaps the machine is—rusty." Then, realizing what she had said and becoming flustered, she went to put her arms around his neck. "Forget I said that, Ben. My darned writer's imagination got in the way of common sense."

"It's OK," he replied, thinking. "And you're absolutely correct, as usual. To prove that nothing weird is going on and that this silly apparatus is a fake, I have to give it the acid test." He stared thoughtfully out the window, following the line of the machine's beam.

"You aren't going to Pittsburgh!" Laura protested, sorry she'd said anything.

Ben didn't answer, and for a moment Laura was frozen, awaiting his reply. "No," he said, finally, "there won't be any time before Mother's funeral. But that's OK. I should think that my sitting for hours with the damned thing turned on, maybe all night long, would be adequate for the skeptics, the neurotic hardheads who insist on believing in such idiocy. Absolute proximity to the device for a full night!" He nodded his head to accent his determination, his bearded jaw set in grim lines as he turned back to Laura. "Once and for all, I'm going to achieve what sensible scientists have sought for years: to put the notion of ghosts and goblins and things that go bump in the night directly into the grave of ancient superstition where all that crap belongs."

When Carola entered again, crossing between the apparatus and the window, they jumped. "Would you like me to go to the funeral home with you, Ben?" she asked him.

Laura responded first: "It would help you to have company, wouldn't it?"

Ben gave each woman a sad, weary smile. "Thank you, both of you, but no. It's—it's something I should handle alone. That and telephoning my brother, Willard." He took their hands. "I appreciate your offering."

"Well," Carola said with forced cheer, "then, it's me for a nice, long weekend of relaxation alone in my apartment."

None of them, including the secretary, heard the shift of sound from the ancient apparatus as it beamed its baleful yellowish light upon Carola.

Three
BEYOND THE REACHES OF OUR SOULS

What may this mean,
That thou, dead corpse, again in complete steel
Revisit'st thus the glimpses of the moon,
Making night hideous, and we fools of nature
So horridly to shake our disposition
With thoughts beyond the reaches of our souls?

Shakespeare, *Hamlet*

There is no doubt that we have established communication with another world.

DR. KONSTANTIN RAUDIVE,
concerning his geniometer with which to receive
the voices of the dead (*circa* 1968)

9

Friday, 8:00 P.M.

It was the kind of day that gathers weight and becomes measureable not in minutes but dollops of distress and sapped strength. Usually Ben liked Fridays, with their school's-out, open-ended promise of a pleasurable forty-eight hours. In recent weeks especially he had come to look forward to weekends because they meant more time with Laura Hawks, the woman with whom, he had realized happily, he was falling in love.

But this Friday evening, when he returned exhausted to his empty office, it was different. Choosing a casket for his mother had been a difficult task, one which he prayed he'd never have to perform again. It had been hellish, he thought, like something out of a tasteless "Saturday Night Live" satire, to wander through two brightly lit rooms of empty coffins—conveyances of the not-yet-dead yawning in readiness to expose their sad, silken contents. And it made matters worse for Ben to realize, standing beside the one he'd selected, that somewhere, perhaps, just such a casket awaited *him*.

Back in his deserted office, Ben made his duty calls, including the one he dreaded most, the one to Willard, his brother. That businesslike soul had anticipated their mother's passing for some time and reacted to the telephoned announcement without a single note of surprise or grief. The mild-mannered Ben found his temper rising yet again in the same day; he was barely able to tell Willard, tightly, that the funeral was set for Monday morning. He listened cheerlessly to Willard's avowed intention to "do the right thing and fly in."

With a sigh, Ben replaced the phone in the polished box on his desk and mused about how unlike brothers could be. Ben was grateful that Willard lived across the country in San Diego, and hoped fervently that the man would find his way back to California quickly.

Before he could decide on his next move and while he was simply looking at the ancient apparatus that continued humming from a corner of his desk, marveling at how well it functioned after all these years, the phone rang. He snatched it up and grunted, "Hello," none too civilly.

"Kellogg, this is Ruben. Is that damned thing running right now?"

Ben didn't need further identification of what the parapsychologist was referring to. "Yes, it is. Harmlessly."

"You can't be sure of that. Laura told me about

your mother, and I'm truly sorry—my condolences—but it is *urgent* that you switch off that machine: *now*."

Ben frowned. It wasn't like Martin Ruben to be demanding. "I'm afraid I can't possibly do that, Martin."

"There is no easy way to know what harm you're doing," Ruben insisted. He sounded, through the phone wires, terribly agitated, scarcely in control of himself. "I beg you to shut it down *at once*."

"Martin, I'm awfully tired, and this is going to be a long enough night. I'll talk with you tomorrow." He replaced the phone in its cradle without further comment.

Suddenly it was unusually lonely, abnormally still, in the office. Time for the lonely vigil, he thought, looking out the window at the bleak night. Rain chattered on the pane and, despite the absence of thunder, Ben thought it was a proper setting for such a night. He pulled his address book out of a desk drawer and thumbed through it until he came to the letter *P.*

Now was the time for the one element of which he'd told Laura and Ruben nothing at all. He hadn't wanted to bother them with what could certainly prove to be a wild goose chase, given the age of the man he planned to phone. Quite possibly the old boy's memory was shot, contained no recollection at all of a winter night in 1920 in Pittsburgh, when he played host to the world's greatest inventor. Quite possibly, too, even though they had corresponded in general terms, the information provided Ben wouldn't amount to a damn.

But, then again, it might. Ben smiled with interest and curiosity. It would certainly be fascinating just to speak with Frederick Parlock, the aged, retired General Electric executive who'd escorted Tom Edison on his visit to 1129 Ridge Avenue. And—if Ben was lucky—maybe old Mr. Parlock would be able to fill in the missing pieces concerning Dr. Adolph C. Brunrichter.

Privately, Ben had become mildly obsessed wondering about Brunrichter and the lack of information concerning him. The name came up every time Ben dug beneath the surface of the mansion's weird tale. Clearly, Brunrichter once had been a tenant of the house. One source said as much. But who, exactly, *was* Adolph Brunrichter? What had he done? All Ben knew for sure was that he wouldn't let Laura finish the book until he knew much more about the mysterious doctor's occupancy of 1129—and old Freddie Parlock might possibly provide the answers.

Ben dialed the old gentleman's number and leaned back in his chair. This was the appointed time—8:05—selected by Mr. Parlock based on his dinner and an hour-long nap. His letter had been very clear on that point, the handwriting rather old-fashioned in style, in that thoughtful, considerate penmanship for which his generation was known. *Let's see,* Ben mused, *if Parlock was in his middle twenties at the beginning of the Roaring Twenties, when he and the legendary Edison visited 1129— why, he'd have to be approaching ninety years of age.* For an instant, getting no answer to his ring, Ben considered hanging up. The poor old chap probably had trouble remembering what he ate for dinner!

Then there was a sudden clap of thunder that rattled his desk simultaneous with a shout in his ear. Ben jumped involuntarily, banging his shin on the desk. "Hello!" the voice yelled. "Parlock here!"

"Mr. Parlock, this is Benjamin Kellogg, the publisher, calling from Indianapolis." There was no immediate reply, and Ben hesitated. "Did you get my last letter?"

"Is it going to be your last letter?" asked the old man. "Too bad. I rather enjoyed them."

Another pause. Was Mr. Parlock being witty? "How are you tonight, sir?"

"Not a great deal different than I was this morning." In the tremorous voice there was a touch of boldness, of authority, that surprised Ben. "I'm sorry if my humor is a trifle caustic, but a man I knew once told me to quit apologizing for everything. I've striven to accept his counsel."

"And who was that man, if you don't mind my asking?"

"Thomas Alva Edison." Frederick Parlock chuckled and added, "I'm not likely to mind a great deal of what you say or do, young man."

"Then you *do* remember your frightening experience with Mr. Edison?"

This time Parlock was still. He cleared his throat tentatively. "I'm going to be ninety-one in November, Mr. Kellogg. I'm not sure how many days that represents, but I've remembered the house on Ridge Avenue every single one of 'em. I suppose, in a way, those recollections are starting to bring me a spot of comfort in recent years. They established for me, you see—once and for all—the ongoing continuity of life, the factual existence of afterlife."

"That's wonderful, Mr. Parlock."

"I guess that depends on whether I'm cut out to haunt this big old house of mine or if I'll be permitted to seek more paradisiacal facilities." A dry chuckle. "But according to your letters, Mr. Kellogg, you are especially interested in knowing more about a perfectly terrible man named Dr. Adolph C. Brunrichter."

Ben's heart skipped a beat. "That's correct." He brought to his lips a small, rubbery suction cup, moistened it and applied it to the receiver. "If you don't mind, Mr. Parlock, I'd like to tape-record this information for use in the book we're doing."

"Everybody's sure careful to tell people about recording things nowadays, young man," Parlock said with a thin laugh. "No, I don't mind. The information I have for you comes in two varieties. One is what I was able to assemble for Mr. Edison from a number of reports reaching back to August of 1901, when I was just a small child. Ghastly information, but it seems valid enough. The other data is what I can vouch for one hundred percent, because in 1927 I collected the information from the current newspapers and made it my business to talk with the investigating officer."

"Investigating officer? Then Brunrichter was eventually put away for his crimes, whatever they were?"

"Not for long, Mr. Kellogg. His type can't be held by mere bars. For all I know, the evil bastard is still living somewhere, ruining the lives of young girls."

"But he'd have to be over one hundred years old," Ben protested.

"True enough, but I'm not sure what I'd put past that awful man."

Ben leaned back, fascinated, and lit a cigarette. Looking out the window, he was unaware of the rain as he tried to fix his gaze on a point eighty years in the past. "Why don't you begin at the beginning, Mr. Parlock?" he suggested gently.

"Well, it was the year President McKinley was shot by an assassin—the fourth president in a row to die at twenty-year intervals without a completed term," Parlock's old voice marveled. "That inexplicable chain kept right on going through most of this century, you know." He didn't give the startled Ben a chance to comment. "Also, in 1901, we built the Panama Canal, and Queen Victoria died. Hitler was twelve that year, and I happened to read his daddy didn't remember to buy the boy a present.

"But I digress. This is about a somewhat different Adolph. . . ."

Maisie Simpson was a stunning nineteen-year-old redhead in 1901, and pretty sure she was pregnant. But lasses in that condition don't care for uncertainty, and Maisie wanted to find out for sure.

Even in Pittsburgh at the turn of the century there was a grapevine that distilled and disseminated information for young single girls who'd committed a costly indescretion. Dr. Adolph Brunrichter would make things go right, Maisie was assured.

She paused at the front door of 1129 Ridge Avenue to consider what she'd heard about the man. He was, people said, a charming, compassionate gentleman of the world who scoffed at houses with ancient curses on them and bought the old house for a song. It had been empty for eight years—deserted—before the good doctor briskly took it over, certain that the age of science could deal with dead madwomen and even-longer-dead Indian braves. He was forty years old, on top of his world, and had the kind of charm that made ladies lose their heads.

When Maisie Simpson met him, she discovered they were right. Dr. Brunrichter had no nurse. Instead, he greeted her personally at the door, bowing to kiss her hand. Then he led her through the foyer and down a cheerful hallway to his study.

Brunrichter was a tall fellow, broad-shouldered in his frock coat, with unusually serious brown eyes. Many of his patients thought he resembled the dreamy Edgar Allan Poe. He sported an inch square of moustache, and his dark hair puffed from the temples in serene waves. Maisie thought he was adorable.

Not that she was an authority on men. For a girl who feared she was pregnant, Maisie had very limited experience. Her father had died in the coal mines when she was twelve, and her brother, Clyde, ten years Maisie's elder, dwelled in Philadelphia; so she rarely saw him. Willie O'Brien was the first boy Maisie had dated, and Willie, they say, reminded Maisie a great deal of Daddy. He also worked in the mines, and the witty tales he told came on the lilt of a pure Irish brogue. His ready humor, surface resemblance to her beloved father and work-forged biceps positively charmed Maisie into carelessness on a Sunday picnic. Neither before nor after had she ever dallied, and she promised God that, if He spared her embarrassment, she'd save herself for marriage and bear twenty little ones to atone for her sin.

In Brunrichter's office she waited for him to begin the conversation, but he was quiet, apparently lost in thought even though his somber brown eyes went on staring into hers. Maisie's gaze strayed nervously to the framed photograph on the doctor's desk, depicting a handsome woman with an aura of command.

"Is that the Missus?" she asked softly.

He laughed lightly. "That? My, no, child; I'm not married. That is, um, a dear friend—Madame Aenotta."

"She looks powerful wise, sir," Maisie remarked gravely.

"Observant child!" He smiled. "She taught me much of what I know."

"About the art of healing?"

He laughed again. "Not exactly. If you are a very, very good patient, I may permit you to know what the Madame has taught me."

The lass shivered and shifted in her chair. "I do believe there's a cold draft in here," she said shyly, lowering her green eyes to her neatly gloved hands. "Isn't that queer, in August?"

"It's difficult to keep this house warm," Brunrichter told her, blinking as he peered around his study, almost as if listening for someone or something. Then he shook away the mood, folded his hands and gazed paternally at the young woman. "I gather you have come to me because you believe you may be in the family way?"

She nodded slowly, reddening. Her confession was barely audible. "It's only been once, Doctor, and I—"

"Quite, quite. I believe you." He seemed so sympathetic and understanding that Maisie nearly cried. "Who recommended my services, child?"

"Sarah Browning," she admitted in a whisper. "Sarah said that you ... assisted her. With *her* problem."

"Ah, yes, little Sarah." He beamed upon Maisie. "Not the most brilliant young woman I've met, but I was glad to, um, 'assist' her."

"I don't suppose any of us who gets this way is too smart, sir," Maisie acknowledged.

"'*Are* too smart,' dear," Brunrichter corrected. "Well, accidents happen in all of life's activities, do they not?"

Maisie was mortified, miserable. "It isn't an accident when somebody knows what can happen and still goes ahead."

Brunrichter's brows were lifted in pleasure and surprise. "Fascinating," he said with delight. "Possibly I have underrated you, Maisie."

"How d'you mean, Doctor?"

"I mean," he said steadily, "that intelligence is what separates man from the simple beast." His brown eyes came alive with animation. "Intelligence is everything, child—everything of any consequence."

"And what of kindness, sir?" the girl asked. "And the God-given soul? Don't they also separate us from the beasts of the fields?"

He literally applauded her in brisk little pattings of his slender hands. "Bravo! Spirit is a close sister to intelligence, and I begin to think you possess both attributes of that precious family!" Suddenly he stopped talking and began rustling through papers on his desk. Finding the one he sought, he placed it atop the others and deftly picked up a pen. "Did you graduate from school, my child?"

Maisie nodded. "I did. With good marks, sir."

"Excellent." He gave her a quick grin of pleasure and made a checkmark, then dipped the pen again in the inkwell. "And do you read much, my girl?"

"Seems like I've spent m'life reading, Doctor," Maisie replied. She had no idea where any of this was leading but felt it was pleasant to be shown such attention by a learned man. "My brother is much older; so I've spent a good deal of time alone."

"And do you read dime novels, Maisie, or genuine literature?"

For the first time during her visit, she laughed, and her green eyes crinkled with charm. "Mother wouldn't allow her daughter to waste herself on cheap books, sir. I read Dickens a good deal, Mr. Poe, and some of the poets, like Lord Byron."

Then the doctor was out of his chair, hurrying around his desk and placing his slim hands on her head. They were shockingly strong hands, and Maisie winced as the fingers dug into her scalp. But he was brisk and brief, stepping back to peer at her with something like admiration.

"I do believe you'll do!" he told her, hands on hips, giving her an open smile. "Madame Aenotta promised this would be a felicitous period for me.

An important query, child: What is your birthdate?"

"April sixth, Doctor." Maisie was confused. "But why—"

"*Aries!*" he exclaimed. "An alert, bright and aspiring sign!" Brunrichter rubbed his hands together with enthusiasm. "This could well be *it!*"

Before she could ask what, he was assisting her to her feet. A twinge of apprehension moved in her mind. "Are you going to be examinin' me now, Doctor?"

"Yes, indeed, I am," he replied warmly. Then he took her left hand and, beaming upon her, tugged the girl toward the door. They passed an examining table, and Maisie pointed to it with a flopping arm.

"What's wrong with that table, sir?" she asked.

"Wrong?" Brunrichter laughed and half dragged her from the room, down the corridor. "Why, everything is wrong with it, Maisie. It isn't right for someone with your capabilities. You deserve special treatment!"

He released her small hand as they stopped before a locked door. Maisie sensed a strange chill. There was something peculiar about this good-looking doctor, it occurred to her for the first time, and she wished she could go home.

But before she could voice her feelings, he had a large metal key in his manicured hand. First tilting his head as if listening for something, he unlocked the door and escorted her inside.

The room was icy cold, frigid. Dr. Brunrichter locked the door behind them and, bending with his back to her, appeared to be involved with more than one lock. Despite her rising concern, Maisie peered curiously about the room.

There was a second examining table in this cubicle, but it looked rather different to her from the first. For one thing, leather straps dangled here and there from the ends and sides of the table. The walls were painted crazily, with different colors; one of them, Maisie saw with surprise, featured a huge circular design. When she squinted at it, she felt as if she were falling directly into the maze, oddly disappearing into the curling center of the design. What was the *matter* with her?

Blinking, she tore her eyes away. There were no windows; the only exit from the room was the door they had entered—the door the doctor was locking so carefully.

I'm being silly again, Maisie thought, chilled both by anxiety and by the tiny room. Her glance drifted downward. Where the physician's study had been carpeted, this floor was sheathed with linoleum and newspapers, stained an ugly dark brown in a few places. Shuddering, Maisie lifted her gaze.

Against one wall, near the table, squatted a grotesque hulk of a machine she had never seen before. At a glance it looked homemade, with a round scooplike thing, peculiar nozzles and tubes protruding rather like lunatic tongues. And it held a range of gleaming, sharp knives—many sizes of them. There was something about the contraption that suggested it had been built and then altered continually, as if its maker weren't yet fully satisfied with it. Maisie hated the machine on sight. If it was possible for a machine to appear heartless, remote, cruel, this one did.

It also aroused her curiosity. But as she began to approach it, Dr. Brunrichter firmly took her elbow and led her to the examining table. There, he partly assisted, partly lifted her onto it. She glanced uneasily at his attentive face.

"Now, then," he said cheerfully, "kindly disrobe."

Maisie cast an anxious look around her. "I—I can't, sir. There's no screen for me to go behind." Her voice was strained to her own ears.

"Come, come, child." The physician laughed harshly. It sounded more like a bark. "Let us have no false modesty, shall we? Consider, if there was a screen, you would still end up upon my table naked—would you not?"

The thought, *Yes, but I'd have a gown on, at first,* occurred to her, but she nodded anyway. There was something very persuasive about this charming man with the boyish moustache—and something, too—now that she considered it—which she did not wish to anger. Flushed, Maisie began to undress. Dr. Brunrichter had turned his back, appearing impatient, and when she chirped a tiny "Ready, Doctor," he turned quickly back to her.

Maisie's red hair had come down around her shoulders in appealing wisps, and her bright green eyes did not know where to look. She tried to shield her nakedness with her arms, but that device was inadequate. Brunrichter adopted a clinical expression.

"You must lie down now, child," he told her, sounding husky. "I cannot conduct my examination with you sitting up."

Maisie lifted her legs to the table slowly, her hand remaining in a discreet position. When she stretched out, she found, with discomfort, what had seemed peculiar about the examining table. It was so constructed that when she reclined, her head was obliged to hang over the edge. The metallic border cut painfully into her poor neck.

"Do I have to st-stay this way long, sir?" she asked.

But he ignored her. "What I must do now will cause you just a moment or two of pain," Brunrichter informed her in a newly brisk tone, doing things she could not see from her awkward position. "I'm obliged to strap you down for your own good."

When Maisie sought to move her right foot, it was gripped by leather. So, she found, was her left foot. And before she could speak, the physician had both her hands strapped.

What she really detested was the way her legs had been rudely forced apart. She was spread-eagled on the metal table with nothing at all to cover her. She glanced down, across the slight rise of her bosom, but Brunrichter was now at the head of the table to place another strap across her neck.

"Doctor, I'm afraid," she blurted, a prisoner of the table now.

Again he ignored her. She could see from the corner of her eye how busy he'd become with his grotesque machine. A motor thrummed to life. His back was to her once more, and she did not see, until he turned at last, the peculiar instruments he'd tugged from the bowels of the machine. All were affixed by wires and tubing, from the round scoop to a many-buttoned length of metal and a shiny scalpel. Then he was again out of sight, humming cheerily to himself.

Maisie sensed an object above her head, but her gaze was upon Dr. Adolph C. Brunrichter, who had come to the foot of the table. A surge of agonized despair and disappointment almost overwhelmed her actual fear—because the doctor was naked. Beaming down at her bare, spraddle-legged body, he mounted the table and for a moment stood towering above her. Beyond him, over his bare shoulder, the design on the wall began drawing Maisie into its evil heart, sapping her will.

"I remarked that I'd tell you about Madame Aenotta, child, if you were good." His moustache twitched. "I'm certain you are going to be quite good, indeed. Madame has been my tutor in matters arcane, matters concerning a world you would consider evil. Together, Maisie, Madame Aenotta and I shall explore the secrets of eternal life. And you, my girl, may be the one to allow us to turn that final page to the ultimate discovery."

Sobbing, Maisie asked why in the world *this* was necessary.

He knelt to her. "Life begins with the thrust of masculinity, the flow of male semen, Miss Simpson." He was between her legs, perspiring. "Everything in existence begins at the moment a male joins with female. It is the history of civilization."

Now Maisie could see nothing but the magnetic design on the opposite wall, its mesmeric heart throbbing as hers joined it in kaleidoscopic rhythm. Her senses reeled; he was hurting her.

And at the instant Adolph Brunrichter reached his climax, the deadly object high above Maisie

Simpson's pretty head lowered with scientific precision. It was sharp; it cleaved true.

Panting, the doctor kissed her breast and withdrew. His homemade machine whined while he began his important work, instantly absorbed and involved, pushing buttons and making adjustments. The shrill voices in his mind plagued him, gnawed at his brain as they had for months now. "Hurry!" they cried with intensity. "*Faster!*"

Then he unlocked the door with some difficulty and hastened to his private laboratory, where he approached his second homemade machine with a feeling of pride, deference and fresh hope.

When it was activated, Brunrichter made the insertions, added the necessary chemical compound and waited. He rubbed a bloody finger nervously across his moustache.

"This is horrible," Ben Kellogg protested into the telephone. "In a way it's even worse than the other Ridge Avenue episodes."

"I quite agree," Frederick Parlock murmured, "but it gets worse."

"How can that be possible?" Ben paused, then risked rudeness. "Are you certain this is factual? That this actually happened?"

"Quite sure, Mr. Kellogg. It happened in real life. Let me tell you *how* we know about it...."

One of the people who heard the terrible screams that day in August was Peter Link, age fifty-one, an attorney. He was one of several neighbors on either side of 1129 Ridge Avenue who rushed out of their homes to see if they could help.

Afterward, Link said, "We looked at one another with fear and then, knowing about all the terrible things that have happened in the house, we more or less turned as one to stare at 1129. Now, you probably cannot believe this, but ask the others if you don't."

A reporter made notes furiously as the attorney continued. "Just as we took a tentative step toward the place, a scary bolt of red lightning shot through the downstairs. We saw it, all the neighbors—like there'd been a dreadful explosion. Frankly, I never saw anything like that bolt in my life. The entire interior of 1129 was illuminated by it, turned a kind of beet red that lasted for seconds. But what really got to us was the earthquake."

The reporter looked up with shrewd eyes and asked Mr. Link what earthquake he was referring to.

"At the same moment the red bolt raced through the house, the earth beneath our feet quivered and shook. Look at the place if you don't believe me."

The reporter noted, indeed, that every window in the ancient house had been splintered to nothingness. Later, he would learn that a slight quake had been measured on the Richter scale.

The fire engines began reloading their equipment, their powerful horses straining restlessly at their reins, anxious to leave the scene. The reporter observed the way their ears were laid back against their heads, as though they were frightened.

He observed, as well, the firemen being carried out of 1129 on stretchers and wondered what in the world had happened. After all, despite the precautions, there'd been no fire. He abandoned Peter Link and wandered closer to the scene, approaching the chief to learn what had happened.

He found out.

Three firemen had rushed into the house, concerned for a possible loss of life if the quake had caused a floor to fall or something to short out. One of the men, Sidney Williams by name, went to the cellar. There he stumbled upon nine graves containing the bodies of young women.

A second fireman, Marvin P. Chatsworth, discovered the body of Maisie Simpson. Still spread-eagled on the examining table and obviously raped, bite marks on her small breasts, Maisie had been decapitated.

Shaken, Chatsworth staggered out into the corridor in search of the third member of the fire rescue party. He found Charlie Crawford, a bulky veteran of more fires than any other man on the department, simply sitting on the floor of the second laboratory. Crawford was crying softly into his huge hands, and when Chatsworth shook his shoulder, Charlie merely looked up, wordlessly, and gestured.

Chatsworth stepped deeper into the darkened room until he observed a strange, clearly homemade hulk of a machine that continued to make sounds even though it was smoldering from several charred wires. The wires were connected to another machine, a contraption of glass with a series of neatly positioned pedestals set along a clean metallic table. There were two rows of pedestals, he saw, five to a row. And upon each of them, enclosed by a glass globe from which extruded snakelike tubing, was the blankly staring head of a young woman.

Chatsworth gaped. Ten globes, ten pedestals—ten severed, human heads. He was too stunned to tear his eyes away from the scene. There was no decomposition to speak of, he noted; all the heads appeared to be in extraordinarily good condition, considering the trauma they'd undergone. The one closest to him was that of a lovely young redhead.

Just before he managed at last to turn away, from the corner of his eye Marvin Chatsworth thought that he saw *a movement of lips!* It was as if the girl were trying to cry out, belatedly, for help.

He took a quick breath and knew that his heart was beating at an unnatural, unsafe rate. "Reflex," he said aloud, his voice echoing in the laboratory. Then he turned away, pleased because he had actually taken the monstrous scene in stride. By the Lord Harry, Marvin Chatsworth thought, *he* was a real man! He paused to glance pityingly down upon his less fortunate friend, Charlie Crawford, and opened his mouth to say something encouraging.

That was when Chatsworth's nerves collapsed and he slid to the floor unconscious, his limbs twitching spasmodically.

He was in the hospital for three days, suffering from shock. Reports had it that Chatsworth was never himself again.

At one time the residents of that neighborhood—especially the youngsters—made up little rhymes about the events at 1129 Ridge Avenue. At one time the children would dash up to the front door, touch it and be proclaimed heroes. But after that fateful August it was only a single, mad boy who would draw near and, rather than being called hero, he was considered quite unforgivably stupid. No one sang songs about the house anymore; no one told jokes. Because everyone knew that the house was one of genuine horror, of genuine haunting.

"But what of Brunrichter?" Ben Kellogg demanded. "Surely they arrested him and tried him."

"Oh, the police searched high and low for the good doctor," Parlock replied in Ben's ear. "Within an hour there was a warrant for his arrest, and an extensive manhunt was mounted that lasted weeks."

"So he got away scot-free?" Ben asked with amazement and dismay.

"For more than a quarter of a century, he did," said Frederick Parlock, and Ben could almost see the old man nod. "But that leads us to the second part of my story, the one that I can recount with absolute certainty as to detail, because I read the newspaper reports, spoke with reporters both in Pittsburgh and New York and also contacted police investigators."

"When was this, Mr. Parlock?"

"The year was 1927—when Babe Ruth and the New York Yankees may have had the greatest baseball team in history! The German economy collapsed that year and, in August—one month before my story begins—Sacco and Vanzetti were put to death. Unfortunately, someone far more terrible lived on."

It was just getting chilly after a summer that

was sweltering even by Manhattan standards, and the bums in the Bowery faced their annual problem. The shrewd ones were cadging and saving pennies and nickels, beginning to think about new autumnal and winter residences. Those who were not clever tended to be found dead of exposure or, if they were a trifle luckier, were eventually scooped up and taken to charity wards in various stages of illness ranging from malnutrition to tuberculosis. There they could die, at least, on clean sheets.

One old fellow hadn't found it easy in recent years. The last strands of dignity clung to him the way his tattered clothing hung from his wasted body. Still, when he raised his gaunt face to stare at the passersby, there remained a glint of intelligence in the red-rimmed eyes. Staying smart was important to that hobo. He still had things to do in this world.

This bum, of course, was the infamous Adolph Brunrichter. But he was, in some ways, a changed Dr. Brunrichter. There remained a few cities in the east where he hadn't posed as a licensed physician until, somehow, they were on the verge of discovering his real name and the fact that the state of Pennsylvania and his medical association had long since lifted his license to practice. Being a doctor was all Brunrichter knew how to do—that is, in terms of earning a living that was acceptable to his fellowman.

It's safe to say that a less proud, less evil individual—one without psychotic pretensions to greatness—might have sought alternate employment or simply starved to death. But that would have meant fearing death, and this old tramp rather looked forward to it. He figured his Master would reward him handsomely one day.

The police arrested him when he tumbled through a storefront window not far from Wall Street and set off the burglar alarm. Somehow he was in no way injured by the broken glass.

Indeed, when they brought him to the station to book him, the old hobo gathered strength and seemed younger. When the man behind the desk called him "pal," the reply was brusque and succinct: "I am not your 'pal,' sir." He fingered a little bundle of gray moustaches and breathed alcoholic fumes and hatred. "I have never been the 'pal' of anyone, living or dead. I'm a professional man."

When he gave his name, it meant nothing to the booking officer. He was more interested in Brunrichter's description of his "residence" as his head. "Where my ideas and plan survive," the doctor told the clerk, "*I* exist." But he confessed that he had lived in Pittsburgh "and elsewhere."

So the booking officer pressed on, a little uneasy both at the old man's attitude and the way he called himself a doctor. "Look, Doc," he said with a sigh, wondering why he always got the characters, "we're gonna run a check to see if there are any wants on you. Why not save us all the time?"

At that point Brunrichter drew himself erect and confessed that the city of Pittsburgh had once sought him mightily, then added: "I believe the charges involved suspicion of murder. Multiple murder."

The clerk's pencil tip broke. "When was that?"

he asked as lightly as he could. "How long ago?"

Brunrichter smiled with a measure of pride. "The year was 1901," he told the policeman. "A bit over a quarter of a century ago. The fools could *never* find me!"

The police put him in a holding cell and contacted Pittsburgh by phone. It took a little digging to learn that everything the old man said was true. But much of the evidence had been lost, most of the witnesses were either dispersed, beneath six feet of earth or, as in the case of one of the three firemen who had discovered Brunrichter's maimed victims, still held in institutions.

Conversations were rattled off frantically in Pittsburgh and New York, and between authorities of the two cities. There was the question of the time that had elapsed. When one considered the advanced age of the prisoner and his tatterdemalion appearance, there was some doubt linked to how eagerly a jury would put him away.

The district attorney's office in Pittsburgh kicked the ball around for over a month in their effort to decide what to ask New York to do with the old physician. On the one hand, they saw that a genuine monster had escaped them, but a "them" that belonged to their fathers' time on the force. Surely, though, Brunrichter would have been put to death after a speedy trial a quarter of a century ago.

On the other hand, a jury might very well feel that the old crackpot had been adequately punished by his postcrime period as an ill-fed tramp and near alcoholic—never mind how many innocent young ladies he might well have slain, not only at 1129 Ridge Avenue, but perhaps in other locations since then. Juries were peculiar things, being composed of people as they were, and a slick lawyer like that young Melvin Belli could probably get the doctor off on a plea of temporary insanity. At best, the district attorney's office calculated, the old boy would be confined in an institution at the taxpayers' expense and live better than he had for years.

While the police pondered, Brunrichter was having the time of his life. Reporters found him barely reticent about discussing his murders twenty-six years ago and listened with horror and fascination to how he lured the young women to his home and genuinely felt that he had almost succeeded in keeping their heads alive. "I had to be circumspect about it, you understand," he told one youthful reporter who was all agog. "After all, there were no volunteers for the job!"

To other members of the press Adolph Brunrichter spoke in lurid details that they could never print of incredible sexual orgies and of torture conducted "to see how long people could remain lucid despite excruciating pain." The Fourth Estate of New York City had never seen the old doctor's like before and prayed they would never see it again—unaware that they would see his work multiplied over the bloody face of Europe in a matter of years.

Who, the press wanted to know, was Madame Aenotta? Brunrichter said that she had urged all his experiments upon him. Pressed, he finally said in a whisper, "She came to me in my bedroom at night and whispered to me. No one else was ever privileged to see or hear her."

When Brunrichter informed reporters of ten

more young women whose graves were scattered all over the east coast, the news was a bombshell. Trouble was, when the graves were located and opened, there was nothing in them at all. The old madman howled with glee when he was told. "Madame's ghouls got 'em!" he shrieked with laughter.

Finally, the authorities in Pennsylvania and New York State concluded that there was nothing to be gained by returning Adolph Brunrichter to Pittsburgh for trial and quietly, in the dark of night, they simply released the evil physician from Blackwell's Island.

Old Mr. Parlock went on, "The Pittsburgh Spookman, the press called him. The Pennsylvania Pervert, the Keystone Killer and Return of the Monster. Bad enough. But let me tell you, Mr. Kellogg, the guards and Brunrichter's fellow prisoners at Blackwell's Island could have told the newspapers *other* stories, as well—tales of how the old man seemed to thrive on prison fare, how he filled out and began to appear twenty years younger. He was, one guard told me, an authoritative reprobate and he appeared positively dapper when he was released."

"When was that, Mr. Parlock?" Ben asked. His nerves sang. "When did they let Brunrichter go?"

The old man laughed. Then his amusement turned to a sigh of resignation. "Well, sir, I don't suppose you'll even believe this; but the honest truth of the matter is that Adolph C. Brunrichter was released during the night of October 31, 1927. Halloween."

"My God," Ben breathed.

"Yes, sir, he donned his state-donated suit with dignity, gave a curt farewell, and left the whole lot of prisoners and guards shuddering after him. He was never heard from again, I believe."

"I've never heard anything like this in my life," Ben admitted.

"There's just a bit more. Frankly, like I said, this old monster acquired a level of evil knowledge and evil lifestyle quite unique in my experience—and I've been around a long time. Whether he's dead or alive, Mr. Kellogg, I wouldn't be surprised if he were around, somewhere. You see, Dr. Brunrichter left a little message on his cell wall before he departed Blackwell's Island."

"A message?"

"It was in bright human blood, even though there had been no open wounds on his body when they checked him over, and I guess it scared the hell out of everyone who saw it scrawled on the wall."

"What did it say?" Ben asked.

"It read, 'What Satan hath wrought, let *men* beware.'"

10

Friday, 8:44 P.M.

It began when Martin Ruben remarked that Ben seemed completely obsessive about experimenting with the Edison apparatus. "I spoke with him, Laura, tried to talk him out of it just a couple of hours ago. But he's adamant."

Laura twisted the telephone cord and considered. Since Ben had not specifically asked her to keep his story in confidence, she decided to tell Ruben the reasons behind the publisher's determination. "He is absolutely convinced that it's his duty to add meaning to his mother's existence by proving that ghosts do not exist," she concluded.

There was just Ruben's breathing at the other end of the phone connection. "I see," he said at last.

"What does *that* mean?" Laura inquired. She liked and trusted Ruben, but his professional way of speaking and personal revelations, combined with his aristocratic and showy Sherlockian mannerisms, riled her at times.

"It means that I sincerely doubt Benjamin knows his own basic reason for going ahead with this. It means I believe there is a far deeper meaning, and I thank you for telling me what he said."

"I rather wish I hadn't now," she exclaimed. "Ben's no liar." She sat up on the edge of her bed and stopped absently patting Nigel's furry head. "If he said it, he believes it to be true."

"Oh, without a doubt." Ruben paused to light a cigarette. As he exhaled, he continued. "*Believes* he is telling the truth, certainly. I suggest, my dear Miss Hawks, that underneath it all Ben Kellogg is terrified at the prospect of spectral apparitions—indeed, of all that he does not understand. I further suggest that he is having you research and write this book in order to provide himself with the chance of *justifying* his mother's insistence that ghosts *do* exist."

"I don't have the foggiest notion how you can conceive of such a thing," Laura said loyally and defensively.

"It's an elementary deduction. First, the idea that he is trying to help his mother by proving her entire life a neurotic fantasy will not hold water. It's patently absurd. Moreover, children who are exposed to the kind of irrational upbringing that Ben experienced seldom entirely lose their fear of the unknown, of the deep shadows—and things lurking there. They tend, quite often, to oppose the paranormal, to avoid horror films and scoff at books related to the occult. In this way, you see, they keep such matters at a safe distance and outwardly maintain an aura of practicality, of feet on the solid earth. Inwardly, of course, they frequently seethe with superstition. Or possibly write novels of terror as a means of purging themselves."

"You make Ben sound almost cowardly," she said resentfully.

"Quite the contrary!" Ruben declared emphatically. "Ben seems to be displaying enviable courage. By injecting himself into such activities as these, he takes the bull by the horns and tries to deal with it." He paused. "Regrettably, he has selected a relatively rare example of genuine manifestations, and I remain deeply concerned. I won't even use my knowledge of astrology to determine where all this will end."

"I want to be candid with you," Laura said slowly. "I can't fully share your apprehension, Martin." Then a thought occurred to her. "Why did you call me tonight?"

"To make certain you were safe," he said simply.

"Why in the world wouldn't I be?" she asked, startled. "I'm at home, my mother is in the kitchen, the doors are locked, and I own a dog the size of a baby elephant."

Ruben laughed. "I'm happy you're skeptical, even though you happen to be quite wrong about the very genuine risks we all are confronting."

"That's rather evasive, 'my dear Ruben,' " she teased him. Laura paused. "You didn't really answer why I might not be safe."

Reluctantly, Ruben explained. "Laura, two women were pivotal—right from the start—in this trying case: Lyda Congelier, who apparently went hopelessly mad, and the Indian servant Essie, who Lyda decapitated. I haven't told you or Ben the details concerning Dr. Adolph Brunrichter because I didn't wish to accelerate Ben's inner terror, but it happens that Brunrichter murdered a minimum of ten young women in cold blood. Hideously."

"Oh, Lord," Laura whispered.

"There may be *other* examples of women in trouble because of the house at 1129 Ridge Avenue."

"Like my relative Julia Murray? Her life was nearly wrecked just by spending a few hours in that awful house." She shivered, hugged herself.

"Precisely," Ruben murmured. "All this explains why I'm concerned for your safety, especially when you say that you spent several minutes in the same room with the Edison device after it was turned on. That alarms me, to be frank."

"D'you really think the—the spirits from the machine might wage some kind of *attack* on me?" she asked. She failed miserably at asking it lightly.

"Probably not," Ruben lied, "but that does not alter the possibility. I want you to promise to phone me instantly if there's the slightest evidence of peril in your home. I'll phone the police and be there rapidly. Will you promise me?"

Laura laughed nervously. "You can depend on it, Martin. Thanks for your concern."

When they had hung up, Ruben arose from his wingback chair and crossed his apartment's front room to a small alcove in which the walls were lined with books. He had never lost his certainty that some central, guiding, evil force was behind the manifestations on Ridge Avenue, propelling them forward and effectively creating the so-called curse that visited every tenant of the house. For reasons he could not explain, even to himself, he felt that some source other than the biblical Satan lay at the heart of the puzzle.

For more than an hour he poured through old leather-bound books, stopping occasionally to read a paragraph, then plowing doggedly ahead to another volume.

Finally, after midnight—not knowing that the evil source he sought had again struck someone he knew—Ruben rubbed his eyes. Suddenly, he stared —stunned—into space.

"Of *course!*" he said aloud, to himself. "It would *have* to be he!"

In bed later, unable to sleep, Ruben tried to tell himself that being forewarned amounted to being forearmed. But how in the name of everything he held dear could he conceivably deal with ... *Demiurge! No one alive had ever done so.*

8:58 P.M.

Carola Glenn had changed her address three times in the past seven months, and now it seemed to her that she would be moving again.

The reason for such frequent uprootings was, Carola felt, quite easily summed up in a word: presumption. Wherever an educated, elegant young black woman dwelled in Indianapolis, it appeared that she was bound to encounter people who drew conclusions presumptuously. As a small child, before she'd even been aware of what it meant to be black, Carola had been sensitive to others. Their moods, their casual remarks, unfailingly left her wondering what they really meant.

By now, rather than merely wondering, Carola had become a person who was almost preternaturally attuned to every nuance of other people. She studied their changing expressions from day to day, hour to hour, and sifted their gestures and comments for innuendos. It had become impossible to feel really at home anywhere. In short, Carola finally had become her own worst enemy. At least until this Friday, when Ben closed the office early and gave her a few extra hours of liberty.

She put on a pot of coffee to take off the chill from the rain, then went into the living room of her apartment and kicked off her slippers. For several happy minutes she lay with her head back on the couch, resting, trying not to hear the prejudiced demons in her head that never allowed her to forget for long that she was different.

Long ago Carola concluded that white men, for her, fell into two categories: those who looked down their noses at her heritage and secretly longed for her sleek, young body beneath them; and those who boasted to themselves of their "open-mindedness" and made lewd propositions ranging from the overt to the covert, but always with a lascivious undertone. It puzzled her that even the most bigoted of the lot would like to have sex with her and sometimes wondered, with a good deal of horror, what sex would be like with a man who basically hated her.

Just where Benjamin Kellogg fitted into all this, since he'd hired her immediately after one interview and still had not made any kind of pass, Carola avoided considering. Sometimes, at her desk in the publishing company or here at home, Ben's face would leap to mind and she'd find herself smiling warmly at it. And then she would grow angry and tell herself that, despite his apparent gentleness and easy, affable ways, he'd manage to show his true colors sooner or later—and one of them was white.

White women simply saw her as a darker threat, Carola was convinced. Whatever overtures of friendship she had made with them in the past were turned away with hostility if even one white dude appeared on the horizon.

That Laura Hawks, now. The girl seemed friendly enough, almost eager to become chums. It was hard not to like her, too. But hell, Carola mused, if Ben so much as touched her nut-brown shoulder, Laura would immediately figure Carola was after him. That made it a waste of time to get friendly with the white girl, really let her hair down and exchange phone numbers and addresses. Whatever bond they formed would just disintegrate sooner or later and make Carola feel even worse.

Of course, the secretary had finally concluded, blacks were nearly as hopeless. The men either treated her with awed respect—as if Carola were an ornate prize none of them could ever hope to attain —or came on like so many goddamn studs. Her most recent date, a few nights before, had been with a professional basketball player. Carola remembered his arrogant grin and active, presumptuous hands even more than his almost seven-foot height. He was the reason she'd decided to move again: the big, dumb oaf wouldn't stop calling and pestering her.

As to friendship with her black sisters, the younger women of her race appeared to regard Carola as hopelessly unfair competition, while the older ones saw her, Carola felt, as some kind of sellout—simply because she attempted to make her risky way in a fundamentally pale business world. More than a few middle-aged black ladies had even implied that Carola kept her present job because she slept with Ben Kellogg.

Never once had it occurred to Carola that she might be guilty of seeing people in stereotypical terms, of drawing conclusions without evidence, without fact, forgetting the importance of each individual regardless of skin color.

And so tonight, because of her mode of thinking about people, Carola was achingly, painfully lonely. On an evening that had become date night throughout the midwestern part of America, twenty-three-year-old Carola Glenn was merely another young woman alone and bored with the life she had mistakenly and inadvertently embraced.

It was almost nine o'clock. She turned on the television set to see what she could find, and as she was aimlessly switching channels, she suddenly sensed something.

Was that a knock at the door? Carola wasn't sure at all, but she did feel—*sense*—that there was something or someone patiently waiting, across the room, on the other side of the door.

She glanced at her watch, conscious of the pulse pounding beneath the strap. The basketball game couldn't even be in the second half yet; she doubted it was her persistent, would-be boyfriend. She drummed her fingers on the arm of the chair. *Why didn't they knock again!* Lordy, it was eerie just sitting and wondering if somebody was out there or not.

Carola began counting softly to herself: One, two, three (surely they'd rap again if they were at the right door), four, five, six (it's probably just my imagination), seven, eight, nine (I *know* there's someone out there).

For another moment she sought to ignore it, but just as she said "ten" aloud, she made a connection: it could be the little boy from downstairs, wanting to borrow sugar or something for his mama.

She sat forward in her chair. Her vividly-colored lounging pajamas clung to her figure. Her gay, fuzzy slippers were beside her bare feet, and her straight dark hair swept silkily round her shoulders. She stared at the front door, willing it to resound with a knock—or, better by far, to be definitely and conclusively *silent.*

She decided impulsively she was stupid and gutless. Putting her slippers on, she hurried to the door and rested her palm on it, quietly. "Yes?" she called in a little-girl voice.

There was no reply.

Her breathing accelerated and, for the first time, a genuine flicker of fear touched her heart. It was so abnormally quiet, so damned frighteningly silent. The sound of the TV set across the room was oddly subdued, as detached as a distant murmuring word escaping an apartment down the hall. Nothing else in the world was making a sound, and she felt trapped, enmeshed in silence, a veritable absence of human sound.

Again she thought she heart a faint rap, and taking a deep breath, getting a lungful of courage, Carola made the worst mistake of her life.

She threw the door open wide.

They were into the apartment like a shot, past her and brazenly standing in the center of the living room floor, almost as if they hadn't moved there but simply materialized. From the front door to the middle of the room, *zap!*

Behind Carola, untouched, the door softly nestled shut . . .

She blinked wildly, momentarily more outraged than frightened.

There were thirteen of them, each man costumed in the white conical hood and sweeping robes of an organization she had feared ever since she was a small girl and her parents began telling terrible, cautionary tales they could never quite complete.

For no reason Carola could imagine, standing before her with an air of malevolent appraisal, was a chapter of the Ku Klux Klan.

"How *dare* you enter my apartment like this!" she hissed, acting on her brave outrage. "What are you doing here?"

No answer.

But one male figure stepped forward, soundlessly, a tube of rolled papers in his pale hands. He unrolled it, holding the top with one hand and the bottom with his other.

Carola was beginning to feel the cold grip of panic. There was something so indescribably confident about this masked man, so completely in

HORROR HOUSE

charge, unconfused by his right to be here. She looked from one hooded head to another, trying to see something human: if not a face, a nod of the head, a simple gesture, even an impression of contained, derisive laughter.

Instead, she realized with greater horror, through the eyeholes in each pointed white hood—with the exception of the man who had moved forward to confront her, the one who grasped the roll of paper—she could see nothing whatsoever. It was as if—as if nothing substantial dwelled in those hoods.

But with the leader, where eyes should be peering meanly back at her with haughty disdain or malefic amusement, there was only a hint of deep shadows.

Then he began punctuating his perusal of the lengthy white proclamation with inclinations of his head, first to one and then another of his fellows.

My God, Carola realized, straining her ears to hear, *he's reading it to them—but there's not a sound coming from beneath that awful hood!*

She was about to cry out when one of the other robed figures stepped forward and, seemingly from nowhere at all, produced a vicious-looking black whip. Then another did the same; and another. Each angry whip had star-shaped tips, cruel things that looked capable of stripping the skin right off a person's body.

—Others have worn costumes like this, Carola thought suddenly, with a stab of agonizing fear. *Witches. Creatures of secret evil attending dark masses. Ceremonies in which pain was inflicted to the reaction of joy; meetings, replete with gory*

torture, with chanted demonic prayers, with sacrifice—human sacrifice!

The figure heading the hooded coven made a series of gestures at the front of his body, at his chest. Carola stared at him, unwilling to believe that she correctly understood his message. Then the figure repeated it, gnarled fingers fumbling at invisible buttons. Carola shook her head. *No!*

Two of the men with whips stepped forward at once, arms raised threateningly. Their meaning was inescapable. Carola shrank back against the door. If she could just get out of here, she might save herself. Slowly, miserably, Carola obeyed their silent orders and began removing her lounging pajamas. As she cooperated, the figure who was their leader gestured the men with the whips to stand still. Carola completed unbuttoning her top and left it open, only to see the leader gesture again. Remove it, his gesture said. Take it off.

She did and stood proudly before them, bosom heaving, seeking to convey an image of a young woman with scorn and without fear, who might do as they commanded but would never give them the privilege of witnessing her terror. Behind her, she groped for the doorknob. Her fingers squeezed gratefully and began turning.

The leader did not seem to see what she was doing. He stepped closer to her and, for the first time, she saw the eyes behind the mask, clearly: red-rimmed, fierce and hungry, they seared unforgettably into her mind—furious, lunatic eyes that swept her half-nakedness even as the leader's hand went out to her to cup, caress and pinch one perfect breast.

Carola made her move. Twisting suddenly, she threw the door open and turned, ready to run for her life—and screamed aloud in piteous fright for the first time.

Standing just outside the door—clearly mad and just as sexually aroused—a trio of huge, slobbering police dogs tensed their legs to leap. Carola caught a glimpse of their great, sharp fangs, the saliva dripping hotly from their mouths; she saw the unsheathed members of the beasts and their powerful flanks; she saw their oddly yellow eyes; she saw their terrible purpose. . . .

She slammed the door against them, and as she did, unwilling yet to turn and face the others, she realized two things which came to her mind because she was intelligent and because, even now, she felt that her good wits would save her: the animals outside had made *no* sound whatsoever—and she had been unable to feel the touch of the hooded leader on her bare flesh.

If she could only pause to think, if she could *only* have the time to let her mind probe, search for the answer to these anomalies, she might yet save herself.

Then she saw that the leader had thrown back the hood from his head and, emitting involuntary muffled shriek, she knew that escape was impossible.

He was old, older than age itself, so ancient that parts of the skin on his face were mottled and barely adhered to the white skull beneath. It was the face of something slithering out of a grave. His expression could not, for a moment, be identified; and then Carola realized that it was a look of tightly contained self-discipline, as if the leader somehow functioned at the order of others and sought to fulfill their commands despite his own base appetite.

"Who," she whispered, "who are y-you?"

Whether the named response came from his cracked lips or not, Carola wasn't sure. But the name was nonetheless, suddenly, *there,* in her mind: *Brunrichter.* The syllables clicked into a chamber of her terrified mind. His name was Dr. Adolph C. Brunrichter.

The ancient gestured again, this time at waist level, pointedly. His hand shook, but not, she realized, from age.

Keep them nonviolent at all costs, Carola thought, remembering advice she'd heard for potential rape victims. *Appear to be cooperative, and at least they may let you live.*

She dropped her pajama bottoms to a heap on the floor and stepped out of them, nude except for her slippers, before thirteen silent figures. *Eyes,* their awful *eyes,* staring, almost groping and touching; *eyes* upon her sleek, rounded buttocks, *eyes* pawing at her high breasts, *eyes* locking finally below her waist, hungrily. The area between her legs felt vast to her; the patch of curly hair seemed to spread and grow as she wished fervently that it would shrink, that it—and she—could vanish from the room. She pressed her legs together, tightly, protecting what she could from their damnable, probing, insensitive *eyes.*

Then, for the first time, she heard sound.

It was not breathing, but something *like* breathing, an *animal's* inhalations—as if these hooded creatures were not only real at all but something of partial reality, some constructs that only required her nakedness and her bottomless terror to assume the guise of life. It was a sucking, almost sobbing sound of distant longing, something with drool in it and a hint of such unmistakable, longing lust that the sound caught at Carola's frantic heart and caused her instantly to cross one arm over her heaving breasts, to rest one shielding hand across her conspicuous sex.

It was that sound of countless entities on the verge of taking some unguessable, utterly loathsome action.

The ancient leader was licking his cracked, toothless lips, the tip of a finger massaging his upper lip where a cluster of white hairs twitched like a small, furry animal. His ancient eyes seemed to sparkle not with life but Untime—with a timelessness surpassing human age or virility or common human passion, moving beyond them all to something that was a *fiendish*—something of the dead made half-alive, and mindless.

As she stared, helpless to move—thoughts frozen with fear as the unhuman breath continued to seep like poisonous gas—Carola saw that the ancient leader was *doing* something to himself.

Two hirsute legs, scrawny and naked, the hair tangled in clots like wire against the background of fishbelly white, splotched skin, were exposed to her gaze.

The leader was lifting his long, white gown. Inch by queerly seductive inch it rose, exposing more, and still ungodly more.

When it was nearly at waist level, Carola Glenn

began screaming again. But this time it was a piercing shriek of terror that bounced off the apartment walls, off the tilting corners of her staggered inner mind—a scream that would go on pounding and reverberating within her shattered mentality for so long as merciless Nature permitted her life.

The leader's member, dangling at first, almost to his absurd pink knees, was developing an erection. A murderous erection. As her terror mounted and the scream began its life-stealing gestation in her throat, Carola saw the thing snap erect.

It was as wide around and sturdy as a large man's arm, throbbing with pumping blood. It was beyond all sick jokes. At its peak, she saw, it reached some four feet beyond the rest of the old man's body, its questing tip oozing—and touching —her own naked thigh as it prodded.

But what was worst—what finally drove Carola around sanity's precious bend—was that penis *tip* —for the thing was *alive*, a thing unto itself, another devil's entity: an enormous rattlesnake's head, green and scaly, a forked tongue restlessly flicking—even while she gaped numbly at it— against the curly mat between her legs.

And then the skirts of the other hooded creatures were rising, ceremoniously; twelve more of them. Lizard heads and the popeyed ones of toads and frogs were revealed, lifting, thrusting, hungry for her.

The breathy, unhuman sound of a desire from beyond the grave skittered through the room.

Carola slumped to the floor, knees rigid and

raised to her chin, hands knotted like cords of steel around her breasts. Her eyes were wide, gaping pathetically; they saw nothing now.

They saw nothing for the plain reason that she was alone and there was nothing there to see. And there had been nothing—nothing else *real*—in her apartment that night. Not even for one second.

The maniac's laugh that other residents of the apartment building eventually swore they heard was one hellish trick wasted on Carola Glenn. She was no longer a part of the real world, either.

11

During the day, on Saturday, Ben was obliged to drive to the funeral home and make sure that everything was satisfactory. That evening, Edna Kellogg would lie in state.

From Ben's standpoint, everything was distinctly *not* satisfactory. His mother scarcely resembled herself. In just a few hours the mortician's art had transformed her into some kind of coiffed, scented, powdered and painted store-window dummy. She had also bizarrely lost several inches in height and other dimensions. And, most incredible of all, she looked at peace.

Nevertheless, "Thank you," he told the mortician, as everyone did. "You've done a good job."

He turned to survey the empty room—Laura had suggested she go, but he felt this was something he should do—and when he saw that only two flower displays had arrived so far, he wept.

Down the decorous hall, as he departed, he

happened to glance into another room and saw a man about his age turning from a casket with tears in his eyes. For the first time in quite a while Ben sensed a feeling of brotherhood with other men.

Meanwhile, in his office above East 56th Street, a machine that had been created when Edna Kellogg was a young woman hummed to itself. Ben had forgotten and left it running.

That evening, at the funeral home, Martin Ruben paid his respects and, before leaving, found an opportunity to draw Ben into an empty parlor.

"Are you satisfied with your experiment?" he asked quietly.

"Not entirely," Ben told his friend, accepting the cigarette Ruben offered him and inhaling with satisfaction. "Nothing happened last night, nothing at all. But I still plan to use the apparatus again, in Pittsburgh."

Ruben soberly studied the bearded face. "I see. You won't leave well enough alone, then? You won't just drop the matter and write your book?"

"No, I can't do that." An expression of something like fear flickered briefly in the publisher's eyes. "I'd like to, Martin. I really would.".

"I believe that," Ruben said simply. He sighed and draped a long arm around Ben's shoulders. "Well, we all do what we must do. We all have our crosses to bear, as the Christian saying goes."

Ben looked sharply at the parapsychologist. "What d'you mean by that?"

"Nothing." Ruben shook his head. "Nothing at all."

All Saturday night, Ben lay in Laura's comforting arms, unable to sleep. He found himself alternating in moods between depression over his mother's death, and the circumstances of it—with recollections of better, happier times when she would somehow brush back the obscuring veil of supernatural fear and play the piano with surprising facility—and a mood of tentative triumph.

But it was a bitter, unfulfilling triumph. He had told Laura everything that had happened in the office Friday night and had played the Frederick Parlock tape so that she might learn of Brunrichter's part in the legend. "Unquestionably, what the old fellow said happened is true," he said from his position beside her. "And doubtlessly Brunrichter was a madman who committed dreadful murders. But that doesn't mean he was driven to insanity by the house or told what to do by some demonic power."

"But supposedly he was a decent and respected general practitioner when he moved to Ridge Avenue," she said mildly, remembering what Martin Ruben had told her.

"Sometimes people carry the seeds of insanity in their minds half their lives before doing anything particularly antisocial," Ben replied a trifle coldly. "You don't have to be a psychologist like Martin to know that. Brunrichter may have become obsessed with his new home, frightened by shadows that moved, until his latent madness broke loose—but I'm sure the house had nothing to do with it." He paused. "The fact is, darling, the apparatus was turned on during my entire stay in the office—and nothing happened at all."

She raised a light-brown brow. "In the office, at any rate."

"Oh, come on," Ben scoffed with a light laugh. "We'd have heard about anything happening by now, if it had. No, Laura, there are no ghosts."

He kissed her on the lips, then with his tongue traced an imaginary circle around one of her nipples, enjoying the way it tightened and lifted to his waiting lips. They had derived an enjoyment from each other that night that was surprising, given the circumstances of Ben's maternal loss. Their release had been unified and immense, almost exhausting—as if each of them celebrated life in order to keep the specter of death at bay. As a result, his limited sense of triumph was mixed now with satiation and a growing feeling of love for the ash-blond writer. "I wish I were ready again," he said wistfully.

"Horny old man," she said, laughing lightly. But she'd always been a person who tended to wring every fragment of possible meaning from a topic before letting it go. "I wish I could be as sure as you that there are no spirits. But I respect Martin so much, and he's so definite about it. *And* about how dangerous it would be to continue investigating 1129."

Ben blinked and turned his face away from her. "Honey, there are a few free people who know they are fortunate to be given the gift of life. They take it and use it fully for eighty or ninety years. Then, quite simply, they become nothing whatsoever." He turned his bearded head to peer searchingly into her lovely face. "But don't you see? That's enough if you've played your cards right. It's enough, and wanting more is simply greedy."

Laura squirmed up until she was high on a pillow against the headboard of Ben's bed, able to look down at him and think. She decided he was a strange combination of wise, mature, talented businessman and naive, thoughtless, willful little boy. He was, Laura thought, everything she had ever really wanted her man to be—but he was more, too, in complex ways she both approved, and disapproved.

Now, at least, she understood his macabre fascination with death as a topic, a subject she avoided except when her writing demanded its consideration. Ruben had made it clear that Ben was whistling his way through a graveyard, trying unconsciously to convince himself that he might live free of his mother's overdone hauntings. But this talk of nothingness after death was more shocking to the privately God-fearing Laura than she cared to admit.

"Benny," she began lightly, "it's easy enough to say there is nothing beyond life." She caressed the top of his dark head gently. "And that this is sufficient. But women who give birth and see life develop from the very beginning can't be quite so cavalier about it. We have born into us a certain knowing of man's fragility, and most of us, I think, also sense continuation. I wonder how you'll feel, yourself, when you're an old man who is obliged to face the fact that death could occur at any moment."

He frowned and rubbed his cheek against her bare, yielding abdomen. "I only hope that I won't be a hypocrite. But, of course, you're apt to be right.

I may grasp at straws then with the best of them. The total loss of self is certainly frightening." He felt a shiver move along his spine and stopped talking for a moment.

"Did you get in touch with your brother?" Laura asked, sensing he would be glad to change the subject.

"Oh, yeah," he muttered. "He's flying in tomorrow night from San Diego for the funeral on Monday."

"I'm glad," Laura said gently. "I'll look forward to meeting him. Was he terribly close to your mother, too?"

Ben sighed. "Willard's close to nothing but his bank balance. He's coming here only to do the right thing and is flying right back out again. I'm afraid Willard uses money the way small children use security blankets and teddy bears. I think if he jumped into a swimming pool filled with dollar bills, he'd feel he was in the right hand of God."

"He uses money the way you use your success as a publisher?" she asked, smiling teasingly down at his upturned face. "The way you advertise all over the nation for quaint old machines and find happiness in planning weird books?"

"No more," he cried. "I surrender!" He slipped lower in the bed and resumed kissing. "From now on, my sweet, the only thing I seek is the heart of your love."

Laura moved spasmodically. "I don't mean to confuse sex with love," she whispered, "but I think your quest is ended."

Neither of them said anything more for some time.

And no words were spoken by the apparatus in Ben Kellogg's office as it went on functioning, crackling and hissing occasionally, gathering force. Gathering *other* things.

12

On Sunday afternoon the police located Ben at his apartment, pointed that way by an address book they found in Carola Glenn's effects. She was alone in Indianapolis, and his name and address were the only ones in the book.

Laura wept, thinking that might be the saddest thing she'd ever heard. Buying an address book and putting one person in it was like having a party and only one friend showing up.

The police were with Ben and Laura for quite a while, asking a barrage of questions even before telling them whether Carola was dead or alive. Finally, satisfied that the publisher and writer had no complicity in the matter, they informed them that Carola had been taken—alive—to Central State Hospital.

Ben's brother, Willard, wasn't due in town until eleven at night—with typical consideration, he had ignored the three-hour difference in their respective time zones—so Ben took Laura to see Carola. Each of them thought it might be possible for the young secretary to be helped, perhaps restored, by their visit.

The temporary quarters in which they found Carola were closer to what Laura had originally expected of such an institution. The room was utterly cheerless and plain, Carola a dark ghost and somehow frailer beneath the sheets.

She stared into space, seeming almost not to breathe, her fists knotted at her breasts. Ben tried to get some useful information from an attendant but encountered the usual tight-mouthed, self-protective attitude of the medical profession.

They stayed an hour. When they rose to leave, worried and depressed, Ben saw the young woman's lips moving but could hear nothing issuing from them. He bent to her, put his ear close to her mouth.

"Snake," she said softly but clearly, nodding and biting her lip. "It was a snake."

Ben glanced at Laura and repeated, in a whisper, what Carola had said. Laura shrugged her shoulders helplessly.

Then Carola spoke again, and both heard her distinctly. *"Brunrichter,"* she said, just once. That was the last word they could get out of her. For Laura it was very nearly enough. Ben refused to discuss it.

Willard Kellogg was only two years older than his brother but appeared much older and was measurably heavier and ridiculously pompous. More than six-three in height, he wore an astoundingly outdated crew cut that matched his dated mannerisms. He had one of those mouths that protrude, with horselike teeth meeting perhaps an inch beyond the nose. The nose itself was an elongated, slightly sunburned affair. Beneath it, the smile that Willard donned at suitable moments was little more than a slash that advertised his frosty, detached disposition.

He had been picked up at Indianapolis International Airport promptly at eleven, Sunday night, and was asleep by twelve-thirty. To Laura's surprise, but not Ben's, Willard had little to say and seemed eager for solitude.

On Monday, at the mortuary, Willard paid Laura slight attention and appeared more obliged to chat with Ben than happy to do so.

For Ben, approaching the open casket again was a chore that clearly pained him. Laura ached for him. Willard, however, seemed to look down from some grandiose height, bestowing no more than a quick, supercilious glance. It occurred to Laura that the entire thing was rather distasteful to Willard Kellogg, not a reason for great sorrow or loss.

The funeral service was mercifully brief. Martin Ruben attended, since he was not only a friend of Ben but had served in a professional capacity to the late Mrs. Kellogg. Afterward, Ben asked Martin to accompany Laura, Willard and himself in the limousine driving to the cemetery. But Ruben declined as graciously as possible, preferring to drive his own car. Laura could tell that the parapsychologist was dreadfully ill at ease and—she suddenly felt, curiously—something more.

Watchful, that was it. She considered the man as she rode between Ben and his brother. Ruben was almost wary. She wondered why he felt a need to be cautious or perhaps actually observant under dismal circumstances that were ordinary enough. It was, Laura thought, as if Ruben half expected something to happen.

Lincoln Park Cemetery stretches for interminable lengths of emerald green, suggesting eternity itself, along an east-west road bisecting Indianapolis. It serves, some police officers have suggested, as a stark reminder to would-be speeders. It is dotted, more with offhand artistry than geometric precision, with the familiar gray squares and rectangles of identifying stones. Here and there a rich man's private vault rises like a hunched Phoenix from the clinging earth. On a more somber day than this, Laura thought, one could imagine unmentionable creatures lurking behind the great stones.

But this was an inappropriate noon for such a lugubrious ride. The sun was bold as brass directly above them; still, to Laura, it seemed oddly ominous, as if the heavens simply waited to come apart and drench them in the Almighty's sympathetic tears.

As the family party arrived at the cemetery, the limousine driver smoothly braked on a ledge of grass, just off the stony, gravel-spinning road, and Ben saw in the distance a canopy raised for the occasion. It struck the publisher as incongruous. Canopies were for circuses, he thought sourly, for moments of youth and merriment. Beneath the thing, he perceived as they ascended a slight yellow-green slope of earth, six neatly aligned folding chairs awaited them. And, of course, the dreadful pit.

By the time the mourners had assembled there, pallbearers already had rested the coffin on the pulley ropes that would lower it, forever, into the uncaring but busily regenerative earth. With a pang, Ben wished he had bought a more expensive casket. As he moved to select a chair, half appraising the minister who stood waiting with open Bible, there came the first surprise.

Willard Kellogg, directly behind Laura and Ruben, gave a gasp and astonishingly whirled about in a half circle, took three steps away from the canopied graveside and sank to his knees in the tailored grass.

Ben lurched toward him, stumbling and dropping to one knee beside the tall man. "What is it Willard?" he asked. "What's wrong—your heart?"

Willard raised his widemouthed face to his brother and absently ran a palm across his crewcut, graying hair. "I haven't been a son for years," he whispered, "and it's just too much of a shock—reality. I'm only a—a businessman."

"Willard, that's your mother over there," Ben said in low tones.

Willard stared straight ahead, at the winding road leading away from the cemetery to East Washington Street. "When I'm overdrawn, I deposit more money. When I start running out of money," he continued, "I sell somebody something or do clever work for them. It's a—a comforting world, Ben, a world without beginnings and endings. Simple, and direct. I can exist in it."

Ben tried to smile. He rested his hand gently on Willard's shoulder but also longed to strike him. He glanced up at the approaching Martin Ruben and Laura. "Willard can't quite cope with all this," he said. There was a faint apologetic note there.

With Ruben's help, Willard raised himself rather brusquely to his feet. When he shook off Ruben's hand, they saw how pale he'd become beneath his California tan. He made an effort to regain his dignity but had to settle for a quite artificial smile. "Mother would understand this. All too well, I think. I—did my duty, coming this far." His voice was embarrassed yet grating, but not at all sorrowful. "Try to forgive me, Ben. I'll be starting back for the airport—now."

"I thought you'd be my house guest," Ben murmured, clutching his brother's bicep in a way he hoped seemed sincere, "at least for a few days."

Willard looked at Ben, then Laura, then at the waiting, frozen tableau beneath the canopy. A gust of wind blew his jacket collar against his neck. "No," he said shortly. "No."

"Whatever you think you should do," Ben replied.

But Willard, without glancing at Laura or shaking Ben's hand, was already turning and wandering off in quest of transportation.

Ben watched until the tall figure dwindled. Tears stood in his gentle eyes. Tears for many people.

Laura was outraged for him. "Is that man always like this?" she demanded.

"No!" Ben exclaimed. Then he turned back to his friends with a heavy sigh and managed a weak smile. "No, Willard wasn't always a coward. Once, when we were just boys, he saved me from drowning in White River during a raft race. But—well, I suppose he's more susceptible to our mother's imagination than I."

Ruben's gaze met Laura's, thoughtfully. Neither spoke.

"What you two don't know," Ben continued while they walked back to the canopy, "is that Willard, like Mother, occasionally claimed to have psychic experiences—back when he was a boy. They alarmed him. I'd hoped to demonstrate for him the apparent failure of the Edison apparatus, show him he had nothing to fear from the other side. Because it doesn't exist."

"I'm not at all sure you've established that, Benjamin," Ruben said. *Demiurge,* he thought; how can I even explain the concept to them?

"But I am sure, now," Ben responded with a nod, "in my own mind."

The minister, who'd witnessed emotional trauma in other men besides Willard, awaited them, an image of patience. *The man could be St. Peter,* mused Laura, half-sardonically. When they'd moved again to the forefront of mourners, Reverend Justin Peacock glanced down at the holy book, began reading aloud from it in sonorous tones.

Ben, looking for solace, rummaged around in what he heard. But as the casket began to settle at the bottom of the ever-frightening depths, Laura made a muffled shriek and raised a trembling index finger.

She had seen the coffin *lurch.* Just faintly.

"Ben," she whispered, "did you see it, too?"

He clutched her arm tightly. "It's nothing," he said flatly. "A trick of the dirt beneath it," he added soberly.

Laura turned swiftly to Ruben and saw again how wary and watchful he was. But now, she could swear, the lean man's intensity had increased immensely, and he was about to speak. "I'm not sure it's just the dirt," he said aloud to Ben, his tone alerted and cautionary.

Ben and Laura looked where Ruben was now pointing, below them.

Oh, God, Laura wailed within herself.

From where she stood, she was able to see the earth beneath the coffin. That conveyance of death, she saw with terror, was hovering a full inch above the ground.

"Mom," Ben said, blurting it out.

He'd fallen pathetically to his knees and was starting to climb down into the pit when Martin Ruben's strong hands caught him just below the shoulders, squeezing, restraining. Around them the canopied scene was filled with amazed stares and buzzing whispers of shocked incredulity.

"Did you," Ruben asked in a rough whisper against Ben's ear, "*did* you turn on that damned machine and *leave* it on? *Did you, Ben?*"

Ben, preoccupied with his mother's casket, glanced up with tears in his eyes; his face was a mask of consternation. "No. Yes. I mean," he began again, slowly, "yes, I think I did leave it on. But how—"

"How did I *know?*" Ruben finished for him, pity and affection mingling with fear in his features. "Because, Kellogg, I was just now *told* that you had! Something whispered it to me, now, as we were walking away from your brother." Then Ruben was tugging at his friend's shoulders. "Come on, Ben, please. We *must* get to your office swiftly!"

Laura not knowing what to believe, heard Ben ask with anguish, "But *why*, Martin?"

"Because we've been *summoned* there," the parapsychologist replied, yanking Ben to his feet and half shoving him toward the road. "And I don't think our host is going to be polite about further invitations!"

Willard had succeeded in catching an early ride back to the funeral parlor, where his rented car had been left. His driver was Fred McThiele, the aging owner of the funeral parlor, and the vehicle was a Cadillac hearse that had been used for a burial preceding Mrs. Kellogg's.

In his mid-forties, Willard was a man who had been obliged to live with the specter of death since before Ben was born. He had become a contract attorney and owner of a small company partly in the hope that his adaptable Gemini mind would lock itself firmly on writs, torts, probation filings and business contracts to the exclusion of the "dark phantom."

For the most part, his plan had succeeded admirably. Although his marriage had dissolved in divorce because of his lugubrious moods and fondness for listening to recorded classical dirges by the hour—and he could no longer look at a pretty face without feeling a peculiar mixture of nostalgia and lust—Willard was proud of the way he functioned. In recent months there were those who urged him to run for state senator in the next campaign, and Willard was sufficiently impressed with himself to consider the offer seriously.

He rested his crew-cut head on the back of his seat beside old Fred McThiele and tried to quit being so nervous and neurotic. *Patience,* he told himself, *you'll be in the big bird back to San Diego very soon.* Seeing his mother again—remembering all the terrible things she'd claimed to witness in bygone years, until he actually felt faint—reminded the tall man of his own occasional predictive visions. He cheerfully despised these moments of far thought, and feared them, especially the one he'd had before awakening this morning in Ben's apartment. He knew that Ben and that girl thought he was calloused, indifferent to Mom's passing, and that was fine with Willard Kellogg. The more people who thought of him as totally practical and substantial, as an unsentimental realist with bright ideas and brighter future goals, the better Willard liked it.

And the quicker he got through this dreadful midwestern day—*God,* the sun was different somehow; it baked you alive in Indianapolis—the sooner he'd know he was wrong about this morning's premonition: The one that said he would die before the day was over.

Martin Ruben, Ben and Laura drove quickly toward Ben's office, barely pausing at the impossibly complex, multiple intersection linking Emerson Avenue and other boulevards. The parapsychologist, at the wheel, sent his aging Chrysler hurtling in front of a semi. They careened onto Kessler

Boulevard, his passengers leaning to help Martin make the curve. Ruben made two brisk turns to the right, with similar velocity and disregard for law and safety. Then the car was skittering down the street. It wound up nearly sideways in the gravel parking space in front of Ben's office.

Laura huddled against Ben, whose fingers shook as he poked the key into the familiar lock and Ruben waited beside them, impatiently, tapping his heels against the concrete landing. When the door sprang open, they plunged into the gloom of the outer office.

It was late afternoon; the interior was dark. Waist-high stacks of usually familiar books became leering troglodytes in the murky shadows. But before Ben could even turn on the lights, Ruben dragged him and Laura toward Ben's private office.

When the door came open, creaking, a steady and surreal glow poured uremically from the old Edison apparatus on Ben's desk. It was enough light to see by. Laura stared at the machine, heard how much more plaintive and yet persistent was the sound issuing from the device. The light rose in yellow, mucous-like wafts of other-worldly curls, like smoke. As the trio stood considering it from just inside the door, getting accustomed to the relative gloom, a form abruptly took shape before them.

"I tried to warn you," it said in a high, faraway voice instantly familiar to Benjamin Kellogg. *"Oh, I tried so hard!"*

Ben choked back the outcry that leaped to his lips.

Hazily, almost translucently, the figure of his

mother assumed shape to the left of his desk . . .

As they were circling the city on 465, and the limousine headed west, Willard Kellogg began to hear peculiar sounds. He glanced at old Fred McThiele; but the mortuary owner was fully involved with his driving. Only he, it seemed, heard the distressing *crunching* sounds—of someone *eating*. He wondered for an instant why it distressed him. Then he realized the noises were coming from directly behind him, from the portion of the hearse that usually carried a coffin—an occupied coffin.

Willard scratched his close-cropped head and tried to ignore the sound, but his heartbeat accelerated.

Then the scrabbling began—right behind him.

Unable to bear it, Willard turned to look . . .

The expression on the old woman's face was one of sadness and abject loss. Ben stared wistfully, lovingly at it, all fear gone. Mother seemed deeply, miserably unhappy, sad to an unfathomable depth of despair that touched Ben to the core.

He took a hasty, helping step forward with his arms outstretched—and recoiled at once, stinking black smoke rising from the singed arms of his suitcoat. He yelped in pain and hugged his wounded arms to his sides and chest. Laura went to him and then the laughter pealed out, filling the room, surrounding them.

"Fool!" the voice rumbled in a seemingly ageless bass roar. "*Imbecile!* At least the other one who called for me—the one you call Tomedison—knew something of my favorite art: science!"

HORROR HOUSE

The pale and adoring face of Ben's mom, Edna Kellogg, contorted and began to alter before their dumbfounded gazes. Staring in disbelief, they saw a series of animal faces appear where once had been the spectral mother's. Each beast revealed a glint of intelligence in its cold eyes, but the nature of that intelligence suggested an evil avarice they found repelling.

"For the time being," the alien voice continued, each creature's lips or beaks mockingly forming the spoken words, "I shall spare you the sight of my own ineffable features. Beings such as yourselves should not be exposed to the complete charm of sheer and ultimate evil. While they yet *live*, that is."

Ben gaped at the altering images and the shadowy form of his mother with consternation and shock, his every private conviction shaken and tottering, the worst of them falling into acceptance. Laura gripped his hand hard and averted her eyes.

But Dr. Martin Ruben stepped closer with uncommon boldness. He folded his thin arms across his chest. "I demand to know just whom we are addressing. Although, I believe I do know."

Some of the sounds that came, then, were familiar names—Lucifer, Baal, even Satan—and some of them were only grotesque grunting sounds, squeezed-out groanings of noise that rasped on the human ear and obviously took shape from languages thousands of years. Then, satisfied with having cited the long list, the voice chuckled.

"Don't you recognize the family resemblance, Doctor? If not that of the face, then that of the style, the method? The *modus operandi?*" Scorn and taunting humor oozed from the deep tones. "Come, come, Doctor! If memory serves, you've met *my son*."

The creature kneeling behind Willard Kellogg seemed, at first, an apelike thing with very short, bristling yellow hair—but only at first glance. It was the shape of the head and the pointed ears, the unselfconscious and contorted limbs that made Willard think of an ape. But the figure, actually, was quasi human—but no more than three feet in height. It crouched, face still averted, its muscular side toward Willard, working busily away and quite intent on its secret efforts.

The thing was naked, obscenely so. From where Willard sat frozen in the front seat, almost hypnotized by the unsettling and implausible sight, he could discern the hairy testicles of the creature dragging like white turds on the floor of the hearse. That is, until the creature twitched its odd tail and moved that long, muscled appendage like a thin hand and arm in order to curl itself beneath the rear portion of the strange body. The motion was bizarrely, incongruously modest. Willard wanted to cry out, to scream, but he felt immobilized by something so completely out of his own norm that he was incapable of relating to it. He could not properly gauge how frightened he should *be!*

A stench arose from the beast, and Willard, who'd never been able to stand foul odors, was revolted. His long nose twisted in fine disdain; he glanced away, then—richly offended—glanced back.

The creature was defecating on the floor of the

vehicle! Involuntarily Willard spoke up boldly. "Say, there!" he shouted in the way he might have called out to a juvenile delinquent scrawling grafitti on a wall. "What are you doing?"

Old Fred McThiele glanced in surprise at his lanky passenger. "What'd you say, mister?"

But Willard wasn't listening to the real world. He was watching as the creature responded, the apelike head turning slowly, *so* slowly, to give him a full view of its face.

And when it did, Willard felt his heart lurch in his chest. His arm shot out in shock, striking the old driver's thin shoulder. There was a slight vehicular skid and a warning from McThiele that went unheard.

The beast's face was a small and imbecilic, utterly avaricious version of Willard's own face! It was like unexpectedly looking into a funhouse distorting mirror—or possibly at the image of one's own soul's darkest, most luridly evil self.

The creature parted its pale, protruding Willard-lips to speak to him in perfect English. "What am I *doing* here? What am *I* doing here?" The voice was his, too, dignified and condescending. "Why, I'm eating." It paused. "Want some?"

The hand holding its snack came up and whipped abruptly toward Willard, thrusting its hideous contents right beneath Willard's aristocratic nose.

It was a human hand, unmistakable, bloodless—and the thumb had been bitten away.

The ape-thing smiled at him in camaraderie. Willard's nerves buckled, broke. Both arms shot out hysterically, carelessly, like weapons. One caught poor old Fred McThiele squarely in the mouth. Willard followed his arms in almost the same motion, virtually vaulting into the old man's lap in the urgent need for protection.

The long, powerful hearse, too bulky, disproportionate and already traveling in excess of sixty miles per hour, went instantly out of control. It described an arc across the interstate dividing island, caromed and was promptly struck by a three-quarter-ton truck heading in the opposite direction. Willard smashed through the windshield like a shot, briefly airborne, then bounced three times on the highway.

Minutes later, they found both Willard and old Fred. There was, however, no evidence of an apelike creature with Willard Kellogg's face nor, mercifully, any sign that a maimed human body had ridden in the back of the demolished hearse. In point of fact, neither had been there at all.

But the police spent quite a while trying to imagine what had brought such an expression of revulsion to Willard Kellogg's very dead face.

"I not only met the Antichrist but defeated him," Ruben said forthrightly. "With help."

"Not defeated, Doctor. *Delayed* is the correct term. You delayed his fine achievements, moving them to another location upon this planet—and a somewhat different time frame became necessary. Except in a sheerly aesthetic sense, I did not appreciate your efforts." The voice added, in tones so calm they were truly words that cursed, "You cocksucking, motherfucking, miserable son of a bitch." The effect on Laura was one of revulsion.

"I am delighted that I ruined your timing," Ruben murmured. "It is the highlight of my life."

"Oh, you may well be pleased, for the nonce," the voice agreed. "However, when I am ready for *you*, Doctor, nothing in your Hebrew heritage or your recent tentative passion for Christianity shall intervene in your behalf." It laughed shortly. "I pass a measure of my time contemplating the ways I shall amuse myself indefinitely at your expense, Doctor. In fact, throughout *eternity.*"

Ruben blinked. Ben moved quickly beside him, only a few feet from the hazy, grayish-yellow image that had burned him. "Just what the hell do you want with us?" he demanded, his beard bristling in outrage.

"That, sir, would appear to be *my* question," came the murmured response from the opened beak of a huge falcon. "After all, *you* called *me.*"

"I did nothing of the kind," Ben denied angrily.

"Ah, but I insist you did, Mr. Kellogg. I was reasonably content, to observe the progress of my clever spirit friends, getting comfortably by—there were, um, little amusements from time to time—but you chose to rub Aladdin's lamp, and I am the genie you've received!" Another harsh chuckle. "You, sir, raised the lever on Tomedison's device and asked us here—*all* of us."

Ben flushed, uncertain whether the implacable bass voice was lying or telling the truth.

Ruben filled the void of silence. "Tell me, if you will: What have you done since Edison liberated you?"

"A very great deal, Doctor, all of it delightful. A subjective view, of course. But don't be too uncharitable to that old man. He only initiated the procedure, beckoned us together as one. It required the gas company explosion to destroy the old house that had imprisoned us, on Ridge Avenue. It took one *other* explosion, as you well know, to bring us our true liberty."

"The atomic bomb," Laura ventured. "Hiroshima. Nagasaki."

"Excellent, my girl! Quite correct." The eyes of an ancient owl surveyed her methodically and so dispassionately it was almost a medical scrutiny. "I shall look forward to receiving *you* one day. I can be quite—how shall I say it?—*inventive* where lovely women are concerned."

"I'll see you in hell first!" Laura exclaimed, frightened and confused.

"So you will, so you will," the voice purred.

"I doubt sincerely that will be Laura's destination," Ben said hastily, how she had paled. "What exactly did atomic power *do* for you? I don't think we understand entirely."

"You understand virtually nothing. But allow me to elucidate. The principle of the atomic bomb involves a chain reaction that begins to develop at a certain stage of concentration." An immense, particularly ugly crocodile chatted with them with a professorial mien that might have been funny under different conditions. "Uranium 235 is an isotope, Dr. Ruben, and it disintegrates in an ongoing way. That disintegration is slow in small masses, but beyond the 'critical mass,' Mr. Kellogg, that disintegration is marvelously accelerated—a chemical cancer of sorts as the missiles of energy thrust out by the atoms strike the nuclei of other atoms, directly. In turn, they disintegrate, the exploding atoms fire still more 'bullets' and hit further nuclei. That, in short, is an atomic explosion. Child's play, of course. It should have been developed a century before it was. Much the same process occurred on behalf of my entities. They were scattered to the four winds, freed at last!" A croc smiled happily.

"But that wasn't the end of the dispersement stage, was it?" asked Ruben in his best conversational tone. He wanted all he could get and had rested against Ben's desk, one hip supported there. He seemed the soul of calmness, confidence.

Laura, staring at the mustached parapsychologist with the Sherlockian face, thought that it was as if Ruben had both dreaded and anticipated this grim encounter for years. He was almost pleased, she felt, that the waiting was over.

The bass voice replied in a tone that was almost amiable. "You are, as usual, relatively perceptive, Doctor. My entities were dispersed, in effect, by air first, then by other means—those of biological reproduction. In the form of your human species. They've become an integral part of countless men and women. Why, because of the cooperative ignorance of your scientists who explore nature's secrets without the slightest regard to the potential consequences, such men and women have become my *personal* envoys of evil upon mankind." The deep voice shook, convulsed, with fierce, scornful laughter. "They stopped my precious war, but they freed my finest soldiers in the process! They bring me fresh souls to devour much as mortals dine on the limbs of helpless animals."

There was silence for several moments in Ben Kellogg's office. At last Ruben cleared his throat, and when he addressed the presence, his own baritone was quietly disciplined and barren of its affected British mannerisms. "You are, as you've admitted, known by countless names. But I believe, if I am not mistaken, that there is one word in particular that suits you best."

"Oh, there *is!* But I doubt that you know the word, Doctor," rejoined the voice.

"I'll be surprised if I don't," Ruben replied quickly. "Your name is—*Demiurge.*"

The creature was rendered speechless. Ben and Laura stared at Martin Ruben, wondering why the presence was stunned and what the alien word meant. But Ruben did not see their startled, questioning glances, because he was continuing to hold the creature's gaze despite its altering, confusing faces.

"*Answer me!*" Martin Ruben insisted. "Isn't it true that you *are* Demiurge?"

A huge reptilian head, like that of the prehistoric Tyrannosaurus, blinked its hooded eyes. "Yes," it confessed, "that *is* an appellation that, if my memory serves, described me aptly. Doctor, you impress me." The chuckle now was utterly humorless; threatening. "You *never* fail to please me."

"Really?" Ruben asked. He pushed himself away from the desk and leveled a lean finger at the ghostly apparition. His smile was tense, taut, in a mood of triumph. "Very well, I shall cease bringing you pleasure with my next comments."

"How?"

"You and your ghostly entities were recalled.

They have been reassembled here—in this very room." Martin laughed with genuine amusement, with open delight, eyes fairly dancing. "You are *captive* here, nothing less! Once again you're just another damned haunted-house nuisance!" Ruben howled with glee and pounded his friend Ben on the back. "You're *confined* to this place, Demiurge, just as you once were in the mansion on Ridge Avenue— and we puny, pathetic mortals can *keep* you confined here forever!"

Ben and Laura realized at once what their friend meant. Ben jumped to his feet and, smiling joyously, clapped Ruben on the shoulder. "Of *course*, Martin! This—this Satanic thing you call Demiurge and all its miserable spooks are perfectly harmless locked away here! *Helpless* because the apparatus has trapped you!"

For one instant it was as if the air had been sucked from the office. The quiet was deathly still, deafening.

Then, very softly, Demiurge spoke from the hideous face of a cockroach: "Not quite helpless."

Stacks of books in the outer office rose up like a horde of pterodactyls, each upside down with the pages wildly flapping; books on Ben's wall shelves in the inner office charged from them, doing the same—dozens of precious, beloved books given terrible life, flinging themselves against the trio of human beings. Laura cried out in pain as a collections of Poe's works struck her head. Ruben lifted an arm to protect his face from the snapping covers of DeVore's *Encyclopedia of Astrology*. Ben dropped to his knees, batting at one of his own how-to books and a ledger. Books appeared to be coming from everywhere, hundreds of them, a winged library of enemies, swooping, striking and snapping. Pens vaulted from Ben's desk to become dangerous projectiles, jabbing into their arms; a paperweight was hurled, narrowly missing Laura's head. Ruben shouted in anger, Laura screamed, Ben batted at the objects fiercely, ineffectively.

Above the tumult, the voice shouted clearly and loudly from the face of a great, snarling black panther, "We can *project* our essences from this office—just as we wish them to appear! Although we may not leave here, our illusory thought forms may yet destroy this mortal world, this hovel of a planet among millions with more intelligent life! *Think* of *that,* Ruben—Kellogg. Try to *imagine* what I shall have my little entities do next—to the unsuspecting, bovine world beyond this office! They'll never know what attacked and annihilated them!"

The psychic war was finished then, with such an absence of warning that the human beings were caught in a tableau of foolishness. But now Demiurge was not in a mood to be amused by them on their knees, cowering in fear. Instead of laughing, it made noises of madness—snuffing, snorting sounds of fury barely under control. The image-creature was that of a lunatic rabbit, red-eyes and fierce, its nose twitching like something apart from it. Laura thought weirdly of *Alice in Wonderland.*

Ben lowered his arms and looked around. Every book he owned was exactly where it belonged. "When we meet again, in this insignificant place of your selection," the basso voice boomed at them, "I shall not beg you to turn off the apparatus and return liberty to us. You will *rush* to it, eagerly, prayerfully, to shut it down and release us. You, yourselves, will let hell descend in all its mighty vengeance upon your own kind—because it will seem preferable to that which you are about to experience in this quaint and defenseless city!"

Ben stared as the shadowy figure of his mother's body and the angry animal heads simply dwindled from view, like the tiny light left when a television set has been turned off.

13

"I don't think I can stay here another minute," Laura said flatly and shuddered. She had nearly fainted and was sitting on the couch where Ben and Martin Ruben had helped her. She glanced at the suddenly qurescent office she once had liked, envied. Now, it had become a Hollywood prop—a false front behind which monsters lurked. Her gaze focused warily on the Edison machine, which continued to thrum steadily. She tensed her leg muscles to rise and found them still rubbery.

"Well, it'll never be the same here again," Ben said in agreement, shaking his head and running a hand along the books on his shelf. They had become his old friends again, but he viewed them with distrust and turned quickly away from them. "I'll have to move, won't I?"

Martin Ruben smiled privately. He knew this kind of mild reaction well, this talk of the commonplace and concern for the ordinary following immediately on the heels of a bad shock. They would be okay. "If we are to confine Demiurge to your office," he said, "it will be necessary for you to keep this building permanently but to locate other working quarters. What we face, the three of us, is the task of guarding this office for the rest of our lives—eventually acquiring confidantes who will carry on when we are gone."

"I don't want to make this hellish place a goddamn shrine," Ben snarled, sitting beside Laura on the couch and taking her hand. "Are you all right now?"

She nodded. "Physically, I feel surprisingly good. Lord, I've never fainted in my whole life." Carefully, she tried again to stand, tested her balance and found it fine. Her head was crystal clear. "You did something fantastic to me, Martin, didn't you?" She turned to him in gratitude.

"Tut, tut!" He smiled. "It was merely a minor Yoga principle I invoked. But your near fainting spell should actually have brought you a measure of rest and lowered your blood pressure, if I did it properly."

"There's nothing minor about it," she exclaimed, squeezing his hand. "It's positively a miracle, after all that's happened."

"Commonplace. But perhaps I shouldn't explain my methods. *'Omne ignotim pro magnifico,'* and all that." He glanced at Ben and took Laura's arm. "Come, I think we'd best remove ourselves to more, um, suitable circumstances to discuss this further. You may have noticed that I made certain cryptic references to that fiend. I presume you're curious."

Ben started after them and then paused at his desk. "Yes, we'd like to know a great deal more about your allusions to Demiurge. Apparently my original assumption that we were literally dealing with Satan was wrong."

"Primarily in name and the duties of his dubious occupation," Ruben answered, watching Ben make sure the ancient apparatus was effectively running. "I suggest you lock this door tightly after us. Not, of course, to keep the presence *in*—but to keep outsiders *out*."

It was deep night when they climbed into Ruben's old Chrysler; stars were faintly peeking from medium cloud cover. Laura glanced back at Ben's darkened office, shivering. She was glad when he draped an affectionate arm around her shoulders.

"Your place or mine, as the saying goes?" asked Ruben, mustering a smile.

"Mine, if you don't mind," Ben replied. "That way you won't have to rouse yourself from your own apartment to take us home."

As the Chrysler grudgingly pulled away from the curb, Laura looked back at the office with an expression of wonderment. "I have the distinct feeling that, a day or a week from now, I'll look back on this awful evening and believe it was all a nightmare. God help me, I hope so."

"We have seen something that few mortals have witnessed and survived," the parapsychologist remarked. "More than a handful of people might have gone mad on the spot."

Ben hadn't spoken for some time. Now he stared straight out the window without turning to them. "I have a confession to make," he said softly. "Down deep inside I rather wanted to prove that there were such things as spectral forms, discarnate entities—so that my mother wouldn't seem to have been quite so bereft of her senses. On an intellectual level, of course, I never imagined that God *or* His adversaries existed in fact."

"My dear fellow," said Ruben, making a left turn, "life is infinitely stranger than anything the mind of man could invent. We would not dare to conceive the things which are mere commonplaces of existence. If we could but fly from the window, hand in hand, hover over this city, gently remove the roofs and peer in at the queer things which are going on, the strange coincidences, the plannings and cross-purposes, the wonderful chain of events, working through generations and leading to the most *outre* results, it would make all fiction with its conventionalities and foreseen conclusions most stale and unprofitable."

"You put it eloquently," Laura said admiringly.

"Alas, I only paraphrase Sherlock Holmes in *A Case of Identity*," Ruben said with a quick laugh. Surprised, they turned and joined him in laughter.

Ben lived alone in his apartment on the far east side of Indianapolis, just off 38th Street but past Mitthoefer Road. It was far enough from the mainstream of city life to deter all but the most sincere friends, which was what the shy publisher had in mind when he moved there. It was also far from being a luxury complex, but Ben had made a friend of Joe Pelholter, the affable young maintenance man; whenever interesting things were left behind in other apartments by departing tenants—

things that would normally be claimed by apartment management—muscular young Joe obligingly lugged them to Ben's place.

As a consequence, Ruben was surprised to see the welter of furniture, lamps, cassette equipment and several TV sets stuffing his friend's apartment. At a glance, he mused, it looked more like a small warehouse than a home. Since his own place was typically Bachelor Modern Mess, he said nothing about it. "What do you do for entertainment this far from civilization," he asked instead, "count couches?"

"John Marshall High School is only a couple of blocks away," Ben replied with a grin. "I used to see lots of basketball and football. Or *did* before Miss Hawks interfered with my scheme of things."

Laura, who had spent the previous two nights here in Ben's arms, made a face at him. She slipped into one of several plump chairs and dangled her long, silken legs over the side. Reaction was setting in despite Ruben's instructions, and she felt exhausted. For his part, the parapsychologist stretched out on a couch—there were three, all apparently new—and was falling asleep when Ben returned with two cups of coffee.

Ruben didn't open his eyes. "where's mine?" he demanded.

"Up to your old deductions again," Ben remarked, grinning. "I put tea on, knowing how much you like it iced."

"Heaven will reward you for your Christian charity, my good fellow," Ruben said loftily, looking contented and a mile long sprawled on the couch. He tugged at his tie, loosening it, and sighed.

"Speaking of heaven," Laura began, sipping her coffee, "reminds me of why we're here. That apparition."

"That," observed Ruben, raising one critical eyelid, "is like Bill Walton, Moses Malone or Larry Bird reminding you of Mickey Rooney."

"Come on, Martin," Ben prompted, anxious for knowledge, "give!"

With a sigh, Ruben forced himself erect and lifted an index finger. "I shall withhold my commentary on Demiurge for a moment. Which is to say, until you bring me my iced tea. Tell me: what did you think of his little alternating-animal-face show? Did you enjoy the presentation or feel it was a trifle gauche?"

Laura made a face. "They were ghastly."

"Not, however, unusual." They stared at Ruben in surprise. "Throughout history, you see, people who believe in the human soul and a hereafter—which is most of our species, I'm pleased to remark—have periodically seen the soul represented as a bird or an animal. As Sir James Frazier said in his famed *Golden Bough*, 'If a man lives and moves, it can only be because he has a little man or animal inside who moves him.' Often, the archetypes discussed by Jung—you remember him?—took an animal form since historic man generally endowed everything with a soul, even trees and flowers."

"I think my research mentioned something about savages, too," Laura put in.

"Yes. Among certain tribes who dive into water or pass through a cleft tree in order to divert a possible haunting, the ghost of a human being often assumed the form of a beast, bird or fish. Such animal spirits are common among the Indians of both North and South America, and some African tribes still think that dead evildoers become jackals."

"That's precisely the kind of mumbo-jumbo that's always turned me against most aspects of the supernatural," Ben muttered. "Let me get your iced tea for you."

Ruben watched him head for the kitchen, then glanced at Laura with a raised brow. "Do you think I should tell Benjamin that we close the eyes of the dead because our ancestors feared their souls might escape through the open eyes?"

"I don't think I'd tell him that," Laura replied with a light chuckle. Ruben's wit was disconcerting now.

"In that case," Ruben continued as Ben returned with the glass of tea and a bucket of glistening ice cubes, "I shall be more pertinent. I shall instruct you both about . . . *expersonation.*"

"That one's new to me," Ben admitted, slipping to the floor at Laura's feet and retrieving his coffee cup. "Expersonation?"

"Good Lord, man! You never read the *Egyptian Book of the Dead?* Aleister Crowley or Alexandra David-Neal?" Ruben arched his neck to stare at Ben in mock astonishment. "Not even Oesterreich or Waite? What about *Demonality, or Incubi and Succubi* by Sinistrari?" Now he clucked his tongue in good-humored derision. "My, what sheltered lives you've led!"

Ben blinked guiltily into his coffee cup. "I'd have been secretly terrified just to open up one of those books."

"Martin, what the hell is expersonation?" Laura demanded.

"How hasty we are all at once to gather the harvest of information!" The lean parapsychologist fixed his keen gaze on a corner of the ceiling and began his lecture. "In the broader sense, expersonation involves transferring one's astral double to the body of another person."

"Astral travel," Ben groaned, hiding his face in his hands.

"*Or,* since you don't care for that," Ruben went on quickly, "expersonation may pertain merely to the intentional direction of one *soul* to the body of another. A form of possession, you see. Its roots may be traced to China, Tibet, India—also to Greece and Egypt. It's quite well documented." He shut his eyes and folded his hands with a small, superior smirk. "In voodoo, certain rites enable a person temporarily to occupy the body of an animal. (Note, please, that I did not split the infinitive.) And Hindu legends have it that *rishis* can assume animal form as well."

"But what we seem to have here," Ben argued, struggling with unfamiliar concepts that left him ambivalently frightened and annoyed, "is a human soul occupying another human's body. That is, where the ghosts themselves are concerned. A *dead* human soul."

"That," Laura observed with a smile, "is a contradiction in terms."

"Well, you know what I mean!" Ben exclaimed. "If I understand your—your Demiurge correctly, his entities are souls of the dead that somehow have been enabled to occupy human bodies at the moment of birth."

"Wonderful, my dear Kellogg!" Ruben applauded sardonically. "You never fail to amaze me with your grasp of the facts."

Ben frowned. "*Do* I understand all that correctly?" he pressed.

Ruben sobered and nodded. Then he sat forward to take a long draught of his iced tea. "You do, Ben. In Tibet they might have called it 'overshadowing'—a superior *literally* taking over for an inferior, or apprentice. And also in the east it's said that black shamans practice expersonation through necromantic rites involving the *reanimation* of the dead."

"Isn't it rather hard to—to dispossess a soul from an adult's body?" Laura puzzled, feeling chills in her spine again.

"That's true. But Demiurge," Ruben said with a tone of revulsion, "has managed for his spirits to do it at the *moment of birth*—when the soul either is quite weak or hasn't quite entered the body yet. In my conjecture, this practice is closest to the kabbalistic practice of Zohar—but that's another jolly little nightmare." He clapped his hands together. "The fact remains that 'expersonation' is the primary term involved and that a monstrous force has, indeed, brought untold agonies of evil to mankind for more than three decades."

Ben, leaning against Laura's smooth leg, glanced toward a sudden motion at the window of his apartment. But it was merely a tree branch scraping against the pane, and he took a long breath to steady his nerves.

"You were going to tell us why you addressed that—that thing as Demiurge," Ben said at last. "You have your iced tea; so perform."

Laura nudged him in rebuke. "I've never heard the word, either."

Ruben showed them a nearly fatherly, benign expression. "I was only teasing you before," he confessed. "There is no reason why most people raised in a Christian or a Jewish environment should know of such grim forces that lurk beneath a world that commonly appears routine and normal. I want to inject a comment along that line before continuing: If either of you attempts to explain what's happening in your office, you will seem mad, commitable." He hesitated, and a chill breeze seemed to pass through the room. "We are, my friends, *alone* in this."

"In *what?*" Ben pressed. "*What is Demiurge?*"

"There's not a great deal left of Gnosticism these days," said Ruben, "which is probably a pity. There are numerous scholars who insist that Jesus Christ was himself a Gnostic or, at any rate, that he studied as a child in one of the numerous Gnostic sects. Try to understand that while we are dealing with something unfamiliar to you, two thousand years is *not* long in the memory of God, and that Gnosticism was once—let us say—as popular as Episcopalianism. It was not at any time antagonistic toward Christianity, although it was used as a basis for the Hebrew kabbalah—in which my own forebears once faithfully believed." He hesitated before charging ahead with his revelation. "Be that as it may, all Gnostic followers believed that the world was *not created by God.*"

Laura's lips parted in amazement. "How could they believe that during such a religious period?"

"Possibly by the evidence of their own senses," replied Ruben, cocking an eye at her. "Life in those times was very cruel. For most people, it was a challenge to survive a day. Gnostics felt that the Almighty was utterly detached from everything we consider as human existence. God—or the 'Abyss,' to use one of His Gnostic names—dwelt in the realm of the Pleroma, or mystical Plentitude, and would never have done anything as grievous as to create a world of intelligent beings who were doomed to suffer!"

"It does answer certain modern agnostic arguments," Ben observed.

"For such an Almighty, our world would be a distortion of Time, an actual injustice to his creatures. Earth, in short, would be a sadistic *unkindness* for the Abyss, or God."

"But if that were true," Laura inquired, "then —*who* made the world?"

"According to Gnostics," Ruben explained, "an arrogant, demonic fool, divine but stupid enough to be evil. Their faith identified wrongdoing with ignorance; it said a brilliant man *could not do* evil. Yet the creator they envision was brilliant enough to build a world he could dominate—that he could operate in a quixotic fashion—quixotic and chaotic—doing what he pleased to man, arbitrarily, without rhyme or reason." Ruben paused to listen momentarily to the wind stirring at the apartment window. "His name, Ben and Laura, was— Demiurge!"

Ben Kellogg scrambled to his feet. He stared

down at his friend Ruben, his bearded face pale. "Martin, it sounds—heretical!"

"*This*," murmured Ruben, "from the fellow who disbelieved the existence of Paradise?"

"But where, then, is the *true* God?" Laura demanded, leaning forward. "Where is *our* God?"

Ruben pursed his lips. "In the Divine Light of Truth. In Knowledge, according to the Gnostic teachings. Man lives in a dreadful earthen prison created by a fallen deity called Demiurge, who does not even accept the fact that he is an archon and not the God whom you mean when you use the term. And in this, as you have seen, Demiurge is absolute evil." Ruben frowned, angry at the monstrous entity they had confined in Ben's office. "He intends that man remain ignorant, disinclined to question or to think for himself—to appraise and draw sensible conclusions. He wants man to worship false 'isms,' to worship mere things, knowing that when this occurs, man is, in fact, worshipping Demiurge himself."

"How do we reach God, then?" Ben asked, surprised to realize he was awed, and whispering.

"Gnosticism teaches that the God whom we all seek is accessible only by free thought, rich imagination; reason, logic and truth; by *creativity*—by the rays of internal light man may bring to this prison world. Contrary to certain old-fashioned tenets of Christianity, knowledge did not create man's fall from grace—but it can be his *salvation* one day!"

It was quiet in the apartment as Ben and Laura thought it through. At last Ben asked, "What does the word *gnostic* mean, Martin?"

"Its derivation?" Ruben qualified. He smiled. "Knowledge, pure knowledge."

Laura had reached a depth of insight and looked at Ruben with near anger, incredulous at what she had discovered in her train of thought. "Are you really saying that when we confront that mad killer behind his tricks of illusion, we're actually speaking to the—the force that created the *universe?*"

Martin Ruben paused to consider Laura's psychological makeup before proceeding. He liked this young woman, liked her enormously. He did not care to offend her or give her data that she could not handle. When he spoke again, it was with an averted gaze and an attempt to smile.

"I fear that I make the mistake of all scholars," he sighed. "My work permits me time to read and study. Other people are obliged to work for a living. Laura, I cannot claim to have the answer to such a fundamental question. But creation occurred not hundreds or thousands of years ago, but *billions* of years ago. Why, my friends, we don't even know with certainty *how old* this little planet is! Creation was before Cro-Magnon and Neanderthal man, before the dinosaurs or the Ice Age. It was when time itself was born—*true* time—and, well, I doubt that Demiurge himself remembers the truth." Ruben scratched his brow. "After all, he is the prince of distortion. And those who distort the truth are themselves distorted entities."

Ruben looked lovingly at Laura and Ben. "I do know that Demiurge is—from the way we look at things—all evil, and that we can be victorious over him only by dispelling his bewildering, crucifying lies and somehow seeing the light of the genuine God's truth and knowledge."

For a time Ben studied his hands, and Laura did not immediately realize that they were trembling slightly. "Are you sure we're wise to contain such an incredible force?" Ben asked finally, the light of wonder in his eyes. "Jesus, Martin, we're just ordinary people! The discarnate spirits haunting Ridge Avenue were themselves more than mortal man could deal with! I'm simply not conceited enough to feel qualified for a task like this."

"Nor I," Laura confessed.

Ruben rose from his chair. His jaw was set inflexibly in determination. "For the moment I am afraid that just the task you describe is in our hands—exclusively." He did not add that he'd begged Ben not to use the Edison device. "We can only do the best we can and pray for guidance. And now I think it's time for old Uncle Martin to totter homeward. I suggest we sleep on this overnight."

Embracing one another for comfort, Ben and Laura saw their tall friend to the front door of the apartment. There, Ruben paused, turning to peer down at Laura with tenderness.

"May I give you a ride home?" he inquired.

Laura reddened but met his gaze evenly. "Thank you, I'll be—leaving *later,* I think."

Briefly, Ruben nodded and gazed at her with something like longing. Ben, watching his old friend attentively, saw a loneliness in him that he'd never suspected before. His heart went out to Ruben.

Then the parapsychologist mustered an easy, affable expression and put out his hand to Ben.

"It's quite possible that you'll wish to phone me tomorrow morning, my dear Kellogg," he observed. "If I am correct, the newspapers are going to surprise you."

Before the startled publisher could ask him what he meant by that, Ruben had taken three steps down the apartment hallway, where he stopped, a tall, dark figure draped in shadows. He looked back at them and, with a voice that sounded both weary and sad, said, "Use my little helpful hints whilst you can, good chums. I can't guarantee how much longer they'll be available."

Then he descended the steps leading to the ground floor. Ben and Laura heard the downstairs door open and shush to a close behind their friend and gave each other a questioning glance. He took her hand and led her, after a pause toward his bedroom.

They made love with something approaching a feverish need to expel their memories of horror. Afterward, Ben turned on his side to Laura and held her face between gentle hands.

"I've never been known for particularly timely or tactful remarks," he began slowly, her love-roughened lips still only inches away, "but some people know me for my sincerity."

"For that and many other things," she replied tenderly, then could not resist adding, "including a tendency toward making speeches."

"Be serious, will you?" Ben complained mildly. He cleared his throat. "I'm fully aware that I'm really too old for you, but I still feel that I must ask . . ."

Laura smiled happily and slid her arms around

his neck. "Yes, oh, *yes!*" she cried almost tearfully into his ear.

"Gee, you don't need to get *that* enthusiastic about retyping the first section of your book!"

Laura pulled away from him and punched his arm as hard as she could.

Ben chuckled and drew her down beside him. "I do love you," he said softly. "So much."

Together, they made the worst of the memories fade in the flow of hope for their personal futures.

Ben and Laura found they shared the habit of reading a newspaper each morning before doing anything else—apart from guzzling coffee.

On Tuesday morning, they propped themselves luxuriously up in bed, sipped steaming Hill Brothers, and Laura was smiling with domestic fondness at Ben when he began reading the front page of the *Star*—

And, slopping coffee onto the other sections of the morning paper, his arms spasmed and he cried, "Good Lord! Laura—the damndest thing has happened!"

"Something terrible?" She wriggled nearer, moving the sopping sports section aside.

Ben's eyes met hers. "That's impossible to say."

Laura drew the front section from Ben's shaky fingers, read the headlines with the feeling that the world had turned upside down overnight. And she wondered why neither of them was able to welcome the news.

While they'd slept, throughout metropolitan Indianapolis and all of Marion County, there's been *no crimes reported*—and presumably, none *committed.*

"Police psychologists are trying to learn the reason behind the sudden absence of violent and illegal acts," one story read. "A period in excess of twelve hours without a single arrest or hint of reported crime anywhere in a large American county seems to be a record unequaled in modern times."

"There were a few arrests for speeding," Ben said grumblingly, "if you read more closely."

She raised her knees from the bed and spread the newspaper across them. "Honey, this is *wonderful!* No crime . . . and it must have something to do with the Edison apparatus!"

"The *apparition* is committed to evil," Ben snapped.

"But what else could have happened in town to—?"

"I follow your reasoning. But why the hell would Demiurge want the laws obeyed?" He poked at a portion of the *Star*. "Peacock, the minister for Mother's funeral, is one of the clergy they interviewed. While he says we should be grateful to God for the blessing of even one night free of man's inhumanity to man, he cautions people against believing that we've all repented overnight." He frowned thoughtfully. "It reminds me, you know, of an old science fiction yarn I read once. In it—I think Fred Brown wrote it—some typesetter is first to notice that they have nothing for the obituary pages from anywhere in the world. At least, so far, it's just Indy."

"But that's *awful* for you to say!" Laura

exclaimed. She'd dialed Ruben and told him, then, who was calling. "You're just upset because it isn't natural. Here; talk to Martin."

"I wondered, when you two would rise and read the newspapers," Ruben said promptly.

"How do you explain it?" Ben asked his friend. He paused. "Could I be right in what I'm wondering?"

"Demiurge? Of course." Ruben replied amazingly. "Isn't it obvious?"

"Not to me," Ben admitted. Laura snuggled closer to try to share the phone and their friend's insight.

"Benjamin, I *predicted* you would call me after reading the *Star*! That damned apparatus has, indeed, removed evil from men and women."

But that's not a terrible thing to do," Ben argued.

"But it *is*. Because, Kellogg, all evil in this city and county has been *gathered in one place*—your office! Just as much of it was confined before Thomas Edison experimented with the device. Our view of the normal world has changed, but the world—this part of it, at least—is simply back to where it was."

"Then—if we can *keep* Demiurge trapped—evil can't plague mankind again!" Ben declared, excited.

"Perhaps . . ."

"We must trap it—them—forever," Ben argued. And Laura, at his shoulder, added, "Let's *bury* the apparatus—bury it deep in the ground for good!"

"It might," Ruben said, "work. And it's interesting symbolism, is it not—humankind's worst qualities buried in six feet of earth like a common corpse?"

"What's wrong?" Ben asked him. "Why aren't you *pleased*, man?"

"I do not believe we should leap to conclusions." Ruben's voice trailed off, left something hanging.

"Once they're buried, what could go wrong?"

Ruben didn't answer at once. Then he sighed. "Use your wits, Benjamin. Ask yourself what Demiurge proposes to *do* in order to force us to release him and his spirits? He swore he would act, convince us—remember?" Ruben's tones were tight with caution. "I beg of you both not to underestimate a power so dark, so rooted in time. We must be exceedingly alert. We must ask ourselves what illusory thought forms Demiurge means to conjure that are so fiendishly inventive and persuasive that we—*any* of us!—could conceivably rush to your office to release him! We *must* be prepared."

Wordlessly, Ben gave the phone to Laura who whispered, "Bye," and replaced it in its cradle. The potential for joy had been destroyed by their friend's cool reason; he'd left them with further challenges.

For some time, they sat among the strewn papers in the bed like bad puppies, occasionally staring at the silent phone with apprehension. They could not even communicate their fears to each other.

"What next?" Ben asked at last, sighing. "What next?"

Four

WHISPER OF WIND: DEPARTURE FROM EDEN

The story of Eden is a greater allegory than man has ever guessed. . . . Time and darkness, knowledge of good and evil, have walked with him ever since . . . For the first time in four billion years a living creature had contemplated himself and heard with a sudden, unaccountable loneliness, the whisper of the wind in the night reeds.

Loren Eiseley, *The Immense Journey*

Psi phenomena seem to threaten the basic concepts of the universe . . . of modern individuals. We live in a perceived world of law and order, of sequential cause and effect—a world in which space and time are limiting factors . . . What then if these basic laws . . . are threatened? What if we are faced with apparent evidence that they may be illusions . . . ?

>   Lawrence LeShan, *The Medium, the Mystic, and the Physicist*

Time is a counterfeit substitute of eternity. The Demiurge created . . . six archons to help him with creation . . . However, there is a spark of hope. Something in man rejects this false world, and longs for its true home . . . Man, then, finds himself in a prison; but . . . he has a chance of escape through knowledge.

>   Colin Wilson, *The Occult*

14

Laura went home to Lawrence Tuesday afternoon, planning to bring her project notes up to date and to begin devising some sort of outline. Ben had agreed with her that the Ridge Avenue murders and hauntings, coupled with what was happening now in Indianapolis, made it necessary to alter the book's format. There'd be an introduction by Ruben on the topic of man's religious attachment to the spirit world and what this portended, psychologically as well as parapsychologically. There'd be a foreword by Laura, sketching in some of the background history of discarnate entities. The main portion of the book would then cover only the terrible events in and arising from the Pittsburgh mansion. Both Laura and Ben felt that there was no way that such an incredible tale should be a mere portion of a collection detailing haunted-house reports.

As a publisher Ben was stimulated by the fact that, at this frightening moment, they had no clear idea how the book would end. Presumably it would involve Demiurge either succeeding or failing in his effort to make Ben turn off the machine.

Another devastating slice of news that became a piece in the puzzle was the death of his brother during the ride back to the mortuary. Despite his feelings about Willard, Ben was stunned when he was notified of the awful crash.

In Ben's mind there was no doubt that the death was intentional, that it was the work, somehow, of 1129's mad sprites. Even the police admitted they had no idea why the hearse had gone out of control. They were operating on the assumption, until the autopsy was completed, that Fred McThiele had suffered a stroke, Willard's autopsy indicated that he'd died of massive heart failure; Ben's interpretation was that he had died of fright. For a moment, in Ben's emotional reaction to the tragic news, he had nearly blurted out his conviction that Willard's loss was supernaturally induced. Then he got control of himself, realizing that no doggedly realistic cop could ever accept such a theory.

He was surprised, too, by how grieved he felt about Willard. When he was driven to the morgue to identify the body, it was almost as if a key part of himself had been amputated. Within a week, both his mother and his only brother had died. With bitter tears in his eyes, Ben swore to himself that they would be properly avenged. The only thing he was spared was the burial of Willard, whose home was in San Diego. Ben made arrangements to have the body sent there and then returned to his apartment, where, for the first time in years, he took out his Bible and opened it at random.

His eyes fell on a segment of Revelation: "And I saw three unclean spirits like frogs come out of the mouth of the dragon, and out of the mouth of the beast, and out of the mouth of the false prophet." Dragon, beast, false prophet—Ben shivered, thinking of Demiurge. He read further: "For they are the spirits of devils, working miracles. . . ."

Early Wednesday morning, the sun sulked beyond the bedroom windows, husbanding its treasure for itself. Sallow light splashed on the carpeted floor and seemed to dull the pattern. Ben hadn't slept well, not only because of his sadness for Willard but because he missed having Laura beside him. It wasn't just that her newly released sexuality and his own brought pleasures that delighted both of them—he missed seeing her ash-blond hair spread on the pillow, feeling her warm breath against his shoulder, enjoying the way she curled up against his narrow back.

The possibility that Laura could be in serious danger because of the apparatus and what it meant troubled Ben enormously as he turned on his side, uneager to face the new day. He wanted badly to send her away, out of this entire mess, but how that could be done he didn't know. He'd seen intimations of her stubbornness; besides, he didn't want to be guilty of male chauvinism by implying that, while he was qualified to handle the situation, Laura was not.

He was still lying in bed, with his face to the wall, when he felt the subtle change in the atmosphere of his bedroom. It was drafty, chilly. His senses were instantly alert, but he stayed in the same position, wary of moving. His nose told him there was a new odor present, something subtle, not unpleasant. But it didn't *belong* there. The short hairs at the back of his neck twitched; his scrotum tightened with anxiety. He listened intently for the warning sound of shuffling footsteps, but heard nothing.

Still, there was someone else in the room; he knew it for a fact.

Or maybe it was *something* else.

His muscles tensed; his beard itched. He waited, holding his breath—and nearly died when he felt the cold hand spreading fingers on the back of his neck.

Ben turned, the covers twisting, catching around his legs. He sat up in bed, heart pounding, staring in terror.

This was not his room. It was not even a bedroom, but a living room, perhaps that of an apartment. He turned his head from left to right, disbelieving. Had he been transported, somehow? Everything here was hazy, half-formed, distorted by shadows that were cast by no visible objects. What he could identify clearly appeared feminine in touch and style, not in the least frightening, but totally alien, unfamiliar.

God, where *was* he?

She took shape slowly, never completely. Her dark body was clothed in a flowing white gown and seemed to be drifting toward him effortlessly, as if the feet were not moving. Straight, dark hair reached her shoulders. As she drew closer, Ben caught the scent again—the fragrance of her.

Carola Glenn?

"Carola?" he asked, his voice scarcely audible. He cleared his throat. "Carola, is that you?"

She did not answer, and Ben thought wildly, *This is ridiculous—absurd. Carola may be very ill, but she isn't dead! What is she doing here? Or what am I doing here?*

When the apparition was within perhaps ten feet of him, her motion ceased. He saw that the full-length gown ended several inches above the floor. Her feet did not reach it. And he saw that portions of her head and body shifted constantly, in and out of focus, testifying to her insubstantiality. But there *was* a constant: where Carola's rounded bosom should have been, there was only a dazzling white light. And when she turned a bit more, aware of him and facing him, he could see through the area of her heart to the unfamiliar room on the other side of her.

"*Danger.*" Whether she actually spoke the word or communicated it by other means Ben could not tell. Her muzzy, sweet eyes held his. "You are in great danger, Ben."

"How do you know?" he whispered, finding his voice with difficulty.

"I know a great deal more—now." Her smile was open and sad. "You are a good and decent man, boss. But they will ask you to turn off the apparatus, and you must be strong. *You must not* do it."

He was again surprised. How could she know of this? "I won't," he pledged. "I've never intended to shut it down."

"Not now, perhaps, but you may think of it. You will want to." She was closer now, and he saw the glittering tears beneath her faraway eyes. How was it that those shining dewdrops of sadness appeared more alive than anything else about her? What unspoken unhappiness or sense of loss troubled her so? "It will cost you a loved one if you turn it off, Ben. And it will—*hurt* people— everywhere. *Very* much." She paused. "*Remember.*"

Time—what had happened to time? It seemed not to be functioning, to be strangely suspended; there was no sense of the passing of seconds, and Ben felt part of a mystic tableau, adrift in space. "I won't, Carola. I won't turn it off," he promised. Then, quietly, he lifted his palm to her cheek, to touch and wipe away the tears that caressed it.

There was the sound of a kiss as her lips met his fingers. He felt only a shiver of something very cool, something very distant—untouchable, alien.

And then she was gone.

Ben's bedroom, instantly, was restored; there was no perceptible transition. He found himself squatting in the middle of his own bed, with his arm raised—to nothing whatever.

The seconds and the sense of them began to flow once more, and Ben stayed where he was a while longer. He tried hard to understand and was surprised that he could not, for a moment, think it had been a dream. An hour later, when the staff doctor phoned from the hospital, he learned that Carola Glenn had died of cardiac arrest during the night.

Laura rose early on Wednesday morning and fixed herself a mug of coffee. Her appetite was gone; she could not remember ever being hungry. She strove not to think about how she missed being with Ben Kellogg. Was it really possible, at the age of thirty, to fall in love with the intensity of a teenager?

Well, maybe not everyone could, she decided happily, but *I* have! Ben's combination of modesty, candor, shyness, ambition, solicitousness, imagination, fear and courage touched some note in her private heart that reverberated with the same need she'd felt for writing. Laura was modern enough to doubt that Ben would ever permanently replace her aspirations for literary achievement and sensible enough to doubt that he should. But, for now, thinking of him kept the terror of 1129 Ridge Avenue at bay.

Until, that is, she drew out her notes and began reviewing them. Everything about the case was simply terrifying, to the extent that her ongoing terror outweighed any consideration of how unlikely it all seemed. It was as if the event at the turn of the century and in the twenties had merged with present developments without any recognition of passing time. To Demiurge and his haunting spirits of evil, it obviously did not matter when they became free to distort and maim, just so long as they *were* free. Whether this meant that time itself was a fiction she could not possibly determine.

At last she began writing, trying to make a start on her foreword. She worked in longhand, her script flowing, curved, moved by impulse to the point that it was a scrawl only Laura could read. Often, she knew, it was possible to make progress better by using a pen at the beginning; then once it was going fluently, she could switch to the swifter typewriter without a break in the continuity of her thoughts.

She reached unconsciously for a tissue from the nearby blue box. Odd. It hadn't felt hot in here at the dining room table when she began. Yet she was breaking out in perspiration, a few drops of sweat dripping on her notebook and making the light-blue lines waver. When she looked up and away from the notes, she felt strangely dazed, not quite herself.

Nigel, her dog, turned his adoring gaze on her, but then quickly turned and padded toward the distant stairway. His huge head was down as if she had shouted at him, frightened him. Laura heard his footsteps as he ascended the steps with uncommon slowness and disappeared. Then there was silence.

She shook her head and again patted her forehead with a tissue. Determined to shake off the mood and make progress, she hurled herself deeper into her efforts.

Now it was easier, she found, at least in the sense of simply putting words on paper. But she had the sensation of floating, even when she looked down and saw that her feet were very much on the floor, the table before her as solid as ever. It was a little like the particularly hard days at college when, exhausted from study and unable to get untracked, she would dimly hear what the instructor was saying. At those rare times, her hand wrote the notes down for her, her mind seemingly disengaged. Returning later to the sorority house, she usually had no idea what those illegible words meant.

She kept working away....

Then Mrs. Hawks was shaking her shoulder, rousing her from sleep. Laura looked up, startled, far more afraid than she should have been. She became embarrassed, laughing with her mother in the way that people do when they have been afraid for no logical reason.

That's when her gaze drifted back to her notes. Only they *weren't* her notes. There was no way they could have been written by her. The handwriting was precise, old-fashioned and crabbed. None of Laura's freeflowing curlicues ornamented a single word.

She stared in growing wonderment; fright began to trickle along her veins, fright born of a confrontation with the unknown. Someone—something strange had used her to write these words. An invader must have entered her mind, taken over her body, commanding her limbs to move, her fingers to grip the pen and write this utterly legible warning:

"My child," it read. "No one can gauge the dimensions of this evil or its power. By a fortuitous chance you have captured it and believe that you now control it. This will be true only by making a great sacrifice and living with many lives upon your innocent conscience. I tell you these things to warn you and because, even now, in another state, I cannot forget my exposure to its ultimate ugliness. Laura, you and your friends must make the sacrifice and let few die that many may live. One of you must, as well, make a more personal sacrifice. Do not turn off the apparatus whatever occurs. Human life depends upon it. I beg of you, do not turn it off."

There was a signature. Laura looked down at it but had to place the notebook on the table, out of her violently trembling hands, to read it.

The message was signed, simply, *Your loving Aunt Julia.*

Wednesday afternoon.

Agnes Brodhugh, at the age of fifty-one, had been a grade school teacher so long that all her early memories, of a neighbor from childhood or a cheery uncle who'd died when she was six, were the property of a girl dimly recalled. Even the memories of her husband, Earl, were smoothly filed away in another mental cabinet that belonged, for all the world, to another woman—yet Earl had died less than two years ago.

There are those women about whom it may safely be said that they dwell too much in the past and who invite senility with every dredged-up memory of Daddy or the senior prom. But there are other women, less advertised for their judgmental mistakes, who dismiss each passing day as something containing nothing of value. Today is all that counts. They dwell in the specific moment, finding—in the sterile safety that exists because *they* still exist—nothing moving or instructive or amusing or tender about yesterday. Today *is*; they *are*.

Such creatures of routine learn little from mistakes, because even success is forgotten, unnecessary. All that is recalled tends to be the product of an off-balance shock: a sudden rumor whispered in their ears, a scanned newspaper article with many false conclusions drawn, an acceptance of the word found in a gothic or cheap romance. Such women are the creatures of hastily formed innuendo and bigotry, but they always "mean well."

Agnes hurried home from school, her plump arms laden with papers to be graded, her mind full of apprehension because, she'd heard on TV, an old woman had been beaten two blocks away just the other night. It irritated her that Joe was too busy with his college tests at Badler University to come and walk her home for a mere few days. Just until they caught that monster. What was being a mother all about if it wasn't for rearing a boy to look after her when everyone else had deserted her? Agnes wasn't so much afraid as cautious just now, and she was irked at Joe. Both emotions caused her to accelerate her pace as she reached the last block, the one that concerned her the most.

After all, foreigners had moved into the neighborhood, in droves, over the past year—and everybody knew what they were like. Not that Agnes was prejudiced, she'd tell you, but foreigners all had the same swarthy skin and dark eyes and black, greasy hair that the rapists had (as if rapists had an association and needed to pass some kind of physical resemblance test) and it just made good sense to be careful. They weren't like her son, Joe, with his light-brown, straight hair and fair complexion, a real all-American boy—even if he *did* put his studies ahead of the good woman who'd seen him through measles and chicken pox and acne and all the bad girls who'd sought to despoil him since he turned sixteen.

Her mind was a turmoil of such notions by the time she drew within fifty yards of the apartment building. A small, pretty dark-haired woman with prominent brown eyes and the impressive dignity of a General Motors president, she did not know that few people, including rapists, even dared to contradict her. She could not gauge the incredible degree to which she had become a prototypical old school teacher.

Eyes. Someone, Agnes knew, was staring at her, following her. The knowledge was so severe and uncontradictable that it solidified at once as dogma in her mind, right along with what she thought she knew about foreigners and rapists. The concept that someone was watching her every move and plotting terrible things, the nature of which totally escaped her rather naive mentality, was a fact at that instant, the same as the multiplication tables she'd taught for nearly thirty years.

But she did not let the eyes make her turn, nor did she slow down a step. Lying in bed at night with cramps or worries about Joe, even when Earl was still alive, Agnes had prepared for just such a moment as this. She knew precisely what needed to be done. And, with that kind of knowledge, any teacher *acts*.

Listening acutely for the sound of nearing footsteps, Agnes walked just a bit faster, reached her apartment building with a relief she couldn't even confess to herself and pushed through the front doors with the single-mindedness of Randy McMillan going through the line or Tony Robinson making a pass for an I.U. basket. She was pushing the elevator button before she even realized she was there, and when the doors closed safely in front of her, she felt a sense of release. But instead of tears rushing to her eyes, Agnes thought grimly, They'll have to get up early in the morning to get Agnes Brodhugh!

Yet when she stepped out on the third floor and bustled down the corridor toward her apartment, Agnes felt the eyes again, and they nearly gave her a heart attack. Once more they were in factual existence; she knew it. When she was ten feet from her apartment door, Agnes let the grade school papers in her arms drop, reached in her purse for the key and ran the rest of the way to the door. By some unerring instinct she had the key crammed into the lock on the first darting motion; it turned, the door opened, and she was inside, slamming and bolting the door, then leaning against it, her ample bosom heaving with terror and relief.

Half a minute later Agnes was telling herself that she had been foolish and that she should go back out into the hallway, pick up all the papers and mark them. That, after all, was what a teacher did.

She had just convinced herself to do that, when there came a knock at the door.

Now there were no eyes, because everybody knew that eyes could not see through doors. There was, instead, a different knowing, a knowing that the man who stood outside her door, knocking, was not only a foreigner—which was bad enough to think about, at *her* front door—but also a *rapist pervert!*

Exactly what such monsters did, Agnes had no more idea than a child in her fourth grade math class, but she knew it was unspeakable. With a simple rapist, you might be injured, even killed, but a handful of people would be sorry it had happened. With a rapist pervert you were so utterly defiled that nobody'd even come to the funeral parlor to see your remains.

Agnes sat down in a chair near the door that was usually employed for the coats of visitors whom she didn't wish to entertain long. She perched on the edge of it, conscious of the area between her legs for the first time in at least ten years. It is to Agnes's credit that she was able to make herself think at such a moment, an indication of how much discipline a teacher is taught by her students over a period of thirty years.

She made herself think of the situation in terms of an equation, and no matter how she pushed it around in her head, X simply would not equal rapist pervert in the realm of her mathematical logic. Her own eyes had seen no one in the apartment lobby, and no one in the corridor outside her apartment door. And rapist perverts rarely knocked at the door and called, as this person was doing, "Hello! Anybody home?"

Agnes nodded to herself. This was no rapist of any stripe. Still, it didn't hurt to have an edge in case the individual at the door had never heard of algebra. She quickly went into her bedroom and rummaged in the closet until she found the gun Earl had given her for protection not long before he died. "Be careful with the thing, Aggie," he'd told her. "It's loaded. But if you have to use it," he'd added, "shoot to kill." Agnes nodded her head again, as if hearing Earl speak, and went back to the front door.

She hesitated for an instant, wishing her apartment door had a peephole so she could see the face of the person who was again knocking. Agnes took a deep breath, gripped the revolver in her hand and opened the door.

His hair was a tangle of black wire, his face very dark in color, his expression sullen, gape-mouthed and clearly foreign. He was well over six feet in height and muscular, much more muscular than Earl had been. He wore work clothes that were filthy, stained, unwashed since they'd been put on the first time. The hand that he put out to hold the door open was callused, dirt under the nails; the hand that he used at his zipper was frantic with lust. He was saying something, something about having forgotten his key, but that didn't make any sense. Rapist perverts didn't make any sense.

Agnes lifted the revolver without aiming and pulled the trigger. Later she remembered being startled by how hard it was to pull. But she got the hang of it quickly and emptied the gun into the man, two slugs tearing into his thick neck and two into his groin and the rest dispersed without any particular preference as to site.

He lay sprawled at her feet, and Agnes felt a thrill of satisfaction at the way gouts of blood streamed from the holes she'd put in his disgusting body. He had fallen on his ugly, filthy foreign face, and she supposed she should make a gesture at seeing if he was still alive. Then she would phone the police for removal of the garbage. Reluctant to touch him, it took Agnes's trembling but triumphant fingers several minutes to tug strongly enough to get the body turned over.

Finally she succeeded, and her son, Joe, looked up at her with incredulous eyes from a face that was white, all-American, and quite dead.

Wednesday evening.

In only three days it would be time for qualifications at the Indianapolis Motor Speedway. The "race," as it is referred to locally without fear of confusion with other races, had been on everyone's tongue since the final week of April. It was considered something approachng heresy not to know which driver had the "fast time" on the track each day of practice. A local show preempted fifteen minutes of "The Tonight Show" every evening to spread the four-wheeled gospel—sometimes longer, if there were more casualties than customary.

Almost anybody from twenty-one to roughly fifty could qualify for the annual 500-mile race;

more than a few leadfoots had actually been eighteen or so when they lied their way onto sacred terrain. As a consequence, a middle-aged "rookie" sometimes will finish third or fourth and then become the favorite for the "pole position" the following year. Unlike other sports, legendary athletes at the 500 tend to be skinny little Italians, reckless Jews who talk faster than Don Rickles, redneck ex-mechanics who smoke cigars too short, and the rare English dandy, who has a knack for speaking in complete sentences rather than monosyllabic grunts.

Among jaded Hoosiers—the name for residents of the state of Indiana, the explanation for which changes from county to county—the race itself is often seen as anticlimactic to the real excitement developing on the first day of qualifications. Such cool experts ignore the likelihood of rain washing out all but an hour or so, thereby regularly holding down the record speeds feverishly anticipated by the sportswriting sages of Naptown. "After you've seen 'em take the green flag a few times," goes the conventional wisdom, "the race itself's just a matter of thirty-three cars gettin' wore out by goin' round in ovals. There ain't nothin' left t'do after twenty-five laps but drink."

Fortunately for the proprietors of the Speedway and the merchants, who speak in reverent tones and with flushed faces about the free-spending Memorial Day weekend, out-of-towners continue to see the 500-Mile Race as one of the only good reasons to visit Indianapolis. This causes sensitive Hoosiers a lot of pique since they've done much about the local image in recent times. More attractive neighborhoods than those in cities of comparable size, an ancient railroad station converted into the most modern of multi-level shopping centers, a low crime rate, and two pro sports franchises that have existed on the verge of playoffs or even championships apparently are inadequate reasons for New Yorkers, Californians or Texans to come to Indianapolis.

Except, of course, in May. Which was when P. J. Layton always departed Dallas to make his qualifying run on the "big track." After eleven races, P.J. no longer thought it necessary to wonder if he'd be in the field. The only reasons he hadn't set a new record for total victories were his ungovernably lousy temper, inexplicable automotive breakdowns and exhaustion from too many nights spent with Dallas cowgirls in the nearby Speedway Motel.

This evening, for example, the stoically and phlegmatically good-looking Texan had every intention of establishing a new kind of personal record. Teensie Abbott was the most gorgeous by-God gal he'd persuaded to go with him to Indianapolis in four or five years, and her appetite for sex surpassed his own hunger for the winner's circle. He figured it was even money whether she'd kill him or not, but it was worth the chance, by God. They called her Teensie, with American illogic, because her breasts preceded her into a room by the length of an indrawn masculine gasp—and for another anatomical reason that P.J. thought was none of your by-God business.

He stopped in nearby Speedway, Indiana, after

the track closed for the day, to pick up a six-pack before returning to the motel. In Speedway the abused townspeople were already showing their anger at the blankety-blank out-of-towners who parked in their front yards, trampled their gardens (and their daughters) and littered the town with beer cans and condoms. Even so, the old, bald dude at the liquor store had to wring P.J.'s hand and tell him how great he was; so the Texan was in a good mood as he dashed across the tiny stretch of West 16th Street to the motel. After all, he'd managed to lure his mount into the 200-mile-per-hour range, with a few largely illicit turns of the screw, and had posted the day's best time. Now, by God, P.J. could relax.

Rain was forming on the horizon, and that, he thought delightedly, meant the track'd be wet tomorrow morning and he could rest up from tonight in the garage area. He could give a lot of bullshit stories to the sports flacks while devouring the free food and booze offered by the management. Happy, he turned away from the front window of his suite with the intention of switching on a light. Then he changed his mind about that. Obviously, Teensie Abbot was in the sack, waiting—her clothes were all over the goddamn room—and hadn't heard him come in. Licking his lips, P.J. took the can opener from his breast pocket, rested it atop the six-pack on a handy table and undressed. What a by-God great way to end a tough man's day!

Girding himself for battle, and naked as a jaybird except for his familiar ten-gallon hat, P.J. tucked the beer under his arm and let himself into the darkened bedroom.

Bless her boobs, she was sleepin' like a babe. He tiptoed across the room and paused to look down at her. Teensie had her pretty face buried in a pillow, but everything else was in plain view, including the pair of reasons for her nickname. He gaped down at her another moment or two, until he began snapping to attention, and then put out a rough hand to awaken her.

In all of us, however thick-skinned and earthbound, there are intimations of our mortality. Some latent strain of risk, some vagrant and illused recollection of eerie moods beyond the palpable hazard of his career froze P.J. Layton's hand inches from the girl's shoulder. It was not so much a feeling of fear that moved his turgid heart as an impression that something had gone wrong—much the way he could sometimes sense a piston starting to go, a tire loosening at two-forty down the backstretch. P.J. nodded to himself. By God, *somethin'* was wrong.

From beneath the snow-white pillow, at the edges, something moved, something dark and forbidding. P.J. got reacquainted with an old enemy, the terrifying feeling he associated with the three bad crashes in his lifetime—that sensation he got when he knew he'd lost it and the fence was rushing up to meet him. The sense of time being grasped by a large hand, halted in its movement and turning to ice. Except then, he recalled dimly, there'd been the thrill of knowing he'd bought it and a vivid impression of how magnificent he looked to the crowd as he rode like a man to his doom.

This was different. This was colder, less glamorous, more terrifying somehow. Confused, P.J. wanted to tell Teensie about it. Placing the six-pack on the nightstand, he stooped to kiss an upthrust breast but got no response. "Teensie, old babe," he called to the sleeping woman. "Wake up, lover. Somethin' by-God strange is goin' on."

Still she did not move. Women and race cars that didn't respond to P.J.'s promptings were anathema, scarier than anything. He reached down boldly and yanked the pillow away from her face and her clutching arm.

His eyes opened wide in astonishment, horror and disgust.

He'd expected to see a peroxided head, an upturned pixie nose, two full, kissable lips and a pair of greenish eyes hot with hunger for him.

Instead, where Teensie's head should have been was the biggest fucking black spider he'd seen in his whole life: it was more than a foot in diameter. Anybody who knew P.J. Layton really well knew that he'd sometimes awaken from a deep sleep moaning from nightmares about the tarantulas that had nearly got him when he was a boy. He'd always hated the little monsters and had been ashamed of his fear for years. It was even part of the reason he drove funny-looking little cars at more than two hundred miles per. And *now*, instead of the sleepy, yearning face of the broad he'd spent a fortune to bring with him, there was this in-fucking-credible thing with wriggling woolly legs and the meanest-looking mandibles he ever laid eyes on.

P.J. grabbed the six-pack, raised it over his

head and slammed it down on the spider with all his strength. Two cans of brew flew loose, one of them spilling its urinelike yellow contents all over the place. Taking the four cans that were left hanging on the plastic doodad, he brought them down on the spider again and again. And when he was down to a single can, he kept pounding away until there was nothing left—nothing but the bloody, demolished face of Teensie Abbott.

Wednesday night.

Ruben sat up in bed and stared into the dark, momentarily sure his apartment was afire. The scent of burning was strong in his fine nostrils, and he already had one leg over the edge of his bed before he realized it wasn't fire he was smelling.

It was an offensive odor, acrid and pungent, but it wasn't fire; and Ruben was glad it was real. Generally, when he awakened this way, it was from another of his recurring dreams. He switched on the bedside lamp and inhaled. The smell was still there, whatever it was; yet he began to relax.

The fear of burning to death in his sleep had been with the parapsychologist since he was a boy, and it was one reason he'd never become a psychoanalyst. He hadn't been able to find the courage to undergo the required analysis himself, which would have taken several years—years in whch they would have tried to expunge his neurotic fear of fire and he'd have had to confront it daily.

Physician, he thought, heal thyself. He smiled scornfully at his own idiosyncrasy. Everybody,

Martin felt, was neurotic. It was just that some people could specify what they were afraid of, and a small percentage of them knew *why* they had the fear. The fact that he didn't know why seldom worried him anymore.

He sat there awhile, exhausted, wondering if he should get up and fix a glass of iced tea. It wouldn't be unpleasant to lie abed reading and sipping the rest of the night. It would be relaxing.

He was just admitting to himself that this was a copout, that he was really afraid that the nightmare flames would return, when the odor and atmosphere in the bedroom subtly shifted.

For one thing, it felt cold. Unconsciously he draped a corner of the blanket over his bare knees. Also, there was a sweet smell in the room now, like certain foods that spoil and lure the unwary into thinking they're still good because they beckon in sugary olfactory tones. He thought, no, he'd left nothing out in the kitchenette that might have spoiled. He'd taken the garbage out yesterday; that couldn't be it. Imagination, he told himself. He wriggled his toes, looked down at them and thought what foolish-looking things feet were, to carry a man the many thousands of miles they did during a lifetime.

"*Dr. Martin Ruben, I believe?*"

He jumped, uncontrollably, his body gone spastic and absurd, an outflung hand nearly knocking over the bed lamp.

Nothing, nothing there to see.

"*Here.*"

Ruben turned in the direction of the sound,

blinking nervously.

Within the frame of his open door, about five and one-half feet above the floor, there was some *activity*—a spiral, spinning madly, colorfully, forming starlike from a gaseous nebula; almost a pattern, like a mandala, as though miles of cold, empty space had been traversed and a living galaxy had taken form through cosmic chaos touched with divine intent.

The outlines of a face, of masculine features, became defined, growing clearer. Ruben's nails dug into the mattress. The form was rushing now to complete itself, some insanely gifted artist completing a moving portrait.

"You are Martin Ruben, are you not?"

The lips moved to form the words, but Martin wasn't sure whether the sound came from the bodiless head or simply assumed shape in his mind. His head nodded automatically, but words refused to come out.

"Allow me to introduce myself."

Ruben found his voice. He stared at the large head, the crinkling blue eyes, the tufted white brows, stared at the string tie just beneath the head, apparently encircling nothing at all.

"I know who you are, who you *resemble*," Ruben said tightly. "You're Edison—Thomas Alva Edison."

Whether it was because there was no reason to fear Thomas Edison or because the image suspended in the doorway projected a mood of relaxation and repose, Ruben felt his fear ebbing away. The cheerful face even essayed a smile, but the too sweet odor remained—and there was no doubt as to its emanation point—and it was peculiarly hot in the room.

Fleetingly, Ruben wondered if this was Edison's legitimate spirit or if, for reasons he could not determine, Demiurge was behind the apparition.

"I'm happy that people still remember me," the head said with a nod. "It's most gratifying."

"And I, sir, am honored that you pay me a visit. How may I serve you?"

"You and your friends have in your possession a device of mine, a little apparatus I created." the bodiless head was as affable as if it had knocked upon and entered the front door. Martin tried to clear away the cobwebs in his mind; he couldn't decide whether the apparition actually spoke with words or succeeded in conveying that impression while telepathically addressing him. He tried, too, to reach his usual logic level, to be coherent and deduce *why* this particular specter saw fit to call upon him. The head continued. "In realistic terms, Doctor, I fear that it is only an elaborate and quite dangerous toy. It *must* be turned off, sir. Destroyed, as well."

"Your achievements, Mr. Edison," Ruben said with deference, still seeking answers, "are of incalculable benefit to mankind."

"The achievement in question is *not* of benefit." The tone, whether through telepathy or vocal cords, had become sharp, biting. "It was the mistake of an old man who should have known better."

"I was saying, sir, that destroying an original

invention of Mr. Thomas Edison would be a wholly corrupt and unthinkable act"—Ruben frowned and realized, dimly, that his fear had not actually dissipated but was being controlled in some way; his pulse was racing at a dangerous tempo—"the destruction of a national treasure."

"I said turn the damned thing *off!*" the head exploded, its mane of white hair whirling with the intensity of its remarks. "You and that miserable Kellogg are the ones who are meddling now!"

The atmosphere in the room was suddenly thick, suffocating. Worse, the temperature had risen sharply, increased alarmingly. Ruben's T-shirt adhered immediately to his thin back, glued there. The sweet smell was overripe, overpowering. Could this be a heavenly visitation, Ruben wondered; could this be someone approaching him with a spirit of kindliness?

"It's possible you lack the objectivity to appreciate our present situation," he said as coolly as he could. "Under no circumstances can we—"

The *head* flew at him, swooped toward his own face in a passion of anger that made Ruben shrink back on his bed until his back was against the wall. The face of the apparition was inches from his own, enormous now, swollen out of proportion. The eyes—God, the eyes! They were bottomless pits into which Ruben could feel the very real danger of falling, tumbling helplessly into—into nothing the paraphyschologist could even imagine. And the flaming, boiling heat against his face and body was consummate, engulfing.

"*That machine must be turned off at once!*"

The words thundered in Ruben's mind, bounded off the walls of his brain like a runaway herd of unearthly animals. They screamed there, penetrated to the core of the man in a way that would replace forever his simple dreams of smoldering apartments.

Ruben, squinting and shrinking in terror, his hands helplessly raised before his face, got the words out somehow: "*Go,*" he said distinctly, "*to hell!*"

Immediately the Edison head exploded in a puff of smoke, disintegrated and dispersed. Before the wisps of gray smoke were gone for good, however, the voice spoke a final time in a harsh and unforgettable whisper: "*Then, the consequences are on your head.*"

Ruben threw himself on his bed, covered his face with his arms and wept.

Thursday morning.

A squad of police was summoned to handle a riot at the corner of Central Avenue and 19th Street.

Several experts had predicted that Indianapolis, fortunate for so long in being spared the worst havoc of racial upheaval, might be in for its overdue portion this summer. There would be many factors, they said, including the lost jobs of many automotive employees, slowness in fulfilling promises for lower housing costs, even disputes over the next presidency.

But no one had thought trouble would begin this early. June still lay ahead and temperatures remained moderate. Yet the report reaching the police concerned dozens of angry, sullen and snarling males in their late teens who were said to be milling around, threatening to burn the neighborhood down. Most of them, the report observed, were black; worse, the poor neighborhood whites were said to be on the verge of fighting back.

It was Sergeant Cornelius Bryan, many times cited by the department, who had left the squad cars parked a block away and arrived on a silent run, with the intention of handling the matter as peaceably as possible. He'd put two SWAT teams on standby, ready and eager to back up the regulars if they were needed, but Sergeant Bryan felt confident that he and his handpicked, well-trained men could "wind this thing up in short order without a loss of blood."

What he hadn't told anyone, including his wife, Betty, was how odd he'd felt all day, how edgy. When his teen-aged daughter, Peggy, had told him she had a date with a Protestant lad that evening, Cornelius had flatly told her to break it. When his younger child, Patrick, eleven, had dropped the milk carton, Cornelius had overreacted and grounded Pat for the rest of the week. Betty had told him, before he left for work, that he might be better off phoning in sick, since he was clearly overworked. But he'd shouted at her, told her he'd be the one to decide when to use part of his sick leave.

Truth was, Cornelius had been spoiling for trouble ever since he got out of bed, despite the fact that everyone who knew him considered him the one cool hand on the force who really hated bloodshed and could sweet-talk the worst heroin-head into giving up without a struggle.

Acting from rote, from years of experience and his basically kind heart, Sergeant Bryan had come with his men to the area of Central and 19th Street. He knew much of what to expect. The area was old and rundown, its homes ranging from dilapidated two-stories that the city fathers were always planning to board up to equally antiquated places that were maintained as well as human beings could manage, given that they barely had enough to eat. It was often said that "what ever you can't buy in that neighborhood ain't worth gettin'," but for the pacifist, law-abiding Cornelius Bryan, anything bought in that region was probably either hot or diseased.

Burly, pink-faced and in his late forties, Sergeant Bryan arrived with troops, on foot, in time to see an aged frame house burst into flames. The frightened shriek of a woman pealed from an upstairs window, and, from where Bryan stood, he could see the roof of the house begin to sag.

"Get the fire boys here, fast!" he commanded a young patrolman named Walker. "Go on—use the radio, and be quick about it!"

He turned back to the scene before him. He did a fast nose count and came up with fifteen young men loitering on the empty school playground, most of them obviously high on something. The three men who had started the fire were defiantly approaching another house. Bryan's jaw tensed. They weren't even bothering to be stealthy about it. They were laughing roughly as they waved burning torches and advanced on the house, completely ignoring Bryan's men.

"You!" he shouted, pulling his piece but aiming it down at the pavement. "You three! Just hold it where you are!"

The largest of the trio turned to him, languidly, insouciantly, his expression mild, but his eyes blazing hatred. He and his friends were also powerfully muscled, and looked to be about twenty-one years old. Each of them held a pistol in one hand and a torch in the other.

"You talkin' to us, baby?" the leader said.

Something in the man's attitude was so disdainful and calm that Bryan paused. Jesus, Joseph and Mary, this big bugger was positively flying on H! "Yes, young man, I am indeed talkin' to you—all three of you. Put your weapons on the ground, very nice-like, right now!" No one moved. "I mean it, gentlemen. *Do it!*"

"Shee-it!" exclaimed the enormous leader. With his glazed eyes still on Bryan, his lips twisted in scorn, he turned almost casually to drop his still-burning torch through the broken window of an old building but paused, the torch still held by two insolent fingers.

Something in Bryan's temple tensed, throbbed. A headache was starting, and he realized that he was angry, as angry as a rookie patrolman who hadn't seen monkey business like this before. Bryan tried to blink away the fury. "If y'keep this up," he said loudly, "you're going to get hurt. C'mon, boys, let's be sensible about this. Put your weapons down—*now!*"

Instantly a dozen similarly huge, equally armed, defiantly relaxed black men formed a loose circle around the trio of leaders. Bryan felt his own men inch forward, frightened and mad. He saw the Saturday-night specials, the gleaming blades, tire jacks and monkey wrenches that would break a strong man's spine, and he knew his men were aware of them too.

The largest man, his arm through the broken window, threw back his head to laugh. Then he released his hold on the torch and withdrew his arm, insolently.

Flame leaped from the flooring inside the house, became a painting framed by the broken window.

Cornelius Bryan saw red, within his mind as well as in the old house. He was about to take action, when the immense leader suddenly leveled his weapon at the officer's broad chest. "Honky bastard!" he shouted.

There was a chorus of shouts, animallike roars. "Kill the Man!" cried a black with a scar angling like lightning through his cheek. "Waste Mr. Charlie!" screamed another, openly charging the policemen.

"*Shoot to kill!*" Bryan shouted at his men, snapping, enraged.

Outmanned, genuinely terrified, the small squad of policemen—less experienced and more frightened than Cornelius Bryan—did as they were told.

The explosions were deafening for nearly a full

minute.

None of the police, not even Bryan, noticed that no one returned the fire. And no one noticed the crimson haze that had settled over the playground until it and the smoke from the police revolvers began to disperse.

A dozen policemen groaned, shrieked in their horror, their anguish.

There was no house on fire. The flames that had appeared to leap from each of the two old buildings were gone. And when Patrolman Walker returned from making his call to the fire department, he was astounded to see the rugged Sergeant Cornelius Bryan on his quivering knees, retching.

Walker's head turned from left to right. Some of his fellow officers were also vomiting; one seemed to have fainted. the rest of the men were bent over bloody, fallen bodies, expressions of grief and shock on their faces.

Because the dead and wounded bodies belonged, not to armed, dope-maddened grown men, but to fifteen small, innocent children, black and white alike, who had been at recess from P.S. 29 when the big policemen arrived and, quite inexplicably, began to fire on them.

In the locked house north of East 56th Street, there was a clatter of self-satisfied laughter pouring gleefully into the street. Passersby hesitated, wondering if they might be passing a lunatic asylum. Then they hurried on without looking back.

Demiurge was happy, ecstatic beyond words.

From corner to corner of Ben Kellogg's office,

cavorting *things* flitted in malefic celebration.

This week was the first time in half a century that they had succeeded in bringing death to the hated living. It was *so* much more direct than simply infiltrating human brains at birth. But shortly, they knew, the Master would summon them together. There were even grander conquests ahead of them, they knew. *Ultimate* conquests.

15

Thursday Afternoon.

They came together on nearly a telepathic wavelength, much as desperados of the old West huddled in a saloon to speak of evading the posse, each sensing that the time had come to lay a course of action.

The restaurant, with booths separated by wrought-iron grilles to heighten the suggestion of privacy, was a link in one of those minor chains that survive by selling franchises to men starving not for food but for self-employment. It wasn't so much a fast-food eatery—it took at least twenty minutes to get a sandwich—as that uniquely American enterprise that stays in business not because the food is delicious or inexpensive, but because it is adequate, prepared to order and not as expensive as that of a genuine restaurant. Also, perhaps, because the stainless steel made it literally squeaky clean (thereby catering to another American compulsion) and the waitresses all managed to look like virgins. From somewhere, sensibly hidden, the strident strains of a rock group permeated the air, keeping customers too abstracted and edgy to think much about the food.

Ben's reason for suggesting the place was its proximity to his office. He knew quite well what he intended to do, whatever objections Laura and Ruben might have, and he wanted his old quarters handy. Convenience helps one to avoid changing his mind. Thus, the three of them took their seats in a circular red plastic booth with the awareness that shades from hell were only minutes away.

Ruben, the publisher thought, looked sallow and drawn, thinner than usual. He was wearing a pressed black suit and new tie but still suggested a certain rumpledness, as though his arms and legs had been clothed independently at different intervals. Laura was even more beautiful when weary—the skin over her rather rounded cheekbones was tighter, somehow more exotic, and her pale lips looked kissed. But, then, Ben looked on her now with the eyes of love.

For her part, Laura thought she saw fever in Ben's eyes. A sudden sound might send him shooting out of the booth like a skyrocket. Her heart went out to him because he'd confessed to her alone, on the phone just that morning, his conviction that he'd brought them all to this state. It weighed heavily on his conscience, and, realizing what a decent man he was, she could imagine that he was crushed by the weight.

Martin Ruben considered that both his friends looked precisely the way they should. Under the circumstances, their harried appearance was normal. Clearly, they also realized that what had been happening was the product of the delusion-sending Demiurge, and he sat nervously in the booth with a sense of relief that they had agreed to a sensible action.

He was shocked and startled by what Ben said without preliminary: "We have to give Demiurge what he demands."

Ruben was about to snap a reply when an eighteen-year-old waitress with a curtain of dyed hair materialized beside the table. Bored, she held the point of her yellow pencil just above the lined pad, ready to get her onerous task done and return to her giggling sisters in the booth at the back. "Help you?"

"Coffee all around," Ben said briefly.

Laura wondered why it was that every truly important event was unfailingly interrupted by something commonplace.

"Make mine iced tea," Ruben amended the order. Changing it was his way of indicating that he was about to get tough. When the waitress had left, he turned back to his friends, eyes blazing, and said succinctly: "*No.*"

Laura, sitting beside Ben, put her hand on his. "What d'you mean—no?" Ben bristled.

"I mean, my dear Kellogg, that we cannot permit Demiurge or his discarnate entities to have their absolute freedom. In the name of humanity, we *dare* not."

"But the *children*," Laura said in an agonized breath. "Surely you've read the papers, heard what's happening. We alone know what's going on. Those—those monsters distorted the brains of policemen, made them *slaughter* little ch-children." She paused as her voice broke, her mouth twisting in shock. "Martin, they're *mad!* They must be stopped."

"I know that," he murmured quietly, "but not by releasing them."

"Martin, it's more than just one incident, you know." Ben fought to remain calm as he worked a fork between his fingers. "The crime rate has stayed down—there's almost none—because the spirits aren't in the minds of millions of people any longer. Of course, that's great. But there are all the other, insidious acts of delusion they're creating. Innocent people are *dying!*"

Ruben sighed. "I know that, too."

"OK, maybe it's your scientific turn of mind," Ben went on with exasperation. "Maybe you can't read between the lines about what's happening. Two girls drowned in a swimming pool with other people only yards away, unable to hear any cries for help and now doomed to torture themselves forever because they did nothing. Mothers and fathers are shooting and beating their children because they think they're burglars or rapists. Think how *they* feel. There are old people—three in just a couple of days—who've starved to death because they couldn't get out of their apartments; yet their relatives *did* come to help and simply couldn't *see* the old folks lying in their beds. That race driver, Layton, took his girl for an enormous spider and smashed her face to bits. And what about poor Carola Glenn? It's clear enough they attacked her to get to me!" Suddenly Ben tossed the fork on the table with anger, tears filling his eyes. "There are dozens of such deceptive incidents, and chances are there's a helluva lot more that's happened—stuff they keep out of the papers. Martin, I cannot see that we have any choice in the matter, none at all. We *must* let them go."

The tall parapsychologist leaned slightly forward across the table, his hawknosed face intense, inflexible. "I am *telling* you, Benjamin Kellogg, *we must never do that!*"

Laura blinked at Ruben's determination. Martin wasn't suggesting, he was commanding.

"Consider this." Ruben inhaled, gathering his old diplomacy and persuasion as he saw that he'd gone too far. "You both told me about the visits you had, visits apparently from beyond the grave, from ghosts."

"You had one, too," Ben snapped.

"Granted." Ruben nodded. "But with distinct and severe differences. Carola came to you, Ben, begging you *not* to turn off the apparatus. Remember? And your automatic writing, Laura—Julia Murray warned you *never* to shut it down, am I right? It was only the Edison face, the specter coming to me, who demanded that it be turned off."

Ben scowled. "Obviously, you're saying that Carola and Miss Murray's appearances were genuine—that they were whom they claimed to be—but that the Edison visitation was merely another of Demiurge's delusions?"

"Exactly."

"OK, how do we know for sure it wasn't just the other way around?" Ben looked satisfied that he'd scored a point.

"Come on, Kellogg!" Martin insisted. "Whose interests are obviously served by shutting down the apparatus? Demiurge has wanted that done since the start."

"He has a point," Laura murmured.

"Did you experience intense heat around Carola, Ben?"

"No," he admitted, but Laura put in, defensively for Ben, "I did."

Ruben shook his head. "That was *before* the automatic writing began, Laura. Heat is often an indication that a psychic phenomenon is soon to begin—it seems to have something to do with an adjustment in your biological systems. But the heat created by the Edison head was *simultaneous with and grew during the phenomenon. I might point out that neither of you was threatened or told what to do. You were pleaded with, instead.*"

"I don't know what to think," Laura sighed.

Ben squeezed her hand and said simply, "I don't either."

"Damn it, Ben," Ruben barked, "are you actually prepared to believe that the kind, sympathetic spirit who came to you wasn't Carola? A sweet entity with *tears* on her cheeks? Well, are you?"

Ben sighed and looked out the window. "No,

I'm not. I was much more than just frightened. At the end, well, I was very moved by her."

He looked back at his friend with reddening eyes. "That was certainly no evil force in my place."

"And you, Laura Hawks," Ruben pressed. "Was that note, written so affectionately and signed 'Your loving aunt,' the work of the same monster we met in Ben's office?"

She gave Ben a guilty glance before replying, "No, definitely not."

Ruben sighed. "Look at it this way," he continued, soothing and conciliatory. "Try to follow my reasoning. The power Demiurge possesses is limited—absolutely, positively limited—so long as he is held prisoner."

Ben's eyebrows rose, and his laugh was unamused. "Limited, is it? Tell that to all those nice people who are dying, who—"

"Kellogg, damn you, listen! Can't you see that it's *localized* power?" His hand gripped Ben's wrist. "Don't you realize that? Everything that's happening is strictly *limited to the city of Indianapolis!*"

The bearded publisher stared a moment at Ruben, startled. "I don't follow you."

"Think for an instant about all you've heard on TV or read in the press. Ben, the *delusions* aren't happening *anywhere else*!"

Laura's lips parted in surprise. She turned to Ben. "Darling, Martin's right. I haven't heard of a single major incident involving harm through misunderstanding or deception in any other city in the country."

"Nor in the world," said Ruben, somewhat

relieved that he'd made his point. "And have you perhaps observed the large number of peace talks that are being planned around the world? Even Moscow and Iran seem to be inclined to be reasonable at last. It's *spreading!* People elsewhere are behaving in a civilized fashion again; they're thinking about the consequences of their remarks and actions. In addition to the crime rate dropping, men and women of the world are conversing peacefully, speaking words of truth for a change—out of mutual respect. Why, there hasn't been a time since the forties with such prospects for worldwide understanding and peace."

"But here—"

"Never mind that for now. Don't just *feel* what's going on—*think* of how wonderful it is in every other location. Crime is disappearing. The peace your Christ sought is coming to the world at last!" He paused, then gave his friend an almost openly calculating smile. "Because of you, Benjamin—because you had the good sense to recover and use Edison's apparatus."

Ben's gaze met Ruben's and held. He hadn't thought of it that way at all. The possibility that he had brought enormous benefits to humankind simply had not occurred to him in the face of the disastrous deceptions throughout the city. He lowered his eyes in thought, his brows curved solemnly, concentrating.

In that moment Laura thought that she would never love him more, knew he was an honest, decent, fair and *caring* human being who had been unjustly asked to handle the responsibilities of an entire world.

Before Ben could give Martin Ruben a reply, even before he had drawn a conclusion, it happened.

At the cash register, the waitress who had taken their order screamed and threw her hands up in fright. Across from her a young, well-dressed black man was registering surprise, both hands in view and each of them empty. "Please don't hurt me!" the waitress cried.

Then, to the surprise of the three people sitting in the booth, the restaurant manager came to the waitress's rescue. Bullnecked, broad-shouldered, still powerful at forty, he ran toward the young black and struck him a blow to the jaw. The man fell and was hit again by the manager, who looked up to ask, for the first time, what had happened.

"He was—he was trying to hold me up," the waitress gasped, her young face contorted with confusion. "His gun. . . ."

"I don't see no goddamn gun," the manager replied, his pawlike hands giving the unconscious customer a quick frisking. "Where the hell *is* it?"

She shrugged, unable to answer.

"Baby, you better come up with some explanation!" The manager, worried now, had brought his customer to a seated position and was supporting him by the back of the neck. "Did he threaten you? What the hell did he say?"

"All I remember is a kind of cl-cloud around me, red and hazy," she said hesitantly, "and sort of *knowing* that he was gonna ask me for money."

"Jesus," the manager mumbled, turning back to his customer with a face of anguish. "Thank God he ain't hurt too bad. Get me some water."

Shortly, Ben saw, the startled young man was on his feet, amazingly forgiving as the manager took his check and tore it in two, talking softly and persuasively. Finally, wondering what had happened but anxious to leave, the customer exited the restaurant. The last Ben saw of him, he was shaking his head in dismay.

"We have here," Ben said to Laura and Ruben, "an angry customer with a bad headache, a waitress who's going to lose her job, and a manager who has lost business." He paused. "If the manager had kept a gun, I'm certain he would have shot that man." He sighed and took Laura's hand in his. "Look, I'm bewildered as hell by all that's happening, I'll admit that. But one thing is certain, Martin. Here in my hometown of Indianapolis, Indiana, innocent people are being injured, haunted with anguish, murdered. Many of them are dying terribly at the hands of otherworldly creatures they *don't even know are here,* and sometimes at the hands of their loved ones and their friends, and their authority figures. I can't possibly accept anything as terrible as this."

Trembling, the young waitress brought them their coffee and iced tea. Badly embarrassed and sure that her job was at an end, she averted her face. When she departed, Ruben returned his gaze to Ben Kellogg's intent expression and spread his hands. "Look, friend, no one rational could accept or condone such horrors. I like to think, however, that I am perhaps the ultimate rational person. And I suggest—quite gently—that you aren't considering the situation on the most rational level accessible to you."

"In what way?" Ben demanded.

"Simply this: You lack the cosmopolitan touch, the broad view. You're too involved with this relatively unimportant town, too much a part of it, and not adequately a man of the world at large." Ruben mustered a teasing, persuasive smile. "It might be difficult for you to see this, my dear fellow, but Indianapolis is merely one city in the midwestern part of the United States of America. The United States itself is merely one nation on a spinning globe containing hundreds of nations. Ben, old friend, this place is a *pea* on the plate of humanity."

Laura frowned. She replied before Ben could. "And we aren't supposed to care if the people of Indianapolis are slowly driven to insanity," she whispered, "or annihilated?"

When Ruben drew in a deep breath, he seemed even more exhausted. "I begin to see that I shall fail in this little exercise in logic, and I am growing tired of feeling like a cold-blooded villain. But, Ben, if you could pass through the boundaries of time, return to 1935 to slay Adolf Hitler—sparing the lives of millions—I earnestly believe you would find the courage to do it."

Ben paled but thought about it. "Yes, I could, happily," he confessed at last.

"Then, if Indianapolis must be sacrificed for the well-being of *billions*," Ruben persisted, "the ratio and the principles are roughly the same: one given for the welfare of a great many. It is only that you *now* enjoy the historical perspective to see the evil Hitler brought to the world and that you lack the *same perspective* on the present evil forces." He pointed an index finger. "Yet the consequences will be much worse."

"I don't necessarily think so," Ben answered stubbornly.

"Please remember the facts." Ruben's voice had grown cold with banked passion, and Laura saw that he was striving to the utmost of his intellectual resources to convince them. "*Entities cannot be killed.* Edison knew it and said as much. They are *eternal*, the evil spirits contained by that machine. The evil they can do to the minds of *trillions* of people, over the unguessable amount of *time* left to the planet Earth, is *literally incalculable!*" Suddenly his iron control broke, and he slammed the palm of his narrow hand on the table. Coffee from Ben's and Laura's cups slopped in reaction, spilling on the tablecloth. Tears had leaped to Ruben's eyes, and Laura felt a rush of compassion for the parapsychologist, realizing, as Ben could not, that Ruben was advocating what he honestly considered the best for all levels of humanity. Advocating it in agony.

"Kellogg," Ruben said after taking a breath, "if we today must sacrifice one city—allow *one* city to fall into the pit—it is a small, almost negligible loss in the face of the gain it represents. If Indianapolis is driven mad, driven to mass homicide and suicide, tortured for years—there may *never be* the nuclear war all sane citizens have feared for over thirty-five years! We shall have peace instead. There will be no more holocausts, no more genocide—in short, no more *war*. And I tell you both, losing one city is literally an insignificant cost to pay for the salvation of all mankind throughout the course of history."

Silence descended in the restaurant. Ruben was perspiring freely; he took a napkin and patted his forehead. Mouth dry, he downed half his iced tea in a swallow. He started to speak, to add an afterthought, then realized he'd been as persuasive as he *could* be. He closed his mouth. His hand trembled.

Out of the corner of his eye, Ben saw the young waitress passing through. She wore a coat and carried her purse; tears glistened in her eyes, but she looked straight ahead as she walked out the door. The lines in Ben's forehead deepened like scars, and he was filled with the notion that he was aging rapidly even as he sat there. He spoke at last, unable to look at Ruben. "Martin, I respect you, and I like you—but I cannot picture millions or, worse, *trillions* of anything at *all*—including people. What I see are individual men and women, boys and girls, and, quite frankly, I think your attitude is disgusting. Repulsive."

"I'm sorry," Ruben said, and meant it. His lean hand shook on his glass.

Ben rested his own palm on Ruben's wrist and looked into his eyes. "I tell you that to your face, candidly, because I feel that way. Your concept is, to me, unremittingly and starkly ugly."

"It is your town, too," Laura murmured.

"I'm a Jew, my dear young lady," Ruben said quietly, with pride. His voice held a tremor; he was more moved than he would have admitted. "I can live anywhere. We've always had to believe that in order to live at all. For the sake of international, eternal peace, I would live . . . nowhere at all. To permit old women to walk their neighborhoods in safety, *always*—to permit little children to reach maturity without the stigma of bigotry, and enable them never to die in some momentarily captivating war—I would be equally content to die, *at once*."

Laura felt like crying. "The only alternative would seem to be notifying the citizens of the city; *evacuating* Indianapolis."

"Half a million people or more?" Ben cried, astonished, even bitterly amused.

"It's just a number," Ruben murmured, "remember?"

"It would be impossible to persuade so many men and women to evacuate a modern city on the strength of a half-century-old machine's reputedly haunting an entire metropolis. That's just a dream, Martin. We couldn't convince a single newspaper columnist or TV reporter of something like this, let alone the mayor. Or can you imagine trying to get the governor to call out the National Guard because an apparatus sitting in a slowly rotting office must be left on forever?"

Martin held his cold glass against his burning forehead. "God knows you're correct about that, Ben," he agreed. A tic began in the corner of one eye. He blinked. "If the people in authority couldn't believe what I told them about the murder of my dear friends at the hands of a small boy, they certainly won't believe what's happening today."

"But I refuse to play a part in your vendetta against evil, Martin," Ben said as gently as possible. "We can't be sure that, if they're released, the entities will succeed in making their way to the *same* people they had inhabited. It may have to be the newly born, at worst—or maybe they won't be able to repeat their damage at all. The threat may have been nothing but a bluff." He shoved himself half-erect, leaning on the table to get closer to Ruben. "But right *now*, Martin, there are people being injured or killed by these distortions and deceptions. *That* much is a fact *now*—not in some dim corner of the future. I'm not speaking of people who *may* come along someday, but actual people— those living in this town *today*."

"Very well, but I wish you wouldn't do it." It was a peculiarly offhand request, his tone that of a man asking his wife not to have liver for dinner. And it was the tone of a man who knew she would. Ruben had given up. "I have no vendetta, Kellogg, no axes left to grind. I only ask that—based on my knowledge and experience—you allow that apparatus to run—indefinitely."

A second passed. "I'm going there now," Ben said flatly. He reached in his trouser pocket for money, threw a wadded-up bill on the table. "I'm going to turn that damned thing off forever, and then I'm going to destroy it. Utterly. I'll be releasing creatures of *shadow* substance, Martin, nothing more, in order to free decent people from today's horror. And, with some fortune, those shadows may not rediscover their way back to those whom they once occupied." Above his bristling beard Ben's mouth was fixed in a grim line. "*I'm* the sap who brought the apparatus here, Martin. It's mine, and all the trouble that's happened is also *my* fault, *my* responsibility. Not yours. That's pretty heavy stuff, and I'm ending it."

"I'll go with you," Laura said, making up her mind just then.

"Are you sure?" he asked her solemnly.

She nodded briefly. "I want to. I *have* to."

They slid out of the booth, and Ben paused to look down at his discomfited friend. Ruben stared into his glass, frowning, as if he could see the future there.

When Ben patted his arm comfortingly, Ruben looked up with infinite sadness in his eyes, eyes that seemed a thousand years old and not likely to get much older. "I won't try to stop you, Ben, old friend. I'm not the physical type, and I've exhausted all the reasoning at my command. I only pray you're right."

Ben stared down at him another instant, then turned on his heel without another word. Laura followed him to the door. Shortly, the publisher's car roared past the restaurant window.

Defeated and deserted, Martin Ruben sat alone in the booth and felt his leg muscles begin to release their knots of tension. They felt sore as he stretched out until his feet touched the other side of the booth. Someone put a record on the jukebox, a Judy Collins ballad, mournful and eerie. Ruben dabbed at his forehead and thought how hot it was, despite the air conditioning. It looked like an early summer, he thought, a hot one. Very hot, here and elsewhere, Ruben realized with a shudder, and the sweat on the small of his back turned clammy.

When another waitress came to see if he wanted anything more, Ruben ordered a second glass of tea and then stared with a certain longing at the woman's retreating figure.

She wasn't a particularly attractive person, but she was woman. Her hips moved in a feminine way; a hand patted the back of her hair, the nails scarlet, screaming for attention; the backs of her calves were slightly plump, pleasing.

Ruben lit a Camel and inhaled until the smoke hurt his chest and he coughed a little. Why is it, he wondered with pain, that every man and every woman must learn the same hard lessons alone, time after time after miserable time? *Why* can't they profit from others' experience and know that one cannot strike a bargain with that which is clearly wrong, and hope to make it work? *Any* compromise with that which was truly, genuinely wrong and not merely a sneer at authority's transient influence was doomed to failure. Worse, it was doomed to backfire, to pay off with anguished hours of repentance and irreplaceable loss.

Across the way his gaze found her again. The waitress bent over the counter, adding up her scribbled figures as if the act were of real importance. Her nurse-white uniform was tight across her buttocks and the blouse bulged forward as she performed her simple task and tapped the eraser end of the pencil against even, white teeth. She swiveled slightly on her heel to call out to the manager, and Ruben saw, for a moment, the sweet tunnel between her breasts, and caught a flash of lacy blue.

God, it was such a long time now that he'd felt alone and an even longer time since he'd loved a woman. It might have been possible with Laura Hawks. The idea throbbed along his veins. It just might have been possible . . .

He slipped from his breast pocket a billfold containing a photograph. A small boy named Robert, now dead, smiled happily up at him. Beside the charming child, a strikingly handsome, short, blonde woman peered out with intelligent eyes that were not, at the instant the picture had been snapped so long ago, hateful and unforgiving—as they'd been when he saw her the final time. They were, Martin Ruben felt with a pang, the faces of angels. Angels whose faces had been shadowed by the gnarled wings of evil, by grotesque and contorted demons who hated all love and friendship, all simple and decent things, and who made a man pay a most exorbitant price for being right.

The waitress smiled and laughed along with a wavy-haired man in his thirties, their self-confidence and shared joy enveloping, obstructive, isolating. Their small, private circle was complete; there was no room in that circle for a middleaged parapsychologist who refused to say he was wrong when he *knew* that he was right.

Ruben went on covertly watching them for

another moment or two, suffused with feelings he had considered dead. Then he made up his mind.

16

Momentarily, after they'd climbed into Ben's car and sped toward the office above East 56th Street, Ben and Laura were silent. Doubt—that queer attribute of man that both saves and condemns more people in a year than medicine or automobile accidents—put in its quizzical appearance, riding with them for some three blocks. Then, since their major decision had been reached and they were acting upon it, they found themselves beginning to chatter excitedly—like magpies, it occurred to the publisher, or like children going to their first football game.

With the birth of the simile, he was ashamed and simply permitted the conversation to die. Laura, he saw, felt the same new constraint. She stared straight ahead, her lips compressed in a mixture of determination and reawakened fear.

If he and Laura had been kids, Ben thought, the

game they were playing was well over their heads and they were *careless* children who had come upon a forgotten atomic bomb in the corner lot. And if this were a football game, the most they could hope for, in all probability, was a viciously played tie—while they prayed fervently against sudden-death overtime.

Ben grinned faintly. He realized that, under more stress than man can endure, his cooperative brain changes topics, eager always to save itself first. In his case, the realization that he always tended to think in picturesque terms amused him. Down deep inside, buried at such lonely depths that no one knew the truth, Benjamin Kellogg had always longed to be a novelist, an important novelist.

Not even Laura knew that beginning his self-publishing mail-order house had been a matter of intentionally setting up a place where—when he was ready at last—Ben might easily publish his Great American Novel. There were times when Fitzgerald and Salinger, his personal idols, appeared to merge instructively in his mind and whisper novel ideas that sounded so marvelous that only fear of failure prevented him from falling eagerly on his typewriter. Just once, several years ago, he'd worked for three days and two nights on a bare scratch of an idea, picking at it, trying to make it bleed into a flowing manuscript. A Pulitzer Prize would be its bandage; he'd win the National Book Award and make it his admission ticket to a human race that always seemed to have kept him on the outskirts, a little boy peeking in. Although no one had kept him from it but himself.

He remembered writing nine complete pages, but the wound had kept healing, scabbing over. His idea gradually receded into doubtful and querulous little corners of psychic pain with every self-indulgent sentence. At last he'd crammed the finished pages into an unmarked manila envelope and hidden it in the bottom of a locked desk—the desk upon which, at this instant, perched a strange machine capable of destroying him and everything he held dear, even the world itself. Unless, when he shut it down, its diabolical contents would simply go away.

A semi whipped by, speeding in the other direction and nearly sideswiping them, and Ben saw that he'd let his own car wander. The reality of the close call chilled him through his shirt and jacket, leaving him damp with fear. Had he ever devised such an idea as that of Demiurge, even the haunted and cursed house in Pittsburgh, he would have cast it aside as a bad dream. He knew, just then—gripped by the grim actuality—that he'd never finish his book and never become a novelist. He only hoped that he could save his friends and himself from absolute disaster.

He tried to clear his mind, patted Laura's hand absently.

She glanced lovingly at Ben, thinking how odd it was, the way things were working out. Did life afford no warning signs at all, give a girl no chance to choose between fantastic possibilities? Was everything destiny? She'd been a person merely looking for a job, a chance to write for pay—and, like a puppet, she had fallen in love with an older, rather impractical man, beside whom she now rode to confront a force that even her rich imagination could never have conceived. She smiled to herself and thought, *Next time I'll go through an employment agency.*

There would, of course, be no next time romantically. Whatever happened today, she belonged with Ben. But suddenly she had no idea whether they were doing the right thing or not. Laura looked out the window and saw that the day was beginning to die. Rather than looking magnificent, the sunset seemed splashed on, splotched and feverish with a riot of colors, the work of a surrealist who had come to detest humanity. She was accompanying Ben because she had no better suggestion to offer and because he was her man—which suggested, she realized, that something old-fashioned in her still preferred for him to take the lead.

But was he right or wrong? It was entirely possible that Martin was correct, that they were consciously ending the only real chance mankind had ever had to know genuine peace. It was also possible that, when Ben released Demiurge and the horde of nightmare entities, it would mark a turn toward a world gone crueler and more vicious than the one in which she had grown to womanhood.

Beyond the window, as they sped past, Laura saw with mild longing ordinary people doing ordinary things. An obese man in an undershirt perspired heavily mowing his lawn. A young mother pushed a child in a stroller, her gaze removed to some light consideration of the future. Two dogs yapped and slapped goodhumoredly at each other with their paws, glad to be alive. In the cars they passed, Laura saw acne-strewn teen-aged faces, flashes of horn-rimmed spectacles on red-cheeked middle-aged faces, an old lady with blue hair driving happily home from the beauty parlor, and two young lovers holding hands, careless of all else in the universe. Everywhere she looked, Laura saw people doing things that were routine, normal, human—of this earth. She shuddered.

All of them were surely incapable of believing for a second the horror in which she found herself now. At once she felt paradoxically envious and proud. Ben's deed would make parents stop inadvertently killing their children. Now, once more, they could do it just because they *wanted* to . . .

She grimaced at her dark thought and turned to Ben. Perhaps she was overreacting as she came closer to that horrid office. After all, Demiurge was getting what he wanted. Surely he would leave them alone now. Ben, she saw with a glance, was lost in thought. She covered his hand on the steering wheel, and he turned quickly to her. She was startled by his expression of relief.

"Thanks," he said softly. "I'd forgotten that I wasn't all alone now. An old self-pitying inclination," he added apologetically.

"I was feeling sorry for myself, too," she confessed.

The glare of dying sunlight when he turned the corner blinded Ben momentarily; he reached up to adjust the visor. "Neither of us, Laura, will ever be alone again. Whatever happens, darling, we're a team. Permanently."

"I love you," Laura said simply. "Ben—do you have any second thoughts?"

He laughed humorlessly. "Dozens of them. But I still think I'm right."

"Good," she said seriously, nodding. "Good."

"You see, a great many fairly decent people were surviving even with 1129's curse dispersed throughout the world and causing monsters like Khomeni and Gadafy to come to power. Despite the chaos, *most* of us got along. Once we learn that all that stuff Grandma taught us and that we saw in films—the GI sacrificing himself for his buddies, the Horatio Alger success stories, the decent-plain-guy-defeats-handsome-brute-to-win-girl fairy tale —the crap about how you succeed inevitably if you've worked harder than the next guy—then we begin to learn self-reliance." His face wasn't so much openly grim now, Laura saw, as forced into a cynical, smiling mask. "Whether you're a middle-class WASP or a Chicano street kid, you learn soon enough to rely on your *own* wits and to be wary of everyone until they prove themselves."

"Ben, stop it!"

He didn't hear her. "You learn the shortcuts to success then, if you're smart: how to climb on the same back you stabbed; how to develop a public 'image.' You get used to your authority figures having feet up to their *waist* of clay and bullshit, and you feel pretty well off if they don't hurt you too much." Ben's face was drained of color; he was driving mechanically once more, but not with nostalgic thoughts of the past. "You get used to the president being no better than your next-door neighbor, your minister hating people who are different, and your employer caring strictly about your performance—or how few waves you make. Finally, you learn that the only standards to hold on to are the ones that would make you a little less human in your *own* opinion if you abandoned them."

"Stop the car," Laura said firmly. "I mean it! *Stop the car.*"

Ben looked over with tears smarting in his eyes and saw that Laura meant it. Sighing, he pulled to the curb and let the motor idle. "What's wrong?"

"I don't intend to risk my life for a man who believes such terrible things." Her eyelashes batted away her own tears.

"Prove them wrong." It wasn't just a statement; it was very nearly a prayer.

She stared back at him intently, then buried her face in her hands. "I *can't*," she sobbed—"but you don't come out and *say* things like that. Never, never, *never!* Ben, we keep those things quiet, hide them secretly within ourselves forever—t-to use as an *excuse* when things go wrong."

"Honesty," he said, staring at the sunset, "where is thy sting?"

She was beside him then, squeezing her arms around his neck, her breath warm in his ear. "Maybe everything you say *is* true, darling," she murmured; "but it's what you left out that's so terrible. Ben, there *are* people who try to do the right thing—always.—And you've left out the fact of *hope*—hope that we can change it all somehow, that we can still begin making things right for everybody. And you left out the fact of *love*."

He held her close, sighed and considered turning the car around. But he couldn't. He thought about Laura and how, across a room from him, her healthy woman's body clear to behold, she seemed so strong and so sturdy—almost immortal harm. Even naked in bed, her arms around his neck and her legs around his middle, she had been powerful in a female, *enduring* kind of way. But now, with her weeping against his cheek, her slender form easily encompassed by his arms, he saw that Laura was more than a woman; she was a frail, breakable human being. And he saw how close he'd just come to rending and breaking the spirit of this woman he loved.

He pulled himself from himself in the touching astral travel that love provides and saw himself as she had seen him then—as a fool bolstering his own guts.

"Everything you said is right," he confessed against the waves of sweet-smelling hair pressed against his whispering lips. "You're absolutely correct. I'm sorry."

When she pulled back from him an inch and turned her tear-streaked, woebegone face to him, she was like a girl again. "A-Are you sure?" she asked, hopefully.

"If I weren't," he replied, dropping the transmission into drive, "I wouldn't be able to go back to my office today. And face—it."

The sun disappeared behind gray clouds as they stopped in front of the darkened office building. There was a hint of spring rain, a suggestion of imminent thunder. Black fingers forced their way relentlessly across the evening sky, undressing brilliant day. A tentative rumble of thunder, to Laura's imaginative writer's mind, seemed like cosmic indigestion, symptomatic of an eternal illness for which there might well be no cure.

"I don't know whether Demiurge is literally mad or not," Ben said, coming around to her door and opening it for her. "If he's *only* evil, we may not be in danger."

She glanced soberly at him as she got out. "*Is* there a difference between madness and evil?"

"I hope so," he replied, leading the way up the lane to the door, "or we may be in for even worse trouble."

He paused before unlocking the door. Then he turned the key, took a deep breath and pushed it open.

They walked inside.

It was dark. Shadows sprawled like sleeping demons. From the office Ben heard the incessant humming of the Edison device and crept cautiously toward the entrance. Laura was at his elbow.

She thought of something Edison had said: "*We do not know one millionth of one percent about anything.*"

Now they had that millionth. As was true of much knowledge, perhaps, it would have been preferable to forget it. But knowledge gained was knowledge never forgotten.

Ben saw no evidence of the illusory, shadowy figure of his late mother or the many dreaded animal faces she had worn the day of her burial. It was quiet, even calm. Except for the apparatus keening on his desk, the office appeared the way it had always been.

Where, then, was Demiurge?

Ben's heart beat rapidly. A memory of himself as a small boy—darting quickly into dark rooms in Edna Kellogg's house, glancing apprehensively behind the door or under beds—flashed through his mind, and he felt a rising anger. Damn it, this was *his* office, *his* place—not a place for itinerant hobgoblins and sinister trolls! "Come out, you miserable bastard!" he shouted suddenly. "Where are you hiding?"

"I suppose they're somewhere else," Laura said, trying not to whisper. She stood close to Ben, her eyes slowly roaming the private office. "Doing something terrible, making someone else violent or wanton."

"That takes *very* little doing!"

It was the all too familiar basso, trembling, Ben thought, on the razor's edge of hysteria—pregnant with the anticipation of conquest. There was something of the thunder in its laugh, Laura felt, a sepulchral echo of nature itself. And when she reminded herself that, if Martin were right, Demiurge bestowed the baleful benediction of tornadoes and earthquakes upon helpless mankind, she sensed a hysteria of her own fingering its way up from her bowels.

It was *alive!* The picture of business leader Peter Drucker, above Ben's desk, had suddenly *come alive!* The flesh seemed real, vibrant, viable.

HORROR HOUSE

But the eyes in the photograph were mad, furious, no longer the quietly intelligent and perceptive ones of the respected authority. And the sneering, cruel lips didn't belong to anyone but the hero of hell, the leader of cruelty's vast legions.

"So!" the grimacing lips intoned. "We finally succeeded in bringing you here. I had not thought it would take so long."

Ben faced the photo, hands on hips. "We're here." He tried to ignore the aching thrum of fear in his chest, the arc of cold shivers. "Because of what you and the entities have done to people in this city, I have no choice. You're even more monstrous than I would have thought possible."

"Thank you." The cold lips flicked a grin in return.

Anger twitched at Ben's temple. "A diabolical, murdering bastard. A true fiend, worse than anything I've ever heard of."

"Thank you, sir!" Now the smile was almost winning, charming.

"A soulless creature, a—a *thing*, with no regard for life or the simplest decency."

"And again, dear sir, my *profound* thanks!" The voice purred insinuatingly. "Just as is the case with Professor Ruben, you have come to know me well, indeed!"

Laura found her voice, husky though it was. "Just what *would* insult you?" she asked, suddenly as angry as she was disgusted or frightened. "Would it offend you to be told you'd committed an act of merciful kindness?"

"My, *yes!* It would break my heart to hear such

words." He made an effeminate face. "I haven't, have I? Is it possible that I've somehow done something for one of you ineffectual or superannuated little beings?"

"Not one damned thing," Ben said tersely.

"Come, now, sweet man," Demiurge teased. "*Many damned things, I'm sure.*" The face shifted with insane haste to one of strength, glacial coldness. "*But enough! I'm quite busy, you know. We could spend days enumerating my singular virtues, I'm sure. Now it is time for you to conclude your tiresome tirade, time to get down to business!*"

Ben's lips twisted in repugnance. "*You call this godless affair 'business'!*"

The deep laugh rumbled once more. "*Perhaps you've forgotten that I am, first and foremost, the finest businessman in all the universe! Buy and sell, buy and sell. Why, I'm the ideal prototype for all businessmen who follow in my footsteps.*"

"You're scum—worse than scum!" Ben growled.

"Enough juvenile word games, Kellogg," the distorted face snarled. "Get on with it. Turn *off* the machine!"

It was quiet in the office for a moment. Ben ruminated a moment, frowning. "I don't think so," he said at last. "No, I don't think I want to do that, after all."

"You *must!*" Demiurge cried, clearly startled.

Was there a hint of desperation in that voice? "Martin Ruben said I should not," Ben replied, at his mildest, "and I believe now he was right."

The vivified eyes blazed. "That filthy Jew swine! Ruben is of no concern to me!"

"That's what's the matter with you," Ben replied, nodding amiably. "You have no concern for anyone but yourself. Well, Martin Ruben is my friend." He slipped his arm around Laura's waist, feeling how she trembled against him. "He is *our* friend."

"What is friendship—what is *love*—in the grand scheme of the universe, you fool? How can it even occur in *my universe?*" When the voice laughed this time, booming, there was nonetheless a suggestion of uncertainty. "You are nothing more than toys, my tools, to do with as I please. You aren't even children to me, Kellogg; you are less threat than the most helpless infant. Even before there was such a thing as time, you imbeciles, *I* existed! *I, alone!*"

"Perhaps that's your trouble," Ben said lightly, almost pityingly, "but *do* go on. After what you've done to people, I rather like the idea of you *begging* to be released. In fact, Demiurge, I *love* it."

The face was the color of dripping blood. "*Begging!*" Its voice was a thunderclap, an ear-splitting blare. As if trembling from an earthquake, the office shook; and objects on desks and shelves began to tumble and fall. "*I* do not *beg*! Turn *off* that machine! Do it now."

Ben pulled Laura close to him, shielding their heads with his upraised arm and hand. Seeing her glance of fearful, loving support, he was strengthened. "And if I don't?" he challenged the immortal. He pointed to the humming apparatus. "What if I bury that thing thirty feet in the earth? What if the two of us simply walk out of this office for good, shut it down and lock it tight, never to return—what then, you misbegotten, bastardly lunatic? *What then?*"

"*You wouldn't dare!*" the bass voice shouted, the sound almost deafening. The bookshelf against the west wall fell face forward, books scattering across the floor. "Two feeble human beings would even *think* of doing that to me?" It thundered a cacophany of ribald laughter. "You wouldn't *dare* walk out on me!" The insane eyes in the transformed photograph became two cosmic black holes in the frigid depths of space.

"Watch us," Ben said, as mildly as he'd ever spoken.

He took Laura's hand and, together, the two of them began striding purposefully toward the open office door, their backs boldly turned to Demiurge's incredulous and furious false face.

Immediately, the door slammed shut ahead of them with a crackling shot of sound, partly splintering. They heard the lock turn with a swift, certain, decisive *click*. Before the mortals could move, the shelf on the floor slid at awesome electrical speed toward the door and slammed against it, barricading it and further confining them.

"*You shall be my guests!*" the voice cannonaded.

Ben didn't look back. Jaw clenched, he released Laura's hand and started toward the barricade, ready to hurl it aside, to break the door down if necessary.

"*Ben!*"

He turned at her scream and, when he saw her, he took a step away in shock.

His beautiful wife-to-be, a look of agonizing pain and terror on her beloved face, was beginning to *bleed*. It started slowly, became a gush—a torrent of crimson streaming from her mouth, her eyes, her nostrils and ears. Her lips parted as if to speak but could only belch out an enormous fistlike knot of blood, her lungs torn and ruined. In an instant she was utterly drenched by her own gore, barely able to remain on her feet; she began to slip, to slide. As Ben stared with horror the blood also began flowing—*pumping*—from between her lovely legs. All that was woman of Laura Hawks streamed in hideous clots of red and pink scraps of ripped internal flesh, down her parted, tottering legs.

Then she was sinking down into the scarlet pool, her knees touching first, almost in supplication. Her whole form moved at snail's pace and glided down into the ocean of gore. Her dear face turned to him, uplifted in a silent scream of such pain that it scarred his soul.

And all the while, Laura gaped at Ben, the man she'd chosen, saw with anguish and revulsion the way his handsome skull was *split* and how, even as she watched in horror, it continued to rip, to rend, tearing his bearded face apart. Giving off a gagging, gaseous odor, his throbbing brain rose into view like a gnarled and tumorous sun. Wormy things of blood-caked gray oozed over the razor-sharp edges of his split skull, staining his forehead and cheeks. His face was hanging at the bridge of his nose even while his agonized, impossibly deviated eyes stared mesmerically into Laura's, beseeching her for help.

Dizziness racked Ben but he tried to move, to reach out for the dying Laura, as he sought somehow to stoop to her aid. Terrible, curling things were tumbling from her lips, wrenched from within, pulsing with bloody life.

Now Ben seemed to come apart before Laura's stupefied gaze. When she began to grope for him, she saw something simply break—through his shirt and the front of his trousers—saw an interior of private tissue *collapsing*. Instinctively, she drew her arm back as Ben's trousers crimsoned; then she bawled out her love, disgust and sorrow upon seeing *things* drop to the floor from the legs of his trousers.

And Laura heard him cry, she thought, *The machine! Save me!*

And Ben thought he heard *her* dying gasp: *Turn it off! For God's sake, that will keep me alive!*

"Yes! Yes!" each of them cried in desperation.

Ben got there first, falling heavily on the desk, fumbling at the ancient apparatus. Quickly he reversed the direction he had originally followed when he'd turned it on that day so long ago. He slammed the lever halfway down, shut it off to save her—releasing the entities again—*unleashing the spirit of hell upon unsuspecting mankind*.

The device droned on another two seconds while Ben and Laura stared. Then it stuttered, briefly, and stopped.

It was still in the office. From the photograph

on the wall issued hysterical, triumphant laughter. Malevolent peals of delight filled the room. It was joined at once by a devilish chorus of dark angel voices—mad forces of death gowned in the clammy folds of death and destruction, their unlyrical hilarity dinning from the pores of the walls.

"*Now, at last!*" shrieked the jubilant Demiurge, his basso piercing human eardrums to linger in the soul. "At *last*—my final solution for *mankind!*"

A silence like that of the tomb invaded the office. Ben Kellogg, on his stained knees, looked dazedly at Laura Hawks, struggling to regain her footing, the heel of her shoe broken. *Neither* of them had been harmed in any manner, in any fashion—not physically, at least.

"Tricked," Ben said, his voice scarcely audible as he crawled weakly toward Laura to take her into his arms. "Thank God, you're all right! But we were deceived, again."

Crying hysterically with relief and more, Laura threw herself against his chest and her arms clung to his neck. With a growing sense of abject remorse, she wept. "We f-failed them. Oh, Ben, we *failed* them—people, everywhere."

Before he could even reply, as their eyes automatically moved to the ancient apparatus with a final hopeful glance, its lever seemed to break *off;* it dropped to the carpeted floor with a soft, meaningful sound.

The machine could never be turned on again.

17

The destroyer, the presence, the patriarch of evil—Demiurge—had won, after all. Despite their valiant, self-sacrificing efforts.

How could we have thought ourselves capable of out-smarting an eternal force? Ben wondered in misery, reaching out for Laura. Martin was right; modern man felt he could do anything he pleased. His ego this time would cost the world its only chance to be at peace. *God,* Ben thought torturously, *what "final solution" did Demiurge intend to visit upon mankind?*

Hugging each other in despair, Ben and Laura did not hear Martin Ruben burst through the unlocked door and rush to them, clutching their shoulders reassuringly in his lean, strong fingers.

Ben stared up at his friend and groaned. "It's all over, Martin," he said sadly. "Did you hear? We're finished, and we've taken everybody with us."

Ruben gave him a merely puzzling glance, nodded briefly, and without comment brushed past them.

He then dropped lithely to his hands and knees, reaching swiftly for the broken lever of the ancient apparatus. Kneeling beside the desk, ignoring them, Ruben began to manipulate the lever—to force it against the silent dial face. Heavy sweat popped out on his forehead while his long, lean fingers worked.

"Is there some hope?" Laura asked from Ben's arms. She'd felt more used up than ever before in her life.

"Of course, there's hope," Ruben said confidently. "I have some idea of what's gone on here, but neither of you have yet grasped the extent of the monstrosity's duplicity." He twisted something with all his strength. "Perhaps I can demonstrate for you that Demiurge—evil—succeeds simply because of deception—and our greed to accept it. The one recourse Demiurge had, restrained, was to *bewilder* you—make you believe things that are patently untrue." His hawk's face abruptly broke into a smile. "*There!* It wasn't broken. All he did was *shake* it loose! The damn thing's as good as new!"

"Switch it on!" Ben rushed to Ruben, face suffused with color—with anger, and thirst for vengeance upon that which had tricked him nearly to the point of madness. "Christ, Martin, you were right all along. Turn it back on and maybe we can recall them and still bury this thing a mile deep!"

"Perhaps. But that *isn't* our next move."

He'd spoken quietly, with regret. Ben frowned at him a bit wildly. "What do you *mean*, Martin? Don't get stubborn now! I was wrong, and I'm prepared to admit it—to put it in *writing* if you want! Damn it, turn the thing back on!"

Ruben stared at his bearded friend's anxious, pleading face, and his slender hands came up to Ben's shoulders, gripping them hard. "No, Ben," he said gently. "*Neither* of us was entirely right—least of all, I. I should have remembered that man must *always* be willing to do battle with what is clearly wrong, whenever and wherever it arises—even if the loss is assured before one begins. I apologize to you both for not remembering such simple truth."

Ben was stunned. "I can't believe I'm hearing this!"

"But you are. It would not be right to bring the evil back and trap it because, as you so properly suggested, it would guarantee the unjust eradication of a whole city. Or"—Ruben paused, the glint of sincerity mingling with a hint of his familiar, sardonic wit—"should it happen that *I* was correct after all, it is still not *decent* for an ordinary human being to arrive at such a cold-blooded conclusion. I no longer wish it on my conscience."

"Then what in heaven's name are we going to do?" Laura asked. She'd joined the two friends before the desk. Peering nervously down at the apparatus, she found its silence as ominous as ever. "What other options—choices—do we *have*?"

Ruben hesitated. He seemed to detach himself mentally from them then, his thoughts wondering to other places, other people. Laura felt that he was quietly steeling himself to put into words a decision he had reached a long time before. It was dark and windy outside the office; a tree branch struck the window with the sound of something striving to get in. Ruben took Laura's hand and pressed it to his lips, looking soberly, fondly into her blue eyes.

Then he knelt again to the machine, taking the replaced lever in his slender fingers before answering. "Edison based this invention of his on long and short waves," he said. His voice had regained its customary oratorical intonations; it was brisk, intelligent, on top of things. "The lever, when you acquired this device, Ben, was *midway* up the dial face. Do you recall? You, quite naturally, pushed it all the way up to *begin* the dissemination of waves. You *increased* its range."

Ben nodded slowly. "Yes. I remember. And I think I see what you have in mind. You're going to *decrease* it, to *lower* the level."

"I am." Ruben nodded decisively. "Edison was clever. I suspect he understood more psychology than the average chap—and that he counted, should his apparatus ever be located, upon the ordinary fellow assuming *up* was *on*! He couldn't know that a psychologist would come along and perceive his intentions." Ruben's cool smile flickered. "Now, then. I want you both to leave."

Laura and Ben exchanged glances, the latter shaking his head. "But what have you done?" Laura asked, touching the kneeling Ruben's shoulder.

The expression he lifted to her was warm, generous, discreetly affectionate. Again it showed flashes of a wit that was remarkable, given the circumstances, and his old confidence; it spoke volumes about him. It occurred once more to Laura, recalling Martin's fight against the Antichrist, that he preferred it this way. That he had somehow anticipated for a long while some sort of bizarre yet also meaningful culmination. That—whatever happened—an extraordinary man named Ruben had reached a free and independent choice: He simply refused to allow a collective and ungodly force to decide things for him and those he cared about.

"I cannot predict precisely what is about to happen, but I have a strong presentiment." He sounded almost amused. Laura, hand clasped with Ben's, felt herself responding to certain precious qualities of uniqueness about Ruben which might once have been a regular part of him, before he'd been obliged to see the reflection of his own soul, and his human mistakes. "Now, my dear Benjamin, take this lady and leave me—at once! There isn't time to waste and I will not be responsible for what occurs in this room . . . once I plunge this level *down*!"

"There must be another option," Ben growled. "Perhaps Demiurge's threats were empty. Perhaps people are inured now to the subversion of their souls by—"

"The average man's soul can be infiltrated by the spirit of a dead *termite!*" Ruben exclaimed. "There *are* no options, and, when you have eliminated the impossible, all that remains—however improbable—is the only damned game in town!" He laughed a trifle hysterically and shifted his weight to press his hand firmly against the apparatus lever. When he swore fiercely at his friends, it was with love in his eyes. "*Now,* damn you!" Ruben roared. "Get the hell away from me!"

Laura moved quickly but paused to kiss him on the lips. The love in Ruben's eyes merged with desire, some last longing. Then Ben had grabbed her by the hand and they were moving in an uncertain but final rush to the door of the office.

Once, the publisher paused to look back, doubtful and concerned, in time to see his old friend assume his natural detachment, turning his keen, disciplined scrutiny to the Edison device. For a compressed instant the office faded into swirls before Ben's eyes; he thought he could just discern the faint, tenuous phantom of a young Indian girl and the implicit shadow of a crouching, mad old man with a moustache. Laura tugged at him, then and he followed her outside.

Together they collapsed wearily onto the grass in the front yard, well away from the one-story building. Each felt that he had run a bleak marathon among the scattered black holes of the universe and been defeated. Laura sighed, sat up and stared around her. She was dazzled by a world that was grotesque because of its stunning normality. Exhausted, Ben raised his head to snatch an instinctive gulp of fresh, evening air and saw, above them—ever undisturbed yet all-seeing—stars atwinkle in the new night. He thought, accurately but illogically for an awful moment, how he was staring at light rays that had left the surface of ancient stars hundreds of thousands of years before. Did anything matter? Perhaps everything did.

"Hold me," Laura whispered.

He did, willingly; he pulled reality into his arms, cherishing its occasional gentility.

When he gently removed her arms and climbed wearily to his feet, her eyes shot up to his face in fresh anxiety.

"I'm sorry, darling," Ben said sadly, staring down at her. "This thing is my responsibility, not Martin's." He reached out to take her chin tenderly in his fingers and kissed her lightly. "Whatever happens, I have to help Martin. I must."

Before Laura could protest, Ben turned and dashed back into the once-familiar building. His heart pounded with dread, but he burst through the outer offices, headed for his own private rooms.

He had just made out the open door to his office when . . . *They* . . . were back.

Appalled, frozen in his tracks, Ben knew at once that the entities had returned. His vision was first assaulted by countless flitting, fleeting images of bleakness issuing from the gaping doorway as silent in their approach as death. While formless, devoid of clear features, they conveyed to him a sense of unknowable loss and the publisher threw up his arm, crying out in queer sympathy without knowing why—or why they'd returned.

Quickly, then, came nose—a whine so perfectly pitched that it was agony to hear. Wincing, he pressed his palms over his ears. The reek of indescribable refuse attacked his nostrils; he felt something damp, and clammy, sprawl suddenly upon his back and shoulders, then scuttle over his head.

Ben's gaze was torn upward. Things, he sensed, flapped on ponderous wings. He whipped his head to the side; from the corner of one eye he detected a miniaturized parade of bodiless heads, bobbing. Too much; he looked away, repelled. Too much.

When he shifted his weight he realized he was on his belly. Furry substances rushed him, scrabbling at his fingers; he squirmed wildly to escape. My *nerves*, Ben thought; the mind can't take this.

"RUBEN."

The roar from the inner office was one of detestation. When it sounded, all else stopped except the echo of its horror. Ben heard muttering that was deranged and then two monomaniacal sentences which slashed the momentary silence and registered on his nervous system for all times:

"Ruben, you *meddler!*" The voice bellowed but also projected its unmistakable dark majesty. "TODAY, YOU SHALL BE WITH ME IN *HELL.*"

The outer office at that second filled with the blackness of a cave cut deep into the heart of the earth. The stark absence of light caused Ben's mind to squeal and gibber in fresh terror. Foul odors engulfed him in a lewd stench; he felt his scrotum tighten, strive to shrink from a cosmos of ugliness. Night and odor clogged his spirit and his nostrils, giving him a foretaste of mortal death.

And when the evil receded, darkness drawing to one point of obsidian ebony in the doorway of Ben's office, several things happened. He heard a nightmare threnody in which awful sound and sight and touch and smell blended in the ear like a lunatic chorus caroling at the end of the world; he saw the haloing effect of red flame enfringing the ebon spot; and he felt a queer blast of turbulent air so ineffably cold that his flesh dimpled and his teeth began to chatter, ache and throb. Mystic shadow forms swam spermlike in the cold gray air of the inner office, darting and chuckling to themselves, singing wordless tunes of annihilation and obsessive hatred before shooting, as one, toward a point well beyond the range of Ben's human vision.

It was quiet then.

When he managed to rise again, with massive effort, his heart thundered in his chest, and he feared for it. He forced his shaken body to fall forward toward the open door.

Just inside, Ben stopped short to gape numbly at the scene he discovered there. His entire consciousness was drenched at once in renewed sickness and a depleting despair that would never fully leave him. His lips formed two syllables: *Martin*.

The ancient apparatus created by old Tom Edison exuded the reek of sulphur and excretion. It was aglow with burnished fire—with flames of perfect ebony that wriggled and curled like taunting, toasting fingers. Then, quite abruptly, the apparatus *melted*. Its searing stuff dripped down Ben's charred desk, leaving an inch-wide tunnel as if molten lava had oozed through the polished wood.

Martin Ruben—what was left of him—lay on the floor beside Ben's overturned chair. His clothing had been burnt into his flesh so that Ben could see his friend's nipples and navel showing, obscenely, through the incinerated black suit and white shirt. A pocket pen-and-pencil set, crossed, were branded crudely into the man's motionless chest. His face was a skull, save for a fleshy remnant of his hawklike nose, and his eyes were hollow caverns burned deep into the charred and sightless sockets. The arms ended in two, smoldering stumps from which protruded bone.

There was something else to be observed in that place.

Seeing it the first time, Ben tried for all he held dear to consider it sanely. But his mind would not focus then on what he'd seen; his glance wandered, leaped. He knew then that the presence that had haunted the house on Ridge Avenue and the phantom entities which were Demiurge's tortured souls could not be destroyed—even as Edison had claimed long years before. Even as poor Ruben had warned, only that day. But solely because of Martin's ultimate act of courage, they *had* been returned—sent where they belonged.

To hell.

With that complete realization, Ben Kellogg summoned his own courage, stepped round his friend's valiant corpse, and reluctantly drew near the bottomless pit that had happened in his office floor.

At once Ben found something hypnotic about the gaping cavity, something that beckoned Ben with sublimely lying lips. Dizzy, weak, human, he was like a man on a ledge one hundred stories above a street scene that looked harmless from that vast distance.

Two feet from the edge, trembling, bathed in sweat, Ben stuck out his head and peered down, *down,* into the steaming entrance to man's worst eternity.

Hell loomed before him. It stretched downward endlessly. He saw tongues of silver smoke; bubbles like pustules on the walls of the cavern, popping; a suggestion of yellow-orange flame which twisted and curled with countless sunlike explosions of intimate pain; shadows thrown by things that writhed and knotted in unutterable and eternal agony. . . .

And Ben thought he heard, in the infinite distance, *the unreasoning, unspeakable rumble of evil laughter.*

It wasn't hard to torch the rest of the building, because there were books, magazines and reams of paper everywhere. Yet every moment he remained in that building was time spent on the precipice of hell. And so Ben hurried as best he could, pawing matches as he darted from one corner to another, mumbling aloud at times, sometimes weeping in little, fevered bursts. He laughed with hilarity when he was reminded of Bradbury's *Fahrenheit 451.* He, a publisher, was suddenly a book burner! And Ben thought aloud, "He *doesn't have* Martin down there; he *doesn't,*" and it was a genuine prayer.

Would the giant pit disappear when the building no longer stood, he wondered? Did the pit even actually exist, or could it have been a final deceit, a last, craven lie? Ben had no idea, though he wondered, lips moving; following a coherent track of thought, then, was impossible. He did not ask *why* he was doing this. But he felt with a religious need he could not have described that God's purifying rite of fire might cleanse a portion of the filthy place.

Finished, for no reason Ben knew but as an act of love and of respect, he stripped off his own ruined jacket and spread it tenderly across his friend's pathetic corpse until it covered the skull-like features. He stood, then, muttering words that threatened to burst into hysterics, urgently hoping Martin Ruben—and God—might hear, understand, and concur.

When the flames were dancing like Essie's Indians painted for battle, Ben tottered outside in quest of Laura Hawks. Their future, undoubtedly, was to be troubled; Ben knew that when his glimpse of her salvaged the shreds of his unraveling sanity. He sank to the ground in semi-consciousness, knowing Laura had taken his hand in hers and that this was the best he could hope for.

In the distance, Laura heard the yowl of sirens, sensed them drawing nearer. She yearned to ask what had hapened to Ben's friend, and hers, yet knew Ben had come back to her alone.

Half dragging him, she got them both safely away from the inferno when the fire trucks began to arrive. "He was the best man I ever knew," Ben whispered. "And the wisest."

Afterward

SOME OF THE FACTS ABOUT "HORROR HOUSE"

Every earnest effort possible was exerted to substantiate fully—or to disprove—the often amazing, consistently frightening and macabre events involving the house on Ridge Avenue. Numerous photographs were gathered, and studied. Yellowing newspaper clippings were found and read. The television script for a local Pittsburgh program which closely investigated the gas company explosion used fictionally in the preceding novel was repeatedly examined.

One consequence of this research was a contact and then an on-the-scene interview with a gentleman who *recalled* the house of horror, despite the many years that have passed since its terrifying heyday.

Still and all, the results of this research have been admittedly mixed. Not telling, in the sense of disproving a thing; not at all. Instead, it has seemed at times as if the Edison "entities" were back again, flashing by at the outskirts of one's vision, almost within clear sight before vanishing like so many will-o'-the-wisps.

In point of fact—just to make it clear—I cannot remember any enterprise in my writing career which was more frustrating and sometimes maddening than endeavoring to gather all the facts in this bizarrely mysterious matter. Evidence that appeared to be surfacing promptly sank like a stone at the instant it was cautiously poked or prodded; many scraps of evidence beneath those stones were slimily coated by the muck of bureaucratic error and insufficiency. Others were discarded— presumably forever—or trashed during a period of time when, without computerdom, file space was at a premium. Often, the research conducted for the writing of *Horror House* pointed the way toward hard data that might well have filled every yawning gap of knowledge with indisputable fact ... and such-and-such a business or agency shut down at the beginning of World War II, and so-and-so had either died decades ago or moved away to parts unknown.

This was worse: Richard Hase, whom I hired to be my on-the-scene legs, eyes, and ears, kept talking on the telephone with or writing to persons who idly confessed that they recalled *just* what had happened on Ridge Avenue—but they seemed to develop a queer kind of amnesia whenever a tape recorder popped into view. Or, in some instances, the people who'd initially boasted of knowing salient details that were both evidential and downright shocking suddenly became bewildered and overcome by second thoughts. Incipient paranoia, more times than not, seemed easier to acquire than a bold and straightforward statement of well-remembered experience. And the more long months that passed, the simpler it was to believe that *someone* was intentionally muddying the waters— obfuscating the pursuit of truth for unknown reasons that, hypothetically, might have ranged from personal gain or threat to concern for people and reputations of the past.

Although the portions of *Horror House* which take place in the present were, by and large, entirely fictitious, I began the research and the writing of this novel with adequate reason to believe that most events occurring in the past were quite genuine; real. Perhaps I may be pardoned if I add that there were weary moments when I found myself wondering, inescapably, if we were not *supposed* to uncover the complete truth—

And if we were prevented from learning it by forces, or personalities, that existed long before Thomas Edison began work on his apparatus ... even long before that priceless gentleman was born.

I have mentioned to you, here, the sense of frustration which accompanied the writing of *Horror House*. I meant rather more by that admission than may meet the eye.

It's assumed by most readers who buy a book

that the author is relatively affluent (if the question of his economic condition occurs to them, to *you*, at all). When I chanced upon the various apparently-factual elements that gave me the desire to create a novel that, originally, I called *Entities,* it was 1979 and I'd sold only one book (*The Ritual*). In common with the overwhelming majority of "first novels," its sale did not approach any sort of record. My career, in my forties, had yet to "take off;" all my best novels, my *Masques* anthologies and Writer's Digest Books "How To"—even most of those short stories in which I would come to take pride—were in the future.

I've never wanted to go anywhere as badly as I desired to fly to Pittsburgh, Pennsylvania, and spend whatever quantity of time was required to pin down the elusive evidence. Other books had been published which, despite the use of similar material and seemingly skyrocketing success, turned out to be controversial, even dubious. I didn't want this, for my book; the fact that the long, later portions of *Horror House* are only based on terrifying incidents of the past and not an ongoing record of what *really* happened pains me to this day. But I still had children at home, and obligations, other offspring would return from time to time, and it was financially impossible to pursue the utterly exhaustive investigation I wanted.

None of which means that Thomas Alva Edison did not invent an apparatus with which to establish a dialogue with spirits, or that his device did not somehow disappear after his demise; nor does it mean that the terrible house on Ridge Avenue did not exist and was not haunted.

And I hope it doesn't mean, either, that none of us will ever have the complete truth in our possession.

Both in interviews and reviews the question of my *intent*—the reason *why* I worked so hard on *Horror House*—has been asked and sought. The primary answer is one that any honest novelist with a single sale (at that time) would provide: I believed the material which seeming "chance" had placed in my path was strong enough to become the basis for an immense bestseller.

Even in that instance, I can see, now, with fascination, that the obfuscation and water-muddying I've written about stood athwart my intent. What you have just read is a fairly thorough revision of this book—thorough enough almost to justify alluding to it as wholly new—and what you *are* reading is a brand-new Afterward. The publisher of the previous version of *Horror House*, unknown to me, was experiencing hard times. Despite the loving editorial care expended upon it by Sharon Jarvis and Nancy Parsegian, the book wound-up with a cover that—in my opinion—more properly would have adorned a Nancy Drew mystery. Little or no promotion was afforded it; not many copies, comparatively, were distributed; and that publisher was soon obliged to go (as they say) belly up! In certain respects, the present edition of *Horror House* culminates a truly remarkable chain of confounding stumbling blocks . . .

But there were other reasons I wanted to bring the story of the Ridge Avenue manse to a reading audience and was delighted when the present publisher expressed an enthusiastic interest in attempting, again, to fulfill my expectations for it.

It seemed to me nearly a decade ago and it seems to me now that the awful house's history, as seeming fact, was much more frightening than the typical ghost story. Instead of moody chain rattling, spiderwebs in the attic, filmy apparitions silently materializing on spiral staircases, sliding panels and locked rooms and quicksand—instead of an imperiled little boy or girl along with a prototypical pair of likeable, amazingly stubborn and obtusely skeptical parents—there were reports of the phantoms of *real* people, and some of them committed bloody murder. Among the ostensibly living cast of characters of the period, Dr. Brunrichter could by himself have been the focal point and antagonist of most such novels; point of fact, I'm uncertain I have used my imagination at any time to create a character of such haunting evil.

A review of *Horror House*'s initial version complained that its writer had stuffed the story full of so many really dark characters that it was unbelievable and added that the critic had expected more of my next novel.

That was his or her right, but the point was completely overlooked, it seems.

This book was based, *is* based—to the best of my knowledge, at least—on fact. And I tend to disapprove of fact-based books that are twisted to suit the author's needs. I am turned off by television movies concerning real people which sometimes go too far in distorting truth to make the production conform to a preconceived format.

HORROR HOUSE

The portions of *Horror House* depicting events of the past are, I think, novelization.

When Ric Hase was eagerly and cooperatively trying to run down leads in his spare time, he recorded an interview with then-71-year-old John Cowell, a man who lived his entire life in Pittsburgh. Mr. Cowell was a former butcher, roofer, factory worker and, eventually, politician.

His residence was at Anne Street—and Ridge Avenue.

Cowell described a boyhood of exuberance, and practical jokes; of running up to the doors of mansions on Ridge and being chased away. Among his young friends were Art and Vinny Rooney, the former owner of the National Football League Pittsburgh Steelers.

"Even the older people didn't go around there," Cowell said of the house of horror. "Everytime we'd go up there, we'd hear ... strange noises." He added, "It was always haunted ... We was always a-scared to go around that corner house, because it was always spooky."

He said that in the case of *that* mansion, he never dared get closer than "about twenty feet—and I run like hell!" It had a caretaker who quit, during John Cowell's boyhood, "And they boarded it all up ..."

And did he "hear any stories" about the infamous house? "Oh, yes," Cowell answered. "There was somethin' going on in that house that the older people wouldn't even go around it." And what were the kinds of rumors he heard? "Well, they was about ... murders. About a doctor who was ... experimentin' on people. We heard when we're kids ... that they were choppin' one fella's head off in there."

It may be mentioned that when John Cowell was ten years old, in 1919, a full eighteen years had elapsed since the reported slaughters of Dr. Brunrichter. The beheadings.

What of the Equitable Gas Company explosion? Was it real? "It 'let go' in 1927," Cowell replied, adding (almost astonishingly), "We was in on it." What he went on to describe was a youthful dash in his Model-T to a nightmarish scene in which "lots of them were drownded" while "paintin' the tanks"—some "fifteen painters," Cowell recalled—and "legs and arms, they was blown all across the river—*everywhere!* I saw half an arm down there."

Belief may be the most powerful force on the planet. Chekhov wrote, "Man is what he believes." Lewis Carroll, who wrote *Alice in Wonderland*, once said he had "believed as many as six impossible things before breakfast."

Although it is modern and "cool" to assert that one is "scientific" and fact-oriented, nearer to the heart are those beliefs which keep that organ pumping with excitement; anticipation; faith. The "need to believe" haunts man, according to William James.

Here in Indianapolis, during my teen years, a house existed which was set far back from a tree-shrouded road on a fenced-in estate. When they were quite brave, and young (of course), people often scurried up and down the driveway, giggling like fools for their daring. I was one of them, and, on my way back down—like Johnny Cowell—I "ran like hell."

It was called the House of Blue Lights, that mansion, and rumor had it that hundreds of half-starved cats stalked the interior while a squad of crack trooper-guards—I heard once they were Nazis—patrolled the grounds unceasingly.

Cats and guards alike were protecting the coffin of the woman who had lived there and loved it, people said. An ethereal, sleeping beauty, she'd reportedly been encasketed before a picture window—and the tableau was eternalized or turned horrific by an eerie, smoky, pure blue lighting.

My friends—Speed, Jack, Bill, Charlie and Don—passed along the rumor, as did I, that a cemetery for the cats lay at the rear of the estate; and there were nights when the moon seemed blue as the eternal light around the half-sleeping beauty and one might hear the strangely forlorn feline howls, and see the woman leave her casket to float restlessly among the small, pale headstones. Her grieving widower, we told one another, arranged all that, for her. Only he and God knew how the pact had been sealed, unless one *other* had been a cardinal part of it . . .

Well, virtually none of the rumors I've related again happens to be true.

But you knew that, didn't you, before I said so—didn't you?

And you rather wish I hadn't cleared it up.

"Why abandon a believe merely because it ceases to be true? Cling to it long enough and

... it will turn true again, for so it goes."

Robert Frost

PRIME VIRGINS...
PRIME CUTS...
PRIME HORROR...

Prime EVIL

By Ed Kelleher & Harriette Vidal

Thirteen years have passed since a victim was dragged to the altar, shackled at the foot of an inverted cross, and prepared for a terrifying and agonizing death.

Thirteen years have gone by since the ritual dagger descended in a silvery arc to plunge swiftly into a still-beating heart.

Thirteen years of renewed life had been granted to the believer who had sacrificed his own blood relative — thirteen years of power and youth to sustain a body centuries old.

Thirteen years have passed, and again it is prime time for prime evil.

_____2669-4 $3.95US/$4.95CAN

LEISURE BOOKS
ATTN: Customer Service Dept.
276 5th Avenue, New York, NY 10001

Please send me the book(s) checked above. I have enclosed $ _____
Add $1.25 for shipping and handling for the first book; $ .30 for each book thereafter. No cash, stamps, or C.O.D.s. All orders shipped within 6 weeks. Canadian orders please add $1.00 extra postage.

Name _____

Address _____

City _____ State _____ Zip _____

Canadian orders must be paid in U.S. dollars payable through a New York banking facility.   ☐ Please send a free catalogue.

SPEND YOUR LEISURE MOMENTS WITH US.

Hundreds of exciting titles to choose from—something for everyone's taste in fine books: breathtaking historical romance, chilling horror, spine-tingling suspense, taut medical thrillers, involving mysteries, action-packed men's adventure and wild Westerns.

SEND FOR A FREE CATALOGUE TODAY!

Leisure Books
Attn: Customer Service Department
276 5th Avenue, New York, NY 10001